THE TICKER=TAPE MURDER

BY MILTON M. PROPPER AUTHOR

OF "THE STRANGE DISAPPEAR-

ANCE OF MARY YOUNG"

DEATH LAY IN AUDUBON COMMON

Soaring ever higher under the skillful manipulation of Philip Nixon, president of American Motors, Audubon Common was creating a sensation in the financial world. Then, at the crucial moment, Philip Nixon was murdered!

Was his death planned by a Wall Street "bear," in order to force the stock down? Or did a band of gangsters "get" their man at last? These and many other motives for the crime make

"The Ticker Tape Murder"
By Milton M. Propper

a rousing mystery story that will delight the most blase reader. Begin it in the

POST-DISPATCH MAGAZINE

TOMORROW

THE TICKER-TAPE MURDER

Milton M. Propper

COACHWHIP PUBLICATIONS
GREENVILLE, OHIO

To My Sister
Madelyn
Whose Interest and Encouragement
Have Been Invaluable

The Ticker Tape Murder, by Milton M. Propper
© 2026 Coachwhip Publications edition

First published 1930
Milton M. Propper, 1906-1962
CoachwhipBooks.com

ISBN 1-61646-636-7
ISBN-13 978-1-61646-636-7

SCHEDULE OF TRAINS
BETWEEN
CAMDEN AND CAPE MAY

Mlge.	Station.			
0.	Camden.	5.20	7.45	9.55
31.	Newfield.	6.07	8.25 lv. 8.30	10.35
41.	Rockton.[1]	6.25	. . . .	. . . . .
72.	Oldroyd.[1]	. . . .	9.20[2]	11.29
82.	Cape May.	7.25	9.35	11.45

[1] Rockton and Oldroyd are fictitious towns, the former located approximately beyond Millville, N. J., and the latter between Cape May Court House and Wildwood Junction.

[2] Stops only on notice to conductor to discharge passengers.

I
THE BODY ON THE TRACKS

The late storm proved no obstacle to the Cape May bound express that left Camden at 9:55 in the evening and was due at the seashore resort at 11:45. Despite the torrential rain and a high, sweeping wind, it was making excellent time. Clattering noisily over switches, its whistle giving a piercing warning of its approach, its headlight cutting the murky darkness, it flew across the low, flat land of South Jersey. Little country stations, closed for several hours, flashed past and dwindled behind in the distance. Now and then, lighted village streets appeared and disappeared, and were replaced by the rolling obscurity of meadows and trees. Again, freight cars loomed into close proximity and were gone; but for the most part, the train seemed to be alone in a black and misty world.

Within the brightly lighted cars, however, the passengers were oblivious of the storm outside. The majority were men; it was the late commuter's train. In the smoking car, Daniel Gilmore, detective-sergeant of the Philadelphia police, slumped in his seat. Though his eyes were closed, he was not sleeping; rather was he absorbed in deep thought. In appearance, Gilmore, strangely enough, revealed his occupation. One might almost be tempted to say that he resembled the typical stage detective. A casual acquaintance would inevitably fail to credit him with much intelligence. He was large of physique, tending slightly to stoutness, with a dull, expressionless face set upon a thick neck. Baldness threatened his graying hair. It was not until one studied his eyes, which were deep-set and alive, never failing to observe every movement about him, that one appreciated and understood his reputation. For he possessed an enviable one, born of an infinite capacity to note even the most seemingly trivial item, and to produce it at the proper time, in its correct position of importance. This, coupled with an obstinate tenacity in clinging to a trail, made him an opponent not lightly to be regarded.

Though not brilliant, he was capable and thorough. He managed always to make the most of good fortune, so that his percentage of successes was unusually high.

A studied consideration of his peculiar mission caused Gilmore to open the paper he held upon his lap, to the financial section. On the front page of the section, in flaring headlines, was an article that strangely held his interest. Early that morning it would not even have attracted his attention; now it held for him a unique and intriguing significance. He read:

CAUSE FOR ASTONISHING RISE
OF AUDUBON MOTORS REVEALED
AMERICAN MOTORS PURCHASING; NIXON SILENT
"SHORT" INTERESTS ALARMED

The cause of the erratic behavior of Audubon common, that has been attracting attention in the financial world, is at last discovered. Beginning May 28th, its value began to sink gradually from a normal of 75 to 55 over a period of 14 days. This, in the face of a steady market, was sufficiently unique in itself; and it was believed that unknown bear interests were responsible. Three days ago, Audubon suddenly jumped 12 points. The following rise was phenomenal: 25 points on Friday, and the same on Saturday; today it has reached a new high of 145. The answer is now revealed; American Motors has been carrying on an extensive purchasing campaign of Audubon stock. For two weeks the corporation has successfully masked its activities; but with the disclosure, Audubon common has taken on a new value to its holders. The purpose of the "corner" is, of course, clear, but the policy behind it is not so certain. Philip Nixon, president of American Motors, has refused to speak. It is generally believed that he is the moving force behind the "corner," personally backing it with his own vast interests. . . .

There was more in a like vein in greater detail. Gilmore read it thoroughly before he returned to his browsing. He was lost in a deep study when, at 10:35, the express reached the first of its two stops, Newfield, thirty miles out of Camden. The second station, Oldroyd, was forty miles farther, and his destination at least ten miles beyond that; he had yet one and a quarter hours of traveling before him. The pattering of the rain on the pane was pleasant and soothing. The voices of the card-players ahead of him dropped to a murmur.

A stranger emerged from the coach in the rear and dropped into the seat beside him. As was his habit, Gilmore observed him closely. He invariably took stock of whoever came to his attention; and the newcomer's arrival aroused him.

Studying the tapering fingers, the slight goatee, the carefully waxed mustache tips, and the pince-nez lightly set upon the bridge of his nose, the detective concluded he was a professional man, probably a doctor. The stranger's coat was spotted slightly with rain. As he settled himself, he peered into the darkness beyond the detective; then he sat back, relaxing himself with a sigh of relief. After a moment of silence, broken only by the monotonous clatter of wheels beneath them, he again stared out the window, shaking his head as though in disapproval of the storm. He smiled bleakly at Gilmore, hesitating to speak. When he did so, his voice was curiously hoarse, as from a cold.

"Dreadful weather we are having, isn't it?" he asked. "Is it still coming down very hard?"

Gilmore obligingly looked from the window. By nature he was not taciturn, and he welcomed the prospect of a conversation.

"I believe it's gradually stopping now," he replied. "The pane doesn't seem to be getting any wetter and you can hardly hear the rain at all."

"I'm glad of that," said the other. "Wet weather isn't particularly inviting at a seashore resort. I suppose that is where you're going, isn't it?"

"For a couple of days, yes." Gilmore nodded agreeably.

"I prefer Atlantic City, but Cape May is a good deal more quiet, and that is always an advantage when one wants a rest."

"I suppose that's true," Gilmore returned. "But I'm not very familiar with Cape May. You see, I've never been there before."

"Indeed?" The other raised his eyebrows slightly. "Then perhaps I might suggest a few hotels. There is the Allshore for rooms and service. However, for meals, the Calledonia might be preferable . . ."

"Thank you, but I doubt very much whether I shall want to stay at any hotel."

"Then you are staying with some people . . . friends perhaps?"

"That's right." Gilmore abruptly changed the subject by producing the newspaper. "I've been reading this article. . . . Do you know anything about the stock market?"

"I'm not very conversant with it, though I suppose we are all more or less interested in it." The other reached for the paper. "What is it, anything special?"

"This demand for Audubon stock. American Motors is buying it on the market. The paper isn't very clear . . ."

He broke off as his companion's glasses accidentally slipped from his nose. The latter hurriedly reached for them, but the paper impeded his progress. They would unquestionably have shattered on the floor had not Gilmore swooped swiftly and caught them.

"Be careful of your glasses, there! That was a close shave."

"Thank you . . . It was very careless of me!" He replaced them and again looked through the window. "Tell me, are we anywhere near Oldroyd yet?"

Gilmore took out his watch. "I'm afraid not," he replied. "We're not due until eleven-twenty or so, and it's not much after eleven. It must be a matter of twenty miles yet."

"Thank you again. Really, I shall have much for which to be grateful to you before our journey is over." The speaker permitted himself a wintry smile. "You were saying, then, something about this article. . . ?"

"Yes—this move on the part of American Motors to control the Audubon corporation. They seem to be buying up all their stock and prices are going sky high."

"I suppose that's what they call cornering the market, isn't it?"

"It amounts to that," Gilmore replied. "Whatever the motive behind it, the stockholders are gaining tremendously by it. But sooner or later something is bound to smash."

The detective's companion scanned the article with interest, Gilmore waiting till he had sufficient time to read it and return the paper.

"Interesting," he commented, "and it implies that this man Nixon is the sole owner of American Motors. It must take a tremendous fortune to accomplish such a feat and . . ."

The stranger never finished the sentence. Without a moment's warning, the headlong, hurtling speed of the train slackened. A sudden lurch followed an equally sudden jerk. Amid the screech of grinding brakes, the shrill cry of escaping air, and the clamor of steel crashing against protesting steel, it came to an abrupt halt. It threw both men forcefully against the forward seats; a second convulsive movement sent them to the floor. Cards and passengers flew precipitously in all directions. Distinctly, above all other noises, came the tinkle of broken glass.

For an instant, pandemonium reigned. Several lights were suddenly extinguished; only a miracle, it seemed, prevented the entire car from being plunged into darkness. Then passengers began to struggle drunkenly to their feet and there was a mad rush for the doors.

Gilmore was the first to recover his feet. As he assisted his companion to rise, he could not resist a startled cry.

"Good God! What in the world has happened?"

Finding that they were in no immediate danger, he swiftly raised the window and gazed the length of the train. Even in that moment of excitement he noticed that it had ceased raining. At the front of the train little red and yellow lights were gathering, flickering fantastically. They cast strange shadows upon the wraith-like figures that carried them. Faint shouts were wafted back to him.

Gilmore drew in his head.

"Something's the matter up front, but you can't see what it is from here. I don't think the engine's gone off the track."

"Not another train . . . ?" the other asked anxiously.

"No, nothing like that. Maybe an open switch. If it is, we're lucky things aren't any worse."

"Perhaps we had better go up and see. This is apt to delay us."

Together they started for the door just as a conductor appeared in the front entranceway. He raised his hand reassuringly, and waited a moment for silence.

"It's all right, ladies and gentlemen." He spoke quietly. "Just some slight engine trouble up front. If you'll only take your seats, we'll be on our way within ten minutes."

He paused and surveyed the passengers.

"Are any of you doctors? Some one has been injured in one of the forward cars . . ."

"I am." Gilmore's companion stepped forward. "Dr. David Curtiss. Can I be of any assistance?"

"Yes, if you'll just come forward."

The train officer led him out of the front door. Gilmore followed. His training told him that he had best be present, even though he had not been specifically called for. Their guide, assuming that he was the physician's companion, made no remark.

They stepped from the car, the ground wet and soft underfoot. There was a fresh coolness in the air, rare in the city they had left behind. The sky, however, was still black and lowering, no ray of light piercing it. Gilmore could barely see the outline of a peaked, sharp roof that was the only habitation in sight.

Guided by the red lamp the conductor held, they proceeded toward the engine. Then their leader spoke.

"The truth of the matter is that we've just struck a man, lying on the tracks. The engineer didn't see him until it was too late, and at the speed we were going he couldn't stop within the length of the train. There's no doubt he's dead; the cowcatcher scooped him right up. Still, a doctor ought to look him over before we go on."

Gilmore was startled. "A body on the tracks—way out in this part of the country? That doesn't sound like an accident."

"No, I should certainly say not," Dr. Curtiss agreed, swiftly. "It seems more like a suicide, I should think."

"I think that's what they said it was," explained the conductor, "but I haven't the details, as I came directly back for a doctor."

Traversing the distance to the front of the train, they came upon a strange tableau. Under the glaring brilliant arc of the locomotive's headlight, the engineer, fireman, and two uniformed trainmen waited silently for them. The lamps they carried flickered feebly against the brighter segment of light that caught back its reflections upon the steel rails, hundreds of feet away. Within the huge iron body of the engine came the labored breathing of the settling mechanism, as though it were complaining of the violence of its unexpected halt.

The tragic remains of a human being lay, a crumpled, bulky object, a few feet from the engine. The trainmen had gingerly disentangled it from the prongs of the "cowcatcher," itself unpleasantly besmirched with red stains. The inert mass, mangled and twisted beyond all recognition by the impact of the towering monster, caused even the detective to shudder; he found it difficult to contemplate.

With scarcely a pause, the physician dropped to his knees between the steel rails and began his examination. Only Gilmore observed his tremor of hesitation at the task and the visible strengthening of nerves; and he admired the experience that permitted such callousness. The fireman's tender of a lamp was waved away; the headlight offered sufficient illumination.

The engineer was anxiously explaining the situation to the others.

"You can't blame me for it, can you?" he asked. "You can't see a thing like that till you're almost on top of it; and then, of course, it's too late to stop, if you're going at any speed . . ."

"That's all right, Bill," the grimy fireman reassured him. "No one's goin' to hold you responsible."

"Well, I couldn't help it. . . ." He was a heavy, gnarled, weather-beaten man, seeking solace in the tobacco he chewed vigorously. "If a person wants to commit suicide, it's a wonder he wouldn't choose another road, instead of messing up my engine and making trouble for me."

"That's right," a trainman agreed. "Or killed himself at home in private, where nobody'd see him."

As Gilmore's gaze swung toward the iron prongs, where further evidence of the fatality, bits of cloth mingled with flesh, were visible, two passengers joined them. They descended from the train chattering lightly; they were shocked into awesome silence by the sight. Two others followed; then, as rumor began to spread, more travelers trickled out upon the scene, first from the nearer cars, and then from those farther to the rear. They crowded about with a ghoulish desire to be witnesses to the tragedy; they experienced a dread satisfaction at being upon the scene. Yet, restrained by the presence of death, none spoke above a whisper.

The detective broke in upon the conversation. "Just a moment," he said. "When you first saw the body, how was it lying?"

The authority of his tone caused the engineer to reply to his query, rather than object to it, as he at first seemed inclined.

"What do you mean—how was it laying? Down, of course."

"Was the body stretched out flat on the tracks, or was it huddled together?"

The other appeared puzzled. "I can't say I noticed it," he said hesitantly. "I was too busy with the train."

"But you must have some impression of it. You see, if a man's a suicide, he'd either meet death standing, or if he had to lie down, he'd stretch out, taut, waiting for the blow. He couldn't help that . . ."

"Are you figuring this wasn't a suicide . . ." one of the passengers began, when the engineer interrupted him.

"You mean—was he in a heap? Now that I come t' think of it, he was sort of bundled up, in the middle of the track. He wasn't stretched out at all."

Gilmore nodded as Dr. Curtiss rose from his examination, wiping his hands on a handkerchief.

"It's almost impossible to tell anything without any instruments or conveniences. But I should say that the body is that of a middle-aged man. Of course, he is dead . . . was dead from the moment the train struck him."

He addressed no one in particular, speaking to all listeners.

"That was what killed him?" Gilmore asked.

"Certainly—at least, as far as I am now able to tell. I don't believe that there is the least doubt it was suicide. His skull is crushed, and his body is quite badly mangled. One arm is almost cut off. There are doubtless many internal injuries, resulting from the impact of the train. The engine must have carried him almost three hundred feet."

"At least that," the fireman agreed.

"From the instant he was struck he was beyond medical aid. I will include that in my report to the proper authorities—the county officers here, I suppose, where the suicide occurred."

"There's no possibility that it could have been an accident?" queried the detective.

Dr. Curtiss looked annoyed at his companion's apparent officiousness, and said sardonically, "The victim would hardly be likely to place himself in the path of a visible oncoming train, accidentally. Not if he had all his senses."

"This fellow seems to have a bug in his ear," the engineer remarked crudely. "What's your idea of it?"

Gilmore could hardly have explained what troubled him. Every appearance of suicide there certainly was. But experience had taught him to view the obvious with suspicion; and where violent death was concerned, he was even less prepared to accept surface impressions. It was the setting—the vast, lonely, bedraggled countryside, sunk under the recent rain. Where had the man come from—how had he reached this spot? Except for the single house, there existed no evidence of habitation. No road approached the right of way, as far as he could see. All about him, there were only illimitable shadows receding into darkness.

Even as he searched the utter desolation of the scene, a light suddenly went on, in the upper floor of the house.

He shook his head, uncertainly. "I may be wrong," he admitted. "Have any of you examined his belongings and found out who he is?"

"Not us . . . we don't want to touch him if it isn't necessary. Maybe the doctor would . . ."

The physician appeared to be further vexed. "I haven't yet—but perhaps you would like to examine him, Mr. . . ."

"Detective—Sergeant Gilmore of the Philadelphia police."

A swift, ominous silence fell upon the spectators as the detective, accepting the challenge, dropped to his knees beside the body. The victim of the tragedy was, as the doctor had said, middle-aged. The crushed skull with the resultant matted hair made a scrutiny of the features virtually impossible. Yet he could see that the hair was gray, the forehead high, and the physique large and strongly built.

The man wore a light spring coat, brown in color, of imported English tweed, over an expensive serge suit.

Both were violently torn in many places, and also damp, a fact to which Gilmore attached some importance. For the rain had stopped just before the train had come upon the body at a few minutes after eleven. Unless the dead man had gotten soaked in reaching this point, he had been unquestionably lying in the rain for a time before the express had arrived. The inside of the coat possessed the maker's label—"Lorch & Taylor."

In the vest pocket, the detective found a watch and chain with a charm attached. The crystal was broken, though not completely smashed, a rather curious fact if the impact of the engine had caused it to break. In such a case, there should have been nothing but a mangled piece of gold left; yet Gilmore could tell that the hands pointed to one minute after nine. It was now thirty-five minutes after eleven; two hours and thirty-five minutes had passed since the watch had stopped.

The charm attached to the watch was an ivory skull, set upon the gold background of a coin. Casually, Gilmore turned it over; unexpectedly, he was staring at it with a fascination that amounted to a hypnotic spell. It was impossible that there were two like that. To the astonishment of the watchers, he seized the torn left arm of the victim and inspected the fingers. On the third finger of the left hand was a thick, gold signet ring. He did not have to study it closely—he already knew the initials printed upon it in ancient English script.

Despite the coolness of the night, beads of sweat stood out upon Gilmore's forehead. His fingers raced feverishly through the coat, seeking the inner pocket of the dead man's suit. The hastily formed fear grew to an absolute certainty as he extracted some letters. He did not need to look at the address upon the envelopes to know that his worst fears were realized.

The dead man was Philip Nixon.

Gilmore rose from the body. His attitude was enough to inform the expectant watchers that something was desperately wrong. The seriousness of the situation was written in his eyes; and he appeared strangely enveloped in a cloak of authority that all spectators were now only too willing to grant him.

"I regret to say, gentlemen," he announced, "that this is neither an accident nor suicide. It is murder. I shall take charge at once, and I ask your cooperation."

2
THE ASSIGNMENT

That Monday morning, Sergeant Gilmore had set out for Headquarters in his usual contented frame of mind. Life on the whole was pretty satisfactory, he mused, for he had the most excellent wife in the world, three children of whom he could well be proud and a position that not only insured their comfort but gave him the stimulus of active mental work and interesting contact with human nature. The police routine was certainly never monotonous, and he wondered vaguely what new developments might be awaiting him.

At the Central Detective Bureau, Captain Thomas, on duty at the day desk, looked up from his perusal of the morning paper.

"The Old Fellow wants to see you, Gilmore. Probably you'll be hauled up on the mat. What've you been doing?"

Summons from the Superintendent usually meant one of two things—a calling down or a new assignment. In the past few weeks, there had occurred nothing of an important or sensational nature, so Gilmore approached his chief with some curiosity.

His knock upon the Superintendent's door was answered by a command to enter. The man in the office was slight and wiry, and despite his graying hair, young for a position of such importance. As the door opened, he swung about from his desk, and motioned Gilmore to be seated.

"Good morning, Sergeant Gilmore. How is Mrs. Gilmore these days? I haven't seen her since that outing last summer."

"She's very well, thank you," the detective replied.

That was Superintendent Wainwright's manner—a personal question to put his man at ease, then an abrupt change to the business in hand.

"I'm glad to hear that. . . . Now, as to my reason for wishing to see you. I believe I have some special work for you, though I cannot say exactly what it is at the moment. Have you ever heard of Philip Nixon?"

"Philip Nixon, sir? We all know his name from that Ferris affair. And, of course, I know he is one of the wealthiest men in the country."

The Superintendent nodded gravely. "That's right, Gilmore," he said. "He is the president of the American Motors Corporation, which combines at least fifteen automobile concerns. Practically controls the company. There are offices both here and in New York, but I believe Nixon makes Philadelphia his real center. He lives at Bryn Mawr and there is a summer place at Cape May."

He paused for a moment as though in deep thought, then went on. "As to the man himself, I had occasion to meet him when the Ferris affair came up. I may as well give you my impressions, for what they are worth. I should place his age at fifty, and I was much impressed by his powerful personality. He is a typical Wall Street success. About fifteen years ago he emerged from obscurity, probably with borrowed money, and engineered a daring financial coup. His sheer bravado carried him through, and gradually he has built up a unique place in the financial world. He is a real power, with the biggest auto concern in the world under his thumb."

Again a pause, while the Superintendent smiled at Gilmore.

"I have to tell you all this, Sergeant, because I want you to get a picture of the man you will deal with. He's a widower now—lost his wife about ten years ago. There's also rumor here and there that he was quite a sport in his younger days, and fond of various ladies. But with a grown daughter, I'm sure he is more circumspect now. That Ferris affair is in itself a proof of his affection for her. Eleanor Nixon is really a great beauty and . . ."

"It was her necklace which was stolen," Gilmore interrupted, "at the reception Nixon gave on her twentieth birthday, wasn't it?"

"Quite right, Sergeant. I see you remember the robbery."

"I didn't have anything to do with it personally, sir. Tommy Rankin had the case, but I remember that Ferris was the ringleader, and he got a heavy sentence, didn't he?"

"Yes, it was Rankin's case, but Ferris's capture couldn't be credited to his efforts. It is the first failure we've chalked up against him since long before his splendid work last year in the murder of that girl at Woodlawn Park."

He turned to some papers to refresh his memory, and then looked up.

"I want to review that case very briefly, Sergeant, for your information.

"In November of last year on Eleanor Nixon's twentieth birthday, her father gave a big reception in her honor. It received an enormous amount of publicity on account of her father's position and on account of a rumor that the girl was to wear a diamond necklace valued conservatively at a hundred and fifty thousand dollars. Of course, the news spread to the underworld, and apparently the Ferris gang took on the job of getting the loot. Whatever else can be said of Lew Ferris, you're bound to admit he has brains. This robbery was admirably planned—and even after he was captured he refused to incriminate the rest of the gang. Once his mouth was closed, nothing could open it; all the third degree in the world was useless.

"He wouldn't even admit who was the fourth member," the Superintendent went on. "Rankin knew there had been four of them in the beginning—Lew himself, Arthur Stahl and Ike Morin, old hands those two, and Monckton. But Monckton was killed two years ago, so there must have been a new man. Rankin couldn't identify him, and couldn't find a sign of any of the others anywhere.

"On the night of the reception, Ferris managed to install Ike Morin and Stahl on the inside, one as an extra servant, one as a caterer's assistant. He and Number Four, in dress suits, hid in the garden. Stahl let them in by a side door, and Ferris joined the long receiving line. When he reached Eleanor Nixon, Morin was to switch off the lights. The other three were to handle the three detectives. The scheme worked all right. Under cover of the darkness, Ferris grabbed the necklace."

The chief concluded his story rather grimly.

"In the uproar, a shot was fired and a woman injured. The gang fled in different directions; two got out the front door. Unfortunately for him, Lew made a mistake. Stahl went through the conservatory windows on the right where a veranda broke the fall and escaped. Lew took the left, a sheer drop of five feet to the garden and sprained his ankle. He was caught limping through the grounds.

"The rest is just a common court case; Nixon pressed every possible charge against Lew, hired expert lawyers and all the rest of it. At the close of the trial, Lew Ferris was sent up for fifteen years, for larceny, burglary, accessory to an attempt to kill, and a few minor charges the prosecution put over."

"It's pretty hard on Lew," the detective commented, "but that Ferris gang has had it coming to them."

"I don't say it wasn't deserved. Certainly from his own point of view, Nixon was justified in pressing his charges to the limit."

Relaxing a little, he smiled quizzically. "I suppose you are wondering, Gilmore, what all this has to do with my sending for you.—Simply this. I received a message from the American Motor offices this morning asking me to send Nixon one of my best men for special service. No hint of the reason. Between you and Rankin, I decided on you because he has failed once already to trace the rest of Ferris's crew."

Gilmore asked no questions. It was for him to handle the matter now, and it might mean distinction in the service and ultimate promotion.

"Thank you, sir," was all he said, as he got up. "I'll report at once at the offices."

The Superintendent held out his hand. "I'll let Nixon know there's a man on the way. It'll be an interesting job, Gilmore, I'm sure of that. And I wish you good luck."

In a very few minutes, Gilmore was on his way to the offices of the American Motor Corporation on South Broad Street. These, he found, consisted of a large suite on the fifth floor of the building, where room after room opened out, filled with clerks, stenographers and secretaries.

The detective gave his name to a young man who seemed to be Nixon's secretary.

"Please come right into the private office," he said, "Mr. Nixon is expecting you. . . ."

He led Gilmore into a room which resembled a living room more than a business office. Paneled in dark oak, with handsome Oriental rugs on the floor, it had a fine, rather somber dignity. Behind the massive desk, the stock ticker stood silent but impressive.

The Superintendent's description of the man who sat at the desk had given Gilmore little conception of the strength and magnificent poise of this great financier. Beneath slightly white hair was the broad forehead of great intelligence. Deep, expressive eyes and well-formed features gave the face charm; the firm sweep of chiseled lips gave it character. In every line of shoulder and body one could see that he was a man of parts, successful, finely tempered, of a dominating nature. He wore no jewelry, except a heavy gold signet ring on the left hand which was spread out in a dramatic gesture on the pad before him.

It was not until Gilmore had observed him closely that he decided the man was either ill or greatly worried. His lips were drawn down as though the teeth were clenched, and the pupils of his eyes showed a curious strain.

The detective's impression was confirmed when Philip Nixon spoke. His voice was thick with heavy tones and somewhat hoarse.

"Please be seated, Mr. Gilmore," he said, when the secretary had introduced them. "That will be all, Donald. Please see that we are not disturbed."

He waited until the door had closed behind the young man, meanwhile studying the detective.

"I think you will be most satisfactory for my purposes, Mr. Gilmore. To put the matter directly, I have sent for you because I want protection. For reasons of my own I did not wish to appeal publicly to the police, but I prefer city detectives to private ones. I want protection, Mr. Gilmore, because my life has been threatened."

He made the statement calmly, as though it were of no importance; yet Gilmore could feel a thrill at the sinister appeal.

"You are aware, of course," Nixon went on, "of the details of the robbery that occurred at my daughter's reception last November. It was a disgraceful thing, and

I naturally used all my influence to make an example of the culprit."

Suddenly the quality of ruthlessness which must have served the man in good stead in his business career rang in his voice.

"Immediately after the conviction," he proceeded more quietly, "I received a threatening letter, quite obviously from the members of Ferris's gang. A second letter came last month. I disregarded both of them. But the third which came this morning was so threatening that I felt obliged to take notice of it."

"Have you those letters with you?" Gilmore asked.

The financier toyed with his watch charm, a gold coin surmounted by an ivory skull, before replying.

"Yes, of course, but I've said nothing about them to my daughter or my friends . . ."

His movement toward an inner pocket was interrupted by the opening of the door. The girl who entered was slender, slight of stature, yet Gilmore had no need of being informed that this was Eleanor Nixon. An air of assertiveness with a quality of audacity increased her strong physical resemblance to her father. Auburn hair and brilliant coloring heightened the impression of her vitality and charm.

Philip Nixon's grim features relaxed when he saw her, and all the harshness seemed to melt away.

"Hello, Dad dear!" she cried in a warm contralto voice, as she ran forward to kiss him. "I'm awfully sorry to interrupt, but I was in town and I did want to come in to see you."

"I'm very glad you did, Eleanor. I want you to meet Mr. Gilmore, dear. This is my daughter. . . . Mr. Gilmore may be our guest for a while, so be nice to him."

She met the detective's bow with a pleasant, but absentminded smile.

"That's fine, Dad," she said. "How is your cold today? Bennett and I don't like it at all, and you ought to be careful."

Philip Nixon smiled gently, more at her concern than at her words. "It's hardly very serious, dear. But to tell you the truth, I'm thinking of driving down to Cape May this afternoon for a little rest and a dash of sea air for my cough."

Distinct surprise crossed Eleanor Nixon's vivid face. "Why, father! not today? How can you get away at the beginning of the week like this? And have you let Mrs. Webster know?"

While she was speaking, Gilmore moved over to the window and watched the shifting panorama below him. The distorted perspective amused him, and the incessant stream of tiny flat objects had something of a hypnotic fascination.

"I don't think I'll have to tell her ahead of time," the financier was saying behind him. "I'll just appear and she can fix me up all right. It probably wouldn't be for very long anyway . . ." Abruptly, he changed the subject. "But what else, besides anxiety for the state of my health, brings you to town?"

"I'm going shopping, and I need some money," the girl replied, "That's one thing . . ."

"Nothing new," smiled her father.

"Then there's a tea this afternoon at the Bellevue and so I'll probably not be home before six. And then I'm going to lunch with Donald and . . ."

"With whom did you say, Eleanor?"

Even before Nixon had spoken, Gilmore felt the change in atmosphere. At this cold, metallic tone, he turned quickly. Here was certainly some family situation never intended for the ears of a stranger. The man's hand was shaking as he rose from his chair with an effort; his face was suddenly pale.

Eleanor Nixon nervously tried to pass the matter off.

"With Donald, father. . . . He asked me whether he could take me to lunch, and of course I . . ."

Her father's voice broke in harshly. "You accepted Gardiner's invitation after my request? I thought I had asked you to see nothing of him. If you persist in disobeying me, I shall have to take sterner measures . . ."

A sudden dangerous blaze flared in the girl's eyes. Gilmore at once realized that the financier was using the wrong tactics. Eleanor Nixon, pampered and protected, would brook refusal no more readily than would her formidable father. Her lips tightened; obstinacy descended like a mask over her features.

"We've gone all over this before," Nixon continued with a trace of weariness, "and there is no need to discuss it again. You know my wishes and I expect you to observe them."

"If he is satisfactory as your personal secretary, he must certainly be suitable for my company," the girl replied with spirit.

"In this case, I will be the judge, Eleanor. Donald Gardiner himself would declare my reasons justified, if he had any principles at all . . ."

"You can't say that, father, without giving Donald a chance to defend himself. I wonder that he remains in your employ!"

"Because he knows well enough he could not get any position elsewhere," Nixon exclaimed.

The conviction of his words silenced Eleanor; bewilderment and pain grew in her startled eyes. For a few moments, both she and her father had forgotten that they were not alone. In the sudden pause, however, Philip Nixon remembered his visitor; when he spoke again, he held his voice in control.

"Have you ever known me, Eleanor," he said evenly, "at any time to have acted against your best interests?"

"No, father."

Her brief reply was weighted with the doubt and uneasiness reflected in her face.

"Isn't it true that you have always trusted my judgment before?"

For answer, she bent her head.

"Then you must believe that what I'm asking is for your good . . ."

The calmness of Eleanor Nixon's voice matched his. "But I resent being treated like a child, father. Whatever they are, I'm able to decide for myself whether your objections are justified. And you can't expect me to respect your wishes, unless you take me into your confidence."

"I haven't told you my objections because I think it would hurt you . . ."

"If it will hurt me, father, I'll take my punishment willingly. If you'll tell me when you come back, I'll promise to do no more than speak to Donald today. . . ."

There was a moment of hesitation, in which Gilmore could see Philip Nixon giving way before her plea. He did not speak, but merely inclined his head. The detective needed no further evidence of his affection for this willful daughter.

Eleanor Nixon folded the money he gave her, and prepared to go. She kissed him again, very softly.

"All right, father," she said, "when you come back from Cape May, we'll settle this. Remember this is a truce, not a surrender."

He smiled until she was gone, but when the door closed, he seemed to age. It was as though some inner light had

been extinguished, and only the shell of the man, hardened and somewhat worn, remained. As he motioned the
detective to a chair, he sank back into his own—a magnificent but strangely defeated figure.

"I'm sorry for the interruption, Mr. Gilmore," he said.
"Shall we continue with business? Here are the letters I
received."

3
THE NIXON HOUSEHOLD

There were three letters that Gilmore took from the financier's hand, arranged as the postmarks upon the envelopes told him, in the order of their arrival. The first two, dated in April and May, respectively, were in the same hand, on crumpled paper and smudged by what looked like grease. The third, with its date of the preceding day, had had another author. It came directly to the point, was neat in its execution, and, the detective felt, was pregnant with a menace that could not be misunderstood. None were signed or dated.

"Unless you help Lew Ferris out of the jam you got him in," Gilmore read, "you will get into serious trouble."

"That first one came just after Lew was sentenced," Nixon explained. "There's no question of who sent it. Ferris's gang, believes—and with some reason—that if I wish, I could do something for him. But I certainly have no intention of helping him."

"There ought to be fingerprints," the other remarked, "though I don't suppose they would do us any good even if there were."

He turned to the second message. "You have disregarded the warning. Unless you act at once, you will be threatened with great danger."

"There's no doubt, at any rate, that this came from the same source. And almost a month ago . . ."

The financier smiled slightly. "It was annoying, but I refused to take alarm at such childish tactics. I gave it no consideration; there was nothing they could do."

"How did you say you received these?" Gilmore asked.

"In my regular personal mail, at home. I found them waiting among my other letters."

"And all of them mailed from the Central Post Office," the detective commented, studying the postmarks closely. "They were very careful to leave no traces. . . . The same is true of the one that arrived today. . . ."

"No more warnings," the note read. "You sentenced Lew Ferris to a living death, and you will pay in the same manner."

"I couldn't very well disregard that one," Nixon said. "I'm not in the least frightened, but I've dealt with desperate men before and it would have been foolhardy to take any chances. Accordingly, I communicated at once with your Superintendent. . . ."

Gilmore agreed that he acted wisely. But even as he spoke, he experienced a strange sense of bewilderment. The financier was not being as frank as his words would have him believe; an intuition for which he could not account, informed him that Nixon was carefully feeling his way, lest he say something he did not want Gilmore to know. His former delay pointed in the same direction. He had not wanted to appeal for aid; not until the Ferris gang had left him no choice had he done so. And then he had asked for only one man. What did he expect of the detective alone? It would have been more sensible to put the matter in the hands of the police in the regular fashion. Yet, for some reason of his own, Nixon had failed to do so.

He put his opinion into words. "Your most practical move, in a case like this, would be to turn the matter over to our regular force, so that they could round up the gang as quickly as possible."

The financier's repudiation of the suggestion told him his suspicions had some basis.

"No, that would never do, Mr. Gilmore," he said. "At least, not for the present. You must recall that when the police were hunting the Ferris gang a few months ago, they could not locate them. They wouldn't be likely to succeed now."

"Nevertheless, they are far more likely to succeed than I, alone, possibly could be," Gilmore went on, as though Nixon had not spoken. "And, of course, I could arrange to have you guarded regularly."

The other again toyed nervously with his watch guard, as though he dreaded Gilmore's keenness.

"If you refuse to act, Mr. Gilmore, then I am afraid I shall have to procure some one else for the purpose. . . ."

"I'm not refusing, Mr. Nixon," the detective said hastily. "That is not my business. I came to serve you, and I am merely trying to learn how I may best do so and exactly what you expect of me."

The sense that there was something concealed below the surface prompted him to yield immediately. But the financier had difficulty in finding words to express his wishes.

"Well," he said, at last, "as I hinted to my daughter, I want you to act as my guest, and accompany me wherever I go, in case anything should happen. You will, of course, stay with me at my home, while you are on duty. All these precautions may prove unnecessary, but then . . ."

"That suits me quite well, Mr. Nixon, and I shall begin duties at once, if you wish. . . ."

The simple statement appeared to take the financier off his guard. He shook his hand briefly in positive negation.

"Oh, no," he interrupted hurriedly, "I shall not want you to join me until quite late this evening. You must have heard me say that my health has not been of the best, and I am considering going down to my summer home in Cape May this afternoon for a short rest."

"Then you expect me to travel down with you. . . ?"

"No, Mr. Gilmore," Nixon replied, "I shall merely ask you to join me there this evening. A train leaving Camden at nine-fifty-five will get you there just before bedtime. I shall be there, myself, by that time, but it is so difficult to foretell exactly when I can get away, that . . ." He left the sentence, unfinished. "Here—that is my address."

The detective took the card that was offered him. "And what will you do, Mr. Nixon?"

"I. . . ? I shall drive down as soon as business permits me to leave. Naturally, tied down as I now am, I would hardly leave, unless I thought my health necessitated my making a change for a few days . . ."

Here, again, the financier was concealing something. It had to do with his intended journey, Gilmore was certain; mention of it appeared to make him uneasy. The detective had first noted that confusion, while Nixon had been discussing his trip with his daughter. Then, when she had questioned him on the subject, he had swiftly spoken of something else. Before others, he might have successfully concealed his feelings; facing Eleanor, he had made a poor liar. His unaccountable distress had been evident to Gilmore; and once more he wondered what the man was hiding. His true plans regarding the journey? The time he intended to leave for the shore? Or had he no intention of leaving at all?

Gilmore could not fathom it, but his words revealed nothing of the disturbance in his mind.

"I think I could best occupy my time this afternoon by becoming acquainted with your household. I could work better if I knew how you live, and whom you employ."

The suggestion seemed to please Nixon. "That can be arranged," he replied, as he looked at his watch. "I'm expecting Parker, my chauffeur, any moment and he will take you home. And meanwhile, I'll let Bennett know you are coming, so that he can make things ready for you."

"That's quite all right, Mr. Nixon. I'll manage, well enough."

"Yes, I dare say you will with Bennett to take care of you. He has been with me fifteen years and is something like a perfect servant. He is exactly like one of the family."

Further discussion was interrupted by the entry of the secretary to announce the arrival of the chauffeur.

"Send him in, Donald," the financier ordered him, "I have some errands for him and I had better explain them myself. . . ."

The financier's words gave no indication of rancor or antipathy against this young man over whom he had quarreled with his daughter and Gilmore took the opportunity to study him more closely. He appeared to be little more than twenty-five and his excellent breeding was apparent. Character was written in the aquiline nose and the eyes; and the seriousness of mien added earnestness to the candor of feature, which Eleanor Nixon had found attractive. He had light unruly hair. His face possessed a strange pallor, however, visible only to the detective's expert eye; but he dismissed as ludicrous one possible explanation of it.

The man in chauffeur's uniform was also good-looking, in a dark, foreign manner. But the heavy, lowering lips were covered by what Gilmore was amazed to interpret as a sneer. He was glaring sullenly at the financier, with a studied insolence that gave him a saturnine and sinister aspect. Studying the newcomer, Gilmore was at a loss to fathom the disrespect written in his attitude.

Philip Nixon spoke to his employee with a cold and deliberate finality.

"Parker, this gentleman is to be my guest and you are to drive him, at once, to Bryn Mawr. I shall speak to Bennett before you arrive, but see that he is made comfortable. Is that clear?"

The chauffeur's curt nod and subsequent silence were as defiant as though he had offensively refused to obey. Nixon must have been aware of his behavior; nevertheless, to the surprise of the detective, he appeared to be persistent in disregarding it.

"After that, Charles," he went on, "I want you to return for me, here. Can you be back by half-past two?"

The chauffeur studied his wrist watch for a moment. "It's after one now, but I think it can be done."

"Very well, then; I'll have further instructions for you when you return," he said in a tone of dismissal.

A moment later, Gilmore had followed Parker into the street. A magnificent, yellow Rolls-Royce awaited him, polished and brilliantly reflecting the sun's rays; no blemish spotted its glistening surface.

Disregarding the rear door which Charles opened for him, he took a seat beside the chauffeur. They drove through the park at a comfortable speed; despite the financier's orders, Parker seemed to be in no hurry. At City Line he leisurely entered the Lancaster Pike boulevard. The car rode smoothly and inaudibly; the friction of the wheels was a steady, soothing murmur.

The hour spent in the financier's office had produced a series of kaleidoscopic impressions, and Gilmore took this opportunity to collect and rearrange them. Too many unconnected matters required his attention; four in particular needed special consideration. There was the Ferris gang, with their threatening messages and Nixon's demand for protection; Eleanor Nixon, beautiful and spoiled, demanding an explanation of her parent's antipathy for young Gardiner; the secretary, himself, apparently a trusted and valued employee; and finally, the strange secretiveness of which the financier had been guilty.

There was some peculiar situation, too, with regard to Nixon's relation to his chauffeur. Though the latter had been deliberately and obviously offensive, the financier had made no objection. Whether he put much faith in him, Gilmore did not know; but he felt that he himself would never trust him. His eyes were shifty and sullen—criminal's eyes, his experience in such matters told him; the thick lips were unpleasantly aggressive.

He proved taciturn and morose, ungraciously refusing to answer Gilmore's questions in more than bare monosyllables.

"You have a wonderful car," Gilmore remarked sociably after a while. "It rides beautifully and you keep it in splendid condition. . . ."

"Yes, it's all right," Parker assented, looking ahead.

"Working for Philip Nixon must be something of a privilege. Have you been with him long?"

The chauffeur's lips tightened as though he was not going to reply. Then, thinking the better of it—

"No, not long; not more than about two months."

"Then you must consider yourself fortunate to have obtained this position. . . ."

A sudden, grim smile appeared on the other's features. "No," he said suddenly. "If you want the truth, I don't consider myself lucky to be working for Philip Nixon, and I'm not stayin' long either."

"You aren't?" The detective voiced his surprise at this outspoken statement. "Why not? I should have thought—"

"I can't be keeping my eye on the wheel, and talking at the same time; but you can tell Nixon, if you want to, that I don't like him any more than he likes me. I guess he knows that already!"

He spoke so venomously that Gilmore was silenced. As a guest of the financier, he could have no reason to ask

further questions. He must of necessity remember his position; it was too soon to attract suspicion to the object
of his visit by an injudicious curiosity in matters which
could not possibly concern him.

After that, no more was said for almost a half-hour.
Then the machine turned off the main highway suddenly,
into an open driveway, hedged on both sides by heavy and
carefully trimmed shrubbery. The first view of the house
was inspiring. It was a tremendous mansion, extending, in
endless gables and corners, into grounds so deep that their
boundaries were invisible. Of white stone, it was covered
by a red-tiled roof, and ivy, covering one of its sides, gave
it an effect of age.

The auto drive approached it by a sharp right-hand
turn, at the main entrance, before it disappeared behind
the house. To the left, Gilmore glimpsed a sunken garden.
Beyond, were tennis courts and further shrubbery, and
then, a rustic summer-house.

Noiselessly, the Rolls-Royce drew to a halt before the
main portal. Gilmore had not stepped from it, when the
door was opened by a kindly-eyed old man in black clothes,
who he at once knew was Bennett. He greeted Gilmore and
bowed him into the house before him.

"Come right in, sir," he said, "I have just learned you
were coming, and I haven't had time to get your room
ready, yet. . . . Mr. Nixon expects you back by two-thirty,
Charles. . . ."

He closed the door behind them both, waving away a
uniformed servant, who waited uncertainly for the luggage. Through a heavily carpeted hallway, they entered a
large room.

"Mr. Nixon wants you to make yourself at home, and I
am to tell you whatever you wish to know. Will you wait
here till your room is finished or come upstairs?"

"I think I'll remain here, Bennett."

The butler bowed himself toward the door. "Very good, sir."

"Oh, just a moment." Gilmore stopped him. "Where is the conservatory?"

"Right off this room, sir, to your right. . . ."

The room he indicated made a protruding ell, one of the picturesque angles of the house. It opened beyond a Gothic arch; French windows occupying the entire outer wall permitted light from every angle. Exotic plants in great profusion covered the parquet floor; their heavy scent penetrated into the next room.

Before the servant's steps had died away on the broad staircase, Gilmore was examining the scene of Lew Ferris's misfortune. The veranda, upon which the French windows opened, extended only half of the length of the conservatory. The other half of the flower room faced the garden; below the windows was a sheer drop to the ground. In the excitement of that moment during the robbery, Ferris had turned in the wrong direction. Instead of crashing through to the veranda, as he unquestionably intended, he had taken the unexpected fall that had resulted fatally for him.

The detective was studying the furnishings of the main apartment when Bennett returned to show him to his room.

"This is a very fine establishment you have here under your care, Bennett—and a large one, too. A huge household like this must require quite a force of servants to keep it going properly."

Pleased at the implied compliment in his words, the butler rose to the bait of Gilmore's suggestions.

"Of course, sir," he replied, "the size of the house makes a large number of help necessary. I have, immediately under me, the footman and Ben, who is the houseman, and waits on the table—both good men, who have been with us for some time. My wife is the housekeeper, and has charge of the kitchen, but in a large measure, I oversee what is

going on there, and what the chef prepares. Miss Nixon has her personal maid, Hilda; for cleaning in general,
we hire extra maids. Outside, we have a gardening force;
they live, with most of the servants, in special quarters set
aside for them, just in back of the house."

He led the detective to a window, and pointed out a
small cottage.

"There, you can see it from here, sir. Hilda, Mrs. Bennett, and I are the only ones who live under this roof."

Gilmore made a mental note of this catalogue. "What
about the chauffeur?" he queried.

"There's Charles to do the driving for Mr. Nixon; and
a young fellow works around the garage. Miss Eleanor
doesn't need anyone . . ."

"That was Charles that brought me here, wasn't it? He
seemed rather a competent fellow."

Bennett looked surprised at his lack of judgment. "He
may be a good driver, sir, but he's not a satisfactory chauffeur. We generally keep our help a long time; but he's only
been with us two months and he's leaving tomorrow when
his week is up."

"Is that so?" Gilmore was casual. "Why, what's the matter?"

"Well, sir, he had quite a bitter argument with Mr.
Nixon yesterday, and he is never one to put up with any
foolishness. I wouldn't have stood him for a moment."

"Have you any idea what the difficulty was?"

"I couldn't say exactly," Bennett replied, "but I do think
that Mr. Nixon caught Charles at something dishonest. He
was always sneaking around from the minute he came—
why, it was enough to give you the chills."

That, then, explained Parker's attitude of deliberate insolence. But it did not render intelligible the financier's
acceptance of that attitude. Unless Philip Nixon had some

immediate use for a chauffeur and could not procure another in time, there could be no reason for retaining him.

The butler could not say what he meant by "sneaking
around." His vague impression was that Parker was seeking
something. Twice, he had found him in parts of the house
in which he did not belong; but the chauffeur always had a
satisfactory explanation for his presence there. Otherwise,
Bennett could not explain his prejudice, except that the
chauffeur "went against the grain." Yet, he had come with
excellent credentials from a lady now living in Europe—an
acquaintance of the family.

It was not until after Bennett had left him that the
detective took stock of himself and his plans. His entire
mission revolved about the attempted robbery of eight
months ago; but his knowledge of it was second-hand and
unsatisfactory. A direct familiarity with all the facts, for-
mulated at his fingertips, was, he believed, desirable. And
he had sufficient time to accomplish this purpose; it was
now barely three o'clock and, according to Philip Nixon's
instructions, he did not have to leave until 9:55.

He informed Bennett that he was returning to town;
and three-quarters of an hour later, he was at Headquarters, going through the archives which gave thorough accounts of every case investigated by the police. The Nixon
robbery case was fairly voluminous reading. Until evening,
Gilmore plowed through the detailed report of the attempt,
the names and criminal records of those concerned, as far
as was known, and the arrest of Lew Ferris. Much of it he
gleaned from the testimony given at the subsequent trial.
When he was finished he possessed a thoroughly rounded
picture of the events that culminated in Nixon's receipt of
the three threatening missives.

Gilmore spent the evening quietly with his family. He
caught the 9:55 express to Cape May.

And at eleven o'clock the speeding train encountered the body of a man on the right of way. When Gilmore discovered that it was the corpse of Philip Nixon, he was certain, with his accumulated knowledge of the day, that the financier's death was due to murder.

4
THE HOUSE BY THE WOODS

At the first instant after he had identified the body, Gilmore felt uncomfortably as though he had failed in his duty. It was an unpleasant sensation of fault, because, in some measure, the responsibility for Philip Nixon's death seemed to rest upon him. But rational consideration informed him how unjust to himself was the idea. It was the financier's lack of candor that was primarily to blame. He had certainly not revealed his hand, either to Eleanor or the detective; and the facts he concealed, Gilmore now believed, would have explained the true cause for his journey to Cape May. Gilmore had offered to accompany him and had been refused; he could not have forced his presence upon the financier. This tragic result gave him an added incentive to capture and punish the perpetrator of the terrible deed.

Dr. Curtiss was the first to recover from the shock of Gilmore's startling announcement.

"Murdered!" he exclaimed. "Are you certain of that? Under these circumstances, any medical man would say this was a suicide."

"And justifiably so," Gilmore agreed. "But I know otherwise. I will explain to you later, Dr. Curtiss, but at the present moment I would appreciate your unquestioned assistance."

The appeal was not in vain. "Certainly, Sergeant Gilmore," the other replied swiftly, "I am at your service."

"Thank you." The detective turned to the engineer. "Can you locate our exact position? How far are we from Philadelphia?"

"Well, sir," the other spoke slowly, "I should say we are about halfway between Newfield and Oldroyd—about fifty miles out of Philadelphia. You see, Newfield is about thirty-one miles from Camden, and our next stop, Oldroyd, is about seventy-three miles. That puts us just between them, twenty miles from both. . . ."

A distant leap, thought the detective—from Philadelphia to a lonely countryside; an even further leap from a human in the full bloom of life to a mangled corpse on the tracks of the Southern Jersey express. The change had occurred in ten hours—hours, the veil of which he would have to pierce.

"Then there's no use in our taking the body to Cape May, since I want to get it back to town as soon as possible," he remarked. "I think it would be best to ship it back to Camden."

"Would you be permitted to do that?" queried Dr. Curtiss.

"Yes, I think so under the circumstances. If it were at all possible, I would have it sent on to Philadelphia, but since this is a Jersey crime, the Jersey authorities must take charge."

"But what of the officials in this vicinity? The place where the crime occurs has the proper jurisdiction over it, and they might object to your moving the body."

In a more normal case, Gilmore realized, the physician's point would have been well made. The ordinary procedure would have been to put the matter in the hands of the nearby county authorities, and withdraw. But in so extraordinary a crime, with the body found miles from any center of population, this could not be done. Camden was far more convenient for his purposes; there the officials would be willing to arrange with Superintendent Wainwright for Gilmore and the Philadelphia police to prosecute the investigation. Courtesy alone demanded that their cooperation be permitted; as a temporary officer, then, of New Jersey, Gilmore would take up a new phase of his assignment—the search for the murderer of Philip Nixon. Because of the greater facilities in Camden, a morgue, and a body of officials who would not obstruct his quest, he felt justified in removing the corpse there, rather than leave it in this lonely section of the state.

"What you say is very true," Gilmore replied to the doctor's objection, "but we can't tell who should have charge here, because we don't know where the murder occurred. There are several possibilities."

"What are they?"

"It might have been committed in the vicinity," Gilmore replied, "and this was the most convenient way the murderer had of ridding himself of the body. Or it might have occurred far away, and the body brought here by machine . . ." He broke off without finishing. "At any rate, we'll be able to deal with the local authorities." To the engineer, he said, "There's another train to Philadelphia tonight, isn't there?"

"Yes, sir—a late one that leaves Cape May at about midnight, and would reach here about twelve-forty or so."

"Excellent! Then I would suggest that we try to find some place to wait with the body until it comes along and I can send it on."

The conductor stepped forward. "I was about to suggest that, sir, myself. We've been delayed forty minutes already; we'll have to be getting along or there won't be a single passenger left in the cars."

"What about that house over there?" the fireman volunteered, pointing toward the dwelling near the tracks. "Will that do?"

"Yes," Gilmore replied, "if the people who live there will be willing to put up with us till then. It's rather difficult to ask them to take a corpse into the house . . ."

He was about to start toward the dwelling, when an illumination on the lower floor cast a shadow across the miry ground. The next moment the door was opened, and two men in shirt-sleeves could be seen against the background of light, approaching the tracks.

"What's the difficulty here?" began the foremost of them. "A breakdown—something gone wrong with the engine?"

He spoke with a hoarse, nasal accent, the words grinding out with a definite effort. He had a huge heavy frame and an ungainly, ponderous manner; his gnarled hands swung loosely almost at his knees. The face was unshaven, the features rough and uncouth; thick eyebrows concealed sharp, darting eyes. The man behind him was younger, and as a noticeable resemblance indicated, his brother. In a crude way, he was handsome, though equally unkempt; nevertheless, he served merely as a background for the striking ugliness of the elder. Farmer folk, thought the detective, but not lacking in shrewdness or intelligence.

Gilmore explained the situation briefly, closing with a request that they allow him to wait in their dwelling, with the dead man, until the Philadelphia-bound train arrived at 12:40.

"And if you have a telephone," he added, "I'd like to use it to get in touch with the city at once."

The newcomers glanced callously at the body, without closer inspection, and looked at each other.

"Humph . . ." came from the elder. "Somebody dead, eh? Well, that's not so nice; I guess I wouldn't like it very

much, 'specially with Martha downstairs. . . . What d'yuh
say, Clem?"

"Well, I don't know," murmured the younger, without
assurance, "If we send Martha back to bed. . . . Martha is
our sister," he explained suddenly to Gilmore, "and you
can't use the phone, because the storm put it out way back,
the first time it blew around, at about half past six."

"Maybe you're right, Clem. . . . All right, mister, bring
it along—it can't do no harm, nor put us out any."

He threw up his hands in swift decision.

"If some one will volunteer to carry the body to the
house," Gilmore suggested to the conductor, "there's no
reason why you should be held up any longer. . . ."

The fireman stepped forward, and with a grunt, the
elder brother joined him. In a moment, they had covered
the victim carefully in his own outer coat, and were proceeding together toward the farmhouse. As soon as they
were well on their way, the detective hastened with a lamp
to the rear of the train, where he paused and lowered the
light to the ground.

His body bent low, he sought for any traces that might
indicate some one had approached the right of way. The
ground was so soggy that if the body had been carried to
the tracks, some trail of the criminals must have been left.
In such a case, there must have been more than one person concerned with the murder. To convey Philip Nixon
bodily even for a short distance would have been well-nigh
impossible for a single man, unless he were exceptionally
strong—somewhat, thought Gilmore, hunting a comparison, like the older brother.

A speedy examination convinced him, however, that
there was nothing to be found. Already he was too late to
find the scene of the tragedy undisturbed. The rain had
been ahead him, washing and sifting through the ground,
destroying old impressions; and new footprints had been

made by passengers as they alighted. There were many such, overlapping each other in a futile maze. Some were already indistinguishable in the spongy earth. And all were valueless.

When he returned, the fireman was back, empty-handed, and the passengers were again boarding the train. Gilmore sought the conductor.

"Of course, I shall stay with the body," he said. "As soon as you reach Oldroyd, I want you to send some telegrams. Or perhaps you will do it, Dr. Curtiss. It's important that they go at once. . . ."

"I think I'll remain with you," the physician replied. "The mistake which I made reacts to my discredit—and I should like to be instrumental in clearing it up."

The detective welcomed his decision and said as much. "And it will be just as well," he went on. "You'll be wanted at the inquest, you know, and it would be quite troublesome all around if you were in Cape May at the time."

Watched by the physician, he scribbled a brief account of the tragedy including the name of the victim and gave it to the conductor. "And here's another."

The second message read, "Arrest Nixon's chauffeur, Charles Parker, at once, and hold him till I return. Gilmore."

It was an act which obviously cried out for accomplishment. Parker was the last man known to be with Nixon; at 2:30 he had joined the financier. Nixon had intended to drive to the shore; that meant that he was making the journey in the Rolls-Royce with Parker at the wheel. And the latter, by his own confession, despised his employer; in addition, according to Bennett, he was a thief or worse. If the murder had occurred on the way . . . or if the financier had been brought to this spot by machine . . . Parker should know much. But in the morning, this valuable witness was leaving. He could not afford to let him disappear; and there was no other means to hold him.

"And don't forget the telegram to Cape May," the detective cautioned the conductor. "We want that midnight train to stop for us. . . ."

Tn company with the physician, he proceeded toward the house. Behind them, the engine discharged a sudden, piercing whistle of belated protest at the delay. Simultaneously it moved forward with slow, belabored puffs that increased into a crescendo of swift chugs; sparks mounted and died in the blackness. As each car slowly passed, its windows cast a reflection upon the travelers trudging through the mud. Then the last car was gone; only the dim light of the cottage was left them.

The younger brother, Clem, unexpectedly joined them in the darkness; but, reserved and shy, did not speak until Gilmore asked him what had attracted his attention to the accident.

The naturalness of the question seemed to put him at his ease.

"We went to bed pretty late tonight," he explained, "on account of the storm. It was a funny storm; it started early around half past six, and kept up for about two hours. Then it quit, but it come back 'bout nine-thirty and blew blazes for more than an hour, I guess. Anyhow, it kept us from sleeping; and then we heard all sorts of commotion from the train. But I didn't get curious till Frank—that's my brother—gets up; and then I follows him. But we made Martha stay in."

"Did you hear anything before that, such as a machine coming along anywhere, across the fields and stopping for a time?"

"Naw, I didn't, and I don't think Frank did either. Anyhow, there's no place a machine could go along here except our dirt road—and that just comes to our house and don't go any further."

"Do you think you would have noticed any such machine, had there been one?" Gilmore asked.

"Couldn't o' helped it. No one could o' come across the field cause there ain't any place smooth enough; and then, there's them woods over there that'd stop a car. Pelham woods, mister—a big place and the easiest thing in the world to get lost among them trees."

He pointed to the left where a darker outline of trees was heavily thrown into relief against the inky clouds that veiled the moon.

"Isn't there any other road—or approach to the tracks?"

"Well," Clem replied, "there's the main road on the other side of Pelham. That runs across the tracks and then keeps on along them, a quarter of a mile over there."

"That's the main highway, is it?"

"Yep—that goes on to Oldroyd and Cape May. . . ."

Clem broke off as they came to a post that marked the boundary of the farmhouse's yard. A rude mail-box clung precariously to it, and Gilmore peered closely to see the name that was painted upon it.

"Name's Marley," Clem observed, noticing him. "Clem Marley."

The dwelling itself was an unpretentious farmhouse such as is often seen along the right of way. It was made of wood, thrown together unsubstantially, with a rude veranda on one side; the sloping roof was of slate. Behind the house was a small barn, the door of which swung partly open; and beyond, to the right, the narrow dirt road, of which Clem had spoken, was barely visible.

As they entered, Frank Marley turned from the fireplace in which he had just lighted a fire. The room combined such comforts as there were of a living room and a dining room. A table covered with a red cloth stood in the center of the room, with an unlighted lamp upon it; beside it were several flimsy chairs. Near the fireplace were a horsehair sofa and a deep armchair; and beside the narrow stairs which led above, a cupboard was visible. A clothes rack, on which hung a single gray topcoat, completed the furniture. Despite its meagerness, the neatness of the room indicated a woman's hand.

"Nasty weather we had tonight," the elder brother remarked. "Draw up to the fire and make yourselves comfortable. It isn't good for the damp to get into your bones."

Gilmore and Dr. Curtiss accepted the invitation, Clem disappearing into a back room.

"Quite right," the physician agreed. "One can sometimes use a fire even in June—especially when it's as damp as it is tonight."

"What about this chap?" Frank went on, conversationally. "What in the world happened to him? It was my sister who first called our attention to the noise outside; until then, neither Clem nor I had heard anything at all. . . ."

Gilmore peered about the dimly illumined room. "Where have you placed the body?" he countered, instead of replying.

"I had it left at the back of the porch. What was it, an accident?"

Dr. Curtiss caught the detective's warning eye. "We're not certain," he replied. "It may have been a suicide—it's difficult to tell anything as yet."

"I understand he was caught under the engine," said the other. "How the devil could he get on the tracks away out here?"

Before Gilmore could answer, another voice spoke in no more than a whisper.

"Are you sure, Frank, there isn't anything I could do for the gentlemen? They must be quite cold and hungry. . . ."

Gilmore caught his breath as he saw the speaker on the stairs, peering over the flimsy banister. A girl was outlined by the flickering fire as a sprite, strangely shadowy and dim. She was slim and delicate, with long, black hair that drooped over her shoulders. Wide eyes shyly looked down upon them, and a pale face searched the room. So ethereal did the light make her that the detective could easily believe she would disappear into nothingness. A dress, carelessly donned, served merely to accentuate the impression.

"Didn't I tell you to stay upstairs, Martha?" her brother replied sourly. "It's no place for a woman down here."

"But can't I make them some tea?" she persisted. And when there was no answer, "What about the man that was hurt? Can't I do something . . . ?"

"No, you can't do anything—he's dead. Now, go back to bed."

Light footsteps echoed above them. Assuming that she had retired, Frank Marley offered his visitors tobacco and, in reply to Gilmore's question, said he had seen no one in the vicinity and no machine was likely to use their private road, for it led nowhere.

The girl was still on the landing, however, peeping carefully about the corner of it. Gilmore caught the slight swish of her dress; and a moment later saw the reflection of her hair in the firelight. She leaned far outward, as though curious to view the visitors; the detective mused that strangers must seem a rare treat.

A pause followed his questions. Then the physician remarked, "This is a rather unique cause for making a call . . . and most tragic."

"We were fortunate in having a place to wait," the detective said.

Frank Marley spat into the fire. "You're welcome to it. The poor fellow has to have a resting place. Have you any idea who he is?"

"Yes," Dr. Curtiss replied incautiously, "A Mr. Philip Nixon, the great . . ."

A sudden, rising cry, like a wail of pain, from the stairs pierced Gilmore to the very core. It ascended into a shriek; horror and fright were its most potent notes. It drowned out Gilmore's exclamation as he leaped to his feet; it was suddenly silenced as the body of the girl hurtled down the stairs into a pathetic heap at the bottom.

Frank smothered an oath. "I told her to get upstairs!" But there was alarm in his tone.

Before any of them could reach her, the younger brother had darted from the kitchen and lifted her in his arms.

"My God!" he exclaimed. "What happened to her?"

"She lost her balance and fell down the steps," said his brother. "She wouldn't go up, when I told her . . . well, she'll go up now, all right."

Though his words were gruffly spoken, Gilmore sensed in them a genuine anxiety. Both the brothers were deeply concerned about the accident, he was certain, despite their uncouth manner.

"You had better examine her," he suggested to the physician, as Clem started up the stairs with his limp burden. "Here, Dr. Curtiss will go up with you, and help you. . . ."

"Certainly," the doctor agreed, "though I doubt if it's anything serious. She has merely fainted; a little water will bring her to. Now, Mr. Marley, if you will show me her room. . . ."

He followed the two brothers to the upper floor, leaving Gilmore alone in the room, to consider once more the problem Philip Nixon's death. There was much to be done at once, which he preferred to do without witnesses—the body to be searched, the financier's papers to be read, the road to be examined. Primarily, there was the question of how the financier's body had come to that lonely spot. As heavy footsteps echoed on the floor above, the detective took the lamp from the table, and stepping from the

house, approached the road. Above, the moon was beginning to be successful in its struggle against the clouds
which veiled it. It was a full moon, bathing the low flat
land in a refulgent glow. Under it, Gilmore could see that
the way was little more than a rocky path, narrowly bor-
dered by grass. The rain had washed it out; little gullies of
water still ran on the sides.

The detective bent closely, holding the flickering lamp
to the earth. It almost went out and then flared brightly. There were auto tracks there, deep in the soft, muddy
earth! He could distinguish the diamond tread, one set of
tracks overlapping the other, indicating that a machine
had entered this road, driven as far as the house and left.
But they were narrow impressions, not like the balloon
tires of Philip Nixon's Rolls-Royce. For a moment, Gilmore was puzzled; it was strange that the Marleys should
have denied any knowledge of a car that had approached
so near them.

Then he saw that the tracks had both their origin and
ending behind the farmhouse, at the barn which he had
observed before. Of course—he was examining the trail
made by the Marleys' own car, which even now was in the
outbuilding that served as a garage. It had been out that
night and during the storm. The hood was still wet; the
sides were spattered with mud and the hubs of the wheels
were literally caked in drying mire. It had made some journey and returned; but these facts were of no importance.

The living room was still empty when Gilmore returned
to it. By the fire, he began to sort through the letters
which had been in the financier's pocket. A memoranda of
business appointments contained no information of whom
Philip Nixon had seen today; some letters were of no
importance; and a list of stock quotations did not help
him. The wallet told him nothing that would assist him in
his quest.

How long, he asked himself, had Nixon been dead when he had been discovered? The dampness of the dead man's suit and coat indicated that he had been lying in the open for some time. The storm had ceased just before they had come upon the body, at eleven o'clock. According to Clem Marley, it had started in this section at 6:30, had blown over at 8:30 and returned an hour later. But these facts brought him no nearer to the solution of his problem. The train schedule, however, aided him. The train that he had taken was the 9:55; the one before that to Cape May left Camden at 7:45, two hours before. Certainly, then, the body had not been on the tracks for more than two hours; else the 7:45 would have passed over it in the course of its journey.

Gilmore drew out his time-table to verify his deductions. In doing so, he caused a small folded sheet of paper to fall to the floor. It had evidently been among the financier's effects, but had thus far escaped examination. Casually he picked it up and opened it. . . .

For an instant, the blood drained from the detective's features. He read it again to make sure that there was no error; it seemed incredible that the financier could have kept this from him.

> Mr. Philip Nixon:
> If we have appealed to you in vain, then we will take further steps. We are not to be trifled with. Unless you meet our demands immediately you will meet grave disaster.

There was no signature.

It was dated the morning of the preceding day. Presumably then, this message had been received by the financier in the same mail in which had come the last of the trio from the Ferris gang. On the very morning when Philip

Nixon had appealed to the police for protection. Those letters he had freely displayed to Gilmore; yet this threat, more alarming and menacing than any of the others, he had kept concealed.

Did that partially explain the financier's nervousness? Had he been afraid to give this to the detective? Or was there another cause for his secretiveness? Was the matter, about which the writer could not be "trifled" with, something that would not bear the revealing light of day? Gilmore again studied the scrawling script through. What demands had been made of the financier? More important than any of these questions, who was the enemy whom Philip Nixon feared to such an extent that he had not even dared to inform the police of his threats?

His thoughts were interrupted by Clem Marley's appearance on the stairs. He descended and would have passed into the kitchen without speaking, had not Gilmore stopped him.

"How is—Miss Marley feeling?"

"She's all right, now." Clem spoke in a relieved tone. "There's no injuries that the doctor can find. . . . Did Frank come down?"

"I didn't see him—I was outside."

The younger brother continued toward the rear of the house, looking troubled as though his sister's condition worried him. Opposite the clothes rack Gilmore had noted when he first entered, he paused. Then he quickly took from it the gray overcoat that hung there and went out.

A moment later Dr. Curtiss joined Gilmore, shaking his head.

"A rather peculiar thing," he commented. "The girl's come to, safely enough, but she isn't the same. She behaves as though she'd had a shock of some sort. . . ."

"A shock?" Gilmore asked sharply.

"That's right. She merely stares at the ceiling and refuses to say a word. . . ."

"Probably she hadn't gotten over her fall, yet. It was a nasty tumble from that top landing."

The physician shrugged his shoulders. "She hasn't been injured as far as I can make out without instruments. She's rather white, of course. I saw her stare just once at her brothers, a look of reproach, if I ever saw one; and after that, she kept looking at the ceiling."

Engrossed though Gilmore was with his own amazing discovery, he realized that Dr. Curtiss was speaking the truth. The accident, if it were merely that, had been a peculiar one. It was possible that by a curious coincidence, it had occurred as the financier's name was being mentioned; but it might well have a deeper significance. Though he did not press the physician on the point, he made a mental note of it. When the time came, this new complication would receive due attention; at the moment, it was but the last of a series of puzzles, all the others of which seemed more closely connected with the tragedy than this one. Especially was this true of the last missive that the financier had concealed. . . .

5

THE FOURTH MAN

It was after 12:40 when the Philadelphia train arrived.
The unpleasant business of moving Nixon's remains was
completed without attracting the attention of passengers;
then when the detective and Dr. Curtiss were comfortably
settled in the last car, the train continued its journey into
Camden.

For an hour and a quarter, they discussed the case
without managing to shed much light upon the puzzle.
Gilmore, with the caution of his profession, did not share
his discoveries with his companion, who was, after all,
a stranger. Nevertheless, the information that both possessed was thoroughly analyzed; but they came to no conclusions.

The express drew into the Camden terminal too late
for Gilmore to accomplish anything further than to make
arrangements for having the body sent to the morgue for an
autopsy. Furthermore, he was tired. As the morrow would
be a busy day, he had best get some sleep while he could.

As they descended together from the car, he uttered an
exclamation of astonishment. Two cars forward, he had
suddenly glimpsed the head of a disembarking passenger.
The head disappeared among the milling crowd so quickly
that, after the first instant, Gilmore was not at all certain he had actually observed it. To the astonishment of

Dr. Curtiss, he darted away, hurling himself rudely through the press in total disregard of a woman who was bringing some sleepy children home. Two of them got in his way; then he had to brush two men aside brusquely. When he reached the forward car, the head was nowhere to be seen; neither was its owner, though Gilmore scanned the platform its entire length to the ferry in search for him.

He rejoined his companion at the ferry slip.

"What was the matter?" the physician asked, puzzled. "What happened?"

"A mistake on my part," Gilmore explained. "I had an idea that I knew some one who got off the car ahead of us. But I must have been wrong. Anyhow, I lost him in the crowd."

But he knew that his eyes had not deceived him. The face that he had seen while descending the steps was that of Philip Nixon's secretary, Donald.

The morning papers already had notices of Philip Nixon's death. Whether culled from the police or from witnesses who spread the tale at Cape May, Gilmore could not tell. Most of the articles were conspicuous for their uncertainty and lack of detail; they made up in vehemence for their deficiency in information. References were made to the other famous Jersey murders—the Hall-Mills case, the Lilliendahl crime, and the various "torch murders"; which, because of the latest victim's prominence, would pale into insignificance beside this case. None of the notices mentioned an arrest; if Gilmore's instructions had been obeyed, this fact had been wisely kept a secret. All were filled with surmises and wild speculation, though none more unusual than those with which the detective had to contend in his own mind.

One advantage of the newspaper reports the detective appreciated deeply. They meant that Eleanor Nixon had been informed of her loss. It would not then devolve upon Gilmore to break the news to her, and he experienced great relief. He had an innate dread of being the harbinger of sorrowful tidings. Despite the disagreement he had witnessed the previous day in the financier's office, he realized that Eleanor must have been deeply attached to her father. The shock of such news was bound to have distressing results. He was spared, at least, her immediate grief and the sorrow that would come with her knowledge of the tragedy's details.

When Gilmore reached Headquarters, he was greeted by Thomas with the expected information that the Superintendent was waiting for him.

He entered the offices without knocking; the interview was of great importance for both of them. His superior's lolling familiar manner of the preceding day was gone, as he nodded Gilmore into a chair; his features were set, displaying deep lines about the corners of his mouth. His eyes were mere pinpoints of light.

"This is a serious business, Gilmore," he greeted him, "a very serious business. . . ."

"I'm fully aware of it, sir," the detective returned gravely.

"Especially with so prominent a man as Nixon, a leader of finance and the president of a tremendous business concern. This morning has been a perfect nightmare of calls from all types of important people. Nixon's daughter sent his secretary, a chap by the name of Gardiner, to find out exactly what had occurred. I told him what I knew from your telegram, but that wasn't much. . . . The stock market will react to it, and I'm afraid the police will be the butt of much criticism from the newspapers . . ."

He raised his hand, as the detective made a move to speak. "Don't misunderstand me, Gilmore, I'm not blaming you in the least. I'm certain the tragedy must have been unavoidable, or you would have prevented it."

He had, he explained, already communicated with the Jersey authorities, and arranged for deputizing Gilmore, and such assistants as he might need, to take charge of the investigation as officers of the other state. Recognizing the greater facilities possessed by the Philadelphia department, already concerned with the case, the Camden officials had acquiesced to permit the former a free hand, ready to offer aid when it was required. The Jersey coroner's physician would make his report to Wainwright as well as to his own police. Throughout the investigation a close contact between the two departments was to be maintained.

The Superintendent then asked Gilmore for the story of the tragedy.

Briefly but completely, his subordinate gave an account of the mission for which the financier had required him, of his journey to Cape May, of the discovery of the body and its subsequent identification. The narrative included facts only; the Superintendent was not interested in impressions. And when he had finished, Wainwright brought his fist down upon his desk with a force that made the inkstand jump.

"So it all comes back to the Ferris gang! Great heavens, they've overstepped the line this time! I'll have the entire force out after them—and as long as it takes to get them . . ." He broke off. "What about this chauffeur, Parker? What has he to do with it?"

"You got him then?" Gilmore countered. "The papers said nothing about it and I wasn't sure . . ."

"Yes, Smith and Jenks were sent out for him. Luckily, they were on time; from Smith's report, had they gotten there a few minutes later, they would have been too late."

The detective bent forward intently.

"Your telegram arrived shortly after midnight"—the Superintendent warmed to his narrative—"and it must have been one o'clock when the two men reached Nixon's place. Without disturbing anyone, they managed to locate the servants' quarters in the rear of the house . . ."

"Yes, I know. They have a separate building."

"Parker was just coming out with two grips packed. He had the car, a magnificent Rolls-Royce, waiting; the engine was running, ready for an immediate escape. They searched his room, which is on the downstairs floor, afterward, without arousing anyone and found that he had gotten rid of all unnecessary belongings; only his clothes, some letters and money were kept.

"Otherwise, his bags contained bearer bonds and some jewelry belonging to Miss Nixon. After he had packed his own belongings, he had visited Nixon's bedroom and robbed his private safe. We found that out from young Gardiner this morning, after he had been told of Parker's arrest. Among the jewels were a diamond bracelet, several rings and platinum watches and a stickpin. I've got the loot all here in the fellow's bag. . . ."

"He probably decided to make the most of his opportunities," Gilmore commented, "while he was making his escape."

The Superintendent nodded. "The diamond necklace was safe because it was in the vaults of the Central National Bank, where Nixon has an account, since the robbery. Parker put up a fight before Jenks managed to sit on him and Smith to handcuff him. Without your tip, Gilmore, we'd never have gotten him; but where in the world does he fit into the murder?"

For answer, the detective reached for a black handbag that rested under his superior's desk.

"You remember, sir," he replied, "when you told me about the attempted robbery, you mentioned that one of the four men who were concerned was a newcomer—at least, he had not been identified by Tommy Rankin, when he was trying to locate the rest of the Ferris gang. Yesterday, after I returned to town, I studied the record of the robbery. I thought I might be able to discover some possible clue that Rankin had overlooked. There was none, but an idea came to me then, having seen Parker and heard something of him from Nixon's butler, that he was one of them. . . ."

"You mean"—the Superintendent moved his chair closer—"that Parker is that fourth man, pulling the strings from the inside, and reporting Nixon's reactions to the others?"

"Exactly, sir. Parker, of course, was the most logical choice for such a plan; he was unknown both to us and to Nixon, and had never been before a court, on any sort of charge. I'm certain that the letter of recommendation he brought with him was forged. Ike Morin was always clever with the pen."

"By God, Gilmore, I believe you're right!" his superior exclaimed enthusiastically. "A very clever piece of work."

"I have no doubt you'll find some proof among Parker's letters, in his bag. . . ."

The detective opened the clasps and began a careful examination of the contents. It was a valise of leather, that had met with much usage; the sides were badly scuffed and scraped, and the clasps unlocked with difficulty. Within, the chauffeur's clothes, originally thrown in hastily, were, with the handling they had subsequently received, now in disorder. A jewel case, which Gilmore did not disturb, and a thin packet of letters lay at the bottom of the bag.

He drew out the latter, and gave a nod of satisfaction.

"I had noticed them, of course," said the Superintendent, "and had intended to go through them before I turned them over."

A few moments sufficed Gilmore to draw the letters from their envelopes and examine them briefly. There were only four, a fact which indicated most of Parker's communications had been made by phone.

"Just as I thought!" he said. "Here's one from Morin with instructions as to sending Nixon the second note; I'll bet Parker himself was responsible for the first two messages. The last was Morin's; next to Ferris, he was the brains of the gang. And here's another—from Stahl, making arrangements to meet in town; but you can't tell when it was written. There, that's sufficient proof. . . ."

The Superintendent took them from Gilmore's hand and read one.

"This is a most important discovery. And you see how well it accords with all our other facts. If Parker can be made to talk, it'll be easy enough to get the others."

"You mean, sir, that you are certain that the Ferris gang is responsible for this outrage?"

The low, doubtful manner of Gilmore's question caused his superior to look fixedly at him.

"Certainly I'm persuaded, Gilmore—I can see no possible doubt. They merely carried out their threat. Parker, you see, had been fired; and after he went, their plan would be twice as difficult to execute. It was a godsend that Philip Nixon should have been taking a journey on the last day of their opportunity to strike while the chauffeur still played his role. They made the most of it. Parker informed them of it; it was arranged that they follow him and at some point on the road, attack the machine . . ."

"But why should they kill him, sir?" the detective asked. "That wouldn't get them what they were after— Ferris's freedom."

"It was done out of revenge, Gilmore; or it might be that though they never intended murder, Nixon resisted and they were compelled to kill him."

"But then they placed him on the railroad tracks. . . ?"

"To make it look like a suicide. And they came very close to succeeding; only the fact that Nixon had called you in yesterday prevented that. Parker didn't suspect you and it was an act they failed to anticipate."

It was more than plausible—it was thoroughly logical. Every statement seemed to be supported by the information which both possessed; yet Gilmore, a deep frown overcasting his features, shook his head in disagreement.

"I'm afraid it's not as easy as all that, sir. Many things will require explanation before this affair is settled. I have an idea that it won't be straightened until every moment between two-thirty yesterday afternoon and eleven last night is accounted for."

"But your objections, Gilmore? The whole thing seems obvious, now that one knows about the Ferris gang."

"Where did they kill him, sir? Stahl and Morin wouldn't have dared to make an attack on the main highway—in broad daylight."

Gilmore's chief lighted a cigarette, extinguishing the match in an ashtray on his desk.

"Parker made some excuse for driving into this narrow road you mentioned. The storm covered the deed—you remember how dark it became, even here in the city. As you've related it, it broke in Jersey, as early as half past six. . . ."

"Mr. Nixon's watch was broken, somehow," the detective pursued, "at one minute after nine."

Wainright shrugged. "That might have been the hour of the attack; it might have fallen from Nixon's pocket—or it may have been broken for days. There are many ways of explaining a shattered crystal."

"Granting, sir, that the gang did capture Nixon, how did they get the body on the tracks without leaving a trace of their presence? There were no signs on the road of Nixon's auto nor of any other strange car."

"But the main highway was only a quarter of a mile away on the other side. They could have returned to it, and come from that direction."

"And carry Philip Nixon's body that distance to the tracks?"

"Why not—in the darkness? There were three of them—and it isn't far . . ."

Superintendent Wainwright lost his patience. Extinguishing his cigarette, he shoved back his chair and drummed his fingers on the desk top.

"Something's troubling you, Gilmore," he said. "What is it? What do you want me to do?"

A reticence the detective could not explain impelled him to say nothing of the message found in Nixon's pockets. While he believed that the heart of the problem was hidden in that note, Wainwright was not likely to be swayed from his theories without stronger evidence; he might even ridicule the importance Gilmore attached to it. Until he was in a position to convince his superior, he wanted to pit his powers against that particular puzzle without assistance. If he could gain his point without revealing this find, Gilmore decided he would do so.

"I'm certain there is more in this murder than first meets the eye," he replied, "and I would like to have freedom to investigate as I please. Tommy Rankin had charge of the case before—of trailing the Ferris gang; he's fully fitted to take up the trail again. If you were to hand over to him Nixon's letters, Parker's letters, his luggage—he could work on that end. Of course, once he has located them, I'll join in the round up; but meanwhile, it will leave me free for other trails."

The other did not reply; instead, he reached into an upper drawer of the desk and produced a cap. There was a slight smile on his face, when he spoke.

"Also this cap; we found it in the rear of the Rolls-Royce. It belongs, I think, to Arthur Stahl."

The cap had served its owner beyond a normal existence. The hood was bent, the lining completely worn out; and it smelled slightly of gasoline. Within was a band, blackened and discolored by grime and sweat; it was only by looking closely at it that Gilmore could make out the faint initials, A. S.

"In the machine—Nixon's machine?" he questioned incredulously. "It wasn't there yesterday afternoon."

"Yes, in the tonneau. . . . You haven't seen the machine, have you?"

The Superintendent's smile broadened into a look of superior amusement as Gilmore replied in the negative.

"Smith and Jenks brought it along with them. It's below, in the City Hall courtyard," he said. "You had better go down and look at it. . . ."

He nodded a temporary dismissal as the phone bell rang. Gilmore did not wait to hear him answer it; this latest information disturbed him, more than he would have cared to admit. It established that Stahl had been in the financier's car the previous day. As Philip Nixon would never have willingly permitted his presence, had he been compelled to tolerate it unwillingly? And Wainwright's attitude was even more disturbing—as though he knew the detective was in error. It was unpleasant to feel that he might have made a fool of himself in his superior's eyes.

Taking the spiral stairs, to the ground floor, the next moment he crossed the courtyard toward the South Broad Street entrance; there, against the inner bastion-like wall, stood a lone yellow car.

No longer did it present the attractive appearance of the preceding day. The burnished sides were coated with mud in much the same manner as the car at Marley's farm had been; rain spots and spattered earth veiled the windshield.

Both sides were badly splashed with hardened mire. The thick, balloon tires were almost incased in mud, hanging from every spoke. No surface had escaped the soiling effects of rain and wet earth. It was obvious that the car had traversed difficult roads in the last twenty-four hours.

But none of these items caught Gilmore's attention. In the rear of the car, just below the lowered hood was a little round, black hole; and close to the rear mudguard was a similar hole. The detective had had too much experience with revolvers not to recognize them. Nevertheless, he could neither believe his eyes nor restrain a low whistle of perplexity.

"Great heavens—bullet holes!"

They were from forty-fives, steel jacketed bullets, used by the police and the crook fraternity. Every discovery made his own conjectures more ridiculous. Every step seemed to indicate that he was willfully closing his eyes to the correct explanation. It was incredible that this should be a mere series of coincidences. Bit by bit, a complete structure was being reared before him; this last item, uncontradictable proof of the attack upon the car and its owner, was the last stone in it. It was impossible to disregard it. Much would depend upon what Charles Parker, when questioned, would have to say; but nothing he could tell would destroy this tangible evidence. Superintendent Wainwright was right; he was floundering about in a tangle of useless theory.

Gilmore returned to his superior's office, to find the latter waiting for him.

"The Central National Trust was on the phone," he was informed. "They wanted to get in touch with whoever was in charge of the Nixon case. I told them you'd be down shortly—after you question Parker." The speaker paused. "What do you think of the car?"

"I would still like to have that phase of the case turned over to Rankin. I'm willing to take all responsibility in the matter. . . . I still believe that I can accomplish more on other tracks."

But it was stubbornness that prompted Gilmore so to reply. He no longer had faith in his own theories.

6
AN ADDED COMPLICATION

The Charles Parker who was ushered into the presence of Gilmore and his chief had undergone a transformation, similar to that of the machine he had driven. No longer was he the trim, natty chauffeur with a jaunty air of insolence. His features sported a blackened eye and a bruised cheek; disheveled hair gave him a most disreputable appearance. His uniform bore equally good evidence of the struggle he had made before submitting to capture. As he entered, he glanced sullenly at Gilmore; but if the detective's presence surprised him, he displayed no indication of his feelings.

Gilmore nodded to the accompanying officer to unlock the bracelets encircling Parker's wrists. He had determined to attempt a familiarly pleasant manner before resorting to sterner measures.

"We meet under different circumstances, Parker," he greeted. "I must say you haven't made the best use of your time. This isn't any too comfortable a position to be in."

Philip Nixon's erstwhile chauffeur gave Gilmore a venomous look.

"I've already said that I don't know anything about Nixon's death—and I don't. I had nothing to do with it . . ."

"No one has accused you—yet," the detective replied significantly, "but you must admit that the circumstances require explanation. There were no bullet holes in the car yesterday, you know."

"Bullet holes? What do you mean, bullet holes?"

"I'm asking you, Parker; I think you are better able to to tell us all about them."

"I don't know what you're talking about."

Gilmore's eyes narrowed; it seemed this fencing would get them nowhere. "Oh, come now, Parker," he said, "you can't expect to maintain that impossible position. You are the only one in charge of the car, and Nixon was killed on his way to Cape May . . ."

The Superintendent nodded his approval of Gilmore's tactics.

"You're intelligent, Parker," he put in. "You must know you'd have difficulty satisfying a jury that you know nothing about it."

"There isn't going to be any jury," the prisoner said uglily, "You haven't anything on me."

"Merely two burglaries for the present. But add a murder to that, and it'll go very hard with you and your pals—unless you talk."

A startled look appeared in Parker's eyes and the blood drained from his face. Inadvertently, his gaze wandered to the black bag resting under the Superintendent's desk.

"We know all about those letters in the grip," Gilmore pursued, pressing the advantage, "that came from Morin and Stahl. Instructions to you, as to when to send Nixon letters threatening his life, Parker—a pretty piece of evidence to put before a jury . . ."

"I never wrote any letters—"

The voice continued inexorably. "And how do you think it will look when we prove that you drove Philip Nixon into Jersey and were there met by other members of the Ferris gang? And then to show how, as soon as the crime was committed and the body disposed of, you hurried back to make your escape?"

"It's not true, any of it," the baited man cried hoarsely. "I'd deny it."

"It would be easy enough to demonstrate that. It was criminally careless of Stahl to leave this cap in the car; it will probably hang all of you."

Beads of sweat appeared on the chauffeur's forehead as he saw the worn cap in Gilmore's hand. His glance shifted to the detective, remorselessly continuing, confronting him with incriminating evidence at every turn; then to the Superintendent, whose very silence and attitude of vigilance was as threatening as the other's questions. He recognized the strong web that had been woven around him.

"And if you were to deny these things," Gilmore was saying, "who would believe you? You had better talk if you want to save your own hide; you won't have the opportunity later."

Parker made a final, futile effort to bluff it out.

"And if I have nothing to talk about . . . ?" he asked.

"If you're innocent," the detective returned, "you should have no hesitation in speaking the truth."

The prisoner made a gesture of defeat. "I'll tell you what I can," he said. "But I'm not admitting anything, remember that. . . ."

"That's more sensible," remarked Wainwright approvingly.

"And even if I did know where you could find Stahl and Morin, I wouldn't squeal on my pals. So that line of questioning is out."

Temporarily, Gilmore had been successful; but he remained alert, not to be deceived by what might be only an apparent surrender.

"As you please, Parker," he said. "You were to call for Mr. Nixon at his office at two-thirty, yesterday afternoon. Where did you take him from there?"

"I took him to the Central National Trust," the prisoner replied candidly. "Mr. Nixon wanted to get there before it closed at three o'clock."

"How long did he stay?"

"Until it closed. He must have been in about twenty minutes. . . ."

"That is, until three. What did you do, meanwhile?"

Parker looked blank, as though he could not understand the question.

"Stayed outside, of course," he replied. "What else did you expect me to do?"

"In front of the bank? Have you any idea what business Mr. Nixon had to transact?"

The chauffeur made a vehement disclaimer, and Gilmore decided to postpone further queries in that direction, until he interviewed the officials of the bank.

"Very well, then," he pursued. "Where did you go after that?"

"I drove Mr. Nixon home. We got there about quarter of four, and then I went upstairs for his overnight bag; I think he had given Bennett instructions from the office to pack it. Then I waited in the garage till I was called back to the house."

"At what time were you called?" Gilmore asked.

"It was about half past four. We started back to town, when Mr. Nixon gave me instructions to drive to Camden"— Parker hesitated for the first time—"to the Pennsylvania terminal. I obeyed him."

"And then . . . ?"

"He bought a ticket for Cape May and took the train."

"You saw him get on the train?"

"I—yes, I did." The reply was defiant.

Gilmore signaled a meaning glance to his superior. Thus far, it would have been folly to lie, since the narrative would undoubtedly be corroborated or disproved by other witnesses—the bank officials and Nixon's household. But they had now reached ground upon which it would be difficult to locate reliable witnesses, and Parker was safe to fabricate a plausible tale.

"He took a train, Parker," the Superintendent put in. "What train?"

Again the prisoner seemed to falter as he replied, "I'm afraid I don't know the exact time it left; but it took us three quarters of an hour to get to Camden, and the train left right away."

"That would be about five-fifteen . . ."

Gilmore drew from his pocket the time-table he had used the preceding day. A hurried glance told him that a local left for Cape May at twenty minutes after five. He nodded for Parker to continue.

"After he went off, I took the machine back to Bryn Mawr and left it in the garage. I never saw Mr. Nixon again, and I don't know anything more about him. And that's the truth. . . ."

"I'm afraid it isn't," the detective said, with a touch of grimness. "You had better tell us what did happen, or it will be so much worse for you."

"I have told you everything . . ."

"You don't know how Stahl's cap got into the car. . . ?"

"Nor who fired the bullets into the back of the machine," the Superintendent put in sternly.

"If you're so ignorant of who killed Nixon, why were you in such a hurry to get away?" Gilmore asked.

The chauffeur gazed at his two tormentors with a look that was both contemptuous and mocking. When he spoke, it was in a tone of finality.

"I've told you all I know. I took the car back to the garage, and spent the evening in town, in the movies, by myself. It's not my fault if you don't know the truth when you hear it. You'll get no more out of me."

From that moment, he refused to open his mouth. Neither cajoling nor threats moved him to add a single item to his story. Tenaciously, he maintained what he had already related. Aware that he was lying, nevertheless, before Parker's stubbornness, Gilmore was compelled to give up the effort.

After the chauffeur had been removed, the detective turned to his superior. "We'll have to turn him over to Rankin; we'll see what he can get out of him, with Smith's help."

Wainright nodded and Gilmore looked at his watch.

"I'd better be getting along to the bank," he said, "or they'll think you forgot about their message."

He opened the office door, to find that the coroner's physician, Dr. Sackett, stood outside with a stranger, about to enter; in his hand he held a sheet of paper, evidently a medical report. Behind them both, to Gilmore's gratification, Dr. Curtiss followed into the Superintendent's office.

"This is Dr. Ralston of the coroner's staff in Camden," Dr. Sackett introduced his companion. "He has just completed a preliminary statement of the condition of Mr. Nixon's body. Dr. Curtiss has joined us for a brief consultation regarding it. . . ."

The speaker was a tall, spare man with a professionally nervous manner; his New Jersey colleague, short, stubby, with a large, comfortable, if not convenient, paunch.

"I can only remain for a short time," Dr. Curtiss put in. "You see, Sergeant Gilmore, I am now fully persuaded that Philip Nixon was the victim of foul play. At the time, however, it was difficult to conceive how it could have been anything but suicide."

Dr. Ralston hastened to the defense of a fellow member of his profession. "It was a most natural assumption under such circumstances. I believe I would have come to the same conclusion, myself. Rigor mortis would not have set in for three hours; and allowing for the fact that the body had been lying in the open in the rain, it must yet have been sufficiently warm to support the belief that death had been recent."

"How long would you say Mr. Nixon had been dead?" Gilmore asked.

"At this late period, we can only approximate the hour of death. I should say he was killed at some time between eight, last night, and half past nine," said Dr. Sackett.

"And we found him at eleven," the detective commented. "He might have been dead between one and a half and three hours. What was the cause of his death?"

For reply Dr. Sackett offered him the written report of his investigation. Stripped of its medical terms, it related that the financier's death had resulted from a blow upon the skull, which had caused a compound fracture of the frontal and parietal bones; a piece of the latter had penetrated the brain. The weapon had been round and blunt, probably a heavy piece of iron or wood; the blow had been given from behind. Other bodily injuries, both external and internal would have been, alone, fatal; but life was already extinct when the locomotive reached the tragic spot.

"How long after the blow did death follow?" Gilmore asked after the Superintendent returned the report.

"Not more than three minutes," Dr. Ralston answered. "Probably he died in less time than that due to the force with which he was struck."

"You have now completed your examination?" Wainwright queried.

"For the present, I have. . . ."

"Then, I suppose you will ship the body over. That was one of the first things Nixon's secretary inquired about."

The coroner's physician agreed. A few moments later the three doctors had taken their leave; and Gilmore, already too long delayed in his errand, followed their example.

On his journey to the bank, he studied the value of these most recent developments. Certain now that the responsibility for Nixon's death lay with the Ferris gang, there remained only to discover the details of the tragedy. He must learn where and at exactly what time the attack occurred, and how it had been arranged. It puzzled him that, according to Dr. Sackett, death had not come until eight o'clock, at least. For if, as Parker claimed, the financier had started out by machine at 4:30, he should have reached his destination, the shore, at 8:00. But the delay on that journey might well be open to some simple explanation.

On the other hand, had Philip Nixon actually taken the 5:20 train to Cape May from the Camden terminal, as the chauffeur claimed, 7:20 would have seen him safely at his summer home. Instead, death had met him on the road at eight or some time after. He could not have fallen from the train at that point fifty miles along the route; the blow on the head negatived such a proposition. Furthermore, it failed to explain Parker's flight, the bullet holes and the presence of Stahl's cap in the machine. Between the 5:20 local and the 9:55 express, which he had taken, was another train, the 7:45, which would have run over the body had it then been upon the right of way.

Cogitating thus, the detective reached his destination. The Central National Trust on Market Street, was one of the most important banking houses in the city. That the financier should have an account there was not unusual; it was probably but one of many accounts.

Within three minutes after he entered Gilmore was closeted with the vice president, a Mr. Folwell, who had made the call to Headquarters.

"I communicated with you," he explained to the seated detective, "because I thought it might interest you to know that Mr. Nixon called yesterday afternoon at about quarter of three, for quite a sum of money. But perhaps I had better let Mr. Manson, the paying teller with whom he dealt, tell you exactly what happened."

Ringing a bell upon his desk, he summoned an office boy. "Tell Mr. Manson I'd like to see him for a few moments." In a short time, the paying teller, upon whom years of indoor toil displayed their effects, appeared. His watery blue eyes, set in colorless features, rested upon Gilmore, as he related the incident for the detective's edification.

Briefly, the financier had called to withdraw from his private account five thousand dollars. He had not mentioned what he intended the sum for, nor, indeed, was he asked. As it was just before closing, he had had time to exchange a few words with the teller.

"I didn't know whether you'd be interested or not," Mr. Manson concluded apologetically, "but I thought the police might want to know, because Mr. Nixon is dead and the papers are calling it murder."

Pleased at finding the first part of Parker's tale verified, Gilmore expressed his approval.

"Do you know Mr. Nixon well?" he then asked.

"We all know him very well," the vice president said. "He has quite an account with us."

"Do you remember whether he has ever called personally for bills before?"

Mr. Manson could not recall any other definite occasion. Generally, he said, the financier withdrew sums by check and he seldom came personally. It was this fact that made his visit so interesting.

"How did you give the money to Mr. Nixon? Do you recall?"

"Yes sir; in fact, I have the numbers, if you would like them. I remember because I had to open a new package to give him what he wanted. There were ten one-hundred-dollar bills, and eight five-hundred-dollar bills—and all new."

"Excellent, Mr. Manson," Gilmore said. "I would like the numbers. They might prove important later on."

He asked a few more questions regarding the financier's private account, Mr. Folwell answering as fully as he was professionally able, and the detective prepared to take his leave.

At the cage of the paying teller, Mr. Manson gave him the list record. The latter's office window was part of a structure of cages that curved in a huge semicircle from the rear of one side of the bank to the rear of the other. Mr. Manson's cage, in the center of the arc, faced Market Street. In front of it and the aisle in which customers transacted business was a huge plate-glass window, through which pedestrians had an excellent view of the bank; and the teller, a complete scene of the street.

"When Mr. Nixon arrived, did you observe who brought him?" Gilmore asked as he took the list.

Mr. Manson hesitated a moment in deep thought. "Yes, sir, I distinctly recall that he was driven up in that conspicuous yellow car of his; and it waited for him right out in front until he came out. I can see many things that go on in the street, through that glass."

But it also enabled Parker to witness the transaction that was going on within. Watching the financier's movements, he had, in all probability, seen the sum pass into Nixon's hands. And that fact he must also have communicated to his colleagues in crime. But what had become of the five thousand dollars? Robbery had not been the motive of the crime; but if the Ferris gang had desired to make it appear so, they would have taken all the personal belongings Gilmore had found on the financier's body. The withdrawal of such a sum was bound to come to light. Had the financier left it in his private safe at home, between 3:45 and 4:30? But then, Parker, in looting it, would have taken the money, and it would have been found upon him, unless Nixon had placed it in some other secret receptacle.

The numbers on the bills, then, took on an unexpected importance. Five minutes after he left the bank, Gilmore was arranging to have the list distributed throughout the country, so that all banks should keep a watch for the notes.

7

QUESTIONS AND ANSWERS—OF A SORT

To Eleanor Nixon, the passing hours of the morning were a nightmare of anxiety and grave suspense, under the strain of which she experienced a sensation of helplessness. From the first awful rumor of her father's death, she had known no peace. The bare fact, verified by the morning newspapers, overwhelmed her. So frantic were her efforts to learn the truth of what had happened that she had no ear for Bennett's information regarding the missing chauffeur and machine. At least, her mind failed to connect them with her loss. Gone altogether were the poise and control which she had inherited from her dominating parent.

It was the first genuine sorrow that she had known and the sensation was a devastating one. Since her mother had died when she was too young to realize the full import of that loss, it had been Philip Nixon who had played the most important part in her life. He had accepted and carried successfully the dual role of father and mother to her. Between them existed an understanding, rare in these days between parents and children; so that even when her own strong will prompted her to disobey him, she informed him of the fact. Whatever the financier might mean to others, to Eleanor it seemed he could do no wrong. When she realized again that her last parting from him had been in anger, after a quarrel, her grief was greatly increased.

Instinctively, she turned to Donald Gardiner for consolation; it seemed most natural to do so. Bennett was himself nearly prostrated by the dreadful tidings; and the soothing ministrations of Mrs. Bennett brought her no comfort. In those anxious hours, facing the question squarely for the first time, she admitted to herself that she loved and needed him. It was ironic that the financier's death should accomplish the very result against which he had so strenuously objected in his life.

Donald Gardiner had attracted her attention at a time when she was wearied of the artificial society of the men who moved in her circle. Like her parent, she was by nature candid and straightforward; like him, she admired directness. In the conversations of her friends, she could find no element of sincerity. But in the young secretary, Eleanor thought she detected qualities similar to her own. His attractiveness was only a minor point in his favor; it was his candor and frankness that beckoned to her as to a kindred spirit. His character intrigued her, so that she welcomed the acquaintanceship.

One characteristic troubled the girl greatly. Several times she caught his mind wandering into strange depths from which he would return as from a distance, apologetic for his lapse. At such times, he appeared to be lost in a maze of tragedy and mental pain that saddened him. Eleanor was certain that in the past he had experienced some dread suffering. But he had never volunteered any fact about himself, and she could not ask; so that she knew only that he was Philip Nixon's secretary and lived with a private family on Roosevelt Boulevard.

Her father's opposition to her association with him was wholly incomprehensible. In all other respects, Philip Nixon appeared to have been well satisfied with him. That he had kept him in his employ was sufficient proof of this fact; it rather puzzled her. Eleanor knew that her father's attitude was not due to the discrepancy in Gardiner's social status. Himself a self-made man, the financier was never influenced by lack of wealth or position. Never before had he crossed her; it was a new experience to find herself refused something.

The opposition increased her already aroused interest, for it is human nature to crave that which is difficult to obtain. The quality of stubbornness, so marked in her father, when faced by an obstacle, was awakened. Inevitably, the two wills clashed; at each encounter, her interest increased, until, with perfect willfulness and independence, the girl admitted that she cared for Donald Gardiner though ignorant of the most commonplace facts regarding him. Thus matters had stood on the preceding day, when she had quarreled with her father.

And now, with his sudden death, she awaited the secretary's report of his visit to Headquarters. As soon as the first rumor had reached her, she had communicated with him. Over the phone, his voice, vibrant and comforting, enabled her to regain her grip upon herself. He had promised to find out everything for her, and join her as soon as possible. But with the tragedy, she knew that innumerable business details would devolve upon him until some responsible persons took the situation in hand. His presence would be required at a hurried meeting of the directors of the corporation; there would be frenzied reorganization to protect the company's finances. It was all in her interest, however, and with the promise, she was content.

Donald had called her once with a brief report of such information as the Superintendent possessed before Gilmore joined him. She sat in the huge central apartment, unconscious of her surroundings; the beauty and comfort of her home were all suddenly meaningless. About her the servants moved on tiptoe, silent and sympathetic: only Bennett or his wife dared to interrupt her sorrowful

meditation. A calamitous pall had descended upon everything, seeming to make even the sunshine that came
through the conservatory stifling and oppressive.

The doorbell rang, and Eleanor heard Bennett's deadened steps move through the hallway toward the door.
That must be Donald now; she started to rise to meet him
as he entered. Then, faintly, she heard voices—the butler's
and another, deeper voice that she could not place. The
words were indistinguishable.

Disappointed, she sank back, as Bennett entered, followed by the stranger she had first met in her father's
office the preceding day.

"Miss Eleanor," the butler spoke gently, "could you see
Mr. Gilmore for a few moments? He says that it is very
important and that he might be able to help us. Otherwise, he wouldn't dream of disturbing you now."

The girl stared into the visitor's face, in dry-eyed
wonder.

"Help us?" she asked numbly. "How can you help us,
Mr. Gilmore?"

The detective bent toward her. "Miss Nixon, I am deeply grieved for you—more than I can express. I would not
think of intruding upon your sorrow now, except that time
is precious and you might be able to tell me something of
value. I'm in charge of this case and if you could answer a
few questions—you and Bennett . . ."

"Then . . . you're a detective?" And when Gilmore nodded without speaking, "You can tell me, then, what happened to father?"

Briefly the detective complied, covering much of the
same ground that he had already covered in the morning
with his superior. He was careful, however, to present few
of the details, lest the girl be seized anew by grief; for he
desired, at that moment, clear minds and direct answers.

When he had finished, they both appeared strengthened as though a weight of uncertainty had been lifted from them.

"Then it was Parker—and those terrible men with him that were responsible for father's death!" the girl exclaimed.

Gilmore's alert ears caught a strange intonation possessed by the words, one totally unexpected under the circumstances. It was as though the girl was relieved. About what—had she feared that the blame lay at another's door? She had no reason for such a fear, unless she possessed some knowledge of the crime.

"We don't know that yet, for sure," the detective replied, "but it is very possible. And we are doing everything to trace the others. If you will tell me whatever you know of Parker, it may give us a clue to their hiding place."

"Everything we can tell you, sir," came from Bennett in a voice filled with emotion. "I've been with Mr. Nixon fifteen years, and a finer, more considerate master no one ever had."

Gilmore nodded a sober approval. "You told me yesterday, Bennett," he then said, "that you thought Parker had been fired because of his dishonesty. Where did you get that information?"

"Day before yesterday, in the evening," the butler related, "I was straightening out this room, when Mr. Nixon came down from his bedroom and asked me to send for Parker. I did, and when he came in, as insolent as you please, Mr. Nixon went with him into the conservatory and shut the door. They were in there for fifteen minutes; and then, just when the door was opened, Mr. Nixon was saying, 'It is understood, then, that you leave when your week is up.' After that, Charles went out, muttering to himself angrily and very red in the face."

"Did you hear anything while Mr. Nixon was in the room with him, Bennett?"

The butler hesitated. "Well, sir, I did hear a word or two from Mr. Nixon—that's what really made me think that Parker had been caught at something. When the door's closed in the conservatory, unless somebody's speaking very loud, you can't hear a thing, but Mr. Nixon raised his voice once or twice."

"And you heard him say?" Gilmore put in.

"Once he said the word 'thief'—and then I heard him distinctly tell Parker that he wouldn't have sneaking around the house. After that he quieted down, and I didn't get anything more that went on."

The detective then put some questions to Eleanor upon the same matter, but she proved ignorant of it. What she did know and could tell Gilmore was that Parker's recommendation as a chauffeur had come from a Mrs. Van Suttart who had gone to France to live, three months before. The girl was not, in fact, acquainted with her, though she was a familiar figure in social circles, but she had heard that Mrs. Van Suttart had dismissed all her servants. When, therefore, Parker had presented her introduction as a capable chauffeur, they had employed him without investigation.

"There's no doubt," Gilmore remarked grimly when she had finished, "that the recommendation was forged." He paused for a moment, before proceeding with an equally important line of interrogation.

"At what time did your father come home from the office yesterday afternoon?"

It was Bennett who answered. "I should say it was about quarter of four; in fact, sir, not more than a half-hour after you left to go back to town."

"Please relate to me carefully what happened. This is very important, Bennett; Mr. Nixon brought home a large sum of money and I want to know exactly where he went and which rooms he visited."

"Yes, sir. When Mr. Nixon called me up to say you were coming, he also instructed me to pack him the overnight bag he usually takes when he goes traveling. I did so, sir, and when Charles brought him, sent him upstairs for it. A little later, Mr. Nixon also went up but only to his own room. He stayed there for about ten minutes, then came down and asked me if Miss Eleanor was in. I told him she was at a tea at the Bellevue-Stratford and wouldn't be in until six o'clock. He instructed me to inform her that he had gone to the shore. After that, he went into the conservatory. And then . . ."

For an instant, the speaker paused and Eleanor broke in.

"Father stayed there for a while and left about half past four. At least, Bennett, that's what you told me yesterday evening when I came home from the tea."

Her statement also verified a portion of Parker's tale. But some quality in the girl's manner, in her abrupt interruption of Bennett's story, caused Gilmore to study her sharply. Her face had taken on a strange whiteness, and he was just in time to catch the mute appeal written in her eyes. The intercepted look sent a perfectly comprehensible message to Bennett, and he responded.

"That's right," he continued, but Gilmore was certain that his words were not those he had originally intended, "Mr. Nixon drove away at half past four . . . And we never saw him again."

"What did he do in the conservatory?" Gilmore's voice was keen and penetrating.

"That, sir, I couldn't say. He closed the doors and I didn't see him again till he came out about twenty minutes later."

Bennett was lying—and the girl, despite her grief, had asked him to do so, as obviously as though she had spoken to him. She was obstructing his investigation, fully as though she did not wish him to learn the truth. Philip Nixon had concealed some important fact from him; did his daughter know what it was and was she making the same effort to keep it from him?

But he could not press the point; he had no grounds for doing so. Yet Gilmore believed that his next question touched the heart of the secret.

"Mr. Nixon was not accustomed to leaving his business for short vacations. Have you any idea, Bennett, why he was going to Cape May?"

"He wasn't feeling well, sir. He was run down and had a cold. I pressed him several times about taking a rest, or he'd have a breakdown, and he finally agreed."

"You know of no other reason, Bennett?"

"No, sir. What other reason should there be?"

"You thought it unusual, Miss Nixon, when your father mentioned that he was going to the shore. Are you aware of any other cause for his journey?"

"Only what he told me in the office, Mr. Gilmore," the girl replied, "that he was in need of a short rest. I don't imagine there was any other reason."

The detective rose from the lounge on which he had been seated and strode toward the conservatory.

"Thank you, Miss Nixon. . . . Now, if I could have some one to help me, I should like to make a search of the house. Your father may not have taken that money with him. I think we will begin in that room."

Eleanor and the old servant joined him in his quest. Together they made a complete investigation of the room that had been the scene of an attempted burglary eight months before. The conservatory possessed almost no furnishings, except the heavy profusion of plants; yet Gilmore did not overlook even the possibility of the money being hidden among the potted shrubs. Only a thorough search convinced him that, whatever events had taken place in that room, the concealment of the bank notes was not among them.

In the tremendous project of searching the rest of the house, the services of Mrs. Bennett and Eleanor's personal maid, Hilda, were also enlisted; nevertheless, it took them more than an hour. They passed from the salon to the dining room, and then to the sun-parlor, the main library and the family bedrooms, upstairs, omitting only such unlikely places as the unused guest quarters. Special attention was given to the financier's wall-safe, of which Eleanor knew the combination; and Gilmore made a thorough inspection of whatever contents Parker had left. He did not expect to find the money there, nor was he disappointed. At the conclusion of the hour of vain searching, he was convinced that Philip Nixon had taken it with him.

Gilmore's final step before leaving the house was the task of interviewing the servants one by one. Beginning with those in the house, Mrs. Bennett, the footman, Ben the houseman, and the chef, Gilmore then questioned the gardeners and the garage man. Even with a series of routine questions, it was fruitless labor; none of them could tell him anything of the financier's movements. Of household gossip, he gleaned a great deal, but none of any use; he heard of Bennett's extreme affection for Eleanor Nixon, of the general unpopularity of the chauffeur, one of the gardeners claiming that he had "opined he was a bad 'un" from the beginning, of Hilda's romance with Ben, of Mrs. Bennett's iron rule over her husband, of the respect in which they all held their deceased employer—and so on, it seemed to Gilmore, *ad infinitum.*

The only item of information came from the garage man. From the time Miss Eleanor had returned from the tea until eleven, he had been in the garage, working upon her car. He was willing to take his oath that, after leaving

with the financier at 4:30, Charles Parker had never returned the Rolls-Royce to the garage. Indeed, he had never
seen the car again. The testimony shattered the chauffeur's
effort to bluff himself out of his difficulties.

Gilmore's final interview of importance during the afternoon proved no more satisfactory than the others. From
the financier's home, he went to the American Motors
offices. There awaited him the interrogation of Philip
Nixon's corps of stenographers and clerks, who knew little
of the financier's movements. Other officers of the corporation were not likely to prove more helpful.

On the way, the detective had purchased the late edition
of the *Evening Ledger* and turned to the financial section.
What he sought stared him in the face, in headlines fully
as prominent as those he had perused on the Cape May
express; and it read exactly as he had expected it to read.
The effect of the financier's death upon the corner he had
been operating was catastrophic. Audubon Common had
opened at 130 instead of its high of 145, at which it had
closed the preceding day. By noon, it had dropped to 120;
by two o'clock, it had gone to 108; and when the market
closed, it was quoted under 100, with values threatening
to plunge even lower on the morrow. It was a disaster at
which the entire money world stood aghast.

Gilmore fully realized the import of the calamity and
its significance to American Motors. The corner had collapsed; and most of the ensuing loss would fall upon the
Nixon estate. The financier had been the moving force of
the corporation as well as the personal financier of the
corner. The detective had no doubt that Philip Nixon's
vast fortune would be sufficient to meet this blow, without depriving Eleanor of her inheritance; nevertheless, the
calamity was certain to lessen it seriously.

It was after he had finished with the company's officers that Gilmore examined Donald Gardiner in his late

employer's private office. The secretary appeared fatigued, with deep rings about his eyes as though the strenuous day had exhausted him. Too, the lateness of the hour of his retirement the night before must have partially contributed to the strained countenance that confronted the detective.

Preliminary questions elicited the fact that while the financier had rivals, none were enemies who would dream of stooping to murder.

"Mr. Nixon had disagreements with several men, to my knowledge," the secretary said. "There was Mr. Paton, of the Starbuck Motor concern, over the matter of concessions. We've had difficulty with the Audubon people constantly. And, of course, there are always cranks, people who try to interest Mr. Nixon in one thing or another . . ."

"Cranks? Anyone of that sort, recently?"

"Not that I remember." Gardiner smiled wanly. "There was a stockbroker who has called Mr. Nixon up constantly within the last few days, about some matter dealing with stocks—a Mr. Russell Stirling. Mr. Nixon instructed me to say he wasn't in the next time he called; and that if he came to the office, he would not see him. But I don't suppose you class stockbrokers with cranks."

"No, hardly," Gilmore replied, interested in spite of himself. "Have you any idea what Mr. Stirling wanted of your employer?"

The reply was in the negative. Gilmore took down all the names given him, as a matter of course; then, pocketing his notebook, he lighted his pipe, a signal that he intended to remain for some time.

"Mr. Gardiner," he said, "did you not consider it unusual that Philip Nixon should have made a journey to the shore yesterday? I am aware that he had not been feeling well; nevertheless, I hardly think it was his custom to leave his desk, even for the sake of his health."

The depth of the question caused the secretary to ponder seriously for a moment before replying.

"You are quite right, Mr. Gilmore; putting it that way, it was rather unusual. But Mr. Nixon asked no one what he should or should not do; he did exactly as he pleased regardless of others. . . ."

Gilmore detected an underlying tone of bitterness in his voice.

"He did not speak to you at all about his journey?"

"He merely mentioned that he was leaving, and that he expected to return tomorrow. That is all he told me."

The other stopped puffing on his pipe, and studied Gardiner searchingly. "You did not discuss any other matter with him? Tell me, Mr. Gardiner, did you speak to Miss Nixon yesterday, when she was in the office?"

On its face, the question contained nothing calculated to arouse emotion; yet the secretary flushed uncomfortably.

"I don't see what that has to do with your investigation."

"It is rather difficult to see the point, at present," Gilmore agreed blandly. "In a brutal murder like this it is impossible to tell what is important as yet. At any rate, you should have no motive for concealing anything."

"Well, then, yes," Gardiner replied, thinking the better of his objection. "I did speak to her."

"After she saw her father?"

"Yes, I suppose it was afterward."

"How long have you been working for Mr. Nixon?"

"About six months," the secretary said.

"How did you get the position?"

Again the other flushed; this time his reply was challenging.

"See here, Mr. Gilmore, I'm perfectly willing to answer all questions within reason; but my personal affairs can be of no concern to your investigation. I would much prefer that, in the future, we do not bring Miss Nixon into the conversation."

The detective shrugged acquiescence. The secretary's nervousness was betraying the very fact he sought to conceal—namely, that he possessed some secret he feared to divulge. But Gilmore could see no reason for pressing the point, at least, not then; sufficient intricacies challenged him without his creating new complications.

"As you please, Mr. Gardiner," he replied. "In fact, I have just one more question to ask, and I am finished."

"What is it?" the secretary asked, as though suspicious of his interrogator's withdrawal.

"I'm given to understand that Philadelphia is not your home town. Will you give me your local address so that I could get in touch with you, if the necessity should arise?"

"Willingly . . ."

He took from his pocket a visiting card on which was printed his name and address.

"I live with a private family—a Mr. and Mrs. Phipps. They are charming people; and it's far superior to a boarding house."

"Thank you," Gilmore said, pocketing the card. "By the way," he added casually, "yesterday evening, did you return the office at any time after closing hours?"

Gardiner looked astonished. "No, of course, I didn't," he replied vehemently. "Why should I go to the office? I stayed—" he broke off, without finishing.

"Oh, you remained in your rooms all evening, then?"

"Yes, I did. I have a typewriter there and I was doing some extra work. The company had been on the verge of declaring a dividend, and at such periods I often have some secretarial work."

"You did not go to the office, or out, at any time, then?"

The secretary replied with what was more than normal vehemence even in the face of Gilmore's persistence.

"I did not leave the house at all," he said without hesitation.

It was a direct falsehood and a deliberate denial by Gardiner that he had made a journey to Cape May the night before. Yet Gilmore was certain that he had come from the resort; the late Philadelphia express had made no stops between Cape May and Camden, except the single halt at the Marley farmhouse. Eleanor Nixon had appeared relieved when informed that the Ferris gang had been responsible for her father's death. Throughout the inquisition, the secretary had lied more than once. Though Gilmore could not, for the moment, conceive how the secretary could have been guilty of the crime, as he lacked the opportunity, nevertheless, this combination of facts was interesting. Interesting enough, Gilmore thought, as he left the office, to set Detective Jenks to watching Gardiner.

8
THE CAPTURE

In the year that had elapsed since Tommy Rankin had successfully handled the case in which a girl had been murdered at Woodlawn Park,[1] he had been concerned with few important assignments. Interesting cases, with the exception of the Ferris affair, were few; for the most part, the stupidity of criminals made them easy prey for the police. The youthful detective's efforts had been expended on matters concerning that realm with which he was so well acquainted—the underworld.

Eight months ago, in the Ferris affair, he had received a distinct setback. Following the attempted robbery, he had taken to the trail of the gang leader's crew. But he had met with no success. Whether they had fled from the city, to return when the first flurry had blown over, or whether they had remained in watchful concealment, he did not know. Certain it was, however, that he had failed to unearth either Stahl, Morin, or the third unknown confederate of the group. His customary channels of inquiry failed him; finally, he was compelled to admit himself defeated.

When a case is not brought to a satisfactory conclusion, it does not indicate that the police have finished

[1] See *The Strange Disappearance of Mary Young*.

with it. Nothing further may be accomplished for a long
time; yet they remain alert for further information which
will set them again upon trail. That event may be some
criminal's confession; or may be another crime which re-
veals the same malefactor's hand. Many crimes are thus
solved through developments that occur years after they
were first committed.

In this case, but eight months had elapsed. And now,
what further facts, upon which to work, did Rankin possess? The information and data of his new assignment did
not appear to promise much. There were merely the letters, and Arthur Stahl's cap. Nevertheless, the detective
believed they presented a previously unsounded line of
investigation.

He set to work with renewed vigor. First, he turned
his attention to the threatening missives Philip Nixon had
received on three successive occasions. Written on ordinary white paper, they gave him no assistance. Parker had
written the first two; and a comparison of the third letter
with a prison copy of Morin's handwriting dissipated all
doubts as to its authorship. All letters had been carefully
posted in town, so that the postmarks—Central Post
Office—were valueless as clues. The Ferris gang had made
no effort to conceal their responsibility for the notes; had
they not once already successfully defied the law?

It was different, however, with the letters found in
Parker's bag. The possibility that they might fall into alien
hands had never occurred to the writer; and he had taken
no precautions in mailing them. The postmarks of all of
them informed Rankin where they had been mailed and
indicated a probable location of the gang's retirement.
They were stamped "Chestnut Hill"; a section, north of
Germantown, and far from the center of Philadelphia. It
was an excellent place of concealment. Logically it was
more than possible that the letters had been posted not far

from where they had been written, and there Morin and
Stahl were.

Carefully Rankin perused them. They were interesting
reading, and valuable as incriminating evidence; but what
he wanted was not included. Nowhere had the men he
sought made a direct reference to the address of their hiding place. They had been too cautious for that. Only one
allusion resembled a clue, and its value was doubtful. It
read:

> ". . . when the time is ready to strike. Arthur
> will throw up his job out here at a moment's
> notice; so you have only to say the word and
> . . ."

From the letters, the detective turned to the cap found
in Philip Nixon's machine. Its size, 7¼, coincided with the
size of Arthur Stahl's head as given by his prison record.
Its plain blue cloth was of no distinctive quality; and due
to the hard usage to which it had been subjected, the maker's label was gone. The initials, faded almost into invisi-
bility, had been written on the sweatband, under the visor.

But it was the fact that the entire headgear was stained
with oil that attracted Rankin's attention. Oil covered the
inside as well as the outside, in heavy smears. There were
also yellowish spots of a glistening appearance which were
easily identifiable as grease spots. By holding the cap to
his nose, the detective caught the same odor of gasoline
that Gilmore had already noted. It was as though it had
been washed in gasoline; the scent on it could have resulted only from a constant association with motor fuel.

Arthur Stahl's prison record labeled him a mechanic.
What conclusions, then, were to be drawn from all these
scattered details with which his new data provided Rankin?
First, that Lew Ferris's accomplices were hiding in that

section of the city known as Chestnut Hill. The postmarks upon the letters written to Charles Parker indicated this. Secondly, that Stahl was working in some industry that brought him in contact with gas, oil and grease. While lying low, he was engaged, under an assumed name, in honest labor—in effect, leading a dual life. The work that he was doing could be only one of two types; he was employed either in a gas station or a garage. The latter was more probable; it gave Stahl a greater opportunity to display the mechanical ability which explained his adeptness with safes and locks.

Finally, the garage in which he worked was also located in the Chestnut Hill district. It was but natural that he should seek employment near his place of lodging. In addition, Morin's letter, written from his place of concealment, referred to Stahl's job "out here," indicating the same locality. Rankin considered it fairly certain that, if he could locate the garage in question, he would be able to lay his hands upon both men.

Indeed, the entire result of his reasoning appeared to promise success. Though admittedly flimsy in parts, it was logically, fairly sound, the assumptions dovetailing nicely. Nevertheless, thought Rankin, he was taking a chance on the entire series of deductions. If any one should prove incorrect, his structure of reasoning would collapse like a pack of cards. And he possessed no means of rebuilding that structure, except through forcing Charles Parker to talk. But that method was distasteful to him; he would not have recourse to it, except as a last resort.

The detective obtained a directory and turned to the classified list of garages in the city. There were thirty-five, he noted, to be found within the Chestnut Hill district; their addresses he listed in such order as he could. It would be tedious work, canvassing through that list and in each garage inquiring about the employees. But there was no help for it; he could only arrange them systematically, so as to avoid retracing the same ground. Thus, he would spare himself some difficulties and save time as well.

Accordingly, armed with the list, and a prison photograph of Arthur Stahl, Rankin set out upon his quest. It was early afternoon, when he entered the first garage to inquire whether an excellent mechanic whose initials were A. S. or who resembled the picture, was there employed. Despite a glib explanation of his search, his queries brought forth suspicious glances until he had revealed their true meaning. Then there was willing cooperation; but there proved to be no such employee there nor could they assist him.

The first failure presaged what was to follow. Through the remainder of the afternoon, Rankin pursued the same general line of inquiry. In some places he successfully dissembled, gaining the information on the pretense that he was seeking a friend whose address he had lost, but who he knew worked in a garage in the vicinity; in other places, he explained his true mission. But no garage appeared to employ anyone answering the description of the man he sought. Twice, indeed, he believed he had come upon a trail, when he located workmen whose initials were A. S.; but each time the man failed to resemble his quarry in any manner.

As afternoon grew into night, failure after failure greeted the detective's efforts. At each, he became increasingly discouraged. The fear that had been rankling in his mind for some time was fast becoming a certainty; namely, that he was somehow proceeding upon a mistaken line of inquiry. Where his reasoning was at fault, he could not tell; a review of his deductions brought him to the same conclusions. He could conceive of no other theory upon which to work. His pursuit promised to end in a complete zero; the twenty-six garages he had already crossed from his list signified failure.

The twenty-seventh appeared no more promising. Its entrance opened into an amphitheater, just wide enough to allow two rows of cars to park, the length of the interior. An elevator led to the second floor, where more machines were stored. Like all the other garages, it was redolent of oil and the choking, heavy scent of exhaust gas.

A sign in the doorway informed Rankin that this was McKenney's. Of the jovial-faced negro in dirty overalls who approached him, he inquired for the owner, and upon being informed that he was in, requested an interview. In a moment, he was ushered into an office on one side of the garage, in which auto accessories almost overwhelmed a desk in one corner.

Mr. McKenney listened to his employee's explanation of Rankin's visit and dismissed him. He was a youngish, portly man of serious mien; studying him the detective decided he could be taken into his confidence.

He took the chair the garage man produced from among a conglomeration of auto fixtures.

"Yes, sir," the other began, "What can I do for you, Mr. —?"

"Rankin," the detective supplied. He offered him a visiting card upon which was also printed "Central Headquarters." The young man sat up suddenly, and he eyed his visitor with greater interest.

"A detective, eh? Well, Mr. Rankin, what's your business?"

"I'm on the trail of a criminal, who I have reason to believe is working in a garage in this vicinity. His name is Stahl, though, of course, he won't be going by that name around here. He's an excellent mechanic; and I would like to know whether you have anyone in your employ whose initials are A. S. or who resembles my man."

"I doubt very much whether he's working here," Mr. McKenney returned. "We employ eight men, but no one with those initials. Now if you would describe him for me . . ."

Rankin concealed the disappointment he felt at what was to be his twenty-seventh successive failure.

"This is his picture—perhaps you will recognize that."

The other studied it casually; then, looking at it again, stifled an exclamation of astonishment.

"That's Clyde Hammond!" he cried. "He was one of our men—we employed him for the last few months. . . ."

With a sinking sensation, Rankin observed that he spoke in the past tense.

"That's Arthur Stahl. You say, he was here; isn't he here any more? If he is, I don't want him to see me; he knows me too well."

"You needn't worry about that. He quit us yesterday without notice; a damned good man he was, too. Who would have thought he was wanted by the police!" The speaker paused. "I thought there was something peculiar about the way he went away!"

"Peculiar?" the detective asked eagerly. "Why, what happened?"

"At about quarter of three yesterday afternoon, a call came for him. After he had answered it, he came to me and asked me to give him the rest of the afternoon off. His hours are daytime hours, and I didn't think I could spare him; but he looked worried and anxious, and he was such a good man besides, that I told him he could go."

"Did he say why he wanted to get off?"

"Not a word—and, of course, I didn't ask him. After I agreed he said he wanted to hire a car for the rest of the afternoon at the regular prices. I told him that if he paid for the gasoline he used, I would be satisfied. So he took one of our cars and went away. . . ."

Here, indeed, was luck. Not only had he found Stahl, but he also traced the car used in following Philip Nixon.

For Rankin had no doubt that the call was from either Parker or from Morin, informing him of Nixon's intended journey and arranging for following the Rolls-Royce from Bryn Mawr into Jersey. Arthur Stahl had procured a car for that very purpose. Every detail pointed to that conclusion; even the element of time fitted into the scheme of the entire plot.

"He came back with the car, of course?" Rankin asked.

"Yes—late in the evening; it must have been eleven o'clock. The car had been out in the storm and needed a cleaning. Then Hammond—as I knew him—told me that he had to leave for good; something had happened that made it necessary for him to go away. I gathered that someone in his family was sick or in trouble, and though I hated to lose him, I said that in such a case he had better go. So I gave him his pay up to the end of this week and he went away. To think, he was really leaving because you were after him!"

The detective nodded as Mr. McKenney closed his narrative.

"You have this Hammond's address—I suppose you know where all your men live in case you should need them for extra work at times?"

"Yes, of course, I do. It's down on my books some-where— if you'll just wait a minute till I find it." He produced a cumbersome ledger, and for some moments searched through its pages. "Ah, here it is! Five-four-six North Ludgate Street—that's only four blocks from here, toward Germantown Avenue. If he's as bad as you say he is, I hope you get him, Mr. Rankin."

The detective noted the address and rose. He had little time for talking; he was anxious to be upon his way. The fact that Stahl had given notice and left was proof that his quarry had taken alarm and were prepared once more to disappear. Indeed, it was possible that they might already have done so, and when he came upon the nest, he would find both birds had flown. He could not chance any delay.

"We've been after him for some time, but so far he's always managed to elude us," he replied in answer to the remark. "Now, after assisting me so splendidly, Mr. Mc-Kenney, if you'll let me look at the car he took out, I'll not disturb you any further. . . ."

"Certainly," the other replied. "If you'll come this way . . ." He led Rankin toward the rear of the garage, where another entrance opened into a back alley. There, against the wall, he pointed out a Buick sedan, the sides of which, though streaked by rain, were not smeared to the same extent as those of the financier's car. It appeared incapable of maintaining the pace of the latter, but Parker, at the wheel of the Rolls-Royce, had assuredly adjusted his speed so that Stahl and Morin, in the smaller car, could follow.

A brief examination of the sedan produced no new facts. The garage owner did not recall at what mileage the indicator had stood when Stahl had taken it out; Rankin had no means of gauging the distance the car had traveled the preceding night. The amount of gas already in the tank when Stahl had taken it was also unknown, so that what was left gave no evidence of the journey's length. In all respects, the car was valueless as evidence of the events it must have witnessed within the last twenty-four hours.

Cautioning Mr. McKenney against mentioning his search to others, Rankin took his departure. It was ten o'clock when he stepped again into the street; it was a quarter after the hour, when, in some suspense, he stood before the address in North Ludgate Street.

The street was a narrow thoroughfare, hardly more than an alley, that was only a single square in length, and from where the detective stood its limited area was completely visible. On each side, red brick houses, all similar in appearance, fronted by wooden stairs, lined the narrow pavement in a row. Number 546 was no different from the others, except that a potted plant upon one window made a futile effort to conceal its meanness. In one window, a sign offered rooms for rent at reasonable rates.

With this excuse to gain an entrance, Rankin boldly knocked upon the door. A grim-visaged woman, in curl-papers, in whose eyes was written worldly understanding, opened it. She waited coldly on the doorstep, studying her late visitor suspiciously.

"I just arrived in town, to take a position in Philadel-phia," he explained apologetically, "and I came out here to look for a room. My baggage hasn't even arrived yet. Your notice and the neatness of your place attracted me; so in spite of the lateness of the hour . . ."

The woman smiled sourly as she decided there was nothing amiss with this handsome, well-spoken gentleman.

"That's all right," she interrupted. "You have to be careful, these days, about strange people, what with so many burglaries and all. . . . My name is Mrs. Hyman. Won't you come in?"

Rankin removed his hat, and stepped into what must have been the living room. It boasted of a piano, with blackened keys, and a sofa; soiled curtains covered the windows, and opposite them, in the center, was a spindle-legged table and some chairs.

"You see, I want a quiet place," he explained, "where I can be comfortable, and meet pleasant people. I like to be sociable, and as I expect to be here for some time, I'll want to know my fellow boarders . . ."

"Oh, I'm very particular who I take in. At present, I can let you have a room on the second floor, because a Mr. Solomon moved out of it a week ago. Mr. Hammond and Mr. Barker are across the hall—and I've never had such nice people. . . ."

Smiling gently, the detective displayed no sign of the satisfaction her words had given him. He was not too late; Stahl and Morin were still there, probably now in their upstairs room. But the landlady's next words informed him how close he was to having lost them.

"I'm afraid, though, Mr. — Mr. —"

"Mr. Malloy, of Erie, Pennsylvania."

"I'm afraid, Mr. Malloy, that you won't have the chance to meet them. You see, they're leaving me tomorrow morning. Mr. Barker has a position somewhere out in Ohio— and Mr. Hammond is going with him. Though why Mr. Hammond should want to give up that wonderful position he has at McKenney's garage, I'm sure I don't know."

"You don't say. Leaving tomorrow. Hm . . . well, there'll be others." Mrs. Hyman assented vigorously to this. "Now as to your terms. . . ."

They discussed terms at length, and Rankin found them satisfactory. Then the landlady showed him up a steep, narrow staircase; at a door at its head, she paused to insert a key.

The bare, uninviting hall was shallow, with only one other door on the same side, that of the bathroom. The detective's interest, however, was centered upon the door opposite. It was tightly shut, but a light issued from beneath the crack in the door and through the keyhole. If he needed further proof that the chamber was occupied, a low murmuring was barely audible in the stillness. Rankin thrilled at the thought that his game was so close at hand, at last.

"That's where Mr. Hammond and Mr. Barker are, is it not?" he asked softly.

"Yes, sir, Mr. Malloy." A bright light suddenly illuminated his room, revealing that it was neat and clean, if somewhat lacking in furnishings. A large brass bed occupied half of the chamber, and a highboy and a washstand filled the rest of it.

The landlady turned down the sheets of his bed.

"I think you'll find everything all right, sir . . . but if there's anything you want, I'll be glad to get it for you."

"There's nothing, thank you, Mrs. Hyman. This will suit me excellently. . . ."

She was about to shut the door, when Rankin stopped her.

"Perhaps I had better tell you, that I expect a visitor in the morning about my position here. He'll be up early—I should say, at about seven o'clock. If it's too early for you, I'll let him in."

"Oh, no," she replied. "I'll be up by then myself and I'll see that he finds your room."

With Mrs. Hyman's footsteps echoing down the stairs, Rankin seated himself on the bedstead to take stock of the situation. On the verge of successfully concluding his assignment, he must make no error, either of being too hasty or too slow. It would be foolhardy to attempt the capture single-handed, nor was this necessary. He could easily have Headquarters send him assistance, and it was for this reason he had informed Mrs. Hyman of an expected guest. He would have preferred to carry it through without attracting any attention; at any rate, he hoped to succeed without a struggle.

Obviously, he must act by early morning, when the culprits would be ready to leave. It seemed to the detective almost a miracle that he was not too late, especially when, as Stahl's behavior at McKenney's indicated, they had intended to escape last night. Rankin believed he knew what had delayed them; they had not heard from Parker. Due to his prompt arrest, he had been unable to communicate with them as they had expected, and make arrangements for flight. The papers mentioned nothing of it; and, in ignorance, his accomplices had waited. But now his very silence alarmed them, and fearing that something was amiss, they were ready to flee in the morning.

At midnight, the detective left the boarding house long enough to make arrangements with Headquarters for the following day. That accomplished, he returned to his lodgings. The murmur in the opposite room was still audible. Without undressing, Rankin extinguished his light, and seating himself in his bed, began a night's vigil. His door he kept sufficiently open to be able to watch the door across the hall. He was taking no chance of his prey stealing away under cover of darkness, an astute move they were capable of making to cover their tracks.

An hour and a half slowly passed. Then the voices opposite ceased; the detective, with ears alert, found himself straining to catch every sound. But there came only the muffled creaks of the house settling itself for slumber, and after a time not even they were heard. It was as though he were suspended in an utter void, pressed in upon every side by a painful isolation. His attitude became increasingly difficult to maintain as the long hours passed; weariness struggled to overcome him. But he fought it off, intensely vigilant, though hearing only the silence. Then, at 3:30, the clattering hoofs of horses shattered it, as the milkman passed up the street, with such a rattle that it was a wonder every sleeper was not awakened. Following another hour of quiet, the first gray signs of the approaching dawn made their appearance, and certain finally, that all was secure till morning, Rankin permitted exhaustion to have its way.

A gentle, penetrating rap awakened him to his complete faculties and a realization of his position. It was seven o'clock; bright sunlight streamed through the window. He leaped from the bed, and opened the door.

Detective Smith entered, closing the door softly behind him.

Briefly, then, he described the two men they were after, how he expected to gain an entrance, and what his colleague was to do, when they had accomplished their first strategic moves.

"As they don't know you," explained Rankin, "you will knock on the door. As soon as it is opened, I'll force it the rest of the way. If we work quickly enough, we'll have them covered in a jiffy."

Smith nodded his understanding. Quietly, they proceeded into the hallway to the tightly closed barrier opposite. Movement and voices issuing from within, told them that their quarry was awake; even now, they must be preparing for flight. Rankin took a position behind his companion, so as not to be visible at first glance; then he placed his foot and the weight of his body firmly against the door. The right hand, in his pocket grasped a bulky object.

Smith knocked lightly.

The conversation within ceased abruptly. From the silence, there issued a gruff, "Who's there?"

"A telegram, sir," Smith replied. "The lady downstairs sent me up with it."

"Get it, Stahl," said a more highly pitched voice authoritatively. "It must be from Parker. Well, it's about time we heard from him. . . ."

There was an audible stirring and a grumbling reply. A bed creaked; shuffling footsteps approached the door, scraping as though made by feet incased in slippers. A key turned in the lock. Rankin held himself taut.

The portal swung open just enough to reveal the smooth-shaven, bruiserlike features of a youngish man clad in a bathrobe and slippers. Arthur Stahl's hand reached out for the message. Simultaneously with the alarm that appeared in his eyes, as he caught sight of two men, Rankin hurled his bulk forward. It met no resistance from the astonished criminal until it was too late; the door swung inward with a resounding crash and the two detectives stood in the room.

"Good morning, Mr. Hammond," said Tommy Rankin, coolly, "I see you are just ready for a journey."

It was an astonishing tableau. The chamber, in the last stages of disorder, bore mute evidence of the activities they had interrupted. The drawers of the two tall bureaus were open; shirts, ties and articles of underclothing hung from them in confusion. Other articles were piled tumul-tuously upon the bed. On the floor lay two open suitcases, partially packed; but not even there existed any semblance of system.

Upon the bed sat Ike Morin, as slender and delicate as his companion was huge, with keen, foxlike eyes and pinched features. He had suddenly paused in the process of dressing, and the Machiavellian smile he usually wore was frozen upon his lips. Stahl, a look of rage distorting his countenance, stood against the door. And Rankin, with Smith at his side, gazed from one man to the other, await-ing the first move.

It was not long in coming. The instant of pregnant silence occasioned by their sudden entry was shattered by Morin's lightning-like move toward his pillow. In his swift-darting hand, an article glinted like a blue flame in the sunlight.

The detective's pocket seemed to speak thunderously. A fiery flash accompanied the ear-splitting crash of the shot. Blood spurted from Ike Morin's hand as his revolver clat-tered the floor; sudden agony twisted his features.

"Damn you, Rankin. . . ." he ground out.

"Don't try it again, Morin," was the ominous reply. "You might as well admit you're caught. We've got you both covered. Move back to the bed, Stahl, quickly, while Smith frisks you."

With a smothered curse, the man at the door joined his companion.

"That's better. . . . Now, it's useless to resist, because you couldn't get away from the men that are waiting for you downstairs."

"You can't arrest us," Morin said bitterly. "You haven't anything on us." He twisted a handkerchief about his injured hand.

"Merely the murder of Philip Nixon," Rankin replied, "You won't have such an easy time with that charge as you've had with some of your lesser crimes."

Mrs. Hyman stood in the entrance behind them, wringing her hands.

"What was that terrible noise I heard? It sounded like a shot. What's going on?"

She broke off in sheer astonishment at the scene before her. By now, Smith had picked up the one revolver from the floor, and was searching Stahl's pillow for another. The latter's companion, having completed the bandage, watched him grimly while his hand slipped beneath the bedding. Rankin, alert for further resistance, covered both his captives. The sheer disorder of the room merely accentuated the strangeness of the scene.

"I'm sorry, Mrs. Hyman," the detective replied, "for this trouble. But these men are criminals, wanted by the police; and they were just about to make their escape. . . . You had best go downstairs—it's much safer there."

Horrified that her respectable boarding house should have been a rendezvous for criminals, and the scene of a disgraceful raid, the landlady obeyed. Once she was gone, Rankin again ordered his prisoners to dress, and under the stimulus of the revolver they robed themselves swiftly.

When both were ready, he turned them over to Smith who led them into the hallway to the steps.

"No slip-ups, there," he cautioned from the doorway. "They've given us enough trouble already."

He shut the door behind him and began a thorough investigation of the room. Beginning with the half-packed bags, he went through the bureaus and then the bed. In the former, he found more incriminating evidence in the form of letters from Parker, and a burglar's kit that undoubtedly belonged to Arthur Stahl. The clothes told him nothing, nor had he expected them to do so. Rankin even made a scrutiny of the floor, looking beneath the scrawny rug for some possible place of concealment. But none existed.

From under the bed, he hauled forth a small-sized valise of brown leather. Within were neat, colored pajamas, of a variegated pattern, an overnight toilet set, and a bottle of medicine. Across its label was written "Philip Nixon"; and all the other articles were initialed with the letters P. N.

It was the overnight bag that Bennett had packed at the financier's order to take along with him on his journey, which Parker had placed in the Rolls-Royce before they had started. And he, Rankin, had found it in this room of Parker's confederates. In that moment he believed there could be no escape from the conclusion of whose hand it was that had struck down Philip Nixon.

9
THE BANK NOTES

CENTRAL DETECTIVE BUREAU
PHILADELPHIA
BANK NOTE WITH NUMBER INDICATED
AS MISSING NOTE LOCATED AT ROCK-
TON N J AT CUMBERLAND COUNTY NA-
TIONAL BANK

GABE SIMMONS
SHERIFF ROCKTON

This brief telegram raised Daniel Gilmore from the slough of uncertainty to the heights of elation. It was waiting for him at Headquarters, on the morning of the second day after the murder. Particularly was it acceptable when he considered that only the preceding afternoon had he broadcast the numbers of the notes Philip Nixon had withdrawn from his account. It was almost incredible that such an immediate communication should follow.

During the evening just passed, while his colleague trailed the Ferris crew, Gilmore had taken a flying trip to Cape May. Though certain that the financier had never reached the resort, there was a chance that he might find some loose strand of the puzzle at that end of the line. There were inquiries to be pursued both at the railroad station at Cape May and at the financier's summer home.

Furthermore, he might unearth the reason for the intriguing behavior of Donald Gardiner, for the journey he had
made and so deliberately denied. Accordingly, he had tak-
en the 5:20 local train—the same that Parker claimed his
employer had taken the day before—to the shore.

In all respects, the effort had proved futile. At the station there was no one who could give him information. The
caretakers at Nixon's shore quarters had not been notified
of the financier's expected arrival, and hence knew nothing of his movements. Twice, indeed, during the course
of the evening—at ten o'clock and at eleven-thirty—some
one, who had left no name, had called to inquire whether
he was there. They had not asked who the speaker was,
nor where he was speaking from—a fact that disappointed
Gilmore, who wanted to know of everyone with knowledge
of Nixon's journey. They had only told him that they were
not aware he was due. And nowhere existed a sign of the
secretary.

Fatigued and discouraged, Gilmore returned to the city
for the second time by the midnight train. In those twenty-four hours, since his first journey, he had done much;
nevertheless he was compelled to admit that he had progressed little. Unaware of the success with which Rankin
was meeting, he realized that, even if Stahl and Morin
were caught, it was likely that they would refuse to speak
a word. Mrs. Gilmore, who waited up for him, was quick
to sense his mood of despondence. Instead of scolding him
for keeping such late hours, she made him a hot drink and
sent him to bed before she retired.

And in the morning there was this new development
that presented untouched and untold possibilities.

Rockton, the town mentioned in the telegram, was, as
he knew, from his journey the preceding night, a village
on the route to Cape May. The 5:20 local had stopped
at it. It was about forty miles out of Camden, ten miles

beyond Newfield, and equally distant from the spot where Nixon's body had been found. His time-table told him that an early morning local left for the shore resort in half an hour; he had just time to telegraph ahead of his expected arrival and catch it.

It took seventy minutes to make the journey of forty miles. It was ten-thirty when the train deposited him upon a bare and unimpressive station, that boasted of a shack and a short gravel platform. As the detective descended, a huge, good-natured and not overly intelligent appearing person with thick goggles approached him and introduced himself as the sheriff. He had a lumbering gait and spoke with a thick, nasal twang.

"Glad to meet you, Mr. Gilmore," he acknowledged the other's introduction. "You sure got here quick enough. . . . It's a funny thing about that note, because even if it didn't turn up, I was goin' to get in touch with you, anyhow."

"You were?" the detective asked. "What about?"

"There's a Mrs. Colby—a widow that lives out along the old dirt road, this side of Pelham Woods—who sent her farmhand in to town to say that she thinks she knows something about the murder. Her house is only about three or four miles from where the body was layin'."

Gilmore's heart leaped. There was no telling what this woman, located near the scene of the crime, might have witnessed.

"As a matter of fact," the sheriff continued, expectorating with marvelous accuracy into a station spittoon, "I was goin' out to see her first; I have to go out that way anyhow to see Jenny Belcher about some early cherries so that my wife can put up preserves. Then, if it seemed important, I was goin' to let you know about it."

"Well," the detective replied, "we can kill two birds with one stone then. As soon as I look into this matter of the money. Where did you say the bank was?"

"Right up the street here—you can see it at the first corner."

Together they started in the direction the sheriff had pointed. The village consisted of a single main street, that stretched only three blocks from the station. The concrete highway changed into a dirt road as it passed through the village. Otherwise, there were only a few scattered houses, on both sides of the street, and upon the intersecting avenues that became mere paths after a hundred feet. A church, a garage, a general store and the bank constituted Rockton's main structures.

Gabe Simmons directed his visitor up the stairs of the small red-bricked building that bore the flaunting title of "Cumberland County National Bank." Once within the doors, he made inquiry at the teller's window, and the young dandy, with plastered hair and a bow tie, led them into the private office of Mr. Sutton, the manager.

"This is Mr. Gilmore, Mr. Sutton," the sheriff said, after the young man had retired, "from the Philadelphia police, come down to see about that note you got yesterday afternoon."

Mr. Sutton acknowledged the introduction, swelling importantly at his connection with the law of so large a metropolis as Philadelphia.

"Just sit down, Mr. Gilmore—and you too, Gabe—and I'll give you the details as completely as I can."

The story he related fully explained the promptness that had greeted the broadcasting of the missing bills. On the preceding afternoon, Mr. Storker, the proprietor of the general store in the village, had entered the bank to make a deposit. It was his custom to make such a weekly deposit his store's earnings, every Tuesday. The young man, to whom the sheriff had spoken on entering, was Mr. Trask, the receiving teller; he accepted the merchant's money and counted it up. In the sum that he counted up was a hundred-dollar bill. It wasn't often that bills of that size made their appearance; at least, they were sufficiently unusual to cause the observant teller to remark upon it. Mr. Storker had agreed that for him it was a large sum, and had observed that he was lucky to have had the change for it at the time. Then Mr. Trask had put the bill away with other moneys.

It was his daily duty to come to work before the bank had properly opened, to prepare accounts for the ensuing day. This morning he had, as usual, been the first to arrive and, as was also usual, he had with him the daily county paper. Due to the proximity of the crime, the interest of the vicinity was aroused to a fever pitch; aware of this fact the paper was printing every item of information it could possibly obtain. And among the items it contained on this day was the affair of the missing notes. It attracted Mr. Trask's attention; recalling the storekeeper's hundred-dollar bill, he had looked at it again. And he discovered, to his astonishment, that the number on the note coincided with one of the numbers in the newspaper account.

"Then," Mr. Sutton concluded, with a dramatic flourish, "he consulted me, and I strongly advised that you people, in charge of the case, should be informed of it."

"Excellent, Mr. Sutton," said Gilmore, who had listened attentively, "I congratulate you and Mr. Trask on your alertness and promptness in dealing with the matter."

The other vouchsafed the detective an inflated smile.

"It was really only a little matter. I am only too glad if we have been able to assist in clearing up this horrible murder. It is a blot upon the name of Cumberland County."

"I think you have helped," Gilmore replied diplomatically. "Mr. Storker is the proprietor of the store across the street, is he not? Did he mention the source of the money?"

"Come to think of it, I don't believe he did. I suppose it must have been some customer. Wait, I'll ask Mr. Trask."

"You might have him bring in the note too. I shall want to see it, and probably shall want it, too."

Mr. Sutton's jaw dropped suddenly, and registered astonishment; it was evident that such a possibility had never occurred to him.

"You mean, you'll want to keep the money—altogether?"

Gilmore was reassuring. "Only temporarily, as evidence. It will be returned to you as soon as possible."

Under instructions of Mr. Sutton, Mr. Trask appeared with the bill, and in answer to the detective's query, informed him that Mr. Storker had not mentioned from where it had come.

"But it's easy enough to find out, sir," he said. "If you want me to go over with you to see him, I'll be glad to do it . . ."

Gilmore did not care to have the young man a witness to subsequent developments; neither did it please his cautious nature to have them bruited about the town as they undoubtedly would be.

"I don't believe it will be necessary, Mr. Trask. And, after the service you have done, I wouldn't like to trouble you further."

The number upon the bill proved indubitably that it was one of those given Nixon by Mr. Manson at the Central National Trust. It was an amazing circumstance that it should make its appearance in this isolated little community. Could the Ferris gang, after having committed the crime and robbed the financier of his money, have made a purchase of Mr. Storker on their return journey? Assuming that they had taken his money, if not his jewelry, it was the only explanation that could possibly account for the phenomenon and accord with the knowledge he already possessed.

After some desultory conversation with Mr. Sutton, Gilmore and the sheriff took their leave. Across the street, they entered the general store. Amid the typical melee of merchandise that little country shops carry, they found the storekeeper. He was a shriveled and bewhiskered old man, whose age was bending him beneath his own weight.

They waited until the customer he was serving was gone. He greeted Simmons cordially in a shrill, thin voice.

"This is Mr. Gilmore, John," the sheriff began. "He's working on the murder case, and he's come to make some investigation out this way."

"Bad business, that is," Storker said. "I hope you get the people that did it. What with gangsters and cutthroats in every third person you meet, nobody's safe these days."

"Mr. Gilmore came in with me to make some inquiries about that hundred-dollar bill you deposited at the bank yesterday. He thinks it might have something to do . . ."

The old man straightened out sharply. "Wasn't anything wrong with it, was there?"

"Oh, no, the note was all right," Gilmore put in. "I merely wanted to inquire where you got it from."

"That's easy." The other was plainly relieved. "Young Clem Marley gave it to me, yesterday afternoon, when he came in to buy food supplies. But shucks, there's nothing wrong with him, or the rest of the Marleys either."

"They're the people who live close by where the body was found," Simmons volunteered. "Where you stopped afterward . . ."

"So they are," the detective remarked evenly. "There are three of them, are there not?"

His demeanor revealed nothing of the sudden mental disturbance into which the storekeeper's reply had thrown him.

"Yes . . . there's Frank; he's the oldest. Clem's his brother. And Martha is the sister—one of the prettiest girls you ever laid eyes on."

"Of course . . . I remember her," Gilmore said. "But Clem—did he say anything, Mr. Storker, about how he came into possession of the money?"

It seemed that he had not. In fact, there were no further details that the storekeeper could give him. His customer had merely pocketed the change, without comment, shouldered his purchase, and left the store. And being made aware of this, the detective followed his example; in company with Simmons, he passed into the street once more.

Clem Marley in possession of money of the financier! On the night of the crime, certain events had seemed curiously to connect him with the family beside the right of way; but none of them had suggested so definite a link as did this latest development. Martha Marley had fainted, it was true, as Nixon's name was being mentioned; but despite Dr. Curtiss's suspicions, it might well have been the accident her brothers claimed it to be. The incident was susceptible of natural explanations. The fact that the Marleys had driven out in the storm gave him no ground for believing something was amiss, even though no other auto tracks approached the railroad on their private road. But this matter of the money was different; it left no doubt of some association with the financier.

Whatever that association, the explanation of it must agree with what he had learned since the murder. He had accepted certain conclusions as to the guilt of the Ferris gang; his discoveries permitted no other inferences, and had forced on him the Superintendent's theory of the crime. In accounting for this latest development, then, he must evolve an intelligible answer that did not cloud that main issue—or he would be merely complicating matters further.

And then, there occurred to him the explanation he was seeking—one that was plausible yet left the real issue clear. The fact that Philip Nixon had not been robbed of his watch, ring and papers indicated that Stahl and Morin had not taken the money either. Had they done so, to complete the deception, they would have removed everything. The bank notes, therefore, were still on the body when Frank Marley had assisted in carrying it into the house. The fireman, who had joined in, had returned immediately to the train; and Gilmore and Dr. Curtiss had not followed him at once to the cottage. For five minutes or more, Frank had been alone with the corpse. What more natural than that he had seized the opportunity to search the remains, and, finding so large a sum, had yielded to the temptation of pocketing the sum as his own.

As though in direct contradiction to Gilmore's thoughts, Simmons was echoing the storekeeper's words.

"There's nothing wrong with the Marleys—they wouldn't o' done anything bad . . . I'd stake my word on that."

The detective turned on him sharply.

"How do you know that?" he asked swiftly. "How well do you know them? Where do they come from?"

Under the barrage of questions, the sheriff was compelled to admit that he really knew little about the Marley family. They were not old inhabitants, but comparative strangers, having moved into the farmhouse by the tracks but two years before. No one could tell where they had come from before that; though they had not held themselves aloof, they had never spoken of their past. At first, people had been curious, commenting upon their peculiar attitude; but later, they had accepted them, and Gilmore would find them well spoken of by anyone he questioned.

"I'm afraid," the detective said, when he had finished, "that we will have to look into it, just the same. It's a very suspicious circumstance, that Clem Marley should have this money. At least, I'll want to hear what he has to say; and in case of an emergency, I think we had better procure a search warrant."

"I suppose you know your business, Mr. Gilmore," Simmons agreed reluctantly. "I'll see about it, right away."

It required more than a little time to procure a warrant and hire a car from the little garage that abutted the
church on the main street. Together, then, they set out
along it, the machine protesting and creaking until the
town limit was reached; then, along the smoother concrete
highway, they rode in silence for four miles.

Jenny Belcher, with whom Simmons had business, lived
at the fork in the road. From the main highway, the dirt
road branched off; the former continued as before, and at
some point not far away crossed to the other side of the
tracks. The latter proceeded, as Gilmore was aware from
Clem Marley's explanations, to skirt Pelham woods, and
on the other side of them, reach the farmhouse and end as
a cul-de-sac, at the garage.

The sheriff stopped the car before the gate of the
farmyard.

"It won't take me more than a minute to settle business
with Mrs. Belcher," he said as he descended. "I'd put it off
till later, only my wife would be sore. . . ."

He was as good as his word; within that time, he emerged
from the house, followed by a grim, lumbering woman
with frowsy hair, whom Gilmore instinctively knew to be
Mrs. Belcher.

"I'll see that you get those cherries, Gabe," she called
as the sheriff reentered the machine. "Where are ye bound,
now? Back t' town?"

"Out to visit the Marleys, Jenny," Simmons replied and
prepared to start the motor.

"It 'pears to me like the Marleys is getting a powerful
lot o' company these days. First, there was that gentleman with two other people just night afore last, and now
you . . ."

Her words suddenly caused Gilmore to turn toward her.
In his uncertainty regarding the status of the Marleys, any

information about them was interesting. And night before last was the night of the murder.

His hand went out to the sheriff's arm. "Just a moment, Gabe. . . . May I ask, Mrs. Belcher, what gentleman?"

"There was a gentleman that stopped here to ask me the way to the Marleys. The storm was comin' up fast and it was gettin' real dark; and, there being no sign here at the crossroad, he didn't know whether to keep on the main road or not. Anyhow, I told him he'd have to take the dirt road for about six miles."

"Can you say when this was, Mrs. Belcher?"

"I should say 'long about half past six—maybe a few minutes earlier, just afore it began to blow up so. I re-member I was just cleaning the supper things, when he knocked at the door."

"You say there were two others with him?"

"Yes, but I didn't see them good, 'cause they stayed out in the car. Just this gentleman spoke to me; you could tell from the very look o' him that he was somebody. . . ."

She spoke with respect; the appearance of the visitor must have impressed her.

"Can you tell me what he looked like?" Gilmore asked her.

His eagerness caused Mrs. Belcher to give him a search-ing look.

"Well, I s'pose so," she replied grudgingly, as though she hated to make the admission. "He was real tall and handsome lookin' with wonderful—well, what you'd call position. Not young, y' understand—maybe forty-five or more, but his age didn't show, except his hair was gettin' gray. He talked like he had a cold; he wore his gray over-coat real tightly wrapped around him . . ."

The man she was describing was Philip Nixon! There could be no doubt that it was Philip Nixon inquiring his way to the very place within a few feet of which he had been found dead. The poise was his, the appearance, the age, the hoarse voice, the gray overcoat. . . .

No, that was wrong. The financier's body had been found in a brown topcoat.

"Gray?" Gilmore interrupted her. "Wasn't it a brown coat?"

Mrs. Belcher was evidently not one to brook doubt. "It was a gray coat," she said indignantly; "I used to own Mr. Storker's place and I know cloth; I guess I can tell a color when I see it."

"I'm sorry, ma'am, but I must make certain. It's very important."

"Well, I know it was gray . . ."

"And you are sure there were two men in the machine? What kind of machine was it—a Rolls-Royce?"

"I wouldn't know a Rolls . . . whatever you call it . . . from a sewing machine," came the curt reply, "but it was a little black five-passenger car like the one you got, there. I didn't have a very good look at it 'cause I was inside the house all the time."

The detective's eyes mirrored his bewilderment. Every reply was opposite to that which he had expected. Mrs. Belcher should have described the huge yellow limousine with its uniformed chauffeur; instead she was telling him of a small black car with two men, strangers as far as she was concerned, driving the financier to the Marley farmhouse.

"You are sure it was a little black car?" was all he could ask. "It wasn't a large yellow one, without a top and driven by . . . ?"

"Look here, Gabe," the woman interrupted, turning to the sheriff, "I don't know whether you expect me to put up with these insults—but that's the second time he's

a-doubtin' my word and if you think I'm goin' to be called
a . . ."

"No, please, Mrs. Belcher, I'm sorry—I don't really
mean to doubt your word at all. . . ."

It required all the tact both the sheriff and his companion possessed to pacify Mrs. Belcher and impress her
with the importance of Gilmore's questions. When she was
again willing to reply to them, she could only repeat her
statements, and she clung to them with a stubbornness
that defied dislodgment. The car had been black. Two men
had sat in the front; they couldn't have been the Marleys,
Gilmore knew, or they wouldn't have inquired the way;
nor Stahl and Morin, for then Nixon would not have been
permitted to do so. For despite all this, despite the gray
overcoat, the man was—could have been—no other than
the financier.

Not until they were well upon their way again did the
detective fully realize the significance of this information.
In it was the complete destruction of a theory of the crime
that had been supported by every fact unearthed. According to all deductions, Parker, followed by his companions
in crime, had driven the financier into a deserted road,
near the spot where the body was found; and there an
attack had been made that had resulted, advertently or
inadvertently, in Nixon's death. But this held true only
if Nixon had made the journey in his own car. For it was
the Rolls-Royce in which the bullet holes had been found,
and in which Arthur Stahl had left his cap. These proofs of
guilt appeared incontrovertible. And now, amazingly, the
financier had made an appearance in a dilapidated black
car, driven by two strangers, who had magically replaced
Parker. When had the change of cars been made—what had
become of the other machine? Where had the two strangers
replaced Charles Parker; how was the chauffeur's attempt

to flee to be explained? More significant yet, what of the bullet holes—of Arthur Stahl's cap? The detective's every conclusion had apparently dissolved into thin air.

And on the other side of the picture, a new theory was beginning to take shape. The financier's objective had been the Marley farmhouse. According to the testimony of the coroner's physician, he had died no earlier than eight o'clock. And at half past six he was but six miles from the Marleys. It followed that he must have reached them; and the murder had occurred more than an hour after his arrival. Then Gilmore recalled the gray overcoat that had hung on the rack at the cottage. Clem Marley had removed it from the detective's sight as though he feared it would be noticed and examined.

Out of the stricken mass of uncorrelated events but one fact remained clearly before him. The Marley family was no longer merely incidental to the puzzle that so baffled him. They were part and parcel of it; they might even be its most vital factor.

10
CONFUSION WORSE CONFOUNDED

Mrs. Colby's tale, when the widow's house at the edge of the woods was reached, merely added to Gilmore's perplexity. It appeared that on the night of the murder, at 6:40, just after the storm had burst in all its fury, she had heard two sharp sounds. At first, she had believed them to be caused by the thunder, but they were too abrupt for that; then she thought they might have been bursting tires, except that it was difficult to imagine who could be on the road in the downpour. Finally, she decided that it was two shots she had heard, not more than a thousand feet away. But she had not been certain of it—not until she had learned of the murder the following morning; and, at the time, she had made no investigation. But now, she felt it was her duty to pass this information to the police, in case it should prove of some importance.

Thanking Mrs. Colby for her service, Gilmore refrained from comments upon her narrative. It was difficult to connect two shots and the attack with the black car in which Nixon was riding, when they were so obviously concerned with the financier's yellow limousine—even though the widow had heard the shots but five minutes after Nixon had passed Mrs. Belcher's cottage. It would be futile, Gilmore knew, to search the road for evidence of what had occurred in the vicinity. Between six-thirty and eleven, at which time the storm had spent its fury, the rain would have successfully obliterated all traces of the car; and subsequent travelers would have completed whatever work the storm had left undone. He could only follow the trail where it led, in hopes that its contradictions would be unraveled.

As to the Marleys, the detective readily realized the inherent weakness of suspecting them of the crime. It seemed incredible that they would have left the body, afterward, directly in front of their dwelling. On the other hand, Frank Marley was sufficiently astute to realize that the sheer daring of such a move was protection in itself; and he might easily have counted heavily upon the appearance of suicide that a body on the tracks must present. How nearly, in fact, had the deception succeeded! Had Dr. Curtiss's natural assumption of suicide been supported by his medical report, the suspicion of murder might never have arisen. Only the fact that he, Gilmore, had been previously consulted and was upon the scene prevented the bluff from being carried out.

Upon Mrs. Colby's invitation, the detective and Sheriff Simmons took lunch with her. They ate quickly however; within twenty minutes, they were once more upon their way toward the scene of the crime.

As the machine jounced along the rough rutted road, Gilmore was impressed by the area covered by Pelham woods. It extended for almost five miles, until it came to its end in the clearing of the Marley farmhouse. The road skirted it in a semicircle; had it gone directly through it, two miles would have been cut off from the journey. The foliage was exceptionally dense; even the sun's rays could not pierce the shadows of the underbrush.

No one was in sight as the auto drew up before the dwelling. Not until its passengers had alighted, and Simmons knocked upon the door, did Frank Marley made his

appearance from within. There was no welcome in the
darting eyes that greeted the visitors.

Behind him, Clem appeared from the kitchen door. The
girl was nowhere to be seen.

The sheriff explained that he and the detective desired
an interview upon an important matter, which he believed
could be explained to everyone's satisfaction. Whereupon
Frank permitted them to enter and had them sit down.

"Well?" he asked.

The single word was spoken in a tone that was both
challenging and hard. Its adamantine quality distressed
Simmons who had not expected resistance; but it merely
informed Gilmore of the verbal struggle that was before
him. He realized that subtlety would be wasted upon this
brother whose stiffening jaw warned of impending battle.

Simmons plunged into what he considered an unpleasant task. "It's about Mr. Nixon that was murdered night
afore last," he said. "We've been given to understand that
he knew you, somehow—at least—well, Clem there—he
had . . ."

"We've come to learn," Gilmore interrupted, as the
other hesitated, "why you pretended that you had never
heard of him, when you were acquainted with him—what
you have to say about an overcoat that your brother hid
from me—how you will explain certain money of Nixon's,
now in your possession . . ."

At every word the younger brother grew more pale; he
supported himself against the wall. But Frank appeared
unmoved.

"I don't know that any of it needs explanation," he said
evenly.

The sheriff looked pained. "Now that ain't no way to
talk, Frank. This here's serious business and you ought to
be willing to help like any good citizen."

"Philip Nixon came to visit you two nights ago," Gilmore went on, "for reasons that I expect to learn before I leave."

"Well, I don't know much about his visiting us, but I helped to carry him into the house 'bout half past eleven, so I guess he was here."

"Don't trifle with me," the detective warned him ominously; "you know what I mean. Before seven o'clock on the night of the murder, he arrived, wearing a gray coat that I saw hanging on that rack over there later in the evening. . . ."

"Who says so?"

"Several competent witnesses saw him on the way. One of them can vouch for his destination, so there's no use lying about it."

"And if he did . . . ?" Frank questioned.

"Not much more than a few hours afterward Philip Nixon was found on the tracks in the vicinity of your house. He was stripped of his coat and his money—five thousand dollars, part of which your brother spent in town. That was a mistake; you might have known it would be traced to you!"

"We didn't take it from him—he gave it to us!"

The words, a sudden cry of dread anxiety drawn from the younger brother, caused Frank to whirl swiftly about. His features were contorted, his eyes blazed with burning wrath, and when he spoke, his voice was harsh and uncontrollable.

"Damn you, Clem—keep your mouth shut! Stay out of this business and let me tend to it!"

Clem Marley shrank before his brother's fury, but Gilmore experienced a sense of triumph at this admission. It was a step forward.

"So Philip Nixon did arrive," he cut in swiftly, addressing Clem. "Why didn't you tell me that before?"

"That's our business, Gilmore," the elder replied uglily. "It was not important, and had nothing to do with the murder. . . ."

"You mean it wasn't important to tell me that Nixon was bound for the very place within a few feet of which he was found dead?"

There were scorn and incredulity in his tone. Frank Marley flushed at the implication, and smothered an oath.

"And the money," the detective went on. "You say he gave it to you. Why should some one regarding whose identity you profess ignorance make you such a gift? Five thousand dollars is a sufficient motive for committing murder. You'll have difficulty in satisfactorily explaining to a jury why you concealed this gift from an officer . . ." He paused and then added, "I want that money and I want Philip Nixon's overcoat."

"Well, you can't have them—we have a right to both of them and we mean to keep them."

"You seem bent on hindering my investigation as much as possible, Marley," Gilmore said. "Then you leave me no choice but to search this house for those articles, and, if it proves necessary, arrest you."

"You can't do it," Clem cried impetuously. "You can't do either without a warrant . . . it's illegal!"

"I have a search warrant with me; and I'll take full responsibility for the arrest. Have you ever heard of resisting an officer in the course of his duty?"

The look in Frank Marley's eyes was sinister and murderous. For an instant, it seemed that his fury would overcome what control remained him; he fairly quivered with rage in his supreme effort to restrain himself. It would have been difficult to predict the result of the situation had not the sheriff spoken.

"Now, Frank," he put in soothingly, "you've known me two years, and you know I don't want no trouble. There ain't no use argering the matter; I don't like this any more than you, but it can't be helped. If you was sensible, this wouldn't be necessary, at all."

In the silence that followed his words, Frank Marley's taut body seemed to relax. A slightly sardonic smile covered his entire countenance. Clem shifted uncomfortably and Gabe Simmons breathed an audible sigh of relief.

"Go ahead and search the house," the elder brother said calmly.

Leaving the sheriff to watch the two men—for he did not altogether trust the apparent surrender—Gilmore ascended the creaking stairs down which Martha Marley had fallen two nights before. At the top he found a short hall that resembled a vestibule opening into three rooms. Two were bedchambers and the third a crude bathroom, lacking many plumbing facilities. The upper floor was a more likely place to keep the money than the lower, as there were almost no receptacles below. And since the topcoat was no longer downstairs, on the rack, if it was anywhere at all, it could only be in one of the closets on the second story.

The first chamber Gilmore entered was the girl's, as the single narrow bed indicated. Besides that, it contained only a bureau and a chair; not even a rug covered the bare floor. Though tidily kept, it was bare of any article that might be considered a luxury. A pitiful effort had been made to add color to the room by means of a tattered scarf on the bureau and a picture on the wall. But the scarf was frayed and the picture soiled, so that the attempt was painfully apparent and unsuccessful.

A hasty search of the bureau convinced the detective that what he sought was not in that room. Most of the drawers contained what little clothing Martha Marley possessed, all of which had seen much wear and encountered the needle more than once. At the bottom was a thin packet of letters addressed to the girl, all quite old. Indeed, the most recent was dated six months back, a missive evidently from an elderly aunt, who signed herself "Aunt Mercy," living in Philadelphia, referring to a visit she soon expected Martha to make her. It was the only one Gilmore had any reason for noting. If an investigation into the unknown antecedents of the Marleys should become necessary, it might prove valuable as a clue to their past and to their relations.

In the bedroom that was occupied by the brothers, Gilmore continued his quest. Here again, except for a huge double bed, there was so little furniture that it would be easy to cover it thoroughly in a very few minutes. But here, there was a closet, an asset the other room had not contained. Again tidiness was the preeminent quality, attesting eloquently to the sister's excellence as a housekeeper.

A single glance in the closet located one object of the detective's search. Carelessly hung in one corner among heavy khaki clothes, and soiled overalls, was the gray topcoat. Satisfying himself that it was what he sought, he removed it from its hook and hung it over his arm. The part it had played in this baffling enigma was yet to be discovered. Why the murderers had deprived the financier's corpse of its own overcoat and replaced it with the brown one—unless in a half-completed effort to conceal its identity—was part of the puzzle to which he must find the solution in the future. For the present, it was enough that he had found it.

Next, Gilmore tackled a highboy. The drawers were loose and ill-fitting, moving with difficulty only after he had made several efforts. The first two contained men's apparel, coarse woolen socks, heavy chambray working shirts and pajamas. But in the third container was his second objective. Crisply green, starkly outlined against a background of white underwear, lay the bank notes. Four thousand nine hundred dollars of them, the detective discovered, counting them swiftly; only one bill was missing.

Under the notes were some further letters. Having found everything he was looking for, there was no need of picking them up. Nevertheless, Gilmore did so. There were several missives of no importance and a half-finished letter that one of the brothers had been writing which contained no information. . . .

But suddenly he found himself staring at it as though petrified. There was nothing significant about either the contents or the writing; the latter was in a scrawling, though legible hand—and, somehow, strangely familiar.

Hastily he drew from his inner pocket another missive; swiftly he made a scrutiny of the two scripts. One was that of the letter and the other that of the note he had found in Philip Nixon's pocket, when he examined the corpse—the note that threatened grave disaster unless certain demands were met immediately.

There was no mistaking the clear, orderly fist. The handwriting was identical.

It was astonishing how many pieces of the puzzle fell into place through this unexpected discovery. It was in answer to this sinister message, written by one of the Marleys, that the financier had left his business and made this unaccustomed journey to Cape May. Primarily, his destination had been the farmhouse by the tracks. Because of it, he had drawn five thousand dollars from his account; that was how the Marleys had come into possession of such a sum. Even more important, the nervousness Nixon had displayed in his office, the lies he had told, were now explained. He was concealing this mission from both Gilmore and his daughter. While he desired protection from the one menace that threatened him, he was not willing to have it at the cost of revealing this other menace. Rather, he would chance the journey alone, and have Gilmore join him at the resort.

Clem Marley had spoken the truth when he claimed that the money had been given him. But the message causing the gift was more criminal than robbery would have been. By extortion, by threats of murder, it had compelled Philip Nixon—a power in his own world—to obey the call of these isolated farmer people. For whatever cause, the Marleys had power to thus make demands, the note fully expressed their cold, devastating hostility toward him. What more likely than that, not satisfied with the money, the two brothers should have wreaked their hatred upon him by murder. Their motive must have been a potent one; else Philip Nixon would never have come. And shortly after his arrival, Nixon was dead, his remains left outside the dwelling. Except for the bullet holes in the financier's car, the behavior of Charles Parker and the shots overheard by Mrs. Colby, Gilmore had a perfect circumstantial case against the Marleys.

But whether or not they were guilty of murder, at least they had committed what amounted to blackmail. He would be failing in his duty if he did not arrest them at once.

Pocketing the money, the detective descended the stairs. The group below watched him approach in silence, Clem sullen, the sheriff ill at ease, but Frank merely impatient, as though he had thought the better of resistance. Gilmore realized that though he might have no further difficulty with him, neither would information be forthcoming from him.

"Which of you wrote this?" he asked, extending the unfinished letter in his hand.

"I did," the elder brother candidly admitted. "It's my writing. What of it?"

"Then this is yours also. . . . I found it in Philip Nix-on's pocket—it was serious error not to have searched the body more carefully."

There was no reply to this direct accusation. Frank Marley gazed emotionlessly at the incriminating message extended before his eyes. Clem gasped suddenly, a choking sob that a contemptuous look from the other cut before it was finished.

"You realize what this means," Gilmore said sternly. "I am compelled to place you both under arrest, and I must warn you that whatever you say will be used against you. . . ."

Again only stillness resulted. Then Frank Marley turned and stalked from the room to the machine outside, with a contempt in his attitude that caused the detective a sensation of uncertainty he could neither conquer nor comprehend. Clem followed his brother's example; and after the sheriff, Gilmore was the last to leave, closing the door to the now deserted cottage.

As the four of them entered the sheriff's car, Martha Marley appeared unexpectedly around the corner of the farmhouse. Despite the studied plainness of her dress, Gilmore was more impressed than ever by the girl's slender, fragile beauty. The sun, playing upon her black tresses, gave color to the pale features he had last seen. From her poise, the joy of living seemed to be written in every movement of her lithe body; but her eyes were ineffably sorrowful, as with a grief that seldom could so have affected youth, and her mouth was tragic with the tragedy of age.

Nevertheless, her greeting was exuberant enough. It was not until she caught the strained atmosphere, from the rigidity of her older brother, and from the sheriff's unresponsiveness, that she stopped. Gilmore was suddenly regretful at the necessity of acts which would bring grief and distress to one who, his senses told him, had already suffered much and deserved respite from her unhappiness.

"What's the matter, Frank?" she cried hurriedly. "Is . . . is something wrong . . . is . . . what's happening here . . . ?"

No one could speak in that awkward, pregnant moment in which apprehension, awakened slowly at first, rose to a certainty that something unaccountable was amiss.

"Where are you going . . . with Gabe Simmons . . . and this gentleman? That man was here the other night . . . the detective, who is investigating Mr. Nixon's . . . Oh, my God!"

The words choked in her throat. Terror, a gripping, uncontrollable terror seized her; her hands went out wildly, to grasp the machine as though for support.

"I'm sorry, Miss Marley," said the sheriff soothingly, "that this has to be done, but they are being arrested . . ."

"For murdering Philip Nixon!" Frank Marley's conclusion was harsh and venomous. Yet Gilmore realized that he spoke in so brutal a manner only in an effort to bring the terrified girl back to a realization of her senses. There was genuine anxiety behind the blunt statement.

"But it isn't true," the reply came fervently. "They didn't do it—they don't know anything about it, I swear that they don't. . . ."

"I'm afraid that it is, Miss Marley," Gilmore said. "I'm sorry but I have no choice left. They will not speak, they have obstructed my investigation, and whether you know it or not, they have concealed important facts regarding the murder."

She seized the detective's sleeve, imploringly, as though to impress him with her denial.

"But I know that they're innocent . . . you must believe me, they couldn't have killed Mr. Nixon. To think that I should be responsible for this terrible trouble . . ."

"Be quiet, Martha," Frank Marley cried angrily. "Don't worry about us; there isn't anything that they can really prove against us . . . if we all keep quiet!"

"But I can't let them take you away! I'll tell Mr. . . . Mr. Gilmore everything, if he only won't do that."

"Don't be a fool, Martha; can't you realize that if you told him *everything you know,* it will only make matters worse for us!"

Every drop of blood drained from Martha Marley's features. Trembling, exhausted, she stepped back from the car, a moan issuing audibly from her colorless lips. But she seemed to recognize the dreadful logic of her brother's statement.

"What shall I do?" she spoke in a sorrowful undertone.

"Stay home and wait for us—go to Aunt Mercy's if you wish; but don't worry. We'll get out of this all right. Come on, Gabe, let's go."

The engine sputtered, drowning out further words. It came to the detective that if he wanted the entire truth, here was the fount of it. This anguished girl, who had sensed instinctively, because of the knowledge she possessed, the cause of the visit, could tell him what her two brothers obstinately concealed. And she was willing to do so. Martha Marley was, in some way, connected with Nixon; perhaps it was on her account that Frank Marley had penned that message. It was easy enough to conjure such a theory, but not easy to follow it through to its end. If the girl had known Philip Nixon, Gilmore found it difficult to picture the circumstances of that acquaintanceship.

At the moment the machine moved off, he was about to order a halt. But, strangely enough, he did not speak. It was not the moment for an inquisition. In the presence of her brothers, Martha Marley would never reveal what she knew; in the presence of her grief, Gilmore would not intrude to add further torment to it. Later, by gently winning her confidence, he would have the entire story of her own volition.

As the auto began to encircle Pelham woods, Gilmore's last view of the girl was of a forlorn, pathetic figure, silhouetted against the ramshackle solitude of the farmhouse.

11

THE BROWN OVERCOAT

If the gray topcoat was the property of the financier, who was the owner of the brown overcoat? In what manner—at what time on the night of the murder—had a change from one to the other been effected?

Back in Philadelphia, at Headquarters, two hours after the arrest the detective gave these questions serious consideration. The two prisoners, stubbornly silent even to his most simple questions, were safely incarcerated in the Cumberland County jail; an immediate train had brought him back to the city; and, with Rankin, he had discussed the details of his successful man hunt. There, too, there had been difficulties; as though fearful of involving themselves in any way, Stahl and Morin had maintained a glowering silence that no inquisition could break. And this fact the two detectives discussed in Captain Thomas's private office, while Gilmore examined the overcoats.

"I never saw anything like it," the latter said, expressing his general dissatisfaction. "In every case I've worked on, there always was someone who had something to conceal; but I'm damned if there ever was one like this, where no one will talk. They can't all be guilty, yet you'd think so from the way they're all behaving."

"In my last case," Rankin replied, "the murder of Mary Young, I had the same difficulty; every fact I discovered opposed every other fact. But in this case it seems to me that finding Nixon's overnight bag in Morin's possession absolutely clinches it."

Gilmore grunted stolidly. "Perhaps—but there's a great deal more that needs explaining. This matter of the overcoats, for instance—it doesn't fit anywhere. I'm having Bennett over to see what he can tell me."

He returned to his scrutiny of the two garments. The gray one, in which were the financier's initials, was of exceptionally fine texture, in a light crisscross pattern that was tasteful without being blatant. The retailer's tag told Gilmore where it had been purchased. These facts were unimportant; but its condition was vitally so. It was soiled in many places, though there had been some effort to clean the spots. There were numerous visible tears, in the outer cloth, tears caused by sheer force as though clutching hands had brutally seized and ripped it. Philip Nixon must have been engaged in a dreadful struggle for his life; and this conclusion supported his colleague's theory of the crime.

The brown overcoat was of equally excellent material. So much so, that the detective discarded his original belief that it was the property of the Marleys. It was impossible that they possessed such clothing. It, too, was violently torn, but by the engine when it had struck the body; and, as Gilmore had already observed, it contained only the maker's label—Lorch & Taylor.

"It oughtn't to be too difficult to trace that coat," Rankin remarked. "If we make inquiries at the Taylor establishment, we are sure to come out on some end of the line."

Gilmore agreed. "This thing has got me worried. . . . As soon as I see Bennett, we'll go off, and try to settle it."

He had just discovered that Lorch & Taylor was an exclusive firm of men's clothiers, located on Walnut Street, when an officer announced Bennett's arrival. In a moment, the butler was ushered into the presence of the two detectives.

He entered hesitantly, casting sidelong glances about the office, and at the desk upon which the two coats lay. The official atmosphere seemed to trouble him, and he waited silently, in doubt as to the meaning of the summons.

Gilmore hastened to put him at his ease.

"Sit down, Bennett—it was very good of you to come. The matter I want to see you about won't take more than a few minutes. . . . This is Mr. Rankin, who is working with me on the case."

"Thank you, sir." Bennett sank heavily into the nearest chair. "It was nothing to come, sir—I'd do much more than that to help you in any way to catch the man who murdered Mr. Nixon."

"An excellent sentiment, Bennett. It's just this—I want to ask you what kind of a coat Mr. Nixon was wearing when he left the house day before yesterday?"

The butler's pained features showed that he considered the question frivolous. "A coat, sir? His regular light gray, summer coat, sir—with a crisscross pattern. . . . Why, that's it, there, on the desk!"

He rose, tremblingly, and indicated that one Gilmore had found in the closet at the Marleys'.

"Are you certain, Bennett, it was the gray coat, and not that brown one beside it . . . ?"

"Of course I am, sir—I took particular notice, and I know Mr. Nixon's wardrobe inside and out. This other coat is of good material, but I never saw it before in my life. I'm certain it was not the property of Mr. Nixon."

"Have you any idea, then, who might be its owner—one of his acquaintances, perhaps?"

"I can't say that, sir—I don't know. May I ask why, sir?"

Deciding that it would be wiser not to reveal the reasons for his inquisition since nothing had come of it, Gilmore gave a casual explanation of the matter, and after a few desultory questions, dismissed him. As the old man moved to the door and started to open it, Gilmore turned about toward Rankin.

"Mr. Gilmore!"

The unexpected and troubled character of Bennett's words caused the detective to whirl about in surprise. The butler's voice choked with an emotion he was unable to control. He was standing in the entrance of the room, one agitated hand closing the door, his features drawn as though in grave pain. The hat he held in his hand was being fast twisted out of shape.

"Yes, Bennett, what can I do for you?"

Words issued in a swift stream. "Mr. Gilmore—there is something I know that I kept a secret from you. And I oughtn't to tell you now, sir, but I can't keep it any longer. Much as I love Miss Eleanor, I loved Mr. Nixon just as much and I won't be responsible for hiding something you ought to know—no, not even for her sake."

"You hid something from me, Bennett?" Gilmore spoke gently lest he should frighten away this confessional mood. "Well, it's not too late to tell me now. It might prove quite important."

"It's about the time," Bennett went on, "that Mr. Nixon came home from his office, at quarter to four, sir . . . on the afternoon he was . . . murdered. I didn't tell you everything about that."

Gilmore recalled the preceding day, when he had interrogated Eleanor Nixon and her servant, how the girl had, by her mute appeal, interrupted Bennett's narrative. Even then, when Bennett had continued it, Gilmore had instinctively recognized that he was falsifying.

"You merely said that Mr. Nixon came home, went upstairs for a few moments, and then spent twenty minutes in the conservatory. Do you mean that he did not go into the conservatory?"

Having made the plunge, Bennett seemed to have gathered courage. "No, sir—that was true enough, all right. Only he wasn't alone, sir. He wasn't there five minutes, when young Mr. Gardiner arrived from the office and asked to see him. I let him into the conservatory . . ."

"Oh, the secretary? At what time did this occur?"

"Well, Mr. Nixon went away at half past four; it must have been fifteen minutes before that. Mr. Gardiner was with him only ten minutes, but that was enough for them to have a most terrible quarrel."

Gilmore could hardly conceal his astonishment. "A quarrel, Bennett? Tell me about it, carefully; be sure not to omit anything—what it was about, what was said . . ."

"You remember, sir, my saying," Bennett interrupted, "that when the conservatory door was shut, you could hardly hear a word? Well, Mr. Nixon shut it tight and whatever I did hear was because they both spoke so loud. So I really don't know what it was about, except that it was real serious. When they came out, sir, I never saw the master's face so red or him so trembling in all my life before. And, as for the young man, he was like a thundercloud, and he tramped out furious, sir, without waiting for me to open the door for him."

"And what did you hear?" Gilmore asked as the other paused.

"Only a few words, sir—but I kept them all in memory. . . . Mr. Gardiner called Mr. Nixon a money grubber; then I distinctly heard the master use the word 'murder,' sir—and Mr. Gardiner said, 'I'm not a murderer,' at least it sounded like that. I couldn't get another word for a long

time, sir; you understand, by then, I was getting alarmed
and beginning to listen. Suddenly the young man said, 'I
could kill him' or 'I could kill you,' I don't know which;
and Mr. Nixon cried out distinctly, 'Damn you, no—not
unless over my dead body!' And that was all. . . .''

"You mean—you couldn't overhear any more?"

"I mean," the butler replied, easing from the high ten-
sion into which the recital had carried him, "that a minute
later, Mr. Gardiner opened the door and came rushing out
like a fury toward the hall. Mr. Nixon had followed; but
he was outside before he could speak."

There was nothing further of the affair that Bennett
could relate. Though pressed for further facts, he could
only repeat that there had been a quarrel of some consequence, that Philip Nixon's secretary had evidently threatened his life and that the financier had replied with a defiant challenge. It was not Gardiner's custom to visit the
house; in fact, as far as the butler was aware, he had never
before been there.

"And Miss Nixon asked you not to inform me of this,"
Gilmore remarked, when the inquisition was finished.
"Why—did she fear I'd suspect Mr. Gardiner of having a
hand in the crime?"

Bennett raised his hand in hurried negation. "No, no.
. . . She didn't know of it, till she came home from the tea
after her father had left, and I told her. But the next day
. . . when you came and asked questions, I could see her
asking me not to mention it. She never said a word, sir—I
did it for her sake . . ."

For an instant, he broke off, deeply distressed; but
gathering strength, he finished his statement, sorrowfully.

"It was either my affection for her—or for Mr. Nixon
. . . I know she loves Mr. Gardiner . . . she told me so yesterday morning. But Mr. Nixon was dead—murdered, and

I couldn't keep it in, sir. It weighed on my conscience too much, that this might be a necessary link."

The detective could well find it in his heart to sympathize with Bennett in his dilemma. But at the same time it was impossible to minimize the importance of what the butler had told him. Adding these facts to his already garnered information regarding the secretary, he realized that Gardiner presented a problem requiring serious attention. At first, he had found his behavior merely suspicious. His emphatic denial of his journey to Cape May on the night of the murder and his attitude under a cross-fire of questions had not been incriminating in themselves. They had merely justified the watch Gilmore had arranged to have made upon the secretary.

Now, however, Gilmore had no choice left but to include Gardiner in his list of suspects. If Bennett had heard aright, it could have been no mere figure of speech that had caused the secretary to deny he was a murderer—a statement that caused the detective much uneasiness. There was no ambiguity in the threat to kill Philip Nixon; and the fact that the financier had been merely infuriated by it served to give it a more sinister aspect. Gilmore did not believe he was stretching his imagination, when he believed young Gardiner strode from the financier's presence with murder in his heart.

And how potent was his motive! As he once more dismissed Bennett, Gilmore mentally upbraided himself for not having realized its importance before. A suitor for Eleanor Nixon's hand—and the tremendous Nixon fortune that went with it—the financier alone stood in the way of his success. In spite of Eleanor's willfulness and the quarrel with her father, Gilmore did not believe she would, in the face of his stern opposition, have disobeyed him. Nixon was, in fact, certain that when she learned the cause of his hostility, she would have nothing further to do with Gardiner. These facts must, then, have been extremely discreditable; and in his, Gilmore's, presence he had promised to tell them to her when he returned from his journey to the shore. After that, therefore, the girl herself would have dismissed Gardiner's suit.

But Philip Nixon never revealed that knowledge he possessed. When the following day rolled around, he had been found foully murdered on the railroad tracks of the South Jersey express. As Eleanor Nixon had spoken to the secretary after her argument with her parent, he must have been aware of the financier's intentions. It was too startling to be a coincidence; all the circumstances cried out for an immediate investigation.

Having made this decision, Gilmore informed his colleague of it.

"Oh, is it as serious as all that?" Rankin asked, giving a low whistle of surprise.

"It's so serious," was the reply, "that, unless I shall have learned some facts about young Gardiner's past in the next ten hours, I shall feel I've encountered a serious obstacle."

"What about the matter of these coats, then? Do you want me to go ahead with that and report developments to you?"

Gilmore hesitated. He couldn't be working on both trails at the same time, but he was anxious for some indication of the trail along which the coats would lead. And as it would not delay him long, he compromised.

"Well, I'll go along with you to Taylor's," he said, "to see what turns up there. After that, we can separate, you to continue with that line of investigation; and I'll take up the other line." He took out his watch. "It's only a little after four. We ought to be able to make it before the place closes."

And so it was that fifteen minutes later the two detectives presented themselves at the building on Walnut Street that housed the tailoring concern. On the first floor, it was fronted by a show window wherein were displayed the newest patterns of cloth for summer wear, and models of sartorially perfect young men, displaying the firm's skill to advantage. As they entered, Rankin carried the brown coat upon his arm as though he was finding it too hot to wear it.

In the main part of the shop, they were greeted by a well-fitted and sprightly gentleman, who rubbed his hands eagerly and desired to know how he could be of service.

"My friend and I," Gilmore related, "have been trying to find the owner of this coat. It was left on a trolley, and Mr. Jones, here, found it. Naturally, he wishes to return it, but the name of the concern is the only way by which we can identify it. We have tried advertising, and gotten no results. As it appears to be a new garment, we thought perhaps you could give us the necessary information."

The gentleman took the coat from Rankin's hands and ran his hands lovingly through the cloth.

"I recognize the pattern," he said. "It's a distinctive one that we carry exclusively, for our customers, for our spring trade. It sold satisfactorily, but as it is only for the best trade, we didn't make many of them. Now, from our accounts, I might be able to find out for you for whom we made this particular coat."

"You make all your clothes to order," queried Rankin, "and specially fitted for your clientele, do you not?"

"Yes, we do—and for that reason we keep the name of everyone with whom we have dealt, so that we can keep them informed of our latest shipment of goods and the newest styles. I ought to be able to trace this garment for you, if you will just excuse me for a few moments."

He disappeared into a back room, through the door of which the two detectives glimpsed, briefly, some young men busily engaged in cutting and pressing. Presently he returned, carrying some papers.

"I remember the sale quite distinctly now," he remarked. "I was speaking to my partner about it, and he refreshed my memory. It was made two months ago to a large, well-attired gentleman who asked for a coat of especially fine quality and was much attracted by this English tweed. So we measured him for his order, and made this coat for him . . . quite reasonably, too . . . yes, this is undoubtedly the coat—a size forty-two. Here is his account and sales record, signed by the purchaser."

Gilmore took them from his hand, not knowing what to expect. At the bottom of one sheet he read "Russell Stirling," and on the other, the address as well—"Garden Terrace Apartments."

There could be no possibility of error, the affable gentleman insisted. The firm kept perfect records, through a well-recognized, accurate system. And presently, reassured, and thanking him for his assistance, Gilmore and his colleague took their departure.

"Now who the devil is Russell Stirling?" Rankin said when they were once more in the street. "And how does he come into this tangle?"

For a moment, Gilmore did not reply. From the instant he had read the name on the firm's records, he was occupied in recalling what he knew of its possessor. Philip Nixon's secretary had mentioned him when quizzed at the office—he was a stockbroker who had, within the last few days, been constantly communicating with the financier. But Gardiner did not know what Stirling had wanted, and said that Nixon had thus far refused to see him. In reality, then, the detective had no information regarding this new astonishing factor of the most difficult problem he had ever encountered.

This he passed on to Rankin in reply to the question. It required all of Gilmore's control to continue with his original course of action, and leave this added enigma to his companion. But Donald Gardiner's behavior presented the older and, as far as he knew, more important aspect of the case; it required his attention ahead of this new development. If, through Rankin's investigation, something came of that, it would not be too late then to carry on.

Accordingly, after they had found out from a directory that the Garden Terrace Apartments were in Germantown, Gilmore set out in one direction, and Rankin in another.

12
ALL TRAILS LEAD TO . . . ?

The events that occurred in Gilmore's investigation of Nixon's secretary, that evening, may best be described from the summary of them that the detective later passed on to his colleague. From the very outset he had decided to move cautiously in his inquiry. It would be an error to reveal his identity or his objective, until he had more than mere suspicion upon which to work. Did Gardiner know that he was the object of surveillance, he might take alarm, and flee before Gilmore had collected sufficient facts to justify a move against him. Accordingly, though he might have learned more by prosecuting inquiries at Nixon's offices or home, he turned his steps first to the secretary's lodgings on the Roosevelt Boulevard—the address of which Gardiner had himself given him.

The house he found to be of a cozy red brick, with a sloping tiled roof and a little inclosed porch, its appearance indicating fair comfort within. It was neater than a boarding house would have been, and fronted by a colorful green plot that was nicely trimmed. The woman who answered his ring was the Mrs. Phipps the secretary had mentioned—stout, of uncertain age, the possessor of several chins and a motherly smile.

Having already ascertained from Detective Jenks that Gardiner was not in, Gilmore had no hesitation in making inquiries about him. He was a friend of his, he explained, from out of town, and as he happened to be in on business, it had occurred to him to surprise the young man by dropping in on him.

Mrs. Phipps was sorry that he had not yet returned from work; the idea of a reunion seemed to please her, and she was certain Gardiner would have liked to see his friend. But she could not say when he would be back; though ordinarily, he was finished much earlier than this, the pressure of work occasioned by the tragic death of his employer had made it consistently necessary for him to remain overtime.

Sociably inclined, Mrs. Phipps was willing to discuss crime in general, and this crime in particular, with this candid, pleasant-spoken friend of her lodger; and this gave Gilmore the opportunity he sought. Clearly, she was thrilled by Gardiner's connection, however remote, with such a *cause célèbre,* basking in a reflected importance which her association with him gave her. The detective was only too willing to discuss the matter with her, without giving her any ideas with regard to it. He listened with respect to her opinions regarding the cleverness of criminals in specific cases, and the corresponding stupidity of the police in others; he agreeably concurred with her highly imaginative theories of Nixon's death. Presently, he had sufficiently won her good graces to be invited into the house for further conversation. And it was not long before he was able to turn the talk to the financier's secretary, and ask fairly direct questions without arousing doubts in the affable matron.

By judicious statements in which he professed not to have seen or heard from Gardiner for many years, he gleaned whatever information Mrs. Phipps had of his recent movements. But this left him no wiser than before, as to the secretary's past. Of his previous history, she knew little, of his previous residence, nothing at all. He had not needed to seek a position when he had come to town— from where, she did not know; his position with the American Motors Corporation had been waiting for him. He was a good worker, often at work upstairs in his room; he had no bad habits as far as she knew, and she admired his perseverance.

The surprise Gilmore displayed at this information appeared genuine. This hardly sounded like the old friend he had known, he explained to her; in the days when they were closely acquainted, Donald had been something of a sport. He had enjoyed going out a great deal, though, of course, on innocent pleasures; and he had never been accustomed to keeping regular hours or retiring early. In fact, on last Monday night, when Gilmore had just reached town, close upon midnight, he had gotten the impression that he had seen his friend on Market Street. He had hurried to speak to him then, but when he reached the corner where he had glimpsed Gardiner, if it were he, he could no longer locate him. Was it possible that the young secretary had been out so late that night?

It was Mrs. Phipps' turn to be surprised. Monday night, she recalled, was the night Philip Nixon had been murdered, and Mr. Gardiner had been working in his room the entire evening. It was true she had not seen him all evening, she said, but he had come in at half past six from work and said he did not want to be disturbed. He had some work to do for the office and intended to be occupied by it all evening. At quarter of seven, Mrs. Phipps had seen him go upstairs and shut his door. As far as she knew, he had not come out again, so that he could not have been on Market Street, or out anywhere else, that night.

The secretary's behavior, as Mrs. Phipps retailed it, resembled the deliberate preparation of an alibi to mask his journey to Cape May. If this evaluation of the facts was true, it put a serious complexion on the case; alibis are not prepared unless they are made in anticipation that inquiries will follow. And inquiries follow only where crimes are concerned. Gardiner must have had a grave motive for concealing his actual movements. It was unlikely that following such a disagreement with the financier as Bennett had overheard, Gardiner would do further work for his employer, or that the latter would employ him afterward. The secretary, then, had carefully secured himself, while he crept away . . . for what purpose . . . ?

Following such a conclusion as this, it was impossible for the detective to leave without an examination of his quarry's room and property. His information was not substantial; and of the secretary's past, about which he was particularly interested, he had discovered nothing. Accordingly, he bent every effort toward persuading Mrs. Phipps to permit him to leave some message of greeting in Gardiner's chamber for him, appealing to her sense of the sentimental. It would please the secretary to find a memento from his friend on his desk when he came home; otherwise, Gilmore explained, as he was leaving town shortly, he would have no other means of communicating with him. And thus entreated, Mrs. Phipps succumbed. Though ordinarily she would have considered the request most unusual, her visitor had made a favorable impression upon her; he had convinced her he was well acquainted with her boarder. She hesitated to interfere with a possible touching reunion, the thought of which warmed her heart.

The room to which she escorted him on the second floor had something of the qualities of a study. The furnishings, though inexpensive, made for a snug, comfortable atmosphere in which one could readily relax. In addition to articles usually necessary to a living room, a typewriter rested upon a small desk, where the secretary evidently did extra work either for himself or for the office. Under the desk was a wastebasket; behind it, a clothes closet, and next to the bed, a chiffonier.

Gilmore wasted no time studying these things; he had to make the most of the period permitted him behind the closed door. As soon as Mrs. Phipps was gone, he turned to the desk—the most natural place to find letters or papers that might give him a clue to the secretary's past. He sorted swiftly through typed business letters, carbon copies, a report of a directors' meeting and a yearbook. In one drawer he found Gardiner's check-book account with a Philadelphia bank, which indicated his deposits to be limited to a small weekly sum out of his salary. Gilmore had the ability to grasp the importance of papers at a glance; the difficulty was that in this case none of it was important in connection with his quest.

In the chiffonier and closet, which came next in his systematic search, he hoped to find some item that would link the secretary to some definite locality. But he was disappointed. The shirts, socks, ties and suits had all been recently purchased at local stores; all of them carried the labels of Philadelphia shops. Most of them were of material of the best quality, but apart from informing Gilmore that Gardiner's salary, if not his bank account, was ample, they were valueless.

Nowhere had he found a single indicium of the secretary's past existence. In the desk there was not even a letter or communication, a fact indicating that Gardiner's correspondence had been practically nil. Otherwise, Gilmore would have certainly found some note, at least from his family, did he have one. But there was nothing of the sort. The bank account and all his clothes were of local origin. Gardiner himself had apparently been so taciturn that even the talkative Mrs. Phipps knew nothing of him.

It was as though his life had begun abruptly from the moment he had reached Philadelphia; beyond that, for all the traces he had left, he might never have been born.

For what reason should Gardiner have made such a determined effort to blot out all evidence of his former life? What was the secret behind the curtain that was so shameful that he sought desperately to cover it, Gilmore had asked himself? Philip Nixon had known it, was aware of facts so disgraceful that he had opposed any relationship between his daughter and his secretary. Although he had kept Gardiner in his employ, that screened past must have been, indeed, discreditable, if it would have turned Eleanor Nixon against him. But the financier took with him those obliterated years; had they been so terrible that he had paid for his knowledge with his life?

The obviousness of its position caused the detective almost to overlook the wastebasket. But just as he was about to open the door and rejoin Mrs. Phipps, he realized his omission. Merely to be thorough, so that he should not have the feeling that he might have missed something, he returned to it. It required less than a moment to search through crumpled scraps, unfinished business notations and rejected sheets.

And then, suddenly he found what he was looking for. Almost at the bottom of the container, crumpled and partly torn, lay an envelope, addressed to Gardiner in a sprawling hand. The postmark was dated June 6, less than two weeks ago; the station stamped on it was Akron, Ohio.

Within was a card upon which was printed in a flowing script, the following announcement:

"Mr. and Mrs. Samuel Denby announce the wedding of their daughter, Ella, to Richard Santell, of Cleveland, Ohio, on the fourth of June, nineteen hundred and twenty-nine, at

the Church of Saint Mary's, corner Little and
Oak Streets, Akron, Ohio."

Here was something tangible, a message from some former friend of Gardiner's; probably the announcement had
been sent either by the groom or the bride, whom he had
known in the past. Not more than two weeks had elapsed
since the betrothal; it was not too late to make inquiries. Here was a starting point that might easily lead to
the clarifying of the entire mystery surrounding the young
secretary.

Pocketing the announcement, Gilmore rejoined Mrs.
Phipps in the living room below. Glibly, but convincingly,
he informed her that he had decided not to leave any message for his friend, but had changed his plans to the extent
of remaining in town another day, and would call on Gardiner at the offices in the morning. As he yet wanted to
surprise him, he hoped Mrs. Phipps would keep his presence a secret, until after he had visited him. The detective
would immensely appreciate this courtesy from her. And
responding warmly to his charming deference, and appeal,
she promised that she would not mention his call until he
had seen the secretary on the morrow.

By the time she did speak of it, Gilmore had reflected
as he took his departure, he would have made some definite progress. Five minutes after his arrival at Headquarters, he had sent a long, carefully worded telegram to the
Akron police, relating the story of the marriage announcement, and asking for such information as they possessed of
all parties concerned—but in particular, Donald Gardiner.

It was close upon eight o'clock, when, in the meantime,
Rankin found himself outside the door of E3, Russell Stirling's apartment at Garden Terrace. He had made the journey to Germantown in his own car, a Dodge that had seen

much service while in his possession. As he drew up before the towering apartment building, the statuary adorning its approach looked aghast to observe anything less than a Packard machine enter the drive. The structure itself, of red brick, decorated with white tile and an ornate frieze, was fifteen stories high, fronted by perfectly planned gardens, a fountain playing in the dusk wind, and little walks that led to a majestic portal. The stockbroker must possess means to reside amid such exclusive surroundings.

In reply to his knock, the door of E3 was opened by a butler whose stately demeanor seemed to proclaim him a gem among servants. It also concealed the smallness of his stature, and the somewhat mean cast of his sharp eyes and ferretlike nose. Below bushy eyebrows were sallow features.

"I don't think Mr. Stirling can see anyone just now," he said when Rankin had stated his business. "He is quite busy, preparing to go out on a dinner engagement."

"This is very important," returned the detective, "and I think he'll see me for a few moments. Tell him that some one from Headquarters wants a word with him."

The butler retired, unable to conceal the fact that he was startled. Rankin was not surprised when he returned in a moment and obsequiously escorted him through a short hall into a living room. Often in his experience, the magic words he had spoken were a touchstone that opened many closed doors.

The chamber, in its exotic luxury, would have done credit to a Sybarite; incidentally, it gave some indication of the type of man its owner would be. Extravagant draperies, painted in riotously modernistic designs, concealed an entrance to the rear; a gold-colored divan furnished the centerpiece of the room, about which were clustered several deep-seated formal chairs. Heavy Persian rugs deadened Rankin's footsteps. A grand piano, covered with a Chinese scarf, occupied one corner. The central lights were out, but a variety of lamps shed upon the furnishings a rich subtle luster.

A moment after he had seated himself the draperies parted. The gentleman who entered was large, and heavily built, resembling, superficially at least, the bodily structure of Philip Nixon. But he lacked the poise and dignity that were the financier's. His features were also large, in a rotund, florid face upon which dissipation and age would have been written had not careful applications of facial creams and powder concealed them. Yet he was not old; Rankin, not favorably impressed, placed his years at forty. He wore felt slippers, and a blue and gold dressing gown, hanging loosely about him in Chinese fashion.

"I must apologize for my appearance," he began, offering the detective a limp, uncordial hand, "but as Higgins told you, I am preparing to go out. No, no, stay seated, Mr. . . ."

"Rankin."

"Yes, Mr. Rankin? I hope you will be brief. I am given to understand that you are from the police. To what am I indebted for this visit?"

The words were urbane and smooth, revealing no sign of nervousness. Yet instinctively, Rankin sensed behind their outer calmness a veiled anxiety to conceal which the speaker was on the defensive.

"I am investigating the death of Philip Nixon," he replied, "of which you must have read in the papers—Mr. Nixon, you know, president of the American Motors Corporation. . . ."

"Ah, yes, I did see something about it; a most unfortunate affair, is it not? And you are investigating the case?"

"We at Headquarters have learned that you were acquainted with him, and on the chance that you might be able to give me some information regarding him, I have come to ask a few questions."

Russell Stirling raised his eyebrows slightly, expressing pained surprise at the detective's recital.

"You've come to me to learn something of Mr. Nixon?" he queried politely. "Mine was a barest acquaintance, and I'm afraid I couldn't possibly know anything that would be of assistance."

Rankin was equally polite, but he made his question pressing.

"However, you did know him, and we are making it a point to question everyone who came in contact with him in any way. You had business dealings with him, I believe . . . ?"

"Yes, but only the slightest; nothing at all of consequence."

"I must ask what sort of business dealings."

"Oh, just a little matter of selling stocks," Stirling returned with every appearance of reluctance. "In addition to my brokerage business, I have a side line of excellent investments, in which I had been hoping to interest Mr. Nixon. Further than that, there was absolutely nothing."

The detective nodded at the glib explanation. "I see; and were you successful in your efforts to interest him?"

"No, I'm afraid not . . . that is, while Mr. Nixon was quite willing to invest, matters had not reached the stage where a sale was effected. His tragic death intervened to prevent that."

"And yet, Mr. Stirling, up to the day of his death, I have it from a reliable source that he absolutely refused to see you! Did you meet him, then, on the day he died?"

For the first time the line of defense was pierced because of a blunder for which the broker himself was responsible. For a moment he hesitated, shaken visibly; only with an effort was he able to speak with the same even tenor he had before employed.

"I'm afraid I must contradict you, Mr. Rankin. I got in touch with Mr. Nixon by phone, at his home, and we met soon afterward, during a lunch hour, outside, several days before his death."

It was a safe reply. Whether true or not, Rankin realized he would be unable to prove or disprove the meeting of two business men at the noon hour, in any eating place, unless he could account for every moment of the financier's time for a week back.

"I see," he replied, as though accepting his defeat, "and you had no further association with Mr. Nixon?"

"Nothing at all, upon my word of honor." Russell Stirling glanced at his wrist watch, and rose with a gesture of dismissal. "I would be glad to help you, but I know nothing further, and it is getting quite late. If there is nothing more, I would ask you to excuse me and . . ."

"Yes, there is just one thing more. Would you say that you were sufficiently familiar with Nixon that he would borrow, or take from you, an article of clothing, say an overcoat?"

There was no denying the apprehension suddenly mirrored in the other's eyes. They wavered, and lowered to sweep the ground in confusion. Stirling dropped back into his chair, as though for support; and, when he spoke, his voice quivered uncontrollably.

"Borrow an overcoat from me?" His effort to seem bewildered was not quite successful. "What a peculiar question, Mr. Rankin! What in the world do you mean?"

Rankin unwrapped the overcoat he still carried, but now wrapped so as not to be seen till he was ready to spring his trap. He regretted the pause that gave the broker the opportunity partially to regain his balance.

"This overcoat, Mr. Stirling, is what I refer to. You lost this, did you not—it was in your possession two days ago."

"I . . . I . . . no, I lost no overcoat . . ." He was striving desperately to control himself. "Wherever did you get such an impression?"

"Whether you lost it or not, it belongs to you," Rankin stated bluntly. "And we found it on Philip Nixon's dead body."

"Is that so? No, it doesn't belong to me, as far as I'm aware. May I see it? . . . Thank you." For a full moment he inspected it, his face bent over it; when he returned it, his manner was tantalizingly suave. "My name is not in it, and as I always put it in for the sake of identification . . ."

"You deny, then, that you own this coat? There is evidence to link you with it, beyond a doubt."

"I can only say that your source of evidence is in great error. Wait, I think we can settle this matter to your satisfaction, easily enough."

Stirling rose, and pulled a thin dangling cord near the draperies, summoning the butler, Higgins.

"Elbert, will you please look carefully at this garment and tell the gentleman whether or not it is mine?"

Higgins complied. "No, sir," he said finally, in positive but mechanical tones. "That is not your coat."

"You know my wardrobe, Higgins. Have you ever seen it before?"

"No, sir, I have not; it is absolutely strange to me."

"That will be all," Stirling said, and when the butler had retired, "You see, Mr. Rankin, there is some mistake; I regret that I cannot satisfy you by claiming ownership. And now, you really must let me complete my dressing, or I shall have a time explaining my tardiness . . ."

And Rankin had, perforce, to permit himself to be ushered out. It was checkmate—a cleverly executed bit of fencing in which the stockbroker was the victor of the first tilt. But at the same time, the detective knew that, for all his cleverness, the man had been falsifying. He had

lied as to his relationship with Philip Nixon; his refusal
to admit his proprietorship of the coat was a lie. And the
entire scene in which the butler had backed up his master's denial was too obviously planted to be natural. More
than that, actually, Stirling had been maintaining a colos-
sal bluff; he knew a good deal more about the case than he
was willing to admit.

The detective was not discouraged by his defeat. It was
just a temporary setback; when he returned the next time
to confront Russell Stirling, he would have evidence and
proofs that the broker could not escape. And Gilmore,
when the two met at Headquarters later in the evening,
was only too willing to give him charge of that phase of
the case, at least, until he had produced something more
substantial than mere suspicion. His own hands were sufficiently full.

13
THE CHAUFFEUR'S STORY

At noon of the following day, as Gilmore sat, engrossed in deep thought in Captain Thomas's office, Detective Smith entered with a message to interrupt his reverie.

The inquest in Camden was just over and Gilmore was in no pleasant frame of mind. It had been a perfunctory affair, and had been adjourned for two weeks to give the police time to acquire further information. Dr. Curtiss had been called to relate the events leading up to the discovery of the body—his journey to Cape May on the 9:45 train, his joining Gilmore and how they were seated together when the train had abruptly halted. Then he told of his having volunteered his services at the conductor's request, and described the scene of the crime as fully as he could. His testimony ended there; the medical details and the causes of death were narrated next by Dr. Ralston in a manner comprehensible to the coroner's jury. Then Bennett was called to identify the body; and further investigation was postponed for a fortnight.

As if Gilmore needed more time to pile up further evidence! It was with some bitterness that he reflected that what he had already collected, so seemingly uncountable in amount, so inextricably tangled in detail, was a useless mass, a jumble of puzzle pieces that did not fit anywhere.

The Ferris gang threatening Philip Nixon's life, the financier's journey by machine to Rockton, the bullet holes and
Arthur Stahl's cap in the machine, and the overnight bag
in Ike Morin's possession; Philip Nixon in a black car with
two strangers, reaching the Marley farmhouse, the Marleys
with their sinister threats against him, taking his money
and afterward concealing these things; Gardiner's behavior, the alibi he had prepared, his concealed past, his
journey to Cape May, and his quarrel with the financier;
finally, the latter's body in Stirling's overcoat, while the
gray one was at the Marleys'. Here was merely a series of
endless complications, no single one of which dovetailed
with any other. When, Gilmore asked himself, would this
thread of trails begin to wind itself in an orderly fashion?

And then Smith brought him the message.

"I've been working on Stahl and Morin for some time," he
informed Gilmore, "but nary a word out of them. But Parker
says he's willing to talk, if that'll help him out any, though
only to you. He won't breathe a word to anyone else."

The other could hardly refrain from shouting. Perhaps
matters would now take a turn for the better and clear
themselves up.

"He'll talk, you say? Great heavens, Smith, send him in
quick, before he changes his mind. . . . It's a wonder that
anybody will open his mouth in this damnable affair!"

In a few moments the chauffeur was ushered in, even
less dapper than when Gilmore had last interviewed him;
two days and nights in prison had not served to improve
him. Besides being badly in need of a shave, when he
spoke, his voice was hoarse and dry.

At Gilmore's order, his handcuffs were removed and
then Smith retired.

"You have something to tell me, Parker?" the detective
asked, when he had motioned the chauffeur into a chair.

"Smith says you have some sort of a proposition to make with me."

"Yes, I have; I've been thinking it over in jail," Parker replied, "and I decided I'm not going to play a martyr for anybody. I know some things, but I don't know anything about Nixon's death. There's no reason why I shouldn't save my own neck; so I'll talk on one condition . . ."

"And what is that?"

"You play me fair, when my case comes up. You've got me on some charges, but I'm going to prove to you that I'm no murderer. Understand, I won't turn state's evidence against Morin and Stahl—I'm not a squealer. But I've got to get out of this jam myself, first, and I'll make a statement if you promise to do your best for me."

Gilmore was only too willing to agree to such a natural request, if it gave him any aid. Without the statement, he might never get any further with the case; and he was certain that Parker's desire to talk was sincere.

"The proposition seems reasonable enough," he replied. "You have my promise to see what I can do for you . . ."

"I guess your word suits me," Parker returned huskily, "because I know you're straight. Understand, this spiel isn't for the purpose of getting into a worse jam; I'm letting myself out."

"You can't object, then, to another witness, so that both of us should be on the safe side. You won't be able to deny anything you've said and I won't be able to claim you said anything you didn't."

At the chauffeur's nodded acquiescence to this proposal, Gilmore opened the office door with the intention of recalling Smith. Outside he discovered Dr. Curtiss standing in the entrance, about to knock.

"Are you busy, Sergeant?" the physician asked. "Captain Thomas told me I could find you here, and I thought

I might have a few words with you before leaving. I've just come from the inquest."

"Come in, doctor. As a matter of fact, I am busy, but . . . you'll do, as well as anyone else. You know a good deal of this affair already; there's no reason why you shouldn't listen in on this."

Briefly Gilmore explained the situation, and when the doctor had expressed his willingness to act as a witness, led him into the room. And when both were seated, he said:

"All right, Parker, go ahead. You mustn't expect me to believe everything you say, without trying to check up on it. But I'll hear it all before I draw any conclusions, you can depend on that."

Without further ado, the chauffeur plunged into his narrative. The first part of it concerned matters regarding which Gilmore had already drawn certain conclusions; but it was valuable that these should finally receive definite verification. Parker admitted that he was a member of the Ferris gang, and had been for some time; but he was shrewdly careful not to admit an active part in the Nixon robbery. Aware that the police had thus far been unable to connect him with it as the fourth member, he spoke, as he had just informed the detective, only to free himself from his present difficulties.

The whole trouble began, of course, with Lew Ferris's capture and sentence. They had all been well satisfied with their leader; he had treated them fairly, and always divided equally with them the profits of their various ventures. His capture had been a terrific blow, but it could have been borne had his punishment been reasonable; the rest of the gang could have shifted along till he had served his term. But due to the financier's power, and the money he spent to make an example of the wrongdoer, the twelve- to fifteen-year sentence had been meted out. And the sentence was Ferris's death warrant; for years, he had been consumptive, so that it was practically certain that if he was forced to serve his term, he would never leave prison alive.

"And that's murder, too," Parker cried angrily, forgetting himself for a moment. "It's judicial murder, Gilmore. A hell of a penalty to pay for a robbery! We couldn't sit by and let the Law kill him, when he didn't have a damn thing to do with shooting that woman."

Accordingly, with Morin and Stahl, he had schemed to compel the financier to free the prisoner. When the opportunity offered he was selected for the position of the financier's chauffeur. Though Stahl was the better mechanic, both he and Morin had been identified by the police, whereas Parker was unknown to all parties concerned. Through a forged recommendation for which Morin was responsible, he got the job. His work was to arrange things from the inside, and report the progress of matters to his colleagues. They were going to try threats first, then turn to more stringent methods; ending perhaps, if forced to it by Nixon's stubbornness, by abducting him or the daughter he loved so fondly. But, Parker took his oath, murder was the last thing they desired, for it would destroy every expectation of ever saving their leader.

Except for the fact that Nixon had disregarded their first two messages, everything had gone smoothly enough until the day before the murder. And then a very serious obstacle was encountered. The financier had been driven home unexpectedly from work in the early evening by a friend, after he had announced he might not be home till late. And, going to his room, he had discovered Parker there. The chauffeur was merely looking about—his ultimate object was too important for him to succumb to the

petty temptation of stealing. The position in which he
was found, however, was as compromising as though he
were guilty of burglary, with the result that, after the hec-
tic argument in the conservatory, he had been summarily
dismissed. But then, Nixon informed him that he was to
stay over till the next day because, as Gilmore now knew,
he needed the chauffeur for the purposes of his journey to
Rockton on that day.

Parker's dismissal was a vital blow to the gang's plans.
As long as he worked for the financier, the latter's movements were well known to it, and schemes arranged
accordingly. After his departure, however, nothing could
be accomplished except with infinitely greater danger to
all concerned. It followed then that, besides sending a
final note of warning, the gang must act in the short period the chauffeur was still employed; if no opportunity
arose to carry out the plans, one must be created within
the twenty-four hours which remained.

Then came the day during which Philip Nixon was
murdered.

"As you know," Parker related, addressing Gilmore, "I
was to call for Nixon at his office at two-thirty in the
afternoon, to take him to the bank. And afterward, as I
told you, I had to take him home, which we left at half
past four. But what I didn't tell you was the fact that, as
we left the office, Mr. Nixon informed me that I would
later drive him to Cape May. The very opportunity that we
hoped would occur, took place! On the journey, there was
no telling what chances we'd have to get at him. And while
Mr. Nixon was in the bank, I called up Ike and told him to
get hold of Arthur and a car and drive out to Bryn Mawr.
From there, they would follow us on the trip; I would go
slowly enough so they could keep up with us, all the time."

Thus far, Gilmore knew he was telling the truth; the
facts fitted in with Rankin's discoveries at McKenney's

Garage. The call for Stahl had come there at about quarter of three.

"Mr. Nixon always gave me my orders before we started out," Parker continued, "so that he wouldn't have to speak again. When we left the house, he said: 'Drive to Cape May by way of Newfield and Rockton, Parker. When we reach Rockton, leave the main highway just beyond the town; we'll make inquiry there, as to the rest of the road.' I just nodded, and when I saw that Morin and Stahl were outside the auto drive, ready to follow, I started."

"So that you knew Nixon was bound for Rockton and beyond."

"That's right . . . only I never took him. Just as we was crossing the Delaware River Bridge, into Camden, Mr. Nixon leans over to me and says, 'I've changed my mind, Parker; I'll take the train to Rockton, and get a machine there. Drive me to the terminal; I can just make the five-twenty train.' Well, that left me flat; I don't know why he changed his mind, for he couldn't very well suspect me of anything. I had been too careful for that. But if he did go by train, unless we could think of something else, we'd lose our last chance for getting at him. Still, I had to obey the order, because we were in the city; so I took him to the terminal and he caught the five-twenty just five minutes before it pulled out."

Was Parker again lying? When he had made this same claim before, Gilmore had not believed it, but since that time he had unearthed facts that indicated it might, nevertheless, be true. Nixon, who believed his chauffeur at least a thief, if not more, had in his pocket five thousand dollars—a sum sufficient to entice a dishonest employee. A journey with him, under those circumstances, was not conducive to the financier's peace of mind. It was natural, therefore, that he should change his mind. More important, the fact that Nixon had turned up near Pelham woods in a machine driven by two strangers might be explainable if, after taking the train to Rockton, he hired a machine to complete his journey.

The chauffeur saw the incredulity mirrored in Gilmore's eyes.

"That's the truth, Gilmore," he said earnestly, breaking off in his narrative. "He did take the train; I never drove him down. The rest of it wasn't right, but that part was true."

"All right, Parker," the detective said reassuringly. "Just keep on going—I'll give you my opinion when it's all finished."

"As soon as he got on, I joined the others who had followed us to the terminal. We talked it over quickly; we didn't have time to waste and we couldn't afford to lose his trail. Yet, unless we all took the train, the only way to get him was to race it to Rockton, beat it there, and somehow, manage to pick him up there, when he got off. But the car Stahl got in the garage where he worked wasn't fast enough; there was just a chance that we could get there first in the Rolls-Royce. Even that might have been impossible, only the train was a local, and took sixty-five minutes or more to make the forty miles. And that meant that we had to make it at forty miles an hour, at the very least. . . ."

For the only time during his narrative, Parker smiled, a grim smile, at the recollection of that thrilling run to beat the train to Rockton. Gilmore was aware that the 5:20 was a local train, nevertheless, he fully realized what a feat Parker had performed if he won his race.

"We started off; and once outside of Camden, on the Black Horse Pike, made up for time lost in the city traffic. Except through towns like Pitman and Glassboro, I must have averaged more than fifty miles an hour for over

twenty miles. The shore-bound traffic wasn't very heavy.
But I wouldn't like to repeat a ride like that again, Gilmore; it was a mighty close thing, and I wasn't letting
anything get in our way. At Malaga—that's about twenty-
seven miles out—we went off the main road to take the
road that paralleled the railroad track through Newfield
t' Rockton; it goes through Millville further on. We got
to Newfield at ten minutes after six, beating the train by
three minutes.

"Outside Newfield, a state cop on a motorcycle came
out of the bushes and tried to stop us. I paid no attention
to him; if we stopped, we'd have an argument on our hands
and, if we got into a jam, Stahl and Morin might be identified. That was a risk we couldn't afford to take. So I sent
him bowling over into a ditch—came near running over
him. It would have been damn good riddance, if I did."
Parker's voice became suddenly malicious. "By the time
he'd got himself together, we were out of sight."

As the speaker stopped for breath, Dr. Curtiss lit a
cigarette. The detective found himself too engrossed to
interrupt with questions.

"We beat the train into Rockton by five minutes," the
chauffeur continued, "getting there about twenty minutes
after six. The storm had begun to threaten us, and it was
getting dark; just the same, I think I hit the last eight
miles at sixty an hour. We had just time enough left to get
to the only garage in the place, hire a car and hurry down
to the station. Then the train came in—"

"Just a moment," Gilmore interrupted, recalling the
only garage that Rockton boasted of. "What was the name
of the garage?"

"The Rockton Center, it was called."

"You arrived at twenty after six; do you know the name
of the man who rented you the car?"

"No, I didn't notice him," Parker replied, "and Ike hired it. He had only time left to pay the deposit demanded and get to the station as quickly as he could. And then the train came in at six-twenty-five; and when Philip Nixon got off the cars, Ike and Arthur were there to meet him. . . ."

Again, the elements of time informed the detective that what he was listening to was absolutely veracious. A bit later than half past six, according to Mrs. Belcher's rough assumption, the financier had made his appearance, in a black car, at the crossroads four miles outside of Rockton. And five minutes later, Mrs. Colby, residing near Pelham woods, had overheard two shots. It all followed with precision.

"At least, you can describe the car, Parker," Gilmore said.

"An old five-passenger black Buick, nineteen twenty-six model; I guess you can find it, if you look it up at the garage . . ."

The detective nodded and Parker resumed his narrative. "Nixon fell for the trap nicely; if he hadn't, at least Ike would have had something to follow him in, wherever he went. Of course I kept the Rolls out of sight, because if Nixon saw that, he'd know something was wrong. There was no car at the station besides the one we hired, and Nixon needed one; besides, the storm was coming up fast and he had to get into shelter somewhere. So when Ike offered him the car, he got in. In case the old man got suspicious at a second man up front, Ike said that his friend lived on the way out of town and he'd take him along. . . .

"As soon as they got him in, I started back to the city. As God is my witness, Gilmore, I don't know what happened to Nixon after that. I had never planned to kill him; and if Morin and Stahl did it, well, you can't lay the murder on me." The speaker extended his hands, and spoke with a sincerity there was no gainsaying. "I never heard of him or the gang again; my one desire was to get back and escape as fast as I could. I knew that there would be inquiries almost at once, and I wanted to get away before my troubles with Nixon came out through Bennett. I knew he was bound to tell.

"And then, Gilmore, I ran into that damned cop again! I had forgotten all about him in my hurry, but he hadn't forgotten me or what I'd done to him. This time, he didn't waste any time trying to stop me; he just came out after me, and when I kept on past him, began to chase me. I was scared then; I wasn't going to be halted and held for a hearing; when the investigation began, I wanted to be out of town. I stepped on the gas and so did he; by that time, it had begun to storm and pour at a terrific rate. We both went through Newfield as fast as it was safe to go on wet roads, and he hung on like grim death right out the other side. It was a wonder we didn't kill somebody.

"On the open road, he began to fire at me. Twice he hit me, once under the hood and once by the mudguard; fortunately for me, he missed the tires; that only made me go faster, and gradually I began to draw away from him. The storm helped me; it was bad enough for me in the open car but much worse for him on a motorcycle with the wind howling at him and the rain streaming down into his face and blinding him. So, after some miles, he fell further behind, and finally I was so far ahead of him that I had lost him.

"But I couldn't afford to take any chances. At a turn in the road, where I was sure he couldn't see me any more, I turned off into a country lane for about five miles, expecting to come out on some other highway. And then I got lost; that's what made me get back to Nixon's place almost at midnight. The lane led only into other narrow muddy paths; and for almost two hours, I twisted along them, with woods on both sides of me and not a house for miles. It was a wonder I didn't get stuck a dozen times in that muck; it was so black and lonely that my brightest lights couldn't pierce the darkness, and so narrow I could hardly get through. But after a while I found a way out; and when I got back, I was too late, as you know, to make a getaway. . . ."

Parker's gesture of finality as effectively concluded the tale as the silence that followed his last words. After a moment, he said:

"Everything I've told you, Gilmore, happened exactly as I've described it. I had nothing to do with Nixon's death."

The detective began to ask questions. Parker could not say exactly where he had left the main pike for the side road, but he believed it was near Clayton, ten miles past Newfield. He had finally come out on a main highway, somewhere beyond Wenonah and from there easily found his way into Camden.

It was not that Gilmore doubted the story though Parker had no witnesses to it. It coincided with all of his own discoveries to a nicety. The disreputable condition of the financier's car was reasonably explained, without involving any attack upon it by the Ferris gang. Nixon's appearance at Mrs. Belcher's, the black car, and the strange drivers, were now all intelligible; and if Nixon carried his overnight bag with him when he entered the latter machine, it might easily have fallen into Stahl and Morin's hands. It was impossible that Parker could have manufactured the story out of whole cloth.

Nevertheless, the detective realized it had not been very helpful to him. Except for the assurance that Parker was eliminated, he was faced with the same problems as before. While the substitution of the machines was explained, the more important substitution of overcoats was still a mystery. More so than ever, the members of the Ferris gang were the most logical murderers; yet in direct contradiction was the fact that Nixon must have reached the Marley farmhouse.

The shots Mrs. Colby reported had been heard at twenty minutes of seven; yet, according to Dr. Sackett, the financier had not died until eight o'clock at the very earliest. The behavior of Gardiner was as inexplicable as ever, while Russell Stirling still remained the unknown quantity of the baffling equation.

But Parker's story, as least, was susceptible of proof. After he had been removed to his cell, Gilmore sent out two telegrams. Dr. Curtiss remained until the answers came to them, an hour later, meanwhile discussing with him the chauffeur's tale from every angle.

Together, they read the replies. The first was as follows:

CORPORAL CANBY OF THE STATE HIGHWAY PATROL REPORTED THAT HE PURSUED AND FIRED UPON A YELLOW ROLLS-ROYCE LIMOUSINE PHILADELPHIA BOUND SOMEWHERE NORTH OF NEWFIELD AT 7:00 ON MONDAY NIGHT HE LOST IT IN THE STORM
    J. J. MORLEY CAPTAIN STATE PATROL

And the second telegram read:

A 1926 MODEL BUICK WAS HIRED AT THE ROCKTON CENTER GARAGE BY TWO STRANGERS AT 6:20 ON MONDAY NIGHT AND WAS RETURNED TO THE GARAGE AT 8:30 IT IS NOT KNOWN WHERE THE MEN WENT LATER
    GABE SIMMONS SHERIFF ROCKTON

14

OUT OF THE PAST

Had Gilmore been informed, at two o'clock that afternoon, that in the evening he would be westward bound, he would have considered the information a joke. But at four o'clock, he had made up his mind to take the journey; and when, at eight-thirty in the evening, the Chicago Flyer drew out of North Philadelphia station, he was aboard and bound for Akron, Ohio.

This astonishing change of plan was due to the receipt of a third telegram, the reply to Gilmore's inquiry in the West. He had looked for little substantial results from it; perhaps some slight information regarding the girl, Ella Denby, who had sent Gardiner the betrothal announcement; he believed it would be necessary to delve further ere he unearthed something of value. For that reason, the suddenness of his immediate success astounded the detective. For the first moment after receiving the message, he stared at it, in mute surprise.

DONALD GARDINER [he read] SON OF JAMES GARDINER WEALTHY AKRON RESIDENT KILLED RIVAL ROBERT FARRELL OF CLEVELAND IN QUARREL OVER THE GIRL ELLA DENBY TRIED FOR MURDER CONVICTED OF MANSLAUGHTER AND

SERVED A TWO YEAR PRISON TERM
NOW IN PHILADELPHIA EMPLOYED BY
AMERICAN MOTORS ANY FURTHER DE-
TAILS NEEDED
        PAUL FREMONT CAPTAIN AKRON
        POLICE BUREAU

It was an unprecedented bit of luck to discover, in one
fell swoop, the cause for Philip Nixon's antipathy toward
his secretary, the latter's secret, and a possible motive for
the crime he was investigating. And what a motive it was!
A crime committed in the past—murder; whether the accusation was justified or not, the very word had an ugly
sound to the detective. It was worth a swift journey to
Akron, he considered, to learn the details at first hand,
though they were incidental to the crime he was investigating. It would be valuable if only for the sake of discovering, from those intimate with Gardiner, his true character; and he was not willing to overlook any possible trail
in this complicated affair.

The detective was pleased to find that the Superintendent, on being consulted, agreed with him as to the necessity of making the journey. And thus it was that midnight
found him tossing about in an upper berth of the Flyer,
his mind too active to permit sleep. It seemed to him a
most curious fact that if the girl, who was now Mrs. Santell, should have been the subject of the quarrel that resulted in the Cleveland man's death, she should have sent
Gardiner this remembrance of her. Perhaps thoughtfulness
had not prompted the deed; it might have been malice.
Another amazing problem, now that he knew the enormity
of the secretary's misdeeds, was the fact that Philip Nixon, who also knew them, should have continued him in
his employ. This was futile speculation, Gilmore realized,
until he had collected further data; and after a while he

obeyed his wife's earnest admonition to try to get some sleep.

The detective was up, however, more than an hour before his train reached his destination, close upon nine o'clock. By the time he had eaten breakfast in the station restaurant, he considered that he could find Captain Fremont at Headquarters; within a half-hour, he was closeted with the officer who had answered his own telegram of inquiry.

The Captain was a grizzled and gray-haired officer, who had seen many years of service. Twinkling eyes betrayed a saving sense of humor and belied the sternness which experience stamped upon stern features.

"You want all the information I can give you about Gardiner, is that it?" he queried when Gilmore had finished with the explanation of his mission. "In order to answer your telegram, I had to collect the records of three years ago, which I have here for you to study. At the time, it created a great deal of scandal hereabouts, but sensations disappear quickly into oblivion. Perhaps you would like to see the accounts . . ."

"You had best give me a brief outline of the affair before I examine those," the detective replied. "First, I want to know exactly who Gardiner is; your message suggested that his family are people of consequence. Secondly, let me have everything you can about this killing and what led up to it. And finally, what can you tell me about him, afterward?"

And Captain Fremont complied. For almost two hours he passed on, in complete detail, all the information he possessed. Gilmore, notebook in hand, listened, for the most part silent; only occasionally he interrupted the other's story with a question. At every moment, his attention was of the keenest.

When the narrative was finished, he said:

"Now, if I may see the records and the newspaper reports of the case, I think that will complete my search here. I'd appreciate it, if you'd get me the addresses of the prosecutor and the attorney for the defense, and of this Denby girl. I want to get as many viewpoints on the matter as I can."

The other complied—and while Gilmore studied the accounts, he procured the other intelligence that had been requested. At the end of an hour spent in reading the records, with a thoroughness that left nothing to chance, the detective discovered that his host had substantially covered all the facts; the press and court reports merely corroborated them in greater detail. Accordingly, after some further discussion, he took his departure.

The purpose of his journey being to discover what he could, incriminating to the secretary—he could not call upon Gardiner's parents or friends. From them, he was unlikely to learn anything; and he would only distress them with his inquisition. Besides, he believed it unnecessary to delve too deeply into matters but distantly related with his quest. Already he had decided that one day would be sufficient for all his investigations; and the two attorneys and the girl could supply him with whatever knowledge he desired.

The public prosecutor was out of town, but Mr. Pastor, Gardiner's lawyer, was in and willing to discuss the trial with the detective. From him, Gilmore gleaned no further details, but much in the way of opinion and surmise, valuable after he had discounted the bias of the informant. These the detective also noted and stored until he could sort them out and evaluate them.

The opportunity came at two o'clock, while he was taking his lunch. There remained only the girl to be interviewed, Gilmore hoping that either she had returned from her honeymoon, or had never gone, and he would find her at the address Captain Fremont had given him. Out of the welter of accounts, evidence and opinions, he weighed the dross and the gold. Mere hearsay, unsupported by either knowledge or evidence, he disregarded altogether. Contradictory facts demanded proper estimation, and a choice between opposing views. Actualities had to be granted their correct values in the scheme of the whole; and finally, after he had sorted and appraised, conclusions had to be reached.

It was not an easy task, but the detective finally had decided the following to be an adequate story of the situation he had come west to acquire:

The Gardiner family, of which the secretary was a member, was one of the most influential and wealthy of Akron families. For years, they had resided in the town, so long in fact that they might have been regarded as one of the first families. Old James Gardiner, having made an ample fortune in rubber and tires, had long since retired to enjoy the ease and comfort to which he was entitled. Stern, strong-willed, and of a somewhat religious turn of mind, he had married comparatively late in life. His wife, a girl from the West, was some years younger, with a taste for the more enjoyable things of life; yet, their married existence had been a happy one.

Young Gardiner, as the only child, was certain to be the heir of his father's immense wealth. Good-looking and popular among those with whom he traveled, he had possessed, from earliest boyhood, everything he desired. As he grew up, he became increasingly handsome; and with that gift, money and adulation were also speedily forthcoming. The result was what Gilmore would have predicted in such a situation. Between a doting mother, who never could refuse him anything, a somewhat strict father, whose objections were never sufficiently authoritative and made him rebellious, and praise from dozens of hypocritical friends,

Gardiner became spoiled and uncontrollably wild. He fell in with a set of fast-living people of a low, undesirable class, that played him, as Captain Fremont had expressed it, "for a sucker."

Perhaps he would eventually have settled down had he not met Ella Denby. She was a variety actress whose people resided in Akron, but who, herself, spent most of her time either in Cleveland or Detroit. The possessor of a rather hard type of beauty, she could be pleasing on occasion, and she effected a coy manner that was agreeable, if not genuine. They first met at a night club in which the girl was working, in Cleveland. From the beginning, Gardiner had been attracted to her, and let it be known that he had taken a fancy to her. She, on her part, appeared to think a good deal of him, though Mr. Pastor had insisted that never was she interested in anything but the young man's prospects. Over a period of several months, the two were constantly in each other's company; so that, had there not been an interruption, an engagement seemed inevitable, if the girl played her hand right.

It appeared that before Miss Denby knew Donald Gardiner she had been intimate with a young man by the name of Farrell, a bookmaker in Cleveland. He had a shady reputation; he also owned and operated a gambling hall, which, though regularly closed by the police, was always a paying proposition. In most of his dealings he had just managed to stay within the law. Farrell was of an exceedingly jealous disposition, and he seemed to believe that the girl belonged to him. The news that she was angling for some one far above his class was an unpleasant shock, both insulting to his vanity and inflaming to his overweening envy. When Ella Denby's disregard for him continued, his anger was aroused.

By one of those coincidences so common in everyday life, the rivals for the girl's love met in one of the club rooms of a hotel in Cleveland. At the time, they had the room to themselves. What occurred behind those closed doors never will actually be known. Afterward, Farrell was found dead, his skull crushed by one of the andirons that lay in the huge fireplace in the center of the chamber. At the trial, the prosecution claimed that Gardiner, in the quarrel that ensued between them, had deliberately struck his victim with the iron bar. His fingerprints were found upon the cross bar. Gardiner admitted only the quarrel; it was his story that Farrell had said something he did not like and he had knocked him down. In falling, the latter's head had collided with the andiron. He refused to divulge Farrell's remark, but it had undoubtedly been insulting to the girl, whose true character he seemed willfully to disregard.

Only the efforts of his parents prevented Donald Gardiner's trial from being a nation-wide sensation; as it was, even with the proceedings hushed as much as possible, it attracted much local interest. On the one hand, Gardiner was a member of a leading family, whose power in the community had to be reckoned with. His parents, shocked beyond measure, stood nobly by him, however, and stinted neither expense nor influence in their efforts to gain an acquittal. On the other hand, the victim was an admittedly criminal character of no particular service to society. Medical evidence supported Gardiner's claim that Farrell had been killed by his fall, and that Gardiner had left his prints on the bar while he bent over to examine the body. If his blow had had sufficient strength, Farrell might easily so have been killed against the andirons. But the fact remained that the two men had quarreled, and one of them had met his death during that quarrel.

The jury was lenient and found it involuntary manslaughter; Gardiner was sentenced to a prison term of from two to five years. It was during the trial that the girl displayed her true character. For whatever had occurred, she had been partially responsible; nevertheless, as soon as notoriety touched her erstwhile lover, she utterly deserted him to his fate. On the stand, she denied any close acquaintanceship with him, or that she was the cause of the disagreement between the two men. Much of her evidence incriminated the prisoner; only because the jury failed to place credence in it did it fail to carry much weight. The young man's lawyer expressed his opinion that not even a two-year sentence was too great a price to pay to be well rid of her.

When this term was completed, it was obviously impossible for Gardiner to have remained at home, the center of gossip and local scandalmongering. James Gardiner's connections in the East, in regard to rubber, had at one time brought him into close contact with the American Motors Corporation, and Philip Nixon in particular; and a friendship had developed between them. It was this connection that enabled Donald to obtain a position as the financier's secretary, the latter having consented for the sake of the father. It was the idea of the old man to give his son another opportunity to settle down, and begin life anew, having been taught a bitter lesson by experience. Because of his wishes, Gilmore now realized, the financier had employed the young man in his office, even while he disapproved of his attitude toward his daughter.

"And yet, I think he did learn his lesson," Mr. Pastor had said. "I'm given to understand that he has been doing most satisfactorily. I wouldn't be surprised if he eventually made good, and earns the right to the Gardiner fortune that originally would have been his."

And according to Mrs. Phipps' favorable report of the secretary, Gilmore realized that this was very possibly true. The entire tale confronted him with the problem of deciding what he should believe about the young man's character. This was one point in his favor. Another was the

fact that Gardiner was not a fortune hunter. A penniless
adventurer would have had much to lose besides a wife, if
the financier's objections had borne fruit; Gardiner, himself of good family, with the likelihood of being wealthy
in his own right, did not seek Eleanor Nixon's wealth. He
would forfeit only the girl he loved.

Nevertheless, Gilmore did not believe that these facts
weakened Gardiner's possible motive for killing Philip
Nixon. Philip Nixon's opposition would have been fatal,
whatever view his daughter might take of the secretary's
fall from grace. The fact remained that Gardiner, unre-
strained and intractable, had killed another man. The detective's knowledge of the law informed him that his quarry had come off most fortunately. Murder was the crime of
premeditated killing without any justification. Whenever
the deed was done, however, under the stress of a justi-
fiable anger, then the crime was lessened to voluntary
manslaughter. A verbal argument, such as Gardiner had
with his victim, was not enough to lower the magnitude of
the crime. And yet, the secretary had been found guilty,
merely of involuntary manslaughter, for killing through
some inexcusable negligence!

It was significant that Nixon had met his death in the
same way that Farrell had; the heads of both had been
crushed by a blow from some heavy weapon.

With all this information, the dilemma had yet to be
faced. Either Gardiner was a much-maligned young man,
who had killed some one through sheer accident, or else
he was an innately vicious villain who had committed one
and perhaps two murders. It would now be for the girl to
swing the balance one way or the other. It was true her
judgment was likely to be colored; but that very merce-
nary shrewdness that prompted her subsequent desertion
of the man, informed Gilmore that she was canny, and
capable of drawing conclusions.

It was middle afternoon before he found himself at the door of the new home of the Santells, a bungalow about which there was already an air of neglect. The little veranda needed sweeping and the garden of dying flowers that fronted it needed weeding. Gilmore required no introduction to be told that the woman answering his ring was the former Ella Denby. She was a youngish hard-eyed woman, whose painted tips were an incongruous contrast to the house dress she wore. The three years that had passed since Gardiner had first met her had not dealt kindly with her; her underlying coarseness was fast becoming apparent on the surface.

Mrs. Richard Santell eyed him suspiciously while she tucked in a few wisps of straggling brown hair.

"Mrs. Santell?" he began. "I'd like to introduce myself and my mission. My name is Gilmore and I've come to make a few inquiries regarding some one whom you once knew quite well, Donald Gardiner. . . ."

He had quickly decided that an appearance of frankness, leavened by a shrewd flattery, would bring best results. The statement appeared to startle her, but she was more curious than alarmed. After a moment, she said quickly:

"Don Gardiner? What 'bout him? What's he been doing now?"

"You know, he's in Philadelphia, now?" and as she nodded, "Well, I represent a Philadelphia merchandising concern—the Cornell silk people; I'm their agent in this district. Some weeks ago we employed Mr. Gardiner on the recommendation of the firm for which he last worked. He has proven quite satisfactory to us, but last week a rumor reached us that, though trustworthy, he was, some years ago, concerned in some sort of difficulty of the most disgraceful nature. For the sake of our reputation we cannot afford to keep him in our firm, if the rumor is true; and

I have been delegated to find out what I can about the matter."

"Well, why do you come to me?" Mrs. Santell asked. "While it's true I knew him, I really don't know him as well as all that."

Now that he saw the woman, Gilmore was certain that she had sent the wedding announcement to reproach the man who had suffered on her account. It was as though she blamed Gardiner for exposing her to unpleasant publicity and wanted him to know that, despite it, she had come out advantageously for herself. But these thoughts the detective kept to himself.

"I wanted to give Mr. Gardiner a fair trial," he replied warmly, "by seeing some one about it who was quite unprejudiced and who has enough ability to form accurate conclusions and express them sensibly."

As he had hoped, Mrs. Santell applied the compliments to herself.

"Oh, all of that you heard was true enough, I'm sorry to say. Don got himself into an awful jam out here, and he only had himself to blame for it, too. As you say, I guess I could tell you all about it, better than some, anyhow. I don't like to make any trouble for Don, but there's no hiding a thing like this. A person who can't hold himself in hand just deserves to get what's coming to him, don't you think?"

And then, as was inevitable, she began to relate the tale Gilmore had already learned, for the sake of justifying the part she had played in it. Her version minimized her own portion in the tragedy, and by so doing she persuaded herself anew that in reality she was in no way responsible for her former lover's death. Gilmore listened intently to her viewpoint, as much to the expression and the nuances of her speech as to the actual words she uttered. Callous and resentful that Gardiner's folly should have embroiled her in such an affair, she was at all times selfishly careful not to involve herself too deeply in her own narrative. In all other respects it was an accurate recital of the facts.

"The whole trouble with Donald Gardiner was," she summed up at the conclusion of the account, "he always had his own way. He never was refused anything—nobody ever stopped him from getting anything he wanted. They didn't dare to, I guess, because he was so wild and uncontrollable. He never knew enough t' keep his head then. Maybe he's different now, but if he'd have learned some restraint, maybe there wouldn't have been any trouble at all."

"He has a bad temper, then?" Gilmore queried interestedly. "You think that caused all the trouble?"

"I guess it did. I can remember once that he got so furious that he didn't know what he was doing. We were at a club in Cleveland, and drinking a little bit, when a waiter accidentally spilt something on him. I honestly believe he'd have brained him with the seltzer bottle if we hadn't held him. And Bob Farrell—I'm sure he didn't mean to say anything really wrong; still, it'd be just like Don to take it the wrong way and see red. . . ."

"I must say, Mrs. Santell, that you were lucky to be rid of him. I'm sure my employers will be glad to hear of all this before it is too late."

She appeared to repent slightly for having created such an unfavorable impression.

"Oh, I don't suppose, Mr. Gilmore," she replied, "that it was a bad streak; it was just the way he was brought up. And maybe he's changed, for all I know—you know, two years in prison must be a pretty tough grind."

"That's true," Gilmore remarked, "but it more often breaks a person than makes him."

"I guess that's so, too. It's hard to tell about these things, I suppose. But I don't think Don would have gotten himself into a jam at all if he'd been more used to hard knocks. Now Dick—that's my husband—doesn't have it so easy, but he makes good money on the racetrack; and like me, he enjoys a good time. We'll get along together, I guess; I don't think Don and I would ever have managed . . ."

After that, she began to discuss her personal life, her marriage and the prospects of the future. Gilmore, realizing that he had elicited from her all the information she possessed regarding his suspect, excused himself as soon as it was conveniently possible. He had acquired as thorough a picture of this complicated series of events in the single day as it was possible to acquire with a week of investigation; and the intelligence gained, though bearing only indirectly upon Philip Nixon's death, might well prove invaluable.

The sum and substance of Ella Denby's tale had told rather heavily against the young secretary. Discounting the petty malice that actuated many of her statements, the detective could, nevertheless, not discard it altogether. Where there is smoke, there is fire; and the account of Gardiner's unbridled temper seemed well substantiated by Bennett's story of the quarrel he had overheard in the financier's conservatory. There was no blinking at facts; the balance of the scales was no longer even. The side to Gardiner's discredit overweighed the items on the credit side.

As Gilmore boarded the train for Philadelphia that night, his brief summary of the day's developments was as follows:

"If I could discover that Donald Gardiner had, in some fashion, the opportunity to commit the murder, I would have him arrested at once."

15

TOMMY RANKIN REPORTS

It took Gilmore the greater part of the forenoon of the following day to collect the threads he had left loose upon undertaking his journey to Akron. There were reports to be received regarding his prisoners, both of the Ferris gang and the Marleys, Jenks to be heard from with a report of Gardiner's activities, and Smith's story of the financier's funeral. From Rankin the detective expected the results of his investigation of Russell Stirling. All these matters engaged Gilmore's attention.

Most of the information proved negative. Arthur Stahl and his accomplice had maintained the same obstinate silence that had characterized their behavior since their capture; no type of inquisition moved them to incriminate themselves. Similarly, the Marley brothers refused to speak; even Clem, when questioned alone, displayed no sign of weakness. As though his older brother had successfully impressed on him the imperative need of speechlessness, he displayed more strength of character in the crisis than Gilmore would have credited him with. Jenks' surveillance of the secretary had been unproductive; his days had been spent in the corporation offices, and his evenings with Eleanor Nixon.

The financier's funeral had taken place the preceding afternoon. Smith, assigned to be present, on the chance that something of importance might take place during the services, had nothing to report. No suspicious-looking characters had been present, no unusual reaction to the sorrowful nature of the occasion—which might have given the police a necessary clue—had occurred. The entire affair had been carried out in a solemnly impressive manner, attended by huge crowds, and witnessed by men famous in politics and financial circles—paying their last respects to one who had played so important a part in the financial life of the country.

Not until noon was Gilmore able to turn his attention to Martha Marley. Inquiry had revealed the fact that she was no longer at the farmhouse beyond Rockton; she had joined her Philadelphia relative, the Aunt Mercy of the letters Gilmore had found in the girl's room. That made it more convenient for his purpose of visiting her, a move that could be delayed no longer. The interview he had resolved upon, at the time he had arrested her brothers, had been postponed too long already. It was unfortunate that the press of complications should have intervened; but equally it had been unavoidable. With the girl, he fully realized, lay his best chance to discover the truth. The information which the two men kept to themselves, of what had occurred during the storm on Monday night, she also possessed. Whether she would give him this invaluable data was another question, but he believed that she would. And that without any more than a little persuasion. The detective knew that he would never use force in her case; rather would he go without the story than to get it by compulsion.

He had just made his decision to seek Aunt Mercy at the address he had found on her letter, when Rankin arrived, breathless.

"Smith just told me you had returned," he announced, "and I hurried in to give you the facts I have as quickly as possible. . . ."

Gilmore had never observed his colleague so excited and, correspondingly, so elated as at that moment.

"You've learned something important about Stirling?" he queried.

"A great deal!" the other returned jubilantly. "I think I know everything about him except where he was on Monday night; and I was just going out to see his butler about that. I knew you'd want to come along, because I haven't the slightest doubt as to what we'll find; so I stopped in first, for you. Hop into my car, and I'll tell you all about it, as we drive along."

Gilmore caught something of Rankin's elation, as they both hastened into the City Hall courtyard, where the machine waited. If Rankin's enthusiasm was any criterion of the value of his information, Gilmore realized he could not afford to miss it; and the postponement of his own plans was only temporary.

"Stirling hasn't had the best of reputations," Rankin remarked, while the car was turning into the Parkway Boulevard, "neither during the past, nor today, among brokers; and quite a few of them told me something about him."

He had gone first, he related, to the American Motors offices, hoping there to unearth some information of Stirling's relations with the financier. The entire morning of the previous day, he had gone through records and questioned the directors, on the matter. Nowhere, however, did he discover an account or memorandum that pointed to any interests, business or otherwise, between them, as far as concerned the financier, at any rate. Gardiner could tell him no more about Stirling than he had already told Gilmore. Rankin had come to the conclusion that, whatever the subject of interest, it had more to do with the broker's affairs than Nixon's, else the latter would not have so discourteously refused Stirling an audience.

Subsequent sources of investigation proved more productive. Stirling occupied a private office of his own in the Albee Building, in the suite of rooms of Sanburg, Pressman & Co., one of the largest investment houses in the East; but he was not connected with the firm in any way. Nevertheless, members of the firm knew something of him, and from them Rankin had received his first information. One of the younger Sanburgs had sent him then to another company which had also offices in Boston, where the detective learned a good deal more. After that, he had made the rounds of other brokers' offices, seeing men of standing in the financial world. These he visited because of their reputations and the likelihood of their knowing about other members of their own profession. And from many he acquired little items that formed the knowledge he had gathered.

Stirling had come to Philadelphia in the fall of 1926, three years before and set up in business for himself. Though he called himself a broker, he had, in these years, been a speculator, in the main gambling on the market fluctuations, arbitraging or selling short. In this last, he had had amazing luck. With an acumen little short of phenomenal, he seemed able to foretell when the value of a certain stock would fall; then he would sell it at its present higher value, borrow to deliver it to the purchaser, and buy it later on the market at its lowered price to return it to his lender, upon an agreed date. It seemed that his intuition never was in error, and having already taken advantage of anticipated drops, he managed to make a tidy little fortune.

Where Stirling had gotten the original capital with which to work, was unknown. In Boston, where he had come from, he had been employed by the brokerage firm of Skorn & Son, as little more than a clerk. Even then, his especial shrewdness on the subject of market fluctuations had attracted attention. One Allen Murray, a man of means who had made money in importing, had made a proposition to Stirling at the time—five years ago—to go into partnership in an investment house. What the partnership articles provided was unknown, but certain it was that Stirling was to supply his experience while his colleague provided the capital. The former accepted the proposal and the investment house of Murray, Stirling & Company came into existence.

For two years, the firm seemed to have prospered. Then, one day, a customer had gone to the city authorities and claimed that the concern had cheated him. Another followed the example of the first, one who had kept silent rather than make public the fact that he had been so cleverly deceived. An investigation was put under way immediately; and it was then speedily revealed that instead of being a legitimate investment house, the concern was a bucket shop. Clients' money, instead of being actually used for the purchase of stocks according to their orders, was merely placed as bets upon certain stocks, gambling upon their rise and fall. A drop of a very few points wiped out the margin provided for by the client's capital; whereupon the stock was theoretically sold, though it had in reality never been purchased, to cover this deficit. Thus customers merely turned over funds that were immediately pocketed. The complainant, however, wiser than the rest, had pierced the swindle; and, as there existed stringent legislation against bucket shops, both partners were arrested.

It developed at the trial that only Murray was guilty of the fraud, his partner convincing the jury that he was altogether ignorant of it. From the books in his possession, Stirling proved that, although he had received purchasers' money, he had turned it all over to Murray to invest; and that for what the latter did without his knowledge he was not responsible. He was able to produce receipts for all sums turned over to his partner, all signed, without a doubt, by the other. Entries in the firm books gave further proof, by the fact that they had been doctored, that Murray had been covering up his swindles and cheating both his partner and the public. On the strength of such evidence, it was useless for him to claim he was innocent; and on Stirling's testimony he was sentenced to three years' imprisonment. As soon as he was convicted, Stirling moved to Philadelphia.

"But that's all past history," the detective concluded his tale. "The more important question is—what do Stirling and Nixon have to do with each other? And I believe I've found the answer to it . . ."

"You have?" Gilmore returned. "Then you've certainly managed to make good use of your time."

His first indication, Rankin related, of a possible connection between the two men had come from his discovery of the corner Nixon had been engineering to control Audubon Motors stock. As Gilmore was already aware, in the early stages of the corner, the American Motors Corporation had tried to keep its purchasing activities a secret. By carefully disseminating rumors that Audubon was due for a fall, and publicly selling large blocks of the stock, it had successfully counteracted the effect of its concealed buying. In fact, in a period over a month, Audubon stock had been depressed from a normal of 75 to a low mark of 55. But on the Thursday of the preceding week, there had leaked out the earliest information of the larger motor concern's intentions. As was natural, Audubon stock took on a new value; after that, it had risen with the demand, by leaps of twenty-five points a day, until, on the day that Philip Nixon had died, it had reached an unheard-of peak of 145.

A month ago, in anticipation of the expected slump, Stirling had sold short 1,500 shares of Audubon Common at $70 a share. He had delivered them that same day to the purchaser, by borrowing them for that purpose from a broker named Caldwell, on a month's loan. The latter was an employee of Nixon and his corporation, in the scheme of cornering the market, and instrumental in forcing Audubon down; and the loan he made to Stirling was merely one of a series of public transactions intended further to depress the stock. For Stirling, it was the biggest gamble he had ever attempted. He confidently hoped to repurchase on the exchange before the month was up, at 50 or even lower, which would mean a $30,000 profit; all the money he had made in the last three years was staked on what he considered a certainty.

When, on the previous Thursday, but a week before his debt was due Caldwell, Audubon common had suddenly jumped to 67, Stirling had not been alarmed. He believed it a mere temporary flurry; as yet, it was under the price at which he had borrowed it. But on Friday the financial world had felt the full effect of the corner; Audubon Common shot up to 92, and on Saturday to 117. And, on the day Nixon had died, it was too late to save himself; two days before the financier himself, acting through his agent, would demand the stock, its price was far beyond Stirling's reach, and he was virtually ruined.

Bit by bit, as Rankin continued with his discoveries, his listener began to realize the ultimate goal of his amazing theory, and the tremendous panorama of activities that so affected the lives of two men; but he made no comment, preferring that the other put it into words.

"And yet," the detective went on, "on this Wednesday, the last day of delivery, Stirling was able to buy Audubon stock on the market at seventy, and fulfill his obligations. He had made no profit, but his fortune was saved. And what had saved it . . . ? Philip Nixon's death. The day after he died, the stock dropped to a hundred; and on Wednesday, before it recovered itself, it went back to seventy. It was practically certain the corner would collapse if Nixon should die—there are many classic examples of tremendous fluctuations, upon the decease of men of standing in money circles. Particularly was such a reaction certain in this case; the corner had been engineered by him and had his own personal support."

"You mean, then," Gilmore queried, "to suggest this as a possible motive that Stirling might have had for murdering Nixon?"

"I mean, first of all, that this was the matter on which Stirling had been trying to see Nixon. In his desperation he might have believed he could prevail on Nixon—who was his ultimate creditor—to come to some settlement with him as to the shares, at a price within his reach. And, failing that, he might even have been driven to commit murder. Stirling was too well versed in the stock market game not to know what would be the reaction if Nixon died and his death appeared a suicide. . . . With Nixon alive, he was wiped out; with him dead . . ."

Rankin's pause was more significant in its implications than if he had completed the sentence.

"But we know," Gilmore objected, "that as far as Gardiner was informed, Nixon had refused both to see and hear Stirling."

"It's possible, however," Rankin countered, "that Stirling finally persuaded him of the importance of the matter without the secretary's knowledge. After all, it would be Nixon's loss as well; if he refused to hear what Stirling had to say, he would never stand any chance of getting back his shares. On a compromise, some adjustment might be possible. You can't get around that overcoat; they must have met somewhere, after Nixon had completed that more important errand at the Marleys'. . . ."

Before Gilmore could reply, Rankin swerved the machine into the long drive that led to the Terrace Garden

Apartments. The conversation was ended; Gilmore, for whom this was the first visit, became too engrossed in the magnificence of the surrounding gardens and of the lobby to talk. As he took it all in, they entered the elevator, and, in silence, ascended to the fifth floor.

At the door of E3, Rankin knocked.

A moment later, the butler Higgins opened the door. For an instant, he was speechless, as his eyes rested on Rankin; then, his sharp countenance a mottled red, he began to shut the door.

"I'm very sorry, gentlemen, but Mr. Stirling is not at home. If you will come in later, perhaps about six o'clock . . ."

Rankin's foot impeded the further progress of the closing door.

"That's all right, Higgins," he interrupted. "We don't want to see Mr. Stirling; we just want to have a few words with you."

"With me, sir?" The butler fell back before the unwelcome visitors, aghast at their rudeness. "I'm sure I don't know what I can tell you. If you'd wait till Mr. Stirling is in . . ."

"Now it's nothing to be alarmed about, Higgins," Rankin said reassuringly. "You just have to answer a few simple questions and we'll leave you alone directly."

"It's nothing that you should have any hesitation in answering," Gilmore put in. "We are merely trying to check up on certain information that we have and we'd appreciate your assistance. If you could tell us how you spent Monday night, I think we would be quite satisfied."

The reassuring manner of the two detectives had the desired effect of assuaging Higgins's fears. Seeing no harm in the simple question, he relaxed, and replied in a manner free from nervousness.

"What I did on Monday night, sir?" He hesitated a moment, and then went on. "Except when I went to take Mr.

Stirling's bag to him at the station and saw him off, I was in all evening, reading."

"Oh, Mr. Stirling went away on Monday night?" Rankin asked calmly, as though it were but a casual point.

"Oh, yes, sir—to Cape May. He called me up about two o'clock in the afternoon to say that he was going, but as he wouldn't be able to get home, I was to pack him a bag and bring it down to the Camden terminal by half past seven. He was taking the seven-forty-five train."

"You saw him get on the train, then, and leave . . ."

"Oh, yes, sir—I waited till it went out, before quitting the station. And then I went home, and, as I said before, I read. . . ."

The 7:45 express—the only train bound for the shore resort, between the 5:20 local which Philip Nixon had taken as far as Rockton and the 9:55 train which Gilmore and Dr. Curtiss had taken. The detective, harking back to his time-table, recalled that it made only a single scheduled stop—that at Newfield at 8:25; though, upon notice to the conductor, it would also stop, to discharge passengers, at Oldroyd, twenty miles beyond the Marley farmhouse and almost ten miles before one reached Cape May. Several times, Gilmore had noted it, in considering the problem of how long Nixon had been upon the tracks before the 9:55 train came along.

"Do you know when Mr. Stirling returned, Higgins?" Rankin was asking.

"He came back the next morning, sir, by an early train so that he could reach the office in time. He called me up from there at nine-thirty to come for his bag. I did, as soon as I had the chance. . . ."

He did not, he insisted, know why the broker had made his journey to Cape May; the master, it seemed, did not discuss either his private or his business affairs with him. He was aware, however, that Stirling had been having difficulties in the stock market, though he admitted this fact only after a repeated catechism; the exact nature of it he could not say, but he believed from something he had heard, that it had to do with an investment known as Audubon Common.

"I can always tell when Mr. Stirling has something on his mind," he went on, confidingly, as he became more sociable. "He gets so worried and moody, when he's not doing well on the market; but so far, everything has always come out all right. Even this time, though beginning with Friday on, it was worse than ever before; I never saw him so nervous and scared. On Saturday, last week, he looked so sick, I thought he'd faint when he came back from work. Over Sunday, and on Monday, when he left, he was that worried, he didn't say a word to me; but after all, it came out all right."

"How do you know that, Higgins?" Gilmore queried. "Did he say anything to you about it later?"

"He didn't need to, sir; I could tell from his pleasant manner when he came home from work, Tuesday, that everything was straightened out, and there wasn't anything more to worry about. . . ."

Rankin sent his colleague a significant glance; his theories were fast receiving the expected verification.

"Now, Higgins," he went on, "as you see, there's been no difficulty about these questions. Just one thing more, and we will be finished." Unconsciously, his voice became stern. "That overcoat I brought here, night before last— that was Russell Stirling's property, was it not?"

The unexpected question took the butler off his guard. For the first time something like terror showed on his face at the realization that all the time these pleasant-spoken gentlemen had been pumping him and leading him toward a trap. His jaw dropped in silent amazement; his fingers intertwined nervously.

"Come now, Higgins," Rankin went on, "we know absolutely that when Mr. Stirling took the seven-forty-five train, he was wearing that coat."

"But I told you before, sir, that . . ."

"Never mind lying. . . . You've told us the truth so far"—the detective was increasingly brusque—"you might as well continue that policy. Or perhaps you would like to tell the story when you are being tried as an accessory to the crime of murder?"

"Murder!" The butler's abject terror was pitiful; his hands groped for support. "I didn't know that . . . I . . . Mr. Stirling, he'll fire me when he knows I've disobeyed him, but I did my best for him, I really did, sir . . ."

"That's right, Higgins, you did. So it was his, then? Why did you lie to me and tell me that it wasn't?"

The other gulped and stammered. "I didn't say it was his, sir."

"You've just admitted it"—Rankin pressed his advantage mercilessly—"and unless you answer my question, I shall place you under arrest. Why did you lie to me before and say that it wasn't?"

"Because . . . because, I had to. Mr. Stirling ordered me to. You're right—he had the coat when he left, sir, on Monday for Cape May; but when he came home on Tuesday, sir, he didn't have it any more. I noticed it and asked him what became of it. He was real sharp and said that he had forgotten it on the train, but, because he didn't want it any more, he wasn't even going to try to get it back . . ."

"Well, that doesn't tell me why you both denied knowing anything about it when I did bring it back," Rankin said.

"Because, sir,"—and Higgins spoke with a desperate effort,—"Mr. Stirling instructed me to do so. He warned me that in case it turned up or anyone brought it around and asked questions about it, I was to say that I had never seen it before. And . . . I didn't want to lose my position, so I had to do as I was ordered. . . ."

Ten minutes later, with the butler completely cleaned of all further details, and gravely warned not to inform his master of their call, the two detectives left. Gilmore had not spoken since his colleague had begun his inquisition on the subject of the coat.

"Well," queried Rankin, as they entered his machine, "have I successfully made my point?"

"Drive me to Abington," was Gilmore's reply. "That is where the Marley girl's aunt lives. You've almost made the point; you've put Stirling on the seven-forty-five train, but you haven't brought him together with Nixon. And yet, he must have met him. There's something diabolically wrong with this whole case. I haven't traced him out of the clutches of the Ferris gang or the Marleys yet, and now I'm trying to prove that he was also at another place at the same time. But where or how, I don't know; and unless Martha Marley can help me, I'll be ready to confess defeat."

16
FROM THE MOUTHS OF BABES

The house Gilmore sought stood alone upon the main highway, set apart from its fellows. Of a generally disreputable appearance, vines and creepers added a picturesque quality to its decay. From a sagging gate a winding path led through a front yard, within which chickens picked a meager sustenance among the scraggly grasses. The dwelling was of weather-worn brown boards, with a slate roof; except for the fact that rag curtains peeped from the windows, one would have considered it an outhouse, rather than a residence.

The detective stood alone as he knocked on the frame door. It would be much easier for him and the girl, if he had no company; the presence of two people would very likely frighten her. Rankin had, therefore, gone on, when he left his companion before the house.

Presently the door was opened by a small, stooped old lady in curl-papers, dressed in an austere gray. Her features were keen and her beady penetrating eyes offered no encouragement to the visitor.

"Miss Mercy?" Gilmore inquired courteously, and when the other nodded, "I've come to see Miss Martha Marley; I had heard she is staying here with you."

Cold suspicion appeared suddenly in the woman's eyes, as she replied in tones extremely forceful for one of her age.

"My niece? Yes, she's here. What do you want of her?"

"I'd like very much to talk with her, on a matter of importance to both of us."

"Humph! . . . You're a detective, and you want to pester the poor child with questions, don't you?" The reply was tart. "Well, you can't have anything of the sort."

"You misunderstand me, Miss Mercy," Gilmore hastened to say. "Believe me, I have no intention of distressing her. She could speak or not as she chose. I think, however, it would be for her benefit if you were to tell her . . ."

The girl's voice interrupted him from within. "Some one asking for me, auntie?" it called, and then, an instant later, "Oh, you want to see me, Mr. Gilmore?"

Martha Marley stood upon the doorstep, against the gloomy shadows of the hall behind her. As she caught sight of the detective, she halted with a barely audible gasp; tears filled her eyes, and she closed her lips to prevent them from quivering.

"If you would—just for a few minutes," was the gentle reply. "I promise you I won't ask you to say anything that you do not care to."

For a moment, she hesitated as though weighing the matter in the balance.

"You don't have to, dear," Aunt Mercy interposed sharply. "Act as you think best, but if you want, I'll send this gentleman about his business very quickly."

The girl smiled wearily. "No, auntie, I think the other is the better way." With this decision, she appeared to acquire confidence. "Won't you come in, Mr. Gilmore?"

She led her visitor through a darkened hallway, into an equally dark parlor, with the shades drawn, the chill dampness of which caused Gilmore to shiver. A spindle table was its centerpiece; a victrola, ancient and dilapidated, kept intimate company with a peculiar little bureau, reminiscent of a washstand. Next to a huge sofa of faded red stood a single lamp. The floor was carpetless and the walls bare.

Gilmore took a seat on the sofa, and the girl opposite him, in a rocker. From the doorway, Aunt Mercy sniffed her disapproval.

"Please, auntie, could you leave us alone just for a few moments . . . ?" And, after the older woman swept into the hall and ascended a staircase, "Now, Mr. Gilmore, you want to see me about . . . Mr. Nixon's death . . . ?"

"Yes, Miss Marley," the detective returned, "I should like to be able to help you, but it becomes so difficult when I have nothing to act upon. The silence of your brothers permits me no alternative but to conclude that they are concealing something of importance."

"They're innocent of his death; you must believe that!"

"How can I when I know nothing of what happened? After all, Frank did write a note demanding money of Mr. Nixon and threatened him if he did not produce it; that, at least, was extortion. And not long afterward he is found, just outside your farmhouse. What am I to think?"

"That note was written for my sake, Mr. Gilmore! I didn't know they had done it and I wouldn't have wanted it, if I had known." The confession was wrung from her in a sudden anguish of emotion. "But I know they didn't commit murder; they couldn't have killed the man I loved!"

The detective spoke to her as though she were an inexperienced, uncomprehending child.

"The man you loved? Come now, Miss Marley, don't you think you had better tell me all of it? I'm not an ogre looking for a victim on whom to place the blame; if your brothers are innocent, I'm just as anxious to prove it as you are."

"Then—then, if they had nothing to do with his death, you won't hold them for . . . asking Mr. Nixon for that money?"

"No, certainly not," Gilmore said, evenly. "I was merely holding them on that until I knew more. But if your
story proves them innocent, I promise you that I shall
press no other charges."

And then, Martha Marley began her narrative. In a tense
low voice, that bore witness to the stress under which she
labored, she unfolded the tale which Gilmore had more
than half expected from all the evidence he had acquired,
from the silence of the girl's brothers, from the fact that
she had fainted on the night Nixon's body was found, from
the financier's secretiveness as to his journey to Rockton,
from the fact that he had brought with him money. A tale
of love . . . and love betrayed.

She had met Philip Nixon a little less than six months
ago, in Philadelphia, during her last visit to Aunt Mercy.
The encounter had been accidental; it had occurred one
day while she was in town doing some shopping. An early
January storm had covered the city pavements with ice and
sleet and made traveling for pedestrians most dangerous.
She had come from a store on Market Street, her arms
laden with packages, and started to cross the street. Too
engrossed in finding safe footing, she had failed to observe
the approach of a huge yellow car until it was too late to
escape it. Despite the fact that the driver had jammed his
brakes until they screeched, and she had tried to leap back,
the car struck her. It threw her back violently against the
curb in a heap and caused her to lose consciousness.

When she had recovered her senses, she was in the
yellow car, being driven to a hospital. Fortunately, she
had not been seriously injured; except for some bruises,
the only unpleasant result of the mishap proved to be a
sprained ankle. After having been treated, she had been
driven home and put to bed. The girl could still smile
faintly at Aunt Mercy's alarm when she had been carried

in, though the accident proved to be the forerunner of all the difficulties that followed.

The owner of the car, who had been seated in the tonneau when she was struck, was, of course, Philip Nixon. The occurrence had distressed him exceedingly, and from the beginning he shouldered all the responsibility for it. It was at his order that the girl had been first carried to the hospital; and he had accompanied her afterward to her home. He had instructed Aunt Mercy to charge all expenses of her treatment to him—a deed which the old woman felt to be a proper one under the circumstances. The day afterward he had sent his own private doctor to examine her and as soon as he was assured that she could see visitors, he had called to express his regret and pay his respects.

After that he became an almost daily visitor, making no secret of his interest in her. When he did not come, he sent his chauffeur with flowers, to inquire how she was progressing. Despite the discrepancy in the ages of the financier and the girl, a friendship grew up between them. Flattered by the solicitude he displayed, she came to look forward to his calls, even when she began to realize that there was a personal element in his conscientious concern of her welfare. He discussed with her, her past life and future prospects and expressed a wish that he might help her. She found herself quick to reciprocate; in her uneventful existence, with her blunt if dependable brothers, she had never before encountered courtly treatment and sensitive understanding.

Some weeks after the accident, when the girl's ankle was fully cured, the financier expressed a desire to entertain her in some manner. Disregarding the danger signals which Aunt Mercy claimed she already observed, Martha had consented. It was a new and fairy world that Philip

Nixon introduced her to. A theater and a visit to a night club—it did not require much to delight her; the color and the life of it fascinated and intoxicated her. The financier seemed gratified at her pleasure and enjoyed her reactions to each delight. Other excursions followed, which she could no more have resisted, having had a taste of pleasure, than steel can resist a magnet. Inevitably there developed, on the part of the girl, a feeling more intimate than friendship. She was grateful for his attentions, and found herself happier in his company than anywhere else. At first she refused to consider this disturbing change of feeling; but then she was compelled to admit to herself that she loved the financier. At no time had he, thus far, become familiar in any manner; rather had he been scrupulously respectful, until she had come to fully confide in him. And matters so approached the danger point, which Aunt Mercy was doing her futile best to prevent. Martha Marley, ignorant of the difficulties that were to follow, was heedless of her warnings; and there came an evening, spent together, when the financier was more than solicitous—fondly and tenderly affectionate, instead.

"But it wasn't his fault," said the girl softly. "After all, shouldn't I have known? Was it not foolish to imagine that one in his position could really love me as I loved him? After all, I was a country nobody; not some one who really mattered. . . ."

Gilmore did not need to hear the sudden break in her voice to tell him that Martha Marley still loved the financier. And she had long since forgiven him. She groped uncertainly for a moment, seeking to collect the wandering thread of her narrative.

"I'm sorry," the detective said, "that this is painful to you. Perhaps you had better not go on with this part of the story."

The girl smiled wanly. "Now that I've started, I might as well finish it . . . you mustn't get the wrong impression. I was only foolish, remember, not bad; I knew so little of people and men."

There was no trace of self-pity in her justification.

After it was all over, she explained, she had feared to tell her brothers anything of the incident. As long as it was possible to do so, she had kept it to herself, nursing her dread in secret. She knew Frank's temper and was apprehensive of what he might do when he learned of it. But there came a time when it was no longer possible to conceal her story, when it would have been revealed without a word from her; and then, torn with anxiety, she had made a full confession.

To her secret dismay, all of her brothers' fury was directed against the financier rather than against herself. Frank raged and threatened all manner of dire things, to avenge himself on the man responsible for Martha's misfortune. His sister pleaded with him in vain to control himself, nor was she successful in her effort to persuade him that the blame was equally hers. Only the fact that any act of his was bound to make the affair public had held him in check and caused him to promise that he would not do anything precipitately. For a time it appeared that there would be no difficulties; but this was merely the ominous calm that precedes a storm. Unknown to the girl, he had sent Philip Nixon a letter, describing her predicament and demanding satisfaction. And when, at the end of two weeks, no answer had been forthcoming, he had sent another, couched in more menacing terms—the note Gilmore had found—which had finally brought the financier to the Marley farmhouse.

The girl paused, and once more there crept into her voice a rending poignancy.

"But I was told nothing about it. I knew nothing of it until Philip Nixon stood on my doorstep at quarter after seven. . . . I suppose Frank meant it for the best, but I would rather have died than be so humiliated. As if money was sufficient to repay me—when all I asked for was to be left alone. . . ."

She was not bitter, but rather deeply injured that Philip Nixon could have so misunderstood her. That Frank's messages were largely responsible for that misunderstanding, Gilmore had no doubt; the financier would never have done anything so crude. In the course of the investigation, the detective had found him to be harsh and ruthless; but he had never discovered that he was small and mean.

"But he came, at least," she went on, "and he would have come in answer to the first letter, but he had been too busy to get away. I know he would never have shirked the responsibility; he was too big a man for that."

Her faith was unshakable and despite what the Superintendent said about Nixon's reckless life in the past, Gilmore was inclined to agree with her estimate of him.

"You are speaking now," he said gently, "of Monday—the day on which Mr. Nixon met his death. Be very careful of your story, and give me every detail, no matter how trifling it may seem. You said that Mr. Nixon reached your farmhouse at quarter after seven . . . ?"

Martha Marley made a conscientious effort to comply.

"Yes, I remember I had just been winding the clock. It was storming then—terribly—with thunder and lightning and such a downpour that a moment outside would have soaked you through. My brothers and I had just finished supper, when there was a knock on the door. I wondered who could be out in such a storm; but I didn't wait to think because there was something so urgent and terribly insistent in the knock that I ran to the door."

Her words were caught up in a choking gasp, and her features were drawn and white. "Philip Nixon stood outside there in the storm! Something terrible had happened to him, I knew from the instant I saw him. . . . He was leaning against the door, barely able to stand; and as Frank helped him into the house, I thought he would fall. The coat he wore—the one you found upstairs—was like a matted rag, and torn as if he had been in a fight in the rain; his clothes and his shoes were full of mud. He had been running madly; he was almost sobbing for breath, and coughing as if his throat would break from the strain of it. He was so exhausted that he could hardly stagger into a chair.

"As to what had happened to him," the girl continued, "I can only tell you what he told us. He had been driving toward our home, on the other side of Pelham woods, when suddenly, just before the road makes the turn, he was attacked. There were two men up front, one of them driving the car; and he brought it to a stop in the shadow of the woods, and turned on him. While he introduced himself, his companion got out and climbed into the rear. What they were after, whether it was the money or not, I don't know, but he introduced himself as the gentleman who had written him several times on a subject of mutual interest; and the other man drew a revolver and cautioned him not to struggle . . ."

"Can you tell me what time this occurred?" Gilmore interrupted.

Martha hesitated. "It must have been a few minutes before quarter of seven. Mr. Nixon said he had been in the woods for half an hour, though it seemed like ages at the time."

The time coincided with that at which Mrs. Colby had heard the two shots. The detective nodded and indicated that the story continue.

"Mr. Nixon could hardly tell afterward how he managed to escape. Even while the one man was talking, he had the presence of mind suddenly to throw himself against the other, getting him by surprise and sending the revolver flying into the road. Then, before he recovered his balance Mr. Nixon had jumped from the car. The first man was too late to prevent him; his fingers only caught hold of his coat as it passed through the door. It ripped in his hand and Mr. Nixon twisted madly through his clutches. His revolver came out, and he fired twice, but fortunately, in the excitement, his aim was bad. The next instant, both men started in pursuit.

"Mr. Nixon plunged headlong into the woods. On every side were heavy thickets, bushes, hindering his flight, but hiding the direction of it. About him was a black darkness; and the rain was a torrent, accompanied all the while by long, dull booms of thunder. Not the kind of crashes that follow blinding flares of lightning; the vague flashes were not illuminating and a constant roll of sound drowned out his crashing footsteps."

As though the girl was experiencing every moment of terror of the man she loved in his dreadful predicament, she dramatized the scene in vivid, indelible phrases. "Can you grasp it, Mr. Gilmore, like a hunted animal, running blindly, into thickets, torn by briars and brambles, dodging and twisting through that terrible storm to save his life . . . ? Running, stopping to listen, believing he heard them on his trail and going on again gasping for breath, stumbling and picking himself up with an effort and running on and on through the woods. Twice he hid as he heard them approach cursing that the storm prevented them from either seeing or hearing him; and when they had struggled by, doubled back again. The first time, they discovered the trick and retraced their steps, knowing that they could not

let him escape after what had already happened. But the
second time, he succeeded in throwing them off.

"It was the darkness that saved Mr. Nixon. As the two
men came nearer, he crouched down in the boll of a split
tree, holding his panting breath with an agony of effort.
They passed him, beating the bushes within two feet of
him, so that he could have reached out and touched them.
But, mercifully, they did not find him and no telltale flash
of lightning gave away his hiding place. Throughout, the
storm protected him well.

"By sheer good fortune, he found his way into our
clearing. During his flight, Mr. Nixon must have been
cutting directly through the woods, all the while. For long
minutes after the footsteps of his pursuers died out, he
remained in hiding, not daring to stir. But finally, certain
that he was safe, he went on in the direction away from the
road where his flight had begun. If he had known what a
large area Pelham covers, he would never have avoided the
road; it is so large that children have wandered about it
in circles, lost for days. But he found his way out . . . he
finally caught a glimpse of our lights near the edge of the
woods; and worn and sick, managed to reach our door."

The recollection of her first view of the financier, in
the pale lamplight that illumined the doorway, caused her
voice to break in a moan of sorrow. The narrative had
strained her nerves to the breaking point; it was not until
Gilmore had procured for her a tumbler of water from the
kitchen that she was able to speak again.

"Perhaps you had better rest a while," he suggested soli-
citously. "I realize that this is not very easy for you and I
wouldn't want you to overtax your strength."

Martha smiled sadly as she returned the glass to him.
"No, no, I'm quite all right now, thank you. I think I can
finish now—there isn't much more left to tell. . . ."

She plunged once more into her narrative. "Mr. Nixon had not recovered from his terrible experience, even after he had dried himself by the fire and rested. While I was out of the room, making tea for him, I suppose it was that Mr. Nixon gave Frank the money he had brought. He was still trembling and coughing; he had not been well and his narrow escape had made his cold much worse. He was in no condition to leave, and when he looked at his watch and said that he must go on, I pleaded with him to wait till he was feeling better. . . ."

"He took out his watch? Did you notice whether it was broken or not? It might have been shattered in his flight through the woods."

"It was perfectly all right as far as I could see," Martha replied after a moment's pause. "It must have been going because it agreed with our kitchen clock. It was quarter of eight, then."

Gilmore nodded and indicated that she continue.

"But Mr. Nixon wouldn't hear of remaining. Even though he wasn't well, he insisted on following what had been his original plan in coming to Rockton. He was going back to Newfield to catch the train to Cape May. He had counted, of course, on being driven back by the two men who had brought him, but now he had to depend on Frank and Clem to get him there. There wasn't much time left, considering that Newfield was twenty miles back and it was already ten minutes to eight."

"Do you know what train he intended to take, Miss Marley?"

"It's an express to the shore," the girl replied. "It gets to Newfield at eight-twenty-five and stays for five minutes, I believe, till an Atlantic City train with which it connects, comes in."

The detective sat up suddenly. The 8:25 train for Cape May, at Newfield, was, at Camden, the 7:45 train which,

according to Higgins, Russell Stirling had taken. At last
he found the first glimmer of consistency in a series of
facts that were, for once, compatible with each other.

"But by going to Newfield," he objected, "Nixon would
be going back toward Philadelphia. Wouldn't it have been
better for him to go in the other direction to the nearest
station toward Cape May, say, Oldroyd, twenty miles further on?"

Even as he asked the question, he recalled that the 7:45
express stopped at Oldroyd only on the request of passengers. That, in itself, explained the peculiar arrangement
by which Nixon doubled on his tracks, but Martha's reply
presented another reason for the plan.

"That wouldn't do, Mr. Gilmore, even though he would
have had till later than twenty minutes after nine to make
the train at Oldroyd; but he said that he had arranged to
meet some one at Newfield, and he wanted to keep the
appointment. I think he was most influenced by a nervous
but natural anxiety to get away, among people again, and
going to Newfield was the quickest way."

Better and better. Rankin's ideas were now beginning
to be corroborated and Gilmore put his next question
eagerly.

"He wanted to meet some one? Did he let anything fall
about whom it was?"

"He merely said he wanted to leave," the girl said, "and
Frank promised to do his best to make the train for him.
As it was still storming, we wrapped Mr. Nixon in blankets, in the machine, so that he would not be cold during
the ride, and to prevent the chance of a complication setting in."

She mentioned nothing further, Gilmore observed,
of the situation existing between her and the financier.
Whether the latter had expressed to her his willingness to
assist her in her difficulties, he did not know; but if he

had, Gilmore believed Martha would have eased his mind
by informing him that she bore him no grudge.

"So Mr. Nixon did not take his coat along, when he
left," he observed. "Exactly what was the reason for it?"

"It was not fit to wear in public any more. You saw
its condition, Mr. Gilmore—ragged and torn and terribly
soiled. If he had that on, it would have attracted attention
to himself at once and told people that something was
wrong. So it was left at our house; but he had blankets
instead. In his condition, he had no business leaving us, but
since he insisted we could only do our best for him. . . ."

There was nothing more she could tell him. It was almost half past nine when Frank had returned with the
information that, by driving recklessly and disregarding
the dangerous wetness of the roads, he had barely reached
Newfield in time to get the train. A journey of twenty
miles in less than forty minutes, it had been something
of an achievement. And after that, she knew nothing of
Philip Nixon until that numbing, dreadful moment, when
she heard Dr. Curtiss name the financier as the victim of
the "accident."

"You see," Martha concluded, "why my brothers said
that if I told anything, I would be making matters worse
for them? I would be giving you the motive that you needed to complete a case against them. And then, of course,
I didn't know that Frank really had taken Mr. Nixon to
Newfield—I had merely his word for it. But then, he must
have—he wouldn't have lied to me."

A moment of quiet followed her last words. Then Gilmore rose and took her hand.

"May I say, Miss Marley, that I admire your pluck tremendously? I appreciate the confidence that you have
placed in me; you may be assured that I shall make no use
of your story except in case of dire necessity. And I shall
remember my promise to you."

She rose, too, a sudden catch in her voice, trembling slightly.

"Thank you, Mr. Gilmore,"—and in her earnestness, her eyes began to fill with tears—"I am tremendously grateful to you—I don't know how to express my gratitude for your consideration. . . ."

Gilmore felt the warm, sincere clasp of her gentle touch after he had taken his leave, followed by Aunt Mercy's somewhat malevolent glances, until he had boarded the street car back to town, and turned his thoughts to his case and the effect Martha's story had had upon it.

That it was true, there was never a doubt in his mind. As far as the girl knew the facts, they were absolutely correct; too many details connected with what he already knew to possibly make it a creation out of whole cloth. The shots overheard by Mrs. Colby, the completed story of Frank Marley's message to the financier and Clem's possession of the latter's bank notes, Nixon's safe arrival at the Marley farmhouse, and how, in his flight, Nixon had left his overnight bag with his attackers—all these things were clarified. It was no coincidence that the Ferris gang should have attacked so near to Nixon's destination. They had just taken the financier from the train; it was their first opportunity, the first lonely road, where they could act under the additional protection of the rising storm.

Even the incident of the overcoat, and how it was left with the Marleys was but a logical sequence to the financier's mad escape through the woods. And following that, in natural order, was his return to Newfield where he could take the train and continue his journey to the shore.

The man whom he had agreed to meet was, of course, Russell Stirling. It looked very much as though Rankin had been correct in his theories. Influenced as much, perhaps, by his own interests in regaining at least some of the shares due him from the broker, as by the latter's desperate insistence, he had consented to hear what he had to say. In all probability, it had been arranged that Stirling would be met at Newfield by Nixon in his yellow limousine, and make the rest of the journey with him by machine. But when the financier had decided to take the train to Rockton, and had no opportunity to inform Stirling of his change of plans, he intended to return by the jitney to Newfield, where he would join Stirling on the train. Together, they would thus continue to Cape May.

But after the meeting on the train, what had occurred? With Audubon shares soaring to ruinous prices, and his debt due within two days, the broker must have been well-nigh despairing. Nixon, though willing to listen, was under no obligation to him; and it was altogether likely that he had refused to compromise the debt owed him in shares, at a sum within reach of the broker's purse. Stirling must then have realized that the financier's death, alone, would save him. It was conceivable, then, that he had lured him to the rear of the train; that Nixon had refused to risk the damp darkness without a coat, and Stirling had, perforce, to lend him his; that, in the excitement of murdering and casting Nixon from the train, the broker had forgotten the incriminating garment on his victim. Afterward, to protect himself, he could only order Higgins to . . .

With a grunt, Gilmore straightened himself in the seat of the car. Like a blow from behind, there came a sudden thought, surprising in its overwhelming importance.

Donald Gardiner had also been on the 7:45 express!

It was the only train Gardiner could have taken to Cape May in time to have caught the midnight train back on the night of the murder. At quarter of seven Mrs. Phipps had heard him go to his room, expressing an intention to remain all evening there. By slipping out at once, he would just have time to reach Camden and catch the 7:45 train. With the promise of the rising storm, he would never have traveled one way by the Reading line and the other, as he had, on the Pennsylvania line. The only other Cape May train was the 9:55 on which the detective and Dr. Curtiss had traveled. But that train, which ordinarily arrived at the seashore resort at 11:45, had been forty minutes late, due to the delay caused by the tragic discovery on the tracks.

It followed, then, that the secretary had taken the 7:45. Did he know, despite his denial, of his employer's intention of boarding the same train at Newfield? Must not the meeting there arranged between Nixon and the stockbroker have gone through the hands of the financier's secretary? The opportunity he sought in Gardiner's case had been found.

But Gilmore realized that he could do nothing against either suspect, until he had actually proven that Nixon had boarded the train at Newfield. It would be dangerous to assume such a fact; he must first prosecute inquiries both at that town and on the train.

17
THE 7:45 EXPRESS

When Gilmore left Martha Marley, it had been but four o'clock, so that he had ample time to procure a photograph of the financier at Headquarters, before traveling to Camden to catch the 5:20 train. The local, which, five days before, had taken Nixon to Rockton, reached Newfield, first along the line, at 6:07; and the two-and-a-quarter hours that intervened until the 7:45 express arrived there at 8:25 would be sufficient to pursue whatever inquiries he might have to make at Newfield. Accordingly, he was aboard the local when it drew out of the terminal.

Newfield, thirty miles out, proved to be an ugly, sprawling little town, the chief importance of which was that it served as a junction for trains running to Atlantic City and those going to Cape May. The station to which Gilmore descended was of old, moth-eaten wood, badly in need of a coat of paint, set upon a triangular platform, from two sides of which the two different lines of tracks branched in diagonally opposite directions.

The detective had already decided to begin his pursuit by questioning the ticket agent. He, more likely than any other, would recall the last-minute passenger of the preceding Monday night, who had barely caught the train. Other possible sources of information were the station porter, if any, the baggage master and the telegrapher. He must also consider jitney drivers or busmen, who might have observed Frank Marley drive up, on that stormy night, almost a week ago, with his passenger.

The ticket agent was an old, whiskered gentleman, whose little, twinkling eyes betokened a sociable nature. He graciously acknowledged the detective's introduction, admitted that his name was Abner Caldwell, and expressed a willingness to be of service.

"How late do we keep open here?" he repeated the other's first query. "Why, generally, till maybe half past ten—that is, till the last train, the nine-fifty-five, bound for the shore, comes in. But I'm the only one that stays till then; the porter closes up at nine and the baggage room, as soon as it gets dark. . . ."

This complete, if somewhat garrulous, reply told Gilmore that his first choice had been a wise one.

"I wonder if you can remember last Monday night well—that is, five nights ago?" he asked.

"Monday night?" The agent paused. "That would be the night of the storm, wouldn't it? Yes, I remember it; what about it?"

"You wouldn't have many customers buying tickets to Cape May on a night like that, would you?"

"Not likely, the way it was pouring. There'd be hardly a soul; I recall now that, 'cause of the rain, I was stranded here till nigh on to eleven, before I could leave the station."

"Then you'd recall," Gilmore said, "whether a passenger came in by a machine on Monday, just in time to make the eight-thirty train for the shore. Think carefully a bit."

He awaited the reply in some suspense, as the agent complied with conscientious effort. After a moment, his face up.

"Oh, you mean Wally Berger from Oldroyd; yes, I remember that. He brought in a passenger to make the train.

Only that was much later than half past eight—somewhere long about half past ten . . ."

"No, I don't mean Wally Berger," the detective returned. "The party I'm concerned with came along, if he came at all, at eight-thirty."

Mr. Caldwell went on as though Gilmore had not spoken. "Nice fellow, Wally is—I've known him ever since he moved to Oldroyd. He made darned good time for that passenger, too, and afterward, he stopped in and talked with me till the rain let up. I ain't seen him for a couple of months before that, so we had a nice, sociable half hour. He's a character—been running a jitney in Oldroyd fer eight years . . ."

Gilmore was annoyed. He had neither time nor patience for reminiscences; there was much ground to cover and minutes were precious.

"The people I'm interested in," he broke in, testily, "must have come much earlier. The driver was a husky, large fellow, with rough sharp features—a farmer, if you get what I mean." He went on fully to describe Frank Marley and concluded by producing the financier's photograph. "And this is the passenger he brought."

The agent studied it carefully. "Never saw 'im afore," was his verdict. "That gent never bought a ticket from me last Monday night, I can swear to that. There was only the fellow that Wally brought, that I can think of now."

This conversation was but a sample of what followed. Passing from the talkative agent to the porter, there again he drew a blank. He had observed nothing of anyone arriving at 8:30 to make the Cape May Express. The baggage master had closed his office at 7:30; and the telegrapher proved to have gone off duty at eight, chancing the storm rather than be stranded half the night in the station. Neither, it seemed, had the jitney drivers observed anything; knowing the slimness of business during wet weather, they had all left the station as soon as the storm had begun.

By no means, however, did Gilmore consider these meager results conclusive proof that Philip Nixon had not made the train. Considering the distance from the Marley farmhouse to Newfield, and the short time which Frank had had, the wonder was that the financier had succeeded at all in making his train. This lack of evidence merely indicated that there had not been left even a moment in which to purchase a ticket; and this very fact should be of assistance later. Some conductor on the train should be able to remember that passenger from Newfield who purchased one from him. Furthermore, it was altogether likely that in the darkness those few who were about the station had failed to notice the arrival.

At 8:25, exactly on schedule, the express upon which all of the detective's interest was centered, puffed into the station. For five minutes it laid over, waiting for connections with an Atlantic City train; and when it drew out, Gilmore was aboard, preparing to make exhaustive inquiries of all the train officials.

Gilmore was not dismayed by the fact that the train was a commuters' train, predominating in male passengers—which was bound to make the investigation more difficult. Setting out from the front car, he resolutely pressed his quest, asking questions in each car, regarding both the financier and his possible companion, Stirling; and each time he produced the former's picture. But it made no impression upon the first few trainmen he questioned; they could not recall having sold its original a ticket on the past Monday night. Yet all assured the detective that had they done so, they would have remembered.

Not till twenty minutes had passed, and Gilmore had reached the car next to the last, did he discover what he sought. The trainman was a dull-featured man, who listened

to the explanation of his quest with something approaching apathy. He listlessly informed the detective that he had
been in charge of the same car on the past Monday night;
yet, when the financier's picture was produced, he recognized it. "Yes, I remember this man," he replied. "As you
say, he got on at Newfield, and he didn't have a ticket. I
had a dickens of a time getting change for a twenty-dollar
bill he gave me for the fare. The man he was with wanted
to pay his fare, but he wouldn't let him. So I had to change
the bill, and, of course, I gave him the usual receipt."

The importance of insignificant items! Had Nixon
pocketed that receipt, instead of throwing it away as he
must have done, for it had not been found on him, Gilmore would have known from the very beginning that he
had been on the train. Instead, it had taken him fully five
days to discover this fact for himself.

"So there was a man with him?" he queried eagerly.

"Yes, there was—and I'll tell you how else I know. When
1 saw they were together, I thought that he'd just got on
the train, too, like his friend. But he explained that he got
on at Camden, and then I remembered he'd already paid."

"Can you describe him for me? Do you think you would
know him if you saw him again?"

But it seemed that the trainman could not be certain
about the appearance of Nixon's companion. That he had
been large, and something of the same build as the financier himself, he was certain; but as to his features, the
color of his hair, or his age, he had formed no impression.
His only mental picture was one of size, and though he
believed he would recognize a picture of the man, there
was little he had noted that he could pass on. He certainly
could not recall the color of his coat. Neither did he know
what had happened afterward to Mr. Nixon or his companion, as he had no further occasion to observe either
of them. Whether they had both left their seats, to go

through the last car to the rear of the train, whether the financier's companion had been alone after such an excursion, and had gone all the way to Cape May, the train official could not say. While it was true that the train had halted at Oldroyd, it had done so at the request of no passenger in his car; hence, he could see no other conclusion, but that both had reached the shore.

It was exactly nine o'clock when Gilmore gave up questioning him and entered the last car. But though there remained the trainman of the smoker to be questioned, he hurried through its length to the rear platform; there was something more important first, to occupy his attention.

He had proven, then, that Philip Nixon had been aboard this train. It was also settled, beyond a reasonable doubt, that from this rear platform, the financier had met his death at one minute after nine. At the exact moment that the express was flying past the Marley farmhouse, he had been struck from behind and thrown from it. That, he now realized, was the significance of the broken watch. The shock of the fall had made it a mute witness to the exact moment of the crime. If the 9:55 train passed this spot at 11:08, the 7:45 could have done so about 9:01. Gilmore upbraided himself for having failed to read its message aright much earlier than this late hour.

There remained only a minute to test the accuracy of his belated deduction. The train, shrieking its piercing whistle, rattled on, raising a breeze that ruffled Gilmore's hair. How black it was! Night, descending like a mantle of mist, concealed everything but the shadowy, wraithlike outlines of the countryside. Except for the deafening clatter of the turning wheels, it was absolutely deserted and still. It seemed incredible that Nixon had met his death here, with the car behind filled with possible witnesses. The detective could picture the scene—the financier leaning naturally over the rear rail, and a blow from behind

while his back was turned; and then his murderer calmly
reentering the car and taking a seat. Unobservant travelers
would have seen nothing amiss in two men strolling to
the rear of the car; neither would they have attached any
importance to the return of but a single man.

One minute after nine. There it was—the Marley farmhouse, deserted, barely visible in the obscure gloom, and
gone as quickly as the detective had seen it. That Nixon
should have been killed in that very spot was one of those
comparatively common but almost unbelievable coincidences that occur in life. But it had not been an important
coincidence; and Gilmore did not permit his mind to rest
on it long. It had not aided him in his investigations in
any manner; it had merely brought him into contact with
the Marley family a day or so earlier than, inevitably, the
bank notes would have done.

What was more important was the question of the
weapon used by the murderer. For the first time since the
investigation began, this matter became a vital one. As
long as there was the theory of a crime, completed in the
financier's limousine, it had been immaterial; any weapon
would have sufficed for the striking of the actual blow.
But here, the criminal must have acted as the opportunity
offered, on the spur of the moment. Unless he had carried
a cane—or a heavy umbrella in the rain—the weapon must
have been picked up during the passage through the car. A
workman's tool, perhaps a wrench, something that could
be found in the rear vestibule of the car. And if such a
weapon were used, and the murderer threw it away afterward—its absence would perhaps have been noticed.

The idea was worth a brief search, at any rate. Reentering the car, Gilmore found the enclosed vestibule almost at the doorway. On the seat was a red flag with its
heavy wooden staff, a plausible weapon in itself, and the
conductor's records. Three red lamps underneath partially

concealed a chest which he drew out. While it was not a custom to carry tools thus loosely, but rather in a locked tool box, there was a chance that some stray irons would here be found. And he was right; within were some heavy emergency implements, a crowbar and a wrench. Whether all were there that should have been there, could only be learned, however, by questioning the trainmen.

He rose from his examination to find himself the object of close scrutiny by a uniformed official.

"What the devil do you think you're doing in there?" came the morose demand.

The speaker was young, with some claims to good looks, except for the startling pasty whiteness of his features and the beady sharpness of the eyes. Gilmore's appearance seemed to have unnecessarily disturbed him; he stood challengingly forward, his attitude was one of truculence, and his manner one of bluster.

The detective parried the question with another.

"Are you the brakeman of this car?"

"Yes, I am," the other replied with a trace of insolence. "What about it? You haven't got any right in this room . . ."

"Perhaps not," Gilmore said evenly. "I was merely wondering whether you remember the trip you made last Monday night—the night of the storm—and whether afterward, you missed anything from here. . . ."

In spite of himself, the man was startled at the question; and he was not able to conceal the fact.

"Missed anything? What in the world do you mean by that?"

"Possibly an iron bar from this chest," the detective went on. "An iron bar or some other implement that could be used to strike a person on the head and kill him."

He had made this unusual statement for the very purpose of noting the other's reaction. To one ignorant of the situation, its strangeness should have occasioned wonderment as to its possible meaning. But the brakeman seemed to have no doubt as to its interpretation. Instead, the words caught him unawares; he recovered from a sudden, curious distress only with an effort. And when he replied, his voice had a tremor in it.

"No, I haven't been missing a thing from here," he said. And recalling too late that he could hardly possess such information offhand, he added hastily, "I'd have to look; but why should anyone bother with the stuff that's in here?"

Gilmore smiled at the success of the ruse, which had made him the aggressor.

"I thought perhaps you could tell me that. You see, I have an idea that a passenger might have taken something for a use for which it was never intended . . ."

Again, the reaction was hardly one of surprise; the brake-man knew as well as he, to what he referred. The detective's immediate intuition, that he had some knowledge he was concealing, was verified.

"No," came the sullen reply, "I can't tell you anything. I don't even know what you're talking about."

"Perhaps, then, you might have observed two gentlemen walking through your car last Monday night, to the rear platform . . . and one of them come back, alone, a little later. . . . As this is your room, I can hardly see how you could have failed to notice them, as they passed."

The brakeman's face became whiter than it had been before.

"Well, I didn't," came his vehement disclaimer. "Do you think I've nothing better to do than watch people parade up and down the car? Say"—and for a moment he seemed to have regained his control—"what business is it of yours, anyway?"

"I'm a detective,"—Gilmore put all the force and command he possessed into the explanation—"investigating the murder that occurred on Monday night, of the body that was found on the tracks. Well, that body was thrown from the platform of this car!"

Even before he had finished, he knew he had failed.

"If it was," said the other antagonistically, "I don't know a thing about it. You don't think, if I did, that I'd keep it to myself? Why wouldn't I have come to you about it?"

The detective wished he could answer that question. Why was the man lying throughout the inquisition and concealing what he knew? Gilmore would have given anything to have been able to compel the truth from him; but he was in no position to accuse him of falsifying.

"Well, I may have been mistaken," he replied, retiring with the best grace he could command, "but we have to make certain of these things, you understand. Now, if you'll just give me your name and address . . ."

"What do you want to know that for?"

Having temporarily won the foray, the speaker's tone was heavy with insolence and defiance.

"In case I might have to get in touch with you. Look here, if you don't know anything, you haven't anything to hide, have you?"

The other looked apprehensive again, as though he feared his inquisitor would gain a wrong impression.

"No, sure I haven't. Didn't I tell you that already?"

And he succumbed to Gilmore's insistence. It seemed that he was Ralph Burke of 3812 Mallory Street, in West Philadelphia; that he lived alone in bachelor apartments and that he did not come on duty until six o'clock in the evening. Thus, he worked on the night shift, returning home at five o'clock in the morning and going out at perhaps four in the afternoon.

By the time the detective had completed his catechism it was 9:20 and the train approached Oldroyd. By disembarking there, Gilmore could catch a Philadelphia bound train that reached Oldroyd fourteen minutes later, whereas at the shore he would have missed it, and hence would have had to wait for the midnight train. Accordingly, at his request, the brakeman gave the necessary signal for the express to stop at the station. Two questions occupied the detective's mind as he descended to the platform. First, what had Ralph Burke seen? Second, why was he silent? Whether he had been a witness of the actual murder, or had merely found an instrument missing and had surmised to what use it had been put, Gilmore did not know. Perhaps he had merely observed the criminal reenter the car— and afterward, on learning of the body on the tracks, had put two and two together. That seemed likely; but why should he have kept his information to himself? Was he attempting to protect the criminal? Was he being paid to keep his mouth shut?—in which case the murderer had a dangerous witness to his deed. Or was Burke deriving some other unknown advantage?

One thing, Gilmore resolved with a grim expression of determination; before Monday had passed, he would find some means of making the brakeman tell what he knew. In fact, before that day was finished, he would compel three to speak and speak the truth—Burke, Donald Gardiner and Russell Stirling.

18
CONFESSION IS GOOD FOR THE SOUL

As though Gilmore's decision of Saturday night had reached one of the people it concerned, upon his arrival at Headquarters on Monday morning, he was greeted with the information that Donald Gardiner and a young lady were waiting to see him. From behind the morning paper, Captain Thomas informed him that they had sought to communicate with him while he was out on Saturday; and failing that, had arranged to come in this morning, to speak to him.

"It looks like something important," he said. "You'd better go in to see them now. When you're finished, I've something to show you that I think you'll find interesting."

As the detective entered the office into which they had been shown, he sensed a quality of tenseness and anxiety in the atmosphere. The secretary, appearing somewhat nervous, nevertheless looked relieved, as Gilmore appeared. Eleanor Nixon, in austere black, waited with her hands folded in her lap, pale but composed. The tragedy with which she had recently been visited still haunted the expressive eyes, but in the vigorous, severe poise which mourning gave her, he recognized more than ever the positive, magisterial qualities of her father.

"You wanted to see me?" They were his only words of greeting. It would be wiser, he decided, to go warily and give no indication of his knowledge regarding the secretary until he had learned the intentions of his visitors.

"Yes, we did, Gilmore—at least, I did, and Miss Nixon came to learn how your investigations were progressing." The young man plunged without hesitation into the purpose of his call. "You suspect me of having a hand in the death of Mr. Nixon?"

The words were an accusation rather than a question, but the detective successfully feigned surprise.

"What makes you think that, Gardiner? What reason have I for suspecting you?"

"That's what I would like to know, but there's surely something behind your behavior. For the last few days, you've had some one on my trail wherever I go. You've been to the offices to ask questions about me. And Mrs. Phipps told me all about my 'dear friend from out of town' who searched my room while leaving a note of greeting."

The detective permitted himself a slight smile that Mrs. Phipps had finally succumbed to her desire to talk.

"That is a rather dangerous proceeding, Mr. Gilmore," the girl broke in sharply. "You had no right to break into anyone's private quarters without a search warrant."

Gilmore, unperturbed, shrugged his shoulders sorrowfully. "It was all in your interests, Miss Nixon. After all, what else am I to do when people conceal the truth from me . . . as you have with regard to the quarrel Mr. Gardiner had with your father."

The statement did not surprise Eleanor Nixon, but it brought her abruptly to a realization of the detective's advantage.

"Yes," she said hastily, "Bennett admitted to me on Saturday that he had told you of that. Knowing that you had that information and were investigating, Donald brought us here today. We have decided that it would have been far wiser to have informed you of everything in the beginning."

"It's not too late now, to do so, Miss Nixon," Gilmore reprimanded, "but your silence and Mr. Gardiner's has greatly hampered my investigations. May I remind you that that is always even a more dangerous proceeding?"

"Eleanor was merely trying to protect me," the secretary said fervently. "Knowing that you had overheard her quarrel with Mr. Nixon, of which I was the subject, she was afraid that if you learned that I had gone immediately afterward to remonstrate with Mr. Nixon, you would suspect me. You see," he added with a touch of sadness, "my past was the cause of our quarrel—and it can hardly bear investigation."

A swift, haggard shadow crossed his eyes, and Eleanor swiftly put her hand out toward him.

"Donald presents it in a much worse light than it really deserves. You were bound to learn of it, Mr. Gilmore . . . and it would be better that you should learn of it from his own lips. If you will not pass judgment until you have the entire story . . ."

As she broke off with an appealing gesture, the detective indicated his willingness to hear Donald Gardiner's narrative. The developments that had brought them both to him, prepared to be frank, assured him that what he now would learn could be believed. Eleanor had intended nothing criminal by her concealment of vital facts; she had merely desired to protect the secretary. But only because of Bennett's breach of faith had they both decided to volunteer any information.

Once more the detective listened to the already familiar story of the secretary's pampered life, and ungovernable temper, of his regard for Ella Denby and the unfortunate quarrel resulting in the death of his rival, of the prison term he had served and the opportunity he had taken to begin his wasted life anew. In telling it, the secretary was not sparing in criticism of his own folly; for the tragedy that had all but blighted his life he blamed no one but himself. It was the fault of his own uncurbed desires, he said, that led up to the tragedy. The unfortunate encounter in the Astor Hotel had been accidental; but the blow that sent his rival against the andirons in the fireplace, though aroused by an insulting remark, had been the result of blind anger.

"I killed him, Gilmore," said the secretary in a heavy voice, "I admit that; and I know there's no justification for it. Farrell had been drinking and was in an unpleasant frame of mind. When he insulted the girl I foolishly thought so much of, my control snapped for a moment, and I struck him a terrific blow across the jaw. When I realized what I had done, he was lying against the irons, his head broken in.

"That's the truth of it, I'll take an oath on it. The prosecution claimed at the trial that I struck Farrell across the head with one of the irons. The fingerprints found on the bar he had struck in falling were placed there when I leaned upon it, as I tried to revive him. . . . I suppose that for my folly, I deserved everything, even those awful days of the trial with people listening hungrily to the scandal about me, the fast life I led, the questionable people with whom I traveled, the women I knew. It was all coming to me for killing that man; but I never intended to do it and murder was furthest from my mind."

Earnestly Gardiner continued his story, telling the detective of the trial and the sentence he served, and reverting to his present determination to make up for his previous failure. At no time did his straightforward account falter, nor vary from the facts Gilmore had learned from Captain Fremont; if anything, the secretary too strongly

condemned himself, even more so than the woman responsible for his difficulties had done. Unaware that Gilmore
already knew the story, it would have been an easy matter
to fabricate one; and the fact that he did not do so seemed
to the detective a perfect test of its truth. It was also
indicative of Gardiner's present sincerity and good faith.

Nor was the story unknown to Eleanor; throughout its
narration her attention was centered only on Gilmore's
reaction to it. When Gardiner had finished, the detective
turned to her.

"You were ignorant of these facts, Miss Nixon," he
said, "a week ago when we both met in your father's office.
When did you learn them?"

"Immediately after I quarreled with Dad," the girl replied. "You remember, I promised him that I would not go
out with Donald until he came back and told me of them.
But I did not say that I would not talk to him. It was then
I learned from his own lips the story of Donald's unfortunate affair. . . ."

As she spoke, Gilmore saw the motive he had attributed
to Gardiner for having killed Philip Nixon disappear. For
if Eleanor Nixon knew Gardiner's secret—before Nixon
went to the shore, the secretary had nothing further to
lose, regardless of how the girl accepted the information.
For, if she took her parent's viewpoint, the harm was already done; and if she viewed the story in an opposite
light, it was immaterial what Nixon told her afterward.

"It was the quarrel that Eleanor had with Mr. Nixon,
that sent me to his home to see him," Donald broke in. "I
wanted to talk the matter over with him. As he had left the
office at half past two, before I had the opportunity, I had
to go to Bryn Mawr. Unfortunately, Mr. Nixon considered me presumptuous and it only made him more furious.
You see,"—a twisted smile played about his lips—"that I
should love his daughter, after my past, was unpardonable

to him. In the end, I lost my temper, and we had the quarrel that Bennett told you about."

"Father judged Donald most unfairly, Mr. Gilmore," said the girl as Gardiner had paused. "But surely you believe this . . . that Donald would never have been guilty of a crime—like murder . . . ? What happened was merely a misfortune that might have happened to anyone, an accident that is now gone and over with."

The detective did not need the sudden appeal in her voice, nor Gardiner's grateful glance, to tell him that she at least had confidence in the secretary and had forgiven him, if there was anything that needed forgiveness. He smiled into her anxious eyes.

"Do you believe that, Miss Nixon?" he asked.

"I do," was her serene reply, "and I have much more to lose than you, by it. For, as soon as possible, we shall be engaged; and if I have been deceived, I shall be marrying a murderer. You simply risk the possibility of failing in this case."

"That's convincing enough to me," the detective said, "but there are other matters requiring explanations, about which nothing has yet been said. Mr. Gardiner went to Cape May last Monday night, and yet swore to me that he had not left the house where he is living."

From the questioning look on Eleanor Nixon's face, it was evident that not even she knew this fact. Gardiner flushed, suddenly abashed; but there was nothing of apprehension or nervousness in his manner.

"You are right, Gilmore," he admitted, "I did make the trip, but I've told no one, not even Eleanor, of it. I kept it from you because I didn't believe you knew much of this matter between Eleanor and myself; and since it had no bearing on Mr. Nixon's death, I could see no necessity for enlightening you about it. It could not possibly concern you. And I didn't tell Eleanor, because nothing came of the journey after I did take it."

"What reason did you have for following Mr. Nixon to the shore?"

"It was on account of that damnable quarrel. I regretted very much that it had occurred, as soon as I had time to get back to my rooms and cool down. I would have given anything if it had never occurred. I had some work to do for the office, but I found it impossible to concentrate on it; the quarrel preyed on my mind so. After all, from his point of view, Mr. Nixon was justified and I couldn't afford to antagonize him; I owed him much for his kindness to me when I was practically down and out. It seemed to me that I could best straighten out matters all around if I apologized, even if it meant traveling to Cape May to do so. That, at least, was action; and I was too distressed to sit still."

"But you told Mrs. Phipps that you were staying in all evening to do some work for the office," Gilmore reminded him.

"When I said that, I had every intention of doing so; but I could not resist the urge to drop everything I was doing, and go out. . . ."

"What time did you leave?"

The secretary hesitated an instant. "It must have been a little before seven," he replied at length. "I got home about half past six, and I don't suppose I stayed in my room very long. At any rate, I left early enough to get over to Camden in time to make the seven-forty-five express to Cape May."

"Did Mrs. Phipps see you leave?" Gilmore queried.

"I don't suppose she did—at least, I didn't notice her anywhere around; I was too occupied with the idea as I came downstairs, and in too much of a hurry besides. Not until I was already on the train did I begin to realize that an apology was not likely to do much good; and I found myself doubting the wisdom of the move. . . ."

Another of the few remaining strands of the case against Donald Gardiner was gone. What had appeared to be a carefully prepared alibi, created for the purpose of masking his journey to the shore, was merely an alibi woven together by the circumstances of the case. Gilmore nodded to the young man to continue.

"The further I went, the less the plan appealed to me. After all, instead of appreciating my intention, Mr. Nixon might have considered it another piece of impertinence. In that case, there was bound to be another scene; and a second argument would do much harm to both Eleanor and myself. Perhaps it would be better to keep out of the way until Mr. Nixon had an opportunity to calm down a bit and reflect. I couldn't afford to antagonize him further.

"You see by what process I had changed my mind. By the time I had reached the shore, I had decided to take the next train back to Philadelphia and let Philip Nixon make the next move. Thus, I could tell my position exactly and gauge the situation from it. And as I was too late to catch any earlier train back to the city—you see, I didn't arrive till it was almost nine-forty—I had to wait for the midnight train."

It was all so reasonable and straightforward that Gilmore could see no cause for doubting it. Gardiner's candor had favorably impressed him; already persuaded by what had preceded, he found all his previous suspicions vanishing before the frankness of the confession. Yet he had better first ask a few questions.

"You say that you had determined to do nothing until Mr. Nixon indicated his stand?" he queried. "Didn't you even attempt to communicate with him at the shore?"

The reply was in the negative; the secretary had done nothing but wait about the Cape May station for the midnight train.

Gilmore bent forward as he put the next question, the most vital point in the entire case.

"Were you aware, Gardiner, that Mr. Nixon had boarded the same shore-bound train at Newfield, and that he had previously arranged to join Russell Stirling there on the seven-forty-five?"

Before he had finished, the young man's intense astonishment—too genuine to be the result of acting—had given him his reply. Gardiner earnestly assured him that he knew nothing of it, nor of any appointment that his employer may have made with the broker. All the information that he possessed regarding Stirling he had given to the detective when questioned at the American Motors offices. During the journey to the shore, he had seen nothing of Nixon or Stirling, and had never left his seat.

The interview was brought to a close when the girl, an attentive listener to the concluding portion of Gardiner's story, rose to thank the detective for his kindness and courtesy.

"There has been a purpose behind my civility, Miss Nixon," Gilmore said. "First, of course, I had to make certain that what I was learning was the truth. But there is also another matter—more difficult to discuss. I am daring to ask a favor in return for what little service I have been able to do for you, in seeking the man responsible for your father's death."

The financier's daughter paused, puzzled by his serious mien.

"A favor, Mr. Gilmore? I should be pleased to do anything within reason to show my appreciation."

For a moment, Gilmore paused awkwardly, as though not certain how to begin, before he made the plunge. "Miss

Nixon, there is a girl in difficulty, who is badly in need
of such assistance and comfort as you could give her . . ."

"A girl in difficulties, Mr. Gilmore?" She was clearly
baffled by his unexpected words.

"Yes—her name is Martha Marley. She had had little
experience," Gilmore said warmly, "and knew almost nothing of the troubles that might follow any indiscretion. At
least, she hardly comprehended the full consequences of
them; so you see, the blame hardly lies with her. She knew
your father well, Miss Nixon."

His eyes met those of the girl. She understood now;
and though she made no remark, he read in them sympa-
thy and distress, as well as wonderment.

"I'm certain your father would have never shirked the
responsibility that properly belongs to him. In fact, one
of the purposes of his journey to Cape May was to help
Miss Marley. I believe I can be just as certain that you will
not fail either; and I only ask for a promise that she will
receive your attention. . . ."

And that, as the saying is, was that. Another suspect, who
proved to be unconnected with the enigma he was attempting to solve, was eliminated. With a feeling of loss, Gilmore suddenly realized that, except for the trainman,
Burke, as a possible witness, Russell Stirling alone remained. And if he also proved a "false alarm," only a blank
wall remained. His eventual quarry must, of necessity, be
the broker, but he could make no error about it. Before he
could arrest Stirling, every clue must be in his hands, lest
the wily one escape. For that reason, Ralph Burke must
be interviewed before he approached the brokerage office
of Sanburg, Pressman & Co.; if he prepared himself with
the vital information which he believed the trainman possessed, there was small hope that Stirling could evade him.

In the outer, main office, as Gilmore returned to it, he found Rankin with Captain Thomas, both perusing the same item in the morning paper. It was at once evident that his colleague was aroused by something, for he seized the paper and approached Gilmore swiftly.

"You said you might have some information that would interest me," the detective began to Thomas, when Rankin interrupted him.

"Take a look at this, Gilmore," he cried, excitedly, "Thomas found it while he was reading the paper. . . ."

The other detective speedily located the spot Rankin had indicated. It was merely a little item, not more than five lines in length, in the lower right-hand corner of the morning *Ledger,* almost at the bottom of the narrow column marked "Personal":

"Unless I receive a call before three o'clock this afternoon at 3812 Mallory St. Apt. C2, from the gentleman whose unusual behavior I noted on the 7:45 Cape May train, last Monday night, his description will be reported to certain authorities. This is the last time I will wait."

The address was that of the trainman of the last car on the 7:45 express. So that was the explanation of Burke's truculent and taciturn behavior! As Gilmore had already deduced, he had observed what occurred on the platform of the car of which he had charge—if not the actual murder, then at least the return of the murderer; and instead of reporting it to the police, he had hoped to make something out of his information by attempting to blackmail him. But ignorant of the criminal's identity, and not having dared to accost him at the time, he could only make use of this method of advertising, in hopes of alarming him into appearing. And the detective's unexpected and disturbing questions on the train had caused Burke himself to become apprehensive, and seek immediate results from his scheme.

"I noticed the first one last Wednesday evening," Thomas was observing, "but it didn't impress me, because I wasn't familiar with the case or what you've since found out about Nixon being on the seven-forty-five. It was inserted each day afterward, and each item was a little more anxious than the last. . . . On Saturday, I caught on to it, but I didn't have a chance to tell you till today."

"Since last Wednesday, and you didn't say a word . . . ?" the detective exclaimed impatiently, though it was doubtful whether even he would have grasped the significance of the insert, so early in the case. "Have you any back numbers of the paper here?"

Luckily the Captain was able to produce from his desk three papers, covering the three previous days; he had been saving them to work out the cross-word puzzles. In their respective advertising sections, he had no difficulty in discovering what he sought. Each item he located was unsigned; and except, as Thomas had observed, that the first were in less threatening terms, were written in the same tenor. All of them requested "the gentlemen whose behavior on the 7:45 express had attracted attention" to communicate with the writer at once, though in the last two the request had become a demand, and in that of the present day there was also the added promise of communicating with the authorities.

If the murderer saw these threatening messages, could he afford to disregard their menacing terms? If the detective was right, and Stirling was the man he was after, the broker dared not fail to heed them. He would be putting

his own head in the noose, if he permitted an actual witness to the crime to report to the authorities a description
of the criminal which they would be able to connect with
him. In fact, the same reasoning held true of anyone else
possibly concerned with the case, whose appearance was
already known to the police. Whether the broker or another was the culpable one, they would be bound to recognize
him from the conductor's observations. Only if he were
some one Gilmore had not yet encountered could he dare
to lay low.

It followed, then, that if the criminal saw the advertisement, Burke would today receive a visitor. Driven from
cover, he would come either to pay the price demanded for
the conductor's silence, or to silence in his own desperate
way the only witness to his deed. In either case, before
three o'clock that day he would be found at 3812 Mallory Street, open to capture, if Gilmore but acted swiftly enough. The conductor could be compelled to assist
Rankin and himself to set a trap; into it, the man they
sought would walk, red-handed, his very arrival an admission of his guilt.

It was almost noon, and the alarming idea that his quarry might already have made his visit, caused the detective
to toss aside the papers.

"Rankin! You get the meaning of this? There might be
a meeting on account of this article at Burke's apartment
. . . and it's likely to end in tragedy. Have you your car
handy?"

The younger man had; it was downstairs in the City
Hall Courtyard.

"Will you go down and get it going?" Gilmore continued. "We want to be present at the meeting, and we're going to have to travel fast if we don't want to be late. . . ."

Rankin, quick to comprehend the possibilities of the
situation, had the machine running and drawn up before

the archway leading to West Market Street when Gilmore joined him. As the latter entered the car, an inexplicable premonition of impending evil seized him. It was a foreboding presentiment that he could neither define nor explain, but he was painfully aware of its existence. The conductor's message was a challenge that had, since dawn, been in the paper to attract the murderer's attention. Gilmore could hardly resist putting his anxiety into words.

"You know the address, Rankin. . . . Never mind the traffic and get there fast. This may be unnecessary, but I'll never forgive myself if we prove to be right—and we didn't act quickly enough. . . ."

The other nodded his understanding, as the car swung into the engulfing traffic of Penn Square. Rankin skillfully engineered the turn between the crossing pedestrians and the swift-moving line of machines. The light at Broad Street, at the base of City Hall, was a bright red; but disregarding it and the traffic officer's signal, he turned at the intersection. A whistle appeared in the officer's hand; but Gilmore leaned out and, in evident recognition, the whistle disappeared.

At Walnut Street, with the signal still against them, they swerved to the right in the direction of West Philadelphia. A stout elderly lady, whose arms were filled with packages, started to cross in front of them; at the sound of Rankin's horn, she came to a complete halt exactly in the middle of the street. By a swift turn of the wheel, the detective barely avoided her, but her packages flew into a heap and she shrieked uncomplimentary things after them.

A jam of trollies and machines blocked them momentarily at the corner of Fifteenth and Walnut streets; and even the delay of a moment served to increase Gilmore's apprehensions. Once they were upon their way again, he remarked to Rankin:

"You had better go down Sixteenth to Pine, as we have to go out that way anyhow. There's less traffic and we'll make better time."

To turn left on Sixteenth Street was bucking traffic, but Rankin obeyed. They encountered no officers, but were the object of much amazement on the part of northbound traffic. Pine Street, at which a right turn was made, was narrower than Walnut; but the lesser number of cars and the absence of trolley tracks enabled Rankin to increase even the astonishing speed he was making through city streets. Amid the sounds of a raucous horn, the intersecting streets flew by at a rate that would have brought his passenger's heart to his mouth.

At Twenty-third Street Rankin turned south again, to South Street, and thence over the South Street Bridge and the Schuylkill River. In West Philadelphia he merely skirted the southernmost portion of the University of Pennsylvania campus; and after another few moments of travel, at every bit of speed of which the car was capable, they had arrived at their destination.

Number 3812 Mallory Street was a small apartment house, in a narrow dingy avenue of imperfectly set cobblestones, the entire length of which was devoid of either shrubbery or yards of any size. The building was four stories high, of dull brown brick, just such a dwelling as might be expected of a man in the trainman's circumstances. Before an entrance, lacking ornamentation of any sort, a baby coach stood and several children played.

Before the machine had been drawn up at the curb, Gilmore was out of it and into the doorway. A plain hallway, with a series of steep stairs, greeted him. Pausing only to verify Burke's address—Apartment C2—at the letter boxes in the vestibule, he took the steps three at a time. Rankin was close behind him; the combined clatter

of their feet brought to the door a housewife in apron from
a second-floor apartment. She stared in astonishment at
the sight of two men dashing past her, up the next flight,
and then followed them.

At the locked door of Ralph Burke's room, Gilmore
knocked thunderously, but there was no reply. He repeated
the knock, this time reinforcing it with a deep command
that it be opened.

"Is it Mr. Burke you're wanting?" the woman volunteered. "He ought to be in now. Generally, he don't get up
till a little before this hour, and I didn't see 'im go out, so
it's funny he doesn't answer."

In the silence that followed her statement, Gilmore
heard a sound within. It was faint, barely audible—like
the sound of a foot placed with infinite caution upon the
floor. Though he listened intently, it was not repeated;
but an instant later, there followed a faint scrape and then
a more audible squeak.

"Rankin—did you hear that?" Anxiously the detective
turned to his companion. "That squeak was a window
opening. . . . Is there any other way of getting in the
apartment besides the front door, madam?"

The woman had difficulty in finding her tongue. "You
can get in the back," she said finally, "where the children
play, by way of the fire escapes, but who in the world is
going to use that, when . . ."

"He's getting out that way," Gilmore exclaimed, cutting her short. "You're quicker than I am, Rankin; see if
you can beat him to it. I hardly think you will, but run
like mad. . . ."

But the younger detective had started as soon as the
woman had begun to reply to the question; and when Gilmore had finished his instructions, he was at the bottom of
the stairs, so that the last words were shouted at him. The
detective's most calamitous presentiment of evil appeared

to have been justified, and basically correct. Wisely, in the agonizing moment of waiting that followed, Gilmore refrained from dwelling upon the significance of that locked door and the sound of that opening window.

Presently, from within, there came again a scraping, followed by distinct footsteps. Then the lock clicked and Rankin stood in the doorway. And from the look on his face, Gilmore knew that they were just too late to prevent a tragedy.

19
DEATH STALKS THE TRAIL

"There was no one in sight," Rankin said brusquely, "either in the back yard or on the fire escapes, when I got around. But the window was open and there's no doubt that he got away through that."

The two detectives, with the door of the apartment closed behind them, surveyed the scene before them. The room in which they stood was obviously the living room and bedroom combined. Simply furnished, a small couch pushed back against a huge closet door, an oblong table with several pine chairs drawn up toward it, one of which was upset, an armchair and a rug completed the equipment. All of it was light, and easily movable, so that at night, it could make way for the Murphy bed which the closet contained. Two doors opened into the remaining chambers of the suite; and on the wall were suggestive prints, in lurid colors.

The adjoining rooms were a bathroom with the usual toilet accouterments—and a tiny kitchen. The latter contained a miniature stove, a cupboard for storing groceries, an icebox and a table, all of it evidence that Burke prepared his own meals. A telephone rested on the floor—the telephone, thought Gilmore, which its owner had probably used to make the appointment which was to end so fatally for himself.

From the window could be seen the route taken by the escaping criminal. The rear of the apartment building was constructed in the form of a letter H, in which the narrow courtyard that divided the two wings extended back to a wooden fence skirting a street in the rear. Flimsy fire escapes clung precariously to the walls in successive tiers, a row of them on each wing; the bottom tier was manipulated by weights, and generally above the ground. But the ground steps on the side occupied by Burke's apartment had been lowered to the earth. Clothes hung from lines across the upper reaches of the court; and the view permitted from the windows of the rooms opposite impressed upon Gilmore the possibility of witnesses having seen the murderer's flight, on this side.

The trainman's body lay sprawled awkwardly on the floor. From the door it was well-nigh invisible, concealed by the oblong table; only the feet protruded. Not until the two detectives had moved farther into the room did they see that it lay face downward, an outstretched arm covering the gaping wound in the head. The other arm had collapsed under the body, in a position that would have been painful except for the fact that life seemed extinct.

"I'm afraid it's all over with him," Gilmore said, and he could hardly recognize his own voice, "but we've got to make sure of it. Get Dr. Sackett, Rankin—the telephone's in the next room. . . ."

The position of the body behind the table and the upset chair made it easy for him to visualize the scene that led up to the tragedy. Two chairs had been drawn up to the table, as though their occupants had been conferring, the criminal seated nearest the apartment entrance. Burke, having just completed his dressing when his visitor had arrived, must have done most of the talking; Gilmore could picture him, making demands, threatening to make public his knowledge unless he was paid for his silence. Apparently, the other had acquiesced to the blackmail—perhaps, even, feigning an apprehension he did not feel, until the brakeman, assured that he had the upper hand, relaxed his guard. At a moment when Burke was bending over the table, and not watching, his visitor had risen and dealt the single terrific blow. The overturned chair attested to the conductor's vain effort to avoid it; he was too late to escape the sweep that silenced him forever.

There was, of course, no weapon to be found; whatever weapon the criminal had used to commit the crime, he would not have consciously left it for the police to discover. Even when Gilmore's startling knock had reverberated upon the door, he had managed to keep his head and took the weapon with him. In fact, his flight had been masterly, with the qualities of a strategic retreat.

Rankin's return from the kitchen interrupted the trend of his colleague's thoughts.

"Couldn't get Dr. Sackett," he reported. "Headquarters says he's out of town and there's no one else around that will do."

Gilmore swore softly to himself; he didn't want a strange doctor puttering about, to whom everything would have to be explained.

"Try to get hold of Dr. Curtiss, Tommy," he instructed. "He knows his business and, besides, he is already acquainted with many facts of the case. . . . I have his address here, somewhere."

He found what he sought and Rankin was just about to carry out the request, when Gilmore stopped him.

"And after that, call Stirling to see whether he is at his office. He couldn't possibly have gotten back there yet as we've hardly been here fifteen minutes. . . . And then you might hunt up Jenks—I haven't taken him off Gardiner's trail yet. Find out where Gardiner was. He left me not more than ten minutes before we started out and I've practically eliminated him; still, it's best to make sure. I've plenty to occupy me here."

Within a few moments, Rankin again returned, with the information that Dr. Curtiss was out, but his housekeeper expected him back at any moment and would send him over.

"That's good enough," said Gilmore. "It'll give me a chance to search the room first. And what about Stirling?"

"He's also out. He left the office at about half past eleven, so the stenographer who answered the phone told me, and she couldn't say where he went. But she said he's expected back at one-thirty. . . ."

Gilmore's face lighted with satisfaction. "That's excellent," he replied. "Since we started out about ten minutes of twelve, Stirling must have been twenty minutes ahead of us; and he couldn't possibly have anticipated our discovery of the advertisement. . . ."

He paused as Rankin, indicating his assent, prepared to leave, to take up his assignment without delay; then he added:

"And if you'd stop at Headquarters and inform the morgue people, I think we'll be ready for them by the time they get here."

He waited till he heard his colleague's footsteps echoing down the stairs, before making a closer examination of the body. The wound that had been the cause of death was a deep one, extending from the temple along the right side of the head, more than an inch in width. On either side, the conductor's brown hair was matted with blood, but otherwise its flow reached only the sleeve of the arm covering the cut. Lifting the body on its side, gingerly, so as not to change its original position more than necessary, the detective made a survey of the under side.

To have been just too late to prevent a second tragedy, to have missed catching the murderer red-handed by
a single moment, was bitter medicine for Gilmore. His
quarry would never have entrusted such an errand to a
professional criminal and thus exposed himself to the very
type of blackmail this crime was calculated to prevent. He
had committed it himself, and had successfully escaped.
While the trainman had brought his death upon himself,
nevertheless, a second murder while Gilmore was in charge
of the case was hardly conducive of favorable comment by
his superiors. In all likelihood, before the day was over,
he would spend a somewhat uncomfortable half-hour in
Superintendent Wainwright's private quarters.

As Gilmore lowered the body to its original position,
the arm, twisted beneath it, was loosened and straightened
out. The detective had to stare twice at the dead hand,
thus far concealed, before he realized that it clutched a
longish black article with an almost viselike grip. Then
swiftly he seized it, and after an effort managed to free
the object.

It was a black check book, ten inches in length and
about three and a half inches wide, folded in the middle,
as bank check books customarily are to fit the owner's
pocket. The yellow checks within had no writing upon
them. But three of them were missing; and upon the stubs
in the book, which testified to this fact, had been scribbled the following notations in this respective order:

> April 1: To Self for H: $100.00
> May 1: To Self for H: $100.00
> June 1: To Self for H: $100.00

The book was a check book of the Boston City National Bank! And Russell Stirling had come from Boston! From
Rankin's investigation, Gilmore recalled that in Boston

had occurred the bucket-shop fiasco, which involved
Stirling, and which had sent his partner, Murray, to prison. The book had been brought along by the criminal,
ostensibly to meet Burke's exorbitant demands; and it must
have been over this book that the conductor bent when
the blow was struck. It was easy to see what had followed.
Subconsciously, his hand closed upon it, as he sought to
avoid the weapon; he swept it under him, as his hold had
tightened in death. And with Gilmore's knock on the door,
the criminal had had no time to recover the telltale article.
What good fortune this was! Regardless of the meaning of
the notations or "H's" identity (perhaps these had been
checks to Higgins, given for some as yet unknown reason),
there could be no doubt that "Self" indicated the broker. It would be the evidence of his own handwriting that
would convict him of his crime.

Carefully pocketing the precious clue, the detective
turned to an examination of Burke's chambers. Both the
living room and the kitchen were productive of ample
proof that the conductor was a bachelor; it was evident,
too, that no one came in to help "straighten out." The
icebox contained no ice; the pantry shelves held a prepon-
derance of canned foods, mainly vegetables and soups; the
rusted stove appeared not to have been used for weeks. In
the washstand in the bathroom, untouched, dirty dishes
were piled; and the Murphy bed, in the living-room closet,
though put away, had not been properly made up. The
dust that lay heavily upon the chairs and the table top
caused Gilmore to search warily, lest he destroy possible
fingerprint impressions that the murderer might carelessly
have left.

But nowhere did he find any note or memorandum made
by the conductor of what he had seen on the 7:45 express
on the night of the murder. He had written down no
description of his observations, but rather had trusted to

his memory to relate them when necessary; and the closed lips carried with them the precious knowledge he possessed. The few papers Gilmore unearthed in the cupboard proved to be bills; and the drawer in the table contained only a few letters indicating that Burke had a married sister in Chicago, who would have to be notified.

He had just convinced himself that his quarry had been too shrewd to have left any fingerprints, when a knock on the door indicated the arrival of Dr. Curtiss.

"I'm sorry to have been so long in coming," he began from the entrance, "especially as it seems something serious. There is a whole crowd of people congregated in the hallway of the apartment, talking it over. . . ."

He broke off suddenly, as he caught sight of the corpse. But he hesitated only for an instant, and once more Gilmore was impressed by his ability to lapse into the customary professional manner.

"I called you in," explained the detective, "because this death is connected with the murder of Mr. Nixon, and I didn't want an outsider who was likely to talk. . . ."

Dr. Curtiss asked no questions.

"If you have finished with the body there, Sergeant Gilmore, will you help me lift it to the couch? I can make an examination much more conveniently on a raised surface."

Together they carried the corpse, the arms of which now hung loosely, to the sofa. The physician made short work of his examination; and presently, rising from his knees, he said:

"There isn't much to report which you probably haven't discovered yourself. The man has been dead for perhaps an hour, I should say—as the result of a blow across the head with a heavy, roundish weapon."

"There's no possibility of suicide, doctor . . . ?"

The physician recognized Gilmore's grim jest, unsmilingly. "Not in this case, Sergeant, though I can see, as you've stated, a definite resemblance to Mr. Nixon's death. The blow was aimed more to the side in this case, but the cause of death is the same. The weapons used are probably of the same type—perhaps a piece of iron pipe, or a blackjack; so it is extremely likely that the same hand dealt them."

"Was there any possibility of the victim's having made an outcry?"

"I think it very doubtful whether there was even a struggle. If he permitted his murderer to stand above him, as he must have, to have so aimed his blow, an instantaneous paralysis of nerve centers must have followed."

As this merely corroborated his own conclusions, Gilmore made no reply, and the physician inquired as to his progress in the search for Nixon's murderer. They were discussing the case, Gilmore telling his companion as much as he considered wise, when the arrival of the morgue wagon interrupted them. Then Dr. Curtiss saw to the removal of the remains for which the detective was thankful, and took his departure immediately, after promising his services in case they should be needed further.

It was not until the death wagon had taken away its tragic burden that Gilmore turned his attention to the important problem of whether anyone had observed, and could describe for him, the murdered man's visitor. At least he would not have to search for his possible witnesses. Like wildfire, the news seemed to have spread until the sensation of it had brought out the entire neighborhood to crowd and stare before the door of 3812. Those who lived in the building were gathered in front of C2 itself, exchanging opinions in lowered tones, making conjectures as to what had occurred. Men, women and children, the detective found in the narrow third-floor hall, craning furiously each time the apartment door was opened, watching the doctor's movements and sighing deeply as the morgue people carried out the covered body.

By informing them in an apparently candid manner that their neighbor had been a suicide, the detective was able to ask questions which might have otherwise aroused suspicion. Out of a welter of gossip, too eagerly volunteered, and too outlandish for credence, it was surprising that he was able to cull any facts of importance. It appeared that Burke, besides living exclusively by himself, had held himself aloof, and refused to be sociable. A morose greeting was all he ever vouchsafed anyone; certainly, he never stopped to talk nor did he speak kindly to the children who lived below. This, with the outlandish hours he worked, "sleeping when decent people were up and doing, and out when they were in bed," had made him somewhat of a mystery. So far as was known, he had no relatives; nor had they ever seen him in the company of a woman, for which he had to blame, in all probability, his unpleasant and gloomy character.

Nowhere did Gilmore discover anyone who had seen the man he sought. At the end of an hour, in which he had questioned each of the dwellers separately, he found that he had drawn a blank. Mrs. Kelley, on the first-floor front, had been busy with her youngest, at the time in question; Mrs. Guilfoyle had been washing clothes in her apartment on the first-floor rear. Mrs. Patchin had known nothing until brought to the door by the footsteps of the detectives, echoing through the halls. Even the children, playing in front of the apartments, had been too engrossed in their games to have noticed the arrival of a stranger.

To learn whether anyone had witnessed the murderer's departure, the detective turned his attention to the inhabitants across the courtyard. And here, after several futile efforts, and becoming the recipient of innumerable family secrets, he succeeded in locating an apparently promising one.

In her kitchen, Mrs. Pretching, a stout, red-faced matron, who, it seemed, was troubled by rheumatism of the back, related to him what she had seen. While she had been hanging clothes from her rear window on a line stretched across the alley, some two and a half hours before, a man had climbed out of the apartment on the third floor opposite and hurried madly down the fire escapes. A moment after the descending gentleman was out of sight, another had appeared below, hastened up the steps and entered the same open window from which the first had come.

"Even then I thought there must be something wrong," she went on, "men running up and down the escapes like that; so I watched 'em both. But I couldn't get more 'n a look at either of 'em. . . ."

"This first man," Gilmore said eagerly, "the one that ran down the steps—can you describe him for me? Was he large or small?"

Mrs. Pretching could describe him and did. The man had been rather large, but she refused to say he was as stout as Gilmore had gathered Stirling to be from Rankin's description. Over his suit, which she had not noticed, he had been wearing a blue summer coat, which had flown behind him like a tail as he hastened down the stairs. A cap of grayish hue had rested on his head and he carried a heavy cane, "like you see some of the sports carry down at Atlantic City."

"That's excellent!" Gilmore said. "Dark blue coat, gray cap and heavy cane. Did you notice what kind of a head the cane had . . . ?"

The woman replied in the negative; the unnecessary luxuries of men she knew little about, and a cane was just a cane to her.

"You haven't said anything about his looks, Mrs. Pretch-ing," the detective went on. "Surely such an observant housewife as you must have noticed his features at once."

"Now that's the one thing I'm afraid I can't say much about," was the reply, "His face was sort of hidden deep down in his coat collar, and I couldn't get a good look at 'im. But I got an idea he was wearing a mustache."

"A mustache? Are you certain of that?"

Stirling had no mustache; the woman must be mistak-en, then, in her impression. The broker would not, melo-dramatically enough, have adopted a disguise before call-ing on his blackmailer; such an act appeared senseless, for Burke knew his appearance.

"Mind, I can't be sure, but that's just what I thought. Anyhow, he wasn't a young man; I should say he was middle-aged, but that's all I can tell you about his looks."

Deciding that she was in error about the mustache, Gilmore persisted with his catechism; but Mrs. Pretching could not say anything more about him. He was still try-ing to jog her memory for more productive results, when Rankin returned with his report.

Together they left the scene of Burke's death; once in the street, the younger detective related what he had done.

"You can make up your mind that Gardiner is out of it. It took a devil of a long time to find Jenks—and he reported that after the young man left City Hall with Miss Nixon, they both went to the offices of American Motors. What clinches it is the fact that they stayed there till almost one o'clock, and then went out to lunch. Then the girl left him and Gardiner went back to the office." He paused and then asked, "Well, what did you accomplish out here?"

Briefly, his colleague related his activities during the course of the afternoon, the discovery of the check book,

Dr. Curtiss's examination and Mrs. Pretching's evidence. And as he went on, Rankin realized as fully as did Gilmore how completely Stirling was cornered. Motive for the crime, opportunity and a possible weapon—the cane that Stirling must have been carrying on the night of the first murder as well as at his second crime—all these had been already discovered. And now, in addition, there was his own handwriting to give him away, and one who had seen him, who was a witness to his flight. It was impossible for the broker to escape all of that.

20
THERE'S MANY A SLIP

It was half past four in the afternoon when, armed with a
warrant and alone, Gilmore reached the brokerage office
of Sanburg, Pressman & Co. Located in the Albee Building
on Broad Street, they occupied a large and luxurious suite
of rooms, as became one of the leading investment houses
in the East. From the central hallway of the building a narrower passage connected a series of offices, all occupied, as
the glass doors indicated, by officials of the company. At
the end of the passage was the board room, where, earlier
in the day, dealers and speculators had watched the progress of stock fluctuations, upon the gigantic board before
them, and, in a turmoil, purchased and sold according to
the movements of respective issues.

To a secretary, the detective told his business.

"Mr. Stirling?" she said. "It's rather late, but I'll see if
he's in. What name shall I say, please?"

She returned a moment later, and ushered him into an
office somewhat isolated from the others, at the beginning
of the passage. It was a well-equipped room; the central
desk of oak, the steel filing cabinet in one corner, and
the luxurious quality of the rug on the floor were elo-
quent witnesses of Stirling's prosperity. A door into the
next room of the suite appeared locked. A stenographer,
who had been working at a smaller desk, left as Gilmore

entered, at the order of her employer who evidently desired no audience at the coming interview.

Gilmore was not more impressed by Russell Stirling
than his colleague had been. The broker, faultlessly attired
in a well-tailored brown suit, an ostentatious stickpin in
his tie, with a cloying odor of perfume on the kerchief
that protruded from his lapel, rose to greet his visitor; but
it was evident that the intrusion did not please him. He
had apparently been about to leave, for his topcoat and
hat lay upon his desk.

With a start, Gilmore realized that the coat was not
blue as Mrs. Pretching had described, but gray; and that
instead of a cap, Stirling was wearing a straw hat. Unless
he could have anticipated his narrow escape from the two
detectives, it seemed incredible that he had had the fore-
sight to have, for the sake of safety, procured new clothes
for himself. The detective was silent so long that the broker began the conversation.

"You wanted to see me, Mr. Gilmore? You're from Headquarters, I understand. What can I do for you now?"

"I came to hear what you have to tell me about Philip
Nixon's death, Mr. Stirling," Gilmore said, his voice grim
and unyielding.

"What I have to tell you? As I've already told Mr.—
what was his name?—Rankin, I know nothing about it. I
regret that you think this necessary; you are merely wasting your time, I assure . . ."

"Mr. Stirling!" Gilmore caught up his suave words
sharply. "I wonder if you realize the seriousness of your
position."

The broker's tone remained painfully tranquil. "I don't
think I know what you mean by that."

"You don't? Then, I'll explain it to you. A week ago,
Philip Nixon was murdered on the last car of the seven-
forty-five express, bound for Cape May. The last man

known to have been with him was you; you had arranged to meet him on that train at Newfield at eight-twenty-five, on a matter of business. When his body was discovered, an overcoat which we have traced to you was found on it. These things you have concealed from us, first denying having had any dealings with Mr. Nixon and then lying about what they were. Then, you denied your ownership of the coat, and even prompted your servant to lie about it. In addition, you said nothing about the meeting. In short, you have done everything possible to hinder our investigation, and unless you convince me that you are innocent of Mr. Nixon's death, I shall place you under arrest for it!"

His original plan had actually been to arrest the broker at once. But the doubt caused by Stirling's coat and hat had given him an unexpected qualm, and disturbed him more than he would have cared to admit.

In spite of every effort to control himself, Russell Stirling became several shades paler as the recital progressed. Only with a visible effort did he still sound unconcerned.

"And what, Mr. Gilmore, is supposed to be my motive for killing some one with whom I merely had business dealings?"

"A very strong motive," Gilmore replied sternly. "The corner Philip Nixon was engineering in Audubon common stock was ruining you. You had sold short in the expectation of a fall in values, to the extent of all that you possessed—and your debt was due last Wednesday, at a time when, if the corner followed its normal course, prices would have been sky-high. Only Nixon, alive or dead, could have saved you; alive, if he was willing to compromise the debt you owed him—dead, because of the resultant reaction that would break the corner. After several efforts on your part, he finally consented to meet you; and then, by refusing you assistance, signed his own death warrant!"

The broker remained silent, as though stunned by the overwhelming case against him, and Gilmore, certain he was pursuing the correct tactics, pushed forward still more vigorously.

"Today, at noon, there was another murder, Stirling, committed by the same hand, to silence a witness to the first crime. Can you tell me where you were at the time it occurred?"

"At noon?" The other seemed genuinely bewildered. "I think I can satisfy you as to that. I went out at half past eleven to take lunch with a Mr. Kassel of the firm of Kassel Brothers, brokers, at the Marlton Club and discuss a deal."

"At eleven-thirty—with Mr. Kassel? How long were you with him?"

"For two hours—it was about one-thirty when I left him. We reached the club at noon and went into the dining room. Mr. Kassel has been a member there for some time; and I'm certain that both the head waiter and the man who served us can vouch for our presence. . . ."

The unexpectedness of this account disconcerted Gilmore completely. This did not sound like an alibi prepared for the occasion; Albert Kassel was well known all over the city, as a respectable business man, a fact that had reached even the detective's ears. He knew, too, the Marlton Club—an organization whose membership included the most successful men in the city. It was impossible that its entire dining room staff could have been bribed to conceal his culpability for murder. If the tale was untrue, the broker well knew that it would collapse under a thorough investigation.

And yet, if it was true, what remained to the detective of the case he had so completely presented against Stirling but a minute before? Somewhere there must be a loophole which, in some manner, he had to discover. In an effort to do so, Gilmore played his strongest—and last—card.

From his inner pocket he drew the black check book, placing it open on the desk before him, so that the first stub was visible.

"If you were with Mr. Kassel," he said, "how did this come to be at the scene of the second murder? It was a most fatal mistake for the criminal to leave it there; it will hang him."

If he expected results, he was not disappointed. For an instant the broker stared at it; suddenly his face became livid. In his eyes, bulging with fear, was written recognition; his hands, clenched on his chair, went white with the pressure he put upon them. He tried vainly to control his voice as he managed to gasp out:

"My God! Where did you say you got that?"

All doubts vanished as Gilmore leaped to his feet. He had him now; there was no question that Stirling knew the writing!

"You know quite well where I found it," he cried exultantly. "At the apartments at thirty-eight-twelve Mallory Street where Ralph Burke met his death today, because he had seen what had occurred on the seven-forty-five train. So you admit this is yours . . ."

"No, no . . ." Stirling broke in, fighting to hold his quivering nerves in check. "I don't know anything about it, Gilmore. It's not my writing—I swear it isn't; but I'll tell you everything I do know and it will be the truth this time . . ."

The detective heard only the single denial.

"Not your writing?" he said incredulously. "You recognize it, don't you? . . . Whose do you expect me to believe it is?"

"I don't know, but it's not mine. Here, I can prove it, easily enough. . . ." Swiftly, the broker seized a pad from a desk drawer and wrote his name across it with his pen; and underneath, a brief sentence. "But if you'll listen, I'll give you everything I know of what happened on the train that night. I kept it quiet because I realized how bad matters could be made to look for me, if all the circumstances came out, just as you've related them; but I'm innocent of Nixon's death, I'll take my oath on it."

There was no resemblance between the two writings. By no possibility could the flowing, slanting style of the checkbook stub, on which the "l" in "self" was at a forty-five degree angle, and the stilted narrow hand on the pad, with its cramped "l" in "Stirling," have been written by the same person, even in a deliberate attempt to disguise his true style. As he stared at them, Gilmore was hardly aware that he had at least loosened the broker's tongue, that Stirling was pouring out his narrative so swiftly that he would have to pull himself together and listen or else he would miss those very facts he desired to hear.

"You were correct in everything you said about the corner," Stirling was relating, "and my many efforts to communicate with Nixon on that account. While it is true that business isn't done that way—one takes one's losses as they come—nevertheless, I was desperate, and I thought I could persuade Nixon to see me because of his own interest in my debt. . . . The worst that could occur to me would be another refusal. So on Monday, I called him again, and had the great luck to get him directly on the phone; but he told me he was going to the shore and had no time for me."

"What time did you call him?" Gilmore asked. "I was with him till quarter after one, that day."

"It must have been between half past one and quarter of two. For when I finally persuaded him to hear what I had to say, and agreed to go anywhere to meet him, because the matter couldn't wait another day, I called up my servant, Higgins, and told him to pack my bag for Cape May. And that was about two o'clock . . ."

This was the truth, the detective was aware, from what the butler had told Rankin and himself. In all probability, Nixon's secretary had been with Eleanor, at the time; and thus he failed to have knowledge of the subsequent arrangements the financier made with the broker.

"We arranged to meet at Newfield, at eight-thirty," Stirling went on, "because the seven-forty-five train stops at Newfield at eight-twenty-five, and by that arrangement I would get there just in time. My butler can vouch for the fact that I made the train, for he brought my bag to the Camden terminal. On the way, we ran into a storm, but we weren't late in getting to Newfield."

"One moment," Gilmore interrupted. "You expected Mr. Nixon to meet you with his machine, did you not?"

The broker's features displayed his surprise. "Yes," he replied. "How did you know that? At least, my impression was that he was driving to Cape May, and after he had accomplished some mission on the road, he would pick me up at Newfield. However, Mr. Nixon must have changed his mind. There was no one at the station to meet me; I got off the train and wandered about the Newfield platform for the entire five minutes the train waits to connect with an Atlantic City train. It was just getting ready to leave, and I, deciding that something had gone wrong, was getting ready to go with it, when Philip Nixon arrived in a little dilapidated auto, with a huge hulking brute of a farmer chap at the wheel. It was the closest thing I ever experienced; we had barely put our feet on the steps before the express started."

Stirling paused as he leaned toward the detective.

"Gilmore—I knew there was something wrong with Nixon the moment I saw him. He was haggard looking, trembling all over, and so utterly exhausted that I had to help him to a seat. He had a hacking cough, that turns the insides out—and, somehow, was like a very old man, weakened by unaccustomed exertion. Obviously, he was sick and shouldn't have been out in that storm; but it was something more than that. There was a look in his eyes, as though . . . he had stared Death in the face!

"I realized at once that in his condition, for all the attention he was capable of giving me, I might just as well save my breath. From the very beginning, Nixon hardly said a word, not even to explain what had happened, or why he arrived at Newfield in that old car. And he continued to be silent when I began to talk, presenting my case to him, and asking him to come to some temporary arrangement with me, about the shares that were due, until I was able to get on my feet again. But I had been right; I doubt if he heard even half of what I said, so great was his discomfort and weariness . . ."

"How long did your conversation last?" Gilmore put in.

Here was a trap he set for Stirling; if the financier had boarded the train at 8:30 and died at 9:01, the broker's argument could not have lasted a half hour. The fact that Stirling successfully avoided it, was, to the detective, proof of his veracity.

"Not more than twenty-five minutes, I should say," Stirling replied, "though I couldn't be too sure. When I had finished, Nixon remained silent for nearly five minutes—and I waited anxiously for his answer. And then, suddenly, he clasped me by the arm and said that he was dizzy and must have air or he would choke. He began coughing, and when I started to open the window, he said that wouldn't do; if I would let him have my coat, so that he wouldn't feel worse after having been in a warm car, he'd go to the rear. Perhaps there, in the wind, he'd be able to breathe more freely and would feel better.

"Naturally, I was alarmed; and after I had given him my coat, I offered to go back with him in case help should prove necessary. But that very suggestion seemed to anger him; and he waved it aside and started down the aisle by himself. That was the last I saw of him, Gilmore, staggering once as the train swayed, then straightening himself and disappearing into the last car. For just an instant after he had closed the door, I caught a view of his back; and then he was gone."

"You were in the next to the last car?" the detective queried. "What happened after Mr. Nixon left you? Surely you must have considered it peculiar that he failed to return with your coat."

"At first, I was so wrapped up in the failure of my attempt to interest Mr. Nixon in my behalf that I didn't give the matter a thought. But you see, Gilmore, that I had no reason for killing him, because he hadn't refused me yet; and it was more than possible that, having heard me through, he might be willing to consider my proposal when he was feeling better. It wasn't till half past nine that I realized he had been gone a half-hour and we were shortly due at Cape May. I knew that he hadn't passed through the car to the front of the train, or I would have seen him; so he must have remained in the rear. You can imagine my surprise, when, on looking for him in the last car, I found that he had disappeared!

"I would have been alarmed then, but I remembered the train had stopped at Oldroyd; and it stopped there only on the request of passengers. I thought perhaps that Nixon had gotten off there because of his illness; and to make sure of it, I questioned the conductor in the last car. He didn't seem very anxious to tell me at first, and by the time he had admitted that Nixon, whom I described, had left the train at Oldroyd, we had reached the shore and I had no further opportunity to discuss exactly what had occurred. . . .”

“The conductor of the last car told you that!” Gilmore exclaimed in his astonishment. “And you believed him?”

It was, of course, a lie, concocted by Burke to discourage further interrogation on the part of Stirling. He had already indubitably settled that Nixon had met his death at 9:01; by no means, then, was it possible for the financier to have disembarked at Oldroyd at 9:20, and returned to the spot where he had been found. But the trainman, having already determined to conceal and profit by what he had witnessed, had used the express’s halt at Oldroyd to avoid further awkward questions. No wonder Gilmore had found Burke discomposed during his examination; he was not the first one to question the trainman.

“Certainly I believed him,” Stirling replied to his question. “It seemed natural enough under the circumstances; and I expected that my coat would be returned the next day. It was not until I saw the papers the following morning, that I realized that the conductor had mistaken my description of Nixon for some man who had actually left the train at Oldroyd.”

The rest of Stirling’s story was swiftly narrated. Upon his arrival at the shore, the broker had taken rooms at the Seaside Hotel. Still troubled about the financier, he had called up Nixon’s summer residence twice—at ten and at eleven-thirty—to inquire whether he had arrived. The caretakers seemed to know nothing about the matter. And, on his return to Philadelphia the following morning, not wishing to become embroiled in the financier’s death as a witness, nor desiring his narrow escape from ruination to become public, Stirling had instructed his butler to deny any knowledge of the overcoat.

“That’s all I can tell you, Gilmore,” he concluded. “You see, I know nothing of the actual crime; and unless you

think it's all false, you can hardly charge me even for with-
holding knowledge of the murder."

And Gilmore was compelled to give credence to the
story. At every point at which it was possible to check with
facts of which he, himself, was aware, it agreed with them.
The portion about Nixon's condition and his arrival at
Newfield station fitted with Martha Marley's story; all the
details of the meeting on the train, with his own investigations; Stirling's movements, with the account given by his
butler; even the broker's calls to Nixon's caretakers was an
item he knew to be true. And, just as important, Stirling's
coat and hat were not the garments Mrs. Pretching had
described, nor were the check book and the writing his.

But he knew he must not capitulate too swiftly; Stirling had not yet been altogether frank.

"All of what you've related to me may be the truth,"
he said, at length, "but you've neglected to tell me everything. You say you know nothing, for instance, about the
second murder? How, then, do you happen to recognize
the handwriting in this check book?"

Stirling's features displayed a bland surprise.

"I never said that I recognized the handwriting," he
replied. "What ever gave you that impression?"

"It was because you saw that check book that you willingly told me everything that occurred last Monday night;
come now, there must have been a reason for it."

"I think you're mistaken, Gilmore; I merely concluded
that it was wrong to withhold any longer such information
as I had, and I was anxious to rectify the error."

The urbane tone told Gilmore he would get no more
from Stirling. He had totally regained his poise; for whatever cause he had been alarmed into a confession, the force
of it was no longer potent. Accordingly, he pocketed the
check book and rose.

"All right, Stirling," he said, with the best grace he could command, "I'll have to take your word for it, for the present. But I'm going to test your story; if I find any discrepancies, depend upon it, I'll return. And in the meantime, you'll be watched closely, I warn you."

"Well, that's candid enough," the broker returned. He accompanied Gilmore to the door. "I suppose I can hardly expect more, considering the difficulties my silence has caused you and Mr. Rankin."

As the detective descended the stairs of the now darkened and deserted office building and passed into the street, he realized that he had reached the stone wall he had so dreaded. Only a single new possibility had suggested itself in the broker's story. Had Philip Nixon's death been an accident and not murder at all? According to Stirling, he had gone alone, a sick man, to the rear platform of the car; could it be that, seized with a spell of dizziness, he had fallen from it, and thus received the injury which had resulted in his death? Could it be that the detective, led astray by the circumstances under which he had taken charge of the case, had been wasting his time pursuing a murderer who did not exist, and making himself the laughing stock of the Central Bureau? It was not improbable that, after all, his premises had been wrong—that no murder had occurred, except in his too fertile imagination. Medically speaking, Nixon's crushed skull could well have been the result of a fall; had not such a thing once occurred in the case of Gardiner's rival, Farrell?

No, there was no obstacle in the way of this theory—except the death of Ralph Burke. But the trainman had been killed because he knew too much of Nixon's death; in his case, there was no doubt that it had been brutal murder. If the financier had died naturally, what could Burke have known that caused his murderer to silence him forever? Nothing at all. It followed then, that Nixon's decease had also been more than accidental, else the trainman could have had no cause for levying blackmail on the criminal. It, too, had been murder.

This conclusion failed to bring Gilmore comfort. He was no nearer answering the more important problem than at the very beginning of the case, and he was in a much worse position. With his suspects, the Ferris gang, the Marley brothers, the financier's secretary, and now Russell Stirling, eliminated, one by one, what was there left for him? Who, then, was the elusive criminal? Was he some unknown, who had thus far not appeared in the case? The difficulty with such a theory was that a stranger failed to fit in; in all his investigations he had located no other enemy of the financier. And no one else, except Bennett, had been aware of the financier's intended journey to the shore. But the butler, with his deep affection for his master, and his love for Eleanor, was clearly out of the question.

Yet his quarry must be some one who was familiar to Stirling. Despite the broker's denial, he had been terrified by the writing. If he would not talk, then Gilmore must trace the ownership of the check book by other methods. A trip to Boston was necessary, while subordinates cleared up the details of Burke's death. But the possibilities of success were slim even then. Out of a bewildering array of suspects and dozens of tangled clues that had baffled him for days, there remained just this little black book, of which he knew only the bank from which it had come!

21
RUSSELL STIRLING'S ENEMY

"I'm afraid, Mr. Gilmore," said Mr. Robinson, the vice president of the Boston City National Bank, "that it will be almost impossible to trace this check book, if this handwriting in it is your only clue. It would mean searching through all of our checks and comparing every one with these stubs; and we have more than eight thousand accounts. If the sums of these checks had been for unusual amounts, they might have attracted attention; but a hundred dollars, withdrawn through some Philadelphia bank, every month—that is a commonplace."

The speaker, a portly, elderly man, with lined features and white hair, gazed regretfully at the detective. The two were seated in his private office, on the second floor of the bank building, a graystone structure on Washington Street, overlooking the rush of traffic below. By assigning the investigation of Stirling's story of his movements in Cape May and his alibi to Jenks, Gilmore had at once been able to make the late-night train to Boston, after having notified both his wife and the Superintendent of the intended journey; and he reached his destination early in the morning. He had had no difficulty in locating the bank responsible for the issuance of his check book clue.

"I suppose I'll have to do it, if there's nothing else," he replied to Mr. Robinson's statement. "You are certain, however, that you have in the bank the check originals of these stubs?"

"Yes, all three of them, I am positive. You see, until we return the checks that come from the clearing house, to our drawers, we keep them together. We send them back with quarterly statements at the end of March, June, September and December. Since all these checks were drawn between March and June—this month—it means that we are keeping them if they come in at all. I'll be glad to show you . . ."

Mr. Robinson broke off and his sudden start of surprise was not lost on the detective.

"That's strange," he went on, gazing at the check book. "We have not been using this type of check book for over two years. The account couldn't have been a very active one, or this would have been used up long ago and we would have supplied its owner with another kind."

Gilmore bent closely, attentive at this first suggestion regarding the man he sought. "How can you tell that?" he questioned.

"By the size of this check book. You'll notice that it is ten inches long and four inches wide—larger than normal pocket size. Some two years ago, through the cooperation of various banking organizations, a standard size for desk checks was adopted universally; and at that same time we made a change in pocket check books to nine inches by three, to meet the demands of our depositors. There had been complaints that the old ones were too cumbersome to handle. I dare say we haven't a hundred customers still using these."

"Then I'm in luck," the detective said eagerly. "That limits my work to only the larger checks; and they ought not to take long. I'd appreciate it, if you'd let me begin with them at once."

Without further discussion, Mr. Robinson led the detective into the sanctum of the bank, behind the bars below; in a very few minutes, he had procured for him a huge collection of canceled checks, and assigned two clerks to assist Gilmore in sorting them. Extremely thankful for the fortunate circumstance that limited his task and gave him some hope of success, he resolutely set to work. With the check-book stubs on the desk before him, he began to go through the checks. The vast majority of them, smaller than the stubs with which he compared them, he put aside at once; the larger ones that fitted his clue, he found with ease, because they protruded noticeably in the pile. Not till he collected all of them—about two hundred—did he begin to examine them. Those dated differently from the stubs, and those made out for sums larger or smaller, he eliminated next, for they could not possibly be the originals of the stub notations. That left but twenty-five out of the original assemblage; and to these, Gilmore turned his attention closely. Painstakingly, he examined each of them, comparing the writing on each with the flowing style of the stubs; and as they failed to agree, he put them aside.

At the end of an hour of constant application, Gilmore had found what he sought—three checks made out to self, each for one hundred dollars, dated April 1, May 1, and June 1, respectively—and all signed by Russell Stirling's erstwhile partner of three years before—Allen Murray!

It was not surprising, then, that the broker had recognized the handwriting on the stubs. Quickly Gilmore recalled what he knew of the partnership, from Rankin's report of the broker's past. Beyond the arrest of the firm for operating a bucket shop under the guise of a legitimate investment house, and Murray's conviction, it was not much; neither he nor his colleague had adjudged the facts to be of much importance. Stirling's ability for gauging the market had attracted the attention of this man, Murray, who had had independent means; they had formed the partnership to which the broker contributed his experience, and which had prospered until an investigation, at the instance of a defrauded customer, revealed the true character of the concern. At the subsequent trial Stirling was able to prove, by the firm's books, that Murray alone was guilty, and that he knew nothing of the swindles that had been perpetrated.

Nothing of Gilmore's mental effort to connect Murray with Philip Nixon's death was apparent as he informed Mr. Robinson of his discovery and requested all the information on Murray that he could supply.

"First, if it is possible," he said, "I want to see his account, and find out his address. After that, I'd appreciate any other facts that you could give me. . . ."

The vice president did not conceal his surprise. "Allen Murray, you say . . . ? That would explain why his account, which we still have, has been inactive and why he uses one of the old books," he echoed Gilmore's own thoughts on that matter. "He has been serving a three-year prison term in connection with a bucket-shop scandal that occurred in the summer of nineteen twenty-six. We have never seen him here since then."

"You know about the affair then," Gilmore queried, "and can give me the story of it in detail?"

"I'm afraid I know no more of it than most people in the business world. I did not attend the trial, nor follow the evidence; I was only aware of the ultimate verdict which sent Murray to jail, and freed his partner of all suspicion."

At Mr. Robinson's order, an account book was brought in by one of the clerks, which the vice president opened to Murray's account.

It had been an extensive one, and fairly active, with deposits and withdrawals of some size entered in the ledger; and the amounts involved affirmed a conclusion Gilmore had already drawn—that Stirling's partner had been a person of some wealth. No doubt, he had accounts in many other banks. It was significant that this one had been untouched for three years, since the three checks he had traced had not yet been entered; the last withdrawal had been in July of 1926. Yet Murray was now free, or else, how had his check book come into Ralph Burke's dead hand? And as it was only June of the year 1929, it indicated that, if Murray had been convicted in the fall of 1926, he had been released before serving his entire term.

The address at the top of the account read: Plaza Hotel, Weymouth Ave., Boston.

"It's a family hotel in the Back Bay district, Mr. Gilmore," the vice president explained, "but, of course, it is an old address, given us when we first opened Mr. Murray's account. If he is not in prison, where he is now, I cannot say. But I'm sure he used to live there, because his wife was an invalid, and incapable of taking care of a household."

"He was married, then?" Gilmore queried interestedly.

"Yes, he was. In fact, I believe there was a child." Mr. Robinson paused, as he tried to recall his knowledge. "His wife died, however, either shortly before his trial or shortly after, I don't remember which. They married late in life—he must have been forty at the time; and Mrs. Murray had never been robust. At any rate, whatever ailed her, I don't think she outlived his conviction."

Who had taken care of the child, then, Gilmore asked both himself and the banker, while the father was in prison? It seemed to the detective that here was the most promising means of tracing his latest quarry; it was unlikely that Murray would have deserted it and left it to be cared for at public expense.

But the vice president's information did not extend to this point; his personal knowledge was limited only to business facts regarding Stirling's partner. Murray had originally been a successful importer of silks; he had retired some six years ago, with enough to maintain his family and himself comfortably. But finding a life of ease not suited to an energetic disposition, he had cast about for some further interest to occupy his time. Attracted by the brokerage business, at the end of a year he had joined with Stirling, then a clerk for the stock house of Skorn & Son, whose offices were on Tremont Street. For two years the firm appeared to have prospered; but then came the investigation, which resulted in such surprising and disastrous revelations.

"I say surprising revelations," Mr. Robinson went on, "because never before had there been a breath of suspicion regarding Mr. Murray's integrity; and he had so little reason for dishonesty. Of course, the urge to make money quickly is often irresistible; but in the case of a man who had once retired, such a development is unusual. But there was the evidence against him—so I suppose his conviction was justified."

"That's very curious," said Gilmore. "But surely there was never any doubt about his guilt?"

"No, not as far as I'm aware. But, as I say, I never followed the case closely enough to say what came out at the trial."

His description of Allen Murray, in answer to the next question the detective put, was necessarily vague and unsatisfactory. He had not seen the man for three years, he reminded Gilmore; and even when he had, it had been for only a few moments at a time. The man was of medium height, and perhaps forty-five years of age; his excellent carriage, however, concealed his years well. The vice president had particularly noted an even-toned, melodious voice and pleasant manner. He thought that Murray had dark hair; but as to his features, he could say little beyond the fact that they were clean-shaven.

Such details were so commonplace as to be valueless; and it was evident to Gilmore that Mr. Robinson possessed no further information. He could not say whether Murray had banking accounts elsewhere, nor could he give the detective the names of people who might have known him. He did not know whether he or Mrs. Murray had had any relatives; nor did he know what affliction it was that had brought about the latter's death. Of the age or the sex of the child, he was not aware. Finally, he could not say where the bank would have sent the canceled checks if it proved that its depositor was no longer at the Plaza Hotel.

"If you want the details of the trial, and these more personal facts of the man's life, you had better see the police," he said, when Gilmore had concluded his questions. "If you will wait a few moments, I'll try to get for you the name of the authorities in charge of the case, and where you can find them now . . ."

The detective had fully intended this to be his next step. As yet he had but scraped the surface of a development so unexpected and incomprehensible that he could not grasp its significance. He needed further intelligence before he could draw any conclusions. And he would wait, this time, until he was sure of himself, before doing so. He would not repeat the greatest error he had thus far made during the course of the case—that of drawing inferences on insufficient basis.

Thus it came about that an hour after the bank official had given him the necessary information, Gilmore found himself entering the Police Headquarters on Berkeley Street and inquiring for Captain O'Connor. He needed only to present his credentials to be ushered into the presence of an officer whose heavy, mustached face and shrewd, searching eyes betokened a successful combination for police work—peculiar discernment with a capacity for constant application to duty.

Captain O'Connor listened to Gilmore's story in silence; but a curious gleam of interest appeared in his eyes as the detective explained his mission and asked the officer for information regarding the erstwhile broker. And when the narrative was completed, he sat back for a moment in deep contemplation.

"It's mighty strange, Gilmore," he said at length, "that your questions about Murray should come at this late date, after he served most of his three-year sentence for running that bucket shop."

The remark, unusual itself, would require some elucidation; but for the moment, Gilmore seized on the more important item.

"Served his sentence? He's been released then?" he queried.

"Yes, he was released early in March, through my efforts and those of Judge Wilson, who tried the case, and who, with me, had never been entirely satisfied with it. You see, the trial occurred in the middle of September, of nineteen twenty-six; and after the jury found Murray guilty, the Judge had no choice but to sentence him to a three-year term. That would have brought him out this following September; but after two and a half years, we managed to get the remainder of the sentence commuted and Murray was let out."

"You can tell me, then, where I can find him?" Gilmore asked. "That's my primary object in coming to you. . . ."

The Captain hesitated a moment. "I'm afraid not, Gilmore; I've heard nothing of him since March. Of an ordinary criminal, we would have certainly kept a record, as far as possible, but his case was different. You might try the Plaza Hotel, where he used to live with his family; I'm

afraid I can't give you any information, because I, personally, never considered it necessary to keep an eye on him."

Nor did O'Connor know anything about the whereabouts of Murray's child—a little girl, Gilmore learned—
nor who had cared for it while Murray had served his
sentence. Aware that the mother had died, the Captain
surmised that it must have been turned over to some relatives of its parents; but who they might be, he could not say.

"There ought to be some method of tracing them down
and finding Murray through them, however," he said, "I'll
be glad to turn over several men to you, if you will want
assistance in your search."

Eventually, Gilmore realized, it might have to come to
this; and accordingly, he accepted the offer, before putting
his next question.

"You say, O'Connor, that you and this Judge—Wilson—were not entirely satisfied as to Murray's guilt. What
gives you any doubts—he was convicted with a fair trial,
was he not?"

"Yes, the trial was fair enough—and raised no questions. It's difficult to say, exactly, what did cause me first
to distrust the evidence, though that seemed clear enough
. . ." He paused as though uncertain of how to continue. "I
suppose that my attention was attracted by a comparison
of the characters of the two men involved."

"Of the characters . . . ? You mean, Stirling and Murray?"

"That's it exactly. On the one hand, you had Allen Murray, a man of some wealth and an excellent business reputation, regarding whose honesty there was never a question.
In appearance, he was a gentleman; he was good-looking,
and exceptionally pleasant and polished, though he had a
certain austere quality about him that kept you somewhat
at a distance. But certainly, he had no criminal's features.
On the other hand, there was Stirling, who had once been
a clerk for the firm of Skorn & Son, but about whom no

one knew anything except that he was phenomenally clever in gauging the stock market. He had a jovial manner that never quite rang true, and shifting eyes that gave one an impression that he was always concealing his true self. Of the two, he fits the role of the guilty party far better; and if you were to meet him, I'm sure you would say so. . . ."

Gilmore found himself deeply engrossed by the suggestions the other's story contained.

"I have met him," he replied, "and, without having seen Murray, I'm inclined to agree with you. But you know that appearances are deceiving; most confidence men and swindlers are outwardly courtly and pleasant-spoken gentlemen."

"I'm not easily taken in, Gilmore, and I think I know the real article when I see it. I'll get Murray's picture and description for you from his prison record, and you can judge for yourself whether or not I'm right."

After having given an appropriate order to an underling, whom he dispatched upon the errand, Captain O'Connor proceeded.

"What occurred at the trial were the next developments that seemed to indicate something was amiss. Only Murray was tried, you know; for Stirling was not only at once able to prove he was innocent, but it was he who insisted upon his colleague's guilt. In fact, his evidence brought about Murray's conviction; and the very vindictiveness of his effort to send him to prison appeared curious.

"Yet it must be admitted that the case against Murray was a strong one. The books of the partnership indicated that the money stolen from its patrons had all been given him to invest; Stirling had receipts, signed in Murray's handwriting, for these funds, when he had turned them over—or claimed to have turned them over—to him. It was conclusively proven that entries in the firm books had been doctored. The junior partner persuaded the authorities that he, younger and presumably more inexperienced, must have been the dupe of the other. The most damning testimony was that of the two customers who had first called the swindles to the attention of the authorities. They gave undoubtedly true evidence that they had given the very funds of which they had been defrauded to Murray personally."

Gilmore pursed his lips. "It would be rather difficult to get around that, I'm afraid."

"Not if Murray passed them on to his partner, for investment. After all, it was Stirling who had the business experience, and the handling of funds must have been his work. Every opportunity for stealing and cheating was in his hands. It was he who produced the evidence of the books—and he who took charge of them. Murray might have signed the various receipts he produced, under the belief that he was signing entirely different types of paper. He trusted Stirling, else he would not have taken him into the business with him, in the first place. So, it wouldn't be likely that he'd inspect too closely everything Stirling did, or demand an accounting."

The officer's theories were plausible, Gilmore considered; and surely, they must have had some basis to have impressed the Judge as well.

"Even with all these incriminating facts," O'Connor went on, "I doubt very much if a conviction would have resulted, had Murray properly pressed his defense or allowed his attorney to do so for him. But, instead, he gave him no assistance whatsoever, and he displayed only the interest of a mere spectator at some one else's trial. Throughout, he maintained an apathetic attitude from which nothing could arouse him; he neither volunteered evidence nor took the stand himself. It became impossible to make any satisfactory efforts in his behalf; and of course, his behavior in court, as well as the resulting weakness of his defense, told strongly against him."

"Exactly what defense did he put up?" the detective asked.

"Bogart, his lawyer, tried to prove his innocence by showing that he had been merely a silent partner of the concern, under the terms of the partnership agreement. But, of course, he found some difficulty there, considering the testimony of the defrauded customers."

"But as a silent partner," Gilmore said, "he would have nothing to do with the management of the concern. Stirling, with an absolutely free rein, could have done as he pleased with Murray none the wiser."

The officer raised his hand swiftly. "Precisely," he said eagerly. "And such a plea, if sufficiently presented, would have vindicated him. But, as though he was not in the least concerned, Murray refused to act in his own behalf or be aroused from the lethargy into which he had fallen."

"Mightn't that be," Gilmore suggested, "simply because the claim wasn't true, and realizing that there was no opportunity of proving it, Murray permitted the suggestion only as a last resort?"

"Certainly not. The real cause, as we found out afterward, was that he didn't care what happened to him. He had just suffered a great shock and loss; and in his overwhelming despair, he ceased to take an interest in life, for the moment. His apathy was the result of grief which dulled every consideration of what was going on around him. Later, when he recovered himself, it was too late; he was condemned to prison bars and four walls for three years."

"The loss that occurred—was his wife's death!" It was more a statement than a question. "I learned at the bank that she had been an invalid and died at the time of the trial . . ."

"Of course, it was that," O'Connor replied. "She died two days before the trial was scheduled. They had not been married more than six years, I understand, and with older people, affection goes much deeper. He must have been extremely attached to her. In the light of this information his actions at the trial were all comprehensible. . . ."

The arrival of the officer with the record requested by O'Connor interrupted the conversation; when he had retired, the Captain passed them to the detective.

"Take a look at that photograph, Gilmore," he instructed, "and tell me whether you don't think my theories justified."

At the first glance, it would certainly appear as though the speaker were correct. The features, obviously those of a person of breeding, were clean-shaven; in a smooth face, shrewd, appraising eyes, and a narrow nose that curved almost imperceptibly, were outstanding. Allen Murray had thin, determined lips and high cheek bones; a marked ascetic appearance was strengthened by a paleness, noted in the record below as a characteristic. He appeared quite youthful. His height was described as medium, his carriage firm; and the breadth of his shoulders indicated a person of powerful and dominating energy.

For the barest fraction of a second, as he studied the picture, Gilmore had a vague and totally inexplicable sensation that somewhere he had seen the owner of those features before. It was a fleeting, almost imperceptible feeling of some likeness that he had at one time encountered. But it was gone, eluding his grasp ere he had fully the opportunity to seize it; and when he looked again, both the impression and the resemblance had faded. He was not even certain then that either had ever existed anywhere except in his imagination. There was only left before him

an altogether strange, if interesting, face. His first indis-
tinct notion he discarded by his positive decision to the
contrary.

Whether or not he had been in error, however, at least
he knew for whom he was searching. Any one of a number of possible trails, branching out in various directions,
might bring the information he required in locating the
missing broker. There were the owners of the building
which housed the firm of Murray & Stirling, and the house
for which Stirling had clerked; also, the lawyer, Bogart,
who had defended Murray at the trial. He must consider,
as well, relatives of Mrs. Murray or her husband, if any
were to be found, nor could he neglect an interview with
Judge Wilson. But more important than any of these was
the finding of the child, for there the whereabouts of the
parent would be known; and in this connection he would
turn his first efforts to the Plaza Hotel.

What, Gilmore asked himself, as he left the Captain
after a further elaboration of the facts already gained, did
his discoveries mean? From the moment he had learned
whose was the black check book, the question had been
running through his mind. The first stub, dated shortly
after Murray had been released from prison, indicated that
Murray had possessed it then; and since the book had been
found in Ralph Burke's dead hand, Murray must have murdered him. But the only reason for killing the conductor
was that he had witnessed the financier's death. It followed, then, that his new suspect had also been on the
7:45 train, having in some manner traced Philip Nixon
there, and murdered him as well. There seemed no escape
from this logical conclusion. But why? What was his motive? What peculiar web of circumstances connected these
two?

Were he investigating Russell Stirling's death, the
whole thing would be comprehensible. There, at least,

existed a powerful motive for which Murray would want to kill his erstwhile partner. If both had been equally guilty of the swindles for which only one was tried, it meant that Stirling had double crossed the other. His testimony had sent Murray to serve a term, while he, presumably, fled with the spoils to Philadelphia. Gilmore certainly considered this sufficient to make Murray a bitter enemy. He well knew the demoralizing effect of prison terms, of days lengthening into years, during which prisoners, locked in their cells, had plenty of leisure to contrive means of retaliation or revenge. Alone, with only their thoughts for company, it was no wonder that convicts were often more vicious and dangerous when released than when they had first entered the jail!

If, as was more probable, Stirling alone was guilty, how much more potent would have been Murray's motive! Not only had he been betrayed by one he trusted; his entire life had been ruined by his partner. Much of his money was stolen, though that was trifling in comparison with the other calamities. His business was ruined, too; and he was ignominiously compelled to stand trial for a crime of which he was innocent. The wife whom he loved died, perhaps because of this disgrace; he was separated from his child. Murray would surely have no more compunction about destroying Stirling than he would have about wiping out a viper. If anything, he would do it as cold-bloodedly. No wonder Stirling had displayed such abject fear at the sight of his partner's handwriting, and yet, dreading any investigation, had refused to divulge his knowledge.

All this conjecture, however valuable in one set of circumstances, was totally useless in the present case. It was Philip Nixon's death he was investigating, not Stirling's. But to find some link between the financier and the Boston broker appeared impossible; nothing that he had thus far unearthed brought that objective nearer. Indeed . . .

The inspiration that suddenly flashed through Gil-more's mind like a brilliant revealing light, left him para-lyzed with astonishment.

Could Murray, intending Russell Stirling to be his victim, have murdered Philip Nixon by mistake?

22
THE SECLUDED COTTAGE

Had such an idea occurred to the detective at the beginning of his investigations into the death of Philip Nixon,
he would have discarded it as being ludicrous and impossible. At that time, with the financier threatened by enemies
of his own, Gilmore would have had his hands fully occupied by the entanglements they occasioned. The ironic
conception that death may have come from some one in
no way connected with Nixon would have appeared ridiculous. It would have added a complication to a problem
already too confused; and if that were not enough, its very
grotesqueness would have condemned it at once in Gilmore's practical mind.

But the situation had changed. No longer were those
involved who might have had a motive for desiring the
financier's death. All of them had been eliminated; and
he was following a slim trail which he could connect with
Nixon in no other manner. Faced by a blank wall, he was
compelled, perforce, to grant to the notion a consideration it did not perhaps deserve. Was it actually possible
that the blow had been intended for another? Great was
Gilmore's amazement to discover that no fact in his possession contradicted the idea; instead, all his knowledge
supported it at every turn.

In the first place, it was far more likely that Murray had been following the broker on the train, than following Nixon. The number who knew of the latter's intended journey to the shore was limited to Gardiner, Stirling, Parker, Eleanor Nixon and Bennett. Only the broker and the Marley family were aware that he intended to complete his trip by taking the 7:45 express from Newfield. On the other hand, Stirling had boarded the same train at its terminal; he may have been followed from Camden. There was no telling how many might have known that he intended to make the trip. His butler Higgins knew of his movements; it was easily conceivable that Murray could have learned of them.

What was far more important, the broker and the financier did resemble each other. It was, true, a superficial physical resemblance that did not extend to the features; but from a rear view, that was sufficient. Both were tall, large and heavily built; approximately, they were alike in size. Rankin, who knew Nixon from his contact after the Ferris robbery, had noted the likeness at his first sight of Stirling. Gilmore had observed it subconsciously; even the conductor of whom the financier had purchased his ticket on the 7:45 had described him as being of the same build as his friend. While they differed in poise, side by side it would have been difficult to find any difference.

Especially in the darkness at the rear of the train—a well-nigh impenetrable blackness that cloaked the countryside and made the Marley farmhouse but a shadow flashing by. Nixon, ill, bending over the railing, presented only his broad back to the approaching criminal—a back upon which he wore the brown overcoat, the property of the intended victim. Circumstances, within the bounds of plausibility, may have prevented Murray from seeing the garment change from Stirling's hands to those of the financier; he may also have failed to see Nixon while the latter passed him toward the end of the train, until it was too late to see him well. Then, however, he had seized the opportunity he sought. The broker's overcoat and the darkness completed a deception already begun by the financier's position as he bent over the rail and his physical similarity. This combination made the resulting error within the bounds of reason.

He was on the right track at last! It was with a buoyancy such as he had not yet experienced that the detective entered the Plaza Hotel. But it was a buoyancy tinged with a caution which must characterize all future steps. Until he was upon ground more firm than that of conjecture, prudence required that he feel his way carefully, and conceal his true character unless he could gain information in no other manner.

The family hotel resembled nothing so much as a large brownstone residence of a private family, typical of the early nineties. But four stories high, it was not even spacious; yet this was an asset which gave it an effect of comfort and coziness. The lobby seemed to be an inviting living room, and the antiquity of the furnishings added a richness more ornate equipment would not have supplied. Only the small desk at the rear and its clerk, whose white hair and elderly features proclaimed him a fixture, informed Gilmore it was a hostelry.

To him the detective explained his mission. The old man's surprise was very evident.

"You want to see Mr. Murray?" he repeated, voicing his astonishment. "Why, he hasn't been staying here since . . ." He began to think aloud. "Mr. Murray was arrested in the June of nineteen twenty-six, and tried in September. His poor wife died just before the trial—her illness and her anxiety together brought it about. . . . That was three years ago, this coming September."

He was garrulous, in a rambling manner that convinced Gilmore that all his knowledge would be speedily forth coming.

"Not here?" His chagrin seemed genuine. "I was given to understand that I'd either find him here or would learn where he is."

"I don't know about that," the clerk said. "As I said, up to three years ago, they were all here, occupying a suite on the second floor; but since Mrs. Murray's death, we've never heard from him, nor known where he went. I'm sure I'd have learned of it, if we had. . . ."

"But what became of the little girl—what was her name, Laura? You remember her?"

"Oh, Mrs. Lorimor took the baby with her, when she left—I suppose through some arrangement with Mr. Murray. Some one had to take care of Anna—her name was Anna, sir—not Laura."

"Of course—Anna—that was it," Gilmore said hastily. "How foolish of me to have forgotten it. But this Mrs. Lorimor, I don't think I quite remember her. Exactly who was she?"

"Well, if you'll recall how sick Mrs. Murray was," was the reply, "you'd see that there had to be some one special to take charge of the baby. Then, too, Mrs. Murray couldn't do everything for herself, either; she couldn't keep house at all, and that's why the family lived here at the hotel, kidney trouble, it was, you know; Mrs. Murray was a lovely woman—it was a shame that she should have been afflicted like that. Murray was certainly in love with her, sir; he was always worried about her, and doing things to make her happy. He brought in the best doctors; I dare say she might be alive this day if it wasn't for the trouble he got into. And he got Mrs. Lorimor as a special nurse to take care of the baby."

"And you say that Mrs. Lorimor was given the baby when Mr. Murray was in prison and there was no one else to raise it?"

"Yes—that was what happened; but I don't think anyone around here knows where they went. Mr. Murray was well off, you know, and he could afford to set them up somewhere together, till he was able to take it himself again. He knew Mrs. Lorimor would take good care of it."

The old clerk described the woman at Gilmore's request. Middle-aged and not good-looking, there had been about her an air of capability that is so often found in nurses and governesses. He did not believe she had been a hospital nurse, in which case the detective might have been able to trace her through the medical register. She had always been very pleasant to him; the Murray family had treated her as one of them, rather than as a mere employee. Certainly, he could recall how attached to her the child had been while they were at the hotel.

"But what became of them since they left," he concluded, "is something I couldn't say."

A younger man, dapper in appearance, who seemed to be, from the clerk's deference towards him, the hotel manager, joined them. He listened to the other's account of Gilmore's quest, and what he had told him regarding the Murray family.

"I was just remarking," said the old man, "that nothing has ever been heard of Mr. Murray or Mrs. Lorimor since they left us. My own opinion is that Mr. Murray is still serving his three-year sentence. . . . I'd advise this gentleman to try some of the doctors who attended Mrs. Murray in her illness. . . ."

"But isn't there some one here," persisted Gilmore, addressing the newcomer, "who might have known Mrs. Lorimor well enough to have learned where she was taking the little girl? She may have mentioned it in the course of conversation with some regular guest or . . ."

The clerk looked slightly exasperated. "I've already said—" he began, when the manager interrupted him.

"What about Mrs. Dolman?" he suggested. "Wasn't she very well acquainted with Mrs. Lorimor? My impression was that they were together a great deal . . ."

"So they were, now that you mention it. They were quite close, weren't they? Funny that it should have slipped my mind, but . . ."

"Who is this Mrs. Dolman?" Gilmore broke hastily into this colloquy. "May I see her? It's very important," he added apologetically, "that I find either Mr. Murray or Mrs. Lorimor."

Mrs. Dolman, it seemed, was the housekeeper, whose duty it was to act as overseer of the bedchambers, particularly concerned with keeping them in order. As "forewoman" of the chambermaids, she had many opportunities for becoming acquainted with the hotel's inhabitants; and since most of the guests remained a long time, she had become quite friendly, at times, with the employees of the wealthier guests. This the woman, when summoned, admitted without hesitation.

She was an outspoken, buxom matron, who, when the manager explained Gilmore's quest, expressed her willingness to assist in whatever manner she could.

Preliminary questions from Gilmore elicited the fact that she had known Mrs. Lorimor very well; in fact, she and "Susan" had become extremely close friends. Mrs. Lorimor, she went on loquaciously, was a widow who had to make her own living as a nurse since the death of her husband. She had had experience with children before; that explained her fondness for the little girl to whom she had given the attention the ailing mother had been unable to give it. And the child reciprocated this feeling, so that Mrs. Murray's death was not so great a tragedy as it might otherwise have been.

"That's why Mr. Murray was so relieved, that it wouldn't be necessary to send it to some home to be raised by strangers," she said. "He could be certain that it would be properly brought up, while he was serving his sentence."

"You can tell me, then," the detective queried, "where Mrs. Lorimor took the little girl?"

"Yes, I believe I can. Of course, I didn't know where she was going when she left; but after she was settled, she wrote me a letter telling me where she was, in case I wanted to visit her. Mr. Murray had taken a little cottage for them both to live in, until he would be able to join them again. Meanwhile, she was to keep house for Anna, send her to school and see that she was brought up properly."

The address of the cottage, which she produced by going upstairs for the letter, was 821 Forum Lane. As Gilmore read it, he experienced a thrill that could come only with the knowledge that he was nearing the last lap. With the finding of the nurse, what must practically be the concluding step was bound to be easy. As soon as he could properly take leave of the hotel officials, he did so; and immediately he set out in search of Forum Lane.

He found both the street and the house without difficulty. In a narrow, bohemian, but sedate little lane on Beacon Hill, the latter nestled, fenced apart from its fellows and completely surrounded by wooden palings. A well-tended lawn and garden fronted it, making it a colorful habitation; creepers, that climbed wire netting at the front of a clean veranda, completed its charm. It was evident Murray had chosen this retreat with a consideration of his daughter's well-being; equally was it evident that he had made no error in leaving her in Mrs. Lorimor's capable hands.

The detective's opinion became a certainty at his first view of the woman who opened the door. Serene, well-preserved in her middle-age, and with an intelligence that it would be difficult to deceive, she waited with no hint of curiosity for him to state his errand. Behind the skirts of the woman's house dress, Allen Murray's daughter peeped out shyly to view the visitor. The child was beautiful, with eyes of perfect blue and rumpled hair of gold; except, perhaps, for his own children, Gilmore had to admit that he had never seen anyone quite so lovely.

For a moment the detective had to steel himself to do his duty. His ultimate objective, he knew, must inevitably bring sorrow to the child; and he was proposing to trick these very people into betraying their loved one. Whenever his profession reduced him to such tactics, he found them extremely distasteful. Particularly in a case such as this; many people would have said that Russell Stirling fully deserved the death that was intended for him. But an innocent man had died instead—there was the difficulty; Philip Nixon, who, as against the murderer, had every right to live, had been the victim. And then there had been another death—a deliberate crime committed merely for self-protection. For these, Allen Murray merited neither consideration nor hesitation.

Gilmore introduced himself as a friend of Murray's, and stated that he wished to see him. That he was safe in making this request, he was confident; his quarry, who had but the previous day committed his second murder, was hardly likely to have returned immediately to Boston.

"I only learned recently, Mrs. Lorimor," he said glibly, "that Allen had been released. I came as soon as I could; and I believed I was almost certain to find him here or learn where he was."

Across the woman's features there flashed a look of doubt that was gone as he had observed it; and she answered graciously enough.

"Mr. Murray isn't here, just now—in fact, he hasn't been staying here at all." She invited him into the attractive snugness of an airy living room and began to elaborate upon her statement.

"Mr. Murray went away after visiting here just once as soon as he was"—she hesitated—"released, in March. He went directly to Philadelphia on some business to which he had to attend, and I haven't heard from him since, except once."

"To Philadelphia?" It was what Gilmore had expected to hear. "Can you tell me where he went or on what sort of business?"

Too late he regretted the pointed directness of his question. The look of doubt returned to her face, this time mingled with suspicion. It was as though she had been warned against people who might ask questions, and she had just recalled this caution. The detective sensed her sudden hostility and the barrier that was effectively raised between them.

"I asked that," he said hastily, "because I also wanted to see him as soon as possible, on business—a most important proposition that has to do with his old line of importing."

His knowledge of her employer's past, evidence that his claims were bona fide, reassured her a little. Nevertheless, her reply was not encouraging.

"I couldn't tell you why he went to Philadelphia, sir, and I can't say where you can find him. I've had no occasion to communicate with him since he left; and he gave us no address. We've been provided here with everything we need."

Glancing about the room, Gilmore agreed pleasantly.

"Yes, this is quite a comfortable place you have here. You've been living here almost three years now, haven't you?"

"That's right." On this subject, the nurse appeared willing to talk. "Mr. Murray made arrangements to rent this cottage for us, immediately after his wife died. As soon as the trial was over, we moved here from the Plaza Hotel, where we were staying."

Again there was a slight hesitation when she spoke of Murray, and this time some color showed in her cheeks.

"I can tell that Allen made no mistake when he gave you the responsibility of raising Anna," Gilmore went on. "She's grown up wonderfully; the last time I saw her, she was only two and now I'd take her for eight years old."

Mrs. Lorimor smiled gratefully. "She's seven, really, you know. I've done my best to raise her the way Mr. Murray would have wanted me to. He wanted Anna to know what a real home was like; and he also wanted her to get away from the place where her mother had passed away. . . ."

"I didn't know Mrs. Murray very well, I'm afraid. It was most unfortunate, her death."

To Gilmore's surprise, her reply was almost callous.

"Of course, unfortunate in a way, because she was taken from her husband. He was very good to her, and very solicitous of her comfort; naturally, she returned his affection. It wasn't surprising, then, considering how ill she was, that the shock of his arrest and trial should have undermined her health completely. Except for that, she might have recovered; as it was, she died just when Mr. Murray most needed support."

The dull, repressed monotone of her voice startled the detective; he had to study her closely to perceive the strange, unexpected stress under which she labored. For a moment he was puzzled, but then he comprehended; and her next words convinced him that his intuition was correct.

"But in another way," she continued, "she had been fortunate. After all, hadn't she won the attachment of the man she loved? As long as she lived, he was hers. That's happiness enough for anyone; and a woman couldn't ask for more than that. If I could . . ."

Mrs. Lorimor broke off suddenly; her eyes met the detective's with a sparkle, not of embarrassment, but of honest and candid admission. In his she read a sympathetic understanding; and though no words passed between them, she knew that her carefully concealed secret had been discovered.

It was because of her love for him that she had so faithfully served Allen Murray; it was that which had impelled her to do everything at his behest. And Gilmore had been the first to find it out. But she did not seem to regret it; indeed, she passed over it in silence, with gentle appreciation for the manner in which he had accepted his information.

"I'm sorry," she said simply, after a pause. "That should never have happened. . . . You wanted to know where you could find Mr. Murray?"

His wordless commiseration had successfully won her confidence; yet, strangely enough, it gave him no satisfaction.

"You told me you didn't know where he was. He gave you no address when he went away?" he inquired quietly of her.

"That is true. He said he didn't wish me to write him unless it was absolutely unavoidable. He was to let me know when he would return, but until then I was to say nothing of his absence."

"You must have considered that a very peculiar arrangement."

"I didn't stop to consider it," Mrs. Lorimor replied quietly. "They were his instructions. That was enough for me."

Gilmore nodded. "But suppose it became unavoidable? Suppose something should happen to his daughter that made it imperative for you to get in touch with him? In such a case, it would have been criminal to leave you no means of doing so."

She smiled at his insistence. "As a matter of fact, he did. You remember, I mentioned that I heard from him once from Philadelphia. That was when I received a letter, telling me where I could send him one; but I was to do so only if, as you suggested, I had something to write him about Anna. It wasn't his address, he said; but if I followed out his instructions, he'd receive it just the same. Of course, he didn't anticipate that I would have to use them; he knew that in my hands, if only for his sake, the child was perfectly safe."

Calmly Gilmore asked, "And where was it, you could reach him?"

In her newborn utter reliance, caused by having shared her secret with one so quietly comprehending, her guard had fallen completely. She appeared oblivious that it was this very thing against which Murray had intended to guard. Had she known the purpose of her employer's journey to Philadelphia, the detective was certain that nothing could have dragged from her the answer she gave him.

"He wrote that a letter sent to Elbert Higgins, Apartment E3, Terrace Garden Apartments, Germantown, would surely reach him."

23
THE VOICE ON THE WIRE

By no possible chance or ingenious scheme could Russell Stirling's butler be the man he sought. Again and again, on his entire return journey to Philadelphia, that very night, Gilmore assured himself of that fact. In the first place, Higgins's features were not those of the picture shown him in Allen Murray's prison record. It was altogether likely that his smooth-faced quarry had adopted a disguise to secure himself while he carried out his mission; the butler wore no disguise whatsoever. What militated more strongly against such an idea was the fact that the stockbroker would not have been deceived. Perfectly well acquainted with the idiosyncrasies of his old enemy, he would, in such close quarters, have recognized them even though Higgins had cleverly concealed his appearance.

The fact that Higgins served as a conductor between Murray and his family, indicated, then, that he was employed in some capacity by the latter. He was acting against his master's interests; but the circumstances of this arrangement were unknown. Gilmore could not tell whether he was aware of the purpose for which he was giving aid; but he swore he would know from Higgins's own lips before he was many hours older.

The train from Boston brought him to Headquarters before eight o'clock in the morning. There, joined by

Smith, he set forth for Germantown, timing himself to reach the Terrace Garden Apartments immediately after Stirling would leave for his office. Gilmore was not anxious to invite the complication that was bound to ensue did the broker learn of his call on the butler.

It was exactly quarter after nine when he knocked upon the door of the apartment.

This time, as Higgins opened the door, there was no greeting; to the butler's intense astonishment, the two visitors stepped directly past him into the hallway. The sheer rudeness of it prevented him from voicing any objection until it was too late.

"Please, sir, you can't come in like this. . . . This is a private house and Mr. Stirling wouldn't like it if . . ."

"Close the door, Smith,"—Gilmore brusquely disregarded him—"and lock it, as we don't want to be interrupted. Bring Higgins along into the parlor; we'll see how easily he can lie himself out of his difficulties this time."

His companion, well coached, obeyed; protesting at every step, the frightened butler found himself hurried into the living room. There, the detective seated himself in the chair that stood near the gold-colored divan and studied the man he intended to question. He instructed him to stand in the middle of the room, before him. Lacking any support, he was at an added disadvantage.

"The last time I was here, Higgins," he began severely, after an ominous pause that distressed the timorous butler further, "I gave you the choice of telling me what you knew or being arrested as an accessory before the fact to the crime of murder. . . ."

"But I did tell you everything I knew then."

Gilmore went on relentlessly as though he had not spoken.

"This time, I'm not going to give you a chance to lie to me. I'm arresting you for murder, as an accessory and I warn you that anything you say will be used against you!"

For a moment, it seemed that the other would collapse. The color receded from his cheeks leaving them a pasty white; his eyes bulged in fear and dismay. So agitated was he that he swayed slightly and only caught himself with a determined effort.

"Murder? Arrest me for murder? I don't know what you're talking about!" he cried at last.

"The murder of Philip Nixon, Higgins. . . . That's a pretty serious charge; it means twenty years at least, and maybe the chair."

"I never heard of Philip Nixon—he's a stranger to me . . ."

"Nor of Allen Murray, I suppose," Gilmore interposed grimly. "You know nothing about an agreement with him to help him against your master, to receive letters for him and to assist him to murder Mr. Stirling as well? Your aid was necessary to his carrying out his plans; he must have paid you well for that."

Much of the charge was sheer guesswork; as he had already reflected, the butler might know nothing of the object to which he was lending a hand. But it had its effect, nevertheless.

As he replied, beads of perspiration stood out visibly on the accused man's forehead.

"That, sir? I didn't mean anything wrong by that, sir; I thought it was all right. I didn't know his name, either, and I only told him of Mr. Stirling's movements. If he went and murdered some one, I had nothing to do with that. I never dreamed that he was anything more than a business rival of Mr. Stirling's."

"He told you that, did he? He intended something much more serious than stealing business secrets. I'm afraid, Higgins, that you're deeply involved. You had better come out with what you know; it will make things easier for you."

The detective's voice was less harsh. Higgins's genuine fright indicated that he was telling the truth; it was unlikely, if he was any reader of character, that the baited man would have dared to take part in the more desperate undertaking.

"I'll willingly tell you what I can," Higgins said anxiously. "But you must believe that I knew nothing about any killing; I only did it because it seemed a harmless way of making a little extra money."

"Well, get on with your story." Gilmore sounded uncompromising. "If it satisfies me, I'll see what I can do for you."

Without further delay, the other plunged into his narrative. Three months previous, toward the end of the month of March, he had received an unsigned letter, making a most peculiar and yet attractive business proposition. Though somewhat vague, it offered the butler a method of earning some money besides that which Stirling paid him, without giving up this job. To whet his curiosity, it suggested that the work would consist merely of speaking on the phone once or twice a day. The anonymous missive concluded by stating that it would give Higgins a few days to consider the offer. In a few days, its author would communicate with the butler once more; and if he proved to be interested in the proposition, further information would be forthcoming.

"You say this occurred in March?" Gilmore interrupted at this point.

Allen Murray had been released in March. It was evident to the detective that he had immediately come to Philadelphia to carry out the scheme of retribution against his betrayer.

"That's right, sir," the butler replied. "It was about March the twenty-fifth, that the letter came."

"What did you do with it? Do you still have it?"

"No, sir, I don't have it any more. I kept it until the writer called me shortly after, and then, at his orders, I destroyed it."

"So he got in touch with you, and you decided to accept his proposition," Gilmore said. "Well, get on with your story."

During the interval between the letter and the call, which had come at exactly ten o'clock in the morning, two days later, Higgins had pondered the offer. He had not wished to do anything wrong, nor to get into difficulties; but it seemed to involve so little trouble that he decided to hear more about it. It seemed that Higgins had parents on a Nebraska farm, whom, as a dutiful son, he was supporting, and any additional income would prove very welcome. Especially since the amount promised him over the phone was almost as much as Stirling paid him. On the first of every month, a hundred-dollar bill would arrive for him, if he merely agreed to keep his unknown employer informed of the broker's movements and what he knew of his business developments.

"It didn't look very bad to me, sir," Higgins explained apologetically. "Even if I wanted to, I wouldn't be able to tell him much; and if he was satisfied with what I did know, it was so much easy money. Mr. Stirling never did business at home, nor discussed it with me. And just to let him know where Mr. Stirling went, wasn't wrong; all he wanted was to hear what he did at home, and away. He suggested that my master might go away to transact business, or have visitors here; so I was to keep him posted as to his hours for going to work, retiring, eating—his habits in general. And I agreed to do what he asked."

"And what did he tell you to do, regarding mail that might come for him?"

"For reasons of his own, he did not wish his mail sent directly to him; accordingly, he had arranged that it be mailed to me in my name," the butler replied. "Anything from Boston was for him, in which case I was to let him know when next he communicated with me. Then we would see about meeting each other, so that I could give it to him. But so far there haven't been any letters."

All transactions, it appeared, had been carried on exclusively by telephone. The butler's mysterious employer had regularly communicated with him daily at the same time as he had done at first—ten o'clock. Every morning at the exact hour, he called to learn both the developments of the preceding day and the news of the coming one. And the calls had not ceased coming since the day on which the financier had met his death. Gilmore found it significant that despite the fact he had killed the wrong man by mistake, Allen Murray was not to be swerved from his original plan. There was something admirable in the tenacity with which he was determined to remove his enemy when the opportunity again offered itself.

"You've never seen your employer, then," Gilmore remarked when Higgins had finished explaining their system of communication. "Can you describe for me his voice?"

"His voice?" The other looked distressed. "It sounded like . . . a . . . voice."

"I know—but was it high-pitched or deep—gruff or refined? Would you recognize it if you heard it in the street?"

"I couldn't say whether I should, sir. It was low, and gentle, as far as I could tell; but you know how metallic everything sounds over the phone."

"How did your money come to you?" the detective asked.

"It came on the first of the month, beginning in April, in single bills of a hundred dollars. The envelopes, addressed to me, were mailed from the Central Post Office, downtown. I don't think you'll be able to get any hint from them, as to who sent them."

Nor did Gilmore. This was but another of the many ingenious precautions that Allen Murray had taken. As swift as the detective to realize the greatest danger to the success of his plans, he had sought to remove it as much as he possibly could. A known enemy of Russell Stirling, it was inevitable that, should the broker perish in any questionable manner, suspicion would point immediately to him. Every effort would be subsequently made to connect him with the crime. Hence, Murray's attention had been brilliantly directed toward erecting a barrier between himself and the crime he planned to perpetrate. He was making certain that no point of contact could be discovered. And how cleverly he labored! Even Higgins, who was his weakest link, had been safeguarded; had Stirling died, the butler was not likely to reveal to the authorities the part he had played, no matter how innocently, in assisting the criminal.

Gilmore next turned to questioning Higgins as to the information he had actually passed on to his secret employer. Until they came to the day of the murder, and Stirling's intended journey to the shore, nothing important developed.

"You told him then that Mr. Stirling was going to Cape May on Monday evening? Exactly what did you say?"

"Simply what I knew, sir," the butler replied; "that Mr. Stirling had called me at two o'clock to order me to bring his bag to the Camden terminal at seven-thirty. But I told him that I didn't know the reason for his trip."

The detective's heart sank suddenly. The most important link, upon which his case stood or fell, failed to connect. If the butler knew nothing of the journey his master was taking until two o'clock in the afternoon of the day of the tragedy, Murray could have had no knowledge of it until ten, the following morning. He could not, therefore, have been trailing the broker aboard the 7:45 express.

But he spoke calmly enough, as he asked, "I suppose you gave this information to your employer, the next morning."

"Oh, no, sir. I told him the same day, at five o'clock, that Mr. Stirling was taking the seven-forty-five train."

"But I thought you said . . ." Gilmore began.

"Since the Friday before that," Higgins explained, "the gentleman had been calling me twice a day—once at ten, and again at five o'clock in the evening. The information I gave him on Friday seemed to excite him a great deal; he said that he would have to keep in closer touch with me, and that he would begin to communicate twice with me. It didn't seem so very important to me, but . . ."

"Never mind that," the detective interrupted impatiently. "What was the information?"

"Simply that I thought Mr. Stirling was in quite serious difficulty on the market. You recall, I said that I could often tell that from his manner, though I could never say exactly what was the matter. But I could make a pretty shrewd guess as to how desperate his situation was."

The circumstance puzzled the detective. Except for a feeling of satisfaction Murray might have experienced in seeing Stirling subjected to the same treatment he had suffered, there appeared no motive for Murray's concern in the broker's ruination.

But, at this moment, there was the more important consideration of taking advantage of the opening offered by his opponent. From the beginning of the butler's narrative, the opportunity that would shortly present itself had been apparent. And swiftly he was evolving a trap which he hoped, with Higgins's aid, to spring. That, to bait the snare, he would have to utilize Murray's natural anxiety for his daughter was regrettable; but there seemed no help for it. Sentiment could not interfere with the necessity of meeting his quarry's cunning with a similar cunning.

There remained but little time to carry his plan into execution. Gilmore's watch informed him that it was ten minutes to ten.

Facing Higgins sternly, he said, "When you began to tell me your story, I promised you that, if it satisfied me, I would see what I could do for you. Well, you've convinced me that your participation in the affair was innocent, and I've decided to release you."

Smith, an attentive listener at the doorway, saw what was coming, and smiled behind his hand.

"Thank you," the relieved butler said fervently, "I appreciate your confidence."

"But I expect something in return. The man you've been helping is twice a murderer, and is planning yet to kill Mr. Stirling. Unless the police are able to capture him, it will be impossible to prevent him, and you are in a position to help us save your master's life."

"I, sir?" Elbert looked surprised and nervous. "But I don't know where he is or anything more than I've told you about him."

"There won't be any danger," the detective went on persuasively. "Your part will only consist in speaking to him over the phone and identifying him later. You'll have the best of guards with you. . . . Come, remember you had best make amends for your past aid to him."

He was doubtful no longer. "I'll do it, Mr. Gilmore, to prove that I never intentionally was guilty of any wrongdoing."

"Very well, then. It is almost ten o'clock now. You are certain that you will get a call at that time?"

"Yes, sir," Higgins said. "At least I have every reason to believe that there will be no interruption in his usual custom."

"Then follow out these instructions to the letter. When the phone rings, you will answer it as usual; as usual, I suppose your employer will ask for information. You will tell him that you have received a special delivery letter from Boston; you must make it seem very important that he should get it as soon as possible. In all probability, he will tell you where to send it or, better still, make arrangements to meet you. In any case, agree to anything that he will suggest to bring you together. After that, you will come with us until it is time for the meeting; then we will give you further instructions. Do you think you can carry it off, successfully?"

"I hope I can, sir—at least, I'll do my best."

Gilmore voiced the importance of the task. "I'm putting a great responsibility into your hands, Higgins; we daren't take any chance of putting him on his guard. Talk as naturally to him as you would on any other occasion. Once he takes fright, it will be impossible to get him."

"I think you may trust me, sir," the other replied.

"Good!" With this exclamation, the detective swiftly shifted the subject. "Where can we find the telephone switchboard?"

"It's under the stairs, downstairs, at the rear of the hallway. There's a girl on duty there, all the time."

Gilmore turned to his assistant; now that his case was nearing its end, his entire concern was turned toward building a case against the culprit.

"Smith, go below and tell the operator that we are expecting a call in Apartment E3 in a few moments, that must be traced to its source. Tell her it's official and urgent, and if she objects, let her know how serious it is for us to learn where it came from."

"I get you, sir," the other detective said. "She'll do it for me if I have to use force to make her do it."

He had barely returned with the information of his success, when, from a corner of the room, there came a tinkling sound. It was light and muffled; yet it seemed to pierce the ears of those who waited for it, like the blast of a siren. The phone rested on a narrow table behind the grand piano; invisible from the doorway, it was hidden from sight by a doll screen, fashioned in the costume of a court lady of the eighteenth century. The wide, flowered, pink hoop skirt served effectively to conceal the ugly black instrument.

The minute hand of Gilmore's watch pointed exactly to the hour.

Before Higgins had time to raise the receiver, the bell peeled forth again, more insistently. Interminably, it seemed to ring while the butler waited for it to become silent, before he began to speak.

"Hello, Higgins talking, sir. . . . Mr. Stirling went out long ago—to the office. . . . No sir, I have nothing new to tell you about him, sir, but a letter addressed to me, arrived from Boston this morning. It's a special delivery letter; it must be for you, because I don't know anyone in Boston. It looks very important, and I don't wish to keep it any longer than I have to. I . . . What's that? . . . A return address on it? Just a minute till I go and see."

"Tell him it came from eight-two-one Forum Lane," Gilmore whispered, as Higgins turned to him. "That will convince him it's authentic."

In the silent spaces, between the butler's speeches, he could hear the metallic, rasping voice at the other end of the wire.

"The address is eight-two-one Forum Lane," the butler continued on the wire. "Yes, sir, I'd like to get it to you as soon as possible. . . . Yes, I could meet you, anywhere

you suggest; that would be the quickest way, wouldn't it?
. . . Any time you say, sir. . . . The Central Post Office at
Ninth and Market streets at four o'clock this afternoon
will be quite convenient. . . . Yes, I shall certainly be on
time. . . . No, there is nothing else, sir, but don't forget
this. Good-bye."

He rang off, and replacing the receiver, turned about.

"At the Central Post Office," he said to the detective,
"at four o'clock this afternoon."

"Very good work," Gilmore warmly commended. "I
couldn't have done better myself. And now, Higgins, Smith
will take care of you until the time you are to meet him.
He will see that you are there with the letter by a quarter
of four. Every safeguard will be taken; you'll have nothing
to fear of any danger."

He waited until both of them had gone, Smith with
the necessary orders, before he searched out the telephone
operator below, and in a narrow cubbyhole under the
stairs, found her.

"Well," he queried, after explaining that he also was a
detective. "Have you traced the call?"

"Yes, just this minute," she replied. "It's a wonder you
wouldn't teach that friend of yours some manners. It's so
much easier to get things done for you if you're nice about
it."

As she spoke, the girl handed to him a piece of paper
on which she had written the results of her efforts.

24
THE TRAP

At last Gilmore knew the entire truth of a crime so brilliant in its plotting and masterly in its execution that never before had he encountered its equal. Reading what was written upon that slip of paper, at first he was frankly incredulous; with a complete comprehension, his surprise turned to admiration. He was too worthy an opponent not to appreciate the cleverness that had led him astray and prevented an earlier solution of the mystery. But he knew that, under the circumstances, it was not to be expected that anyone could have done better. Until given the proper clue, the ingenuity with which the crime had been carried out was beyond one's normal conception of things.

Knowing all the facts, there was nothing to prevent him from arresting the criminal immediately, rather than waiting for the meeting at four o'clock. Nothing but the abominable weakness of his case against Allen Murray. Gilmore was suddenly appalled by the realization that, despite all the information he had gathered, he had not one item of evidence with which to bring the man's guilt home to him. Elbert Higgins could only prove that he had been hired by Murray for some unknown and, as far as he could show, harmless purpose. His own evidence at no point connected Murray with Philip Nixon. Already he could picture the attorney for the defense ridiculing his theory of the crime. "Gentlemen of the jury, the prosecution's motive for the crime it claims Allen Murray committed, is that he intended to kill some one else. You are asked to believe that when one sets out to commit murder, he does not know his chosen victim!"

Gilmore had, therefore, to rely upon the effect of surprise, as a substitute for facts. As long as the criminal maintained a stony silence, he was safe; but it was possible that a capture under the circumstances the detective was planning would loosen his tongue. To thus arrest him when he believed himself most secure was bound to make him believe that the police had an unbreakably strong chain of evidence against him; at the moment of detention, his confusion might betray him into revealing more tangible evidence. Certainly, the entire arrest would be far more effective than if Gilmore were to carry it out immediately.

If only he could uncover the weak link in his opponent's armor! He knew now that Murray had left the 7:45 express, after having committed the crime, at Oldroyd; it was at his request—to the conductor he had subsequently murdered—that the train had halted to allow him to disembark. But the only person who could prove it was dead, and no one at Oldroyd was likely to have observed him. What Gilmore urgently required was evidence indubitably establishing his connection with the crime. If there were only some eyewitness whose story would satisfy a jury! But it was impossible to produce what did not exist or wish for what. . . unless . . .

Out of a clear sky there came the recollection that told him how blind he had been. The words of the talkative ticket agent at Newfield station! With the reviving of the dormant memory of that conversation came the realization that it was the answer to the very problem which now confronted him. At the time, when he had questioned the station master about the arrival of Frank Marley and his passenger, he had disregarded his garrulously surplus talk; he had not the time to listen to local gossip. And yet, it was that very gossip, casually dropped by the agent, that supplied the priceless item of evidence he needed!

But that evidence, with which he hoped to confront Allen Murray, was seventy-five miles away. Already, it was 10:15, and in the interim of less than six hours until the meeting between Higgins and his secret employer, no trains would enable him to procure it in time for the meeting. On the other hand, if it were at all possible, he alone could bring it back. By machine, it might be made if he started without delay, and there were no difficulties on the road. It would, however, be a close thing, when the distance to be traveled in the remaining time was considered. Could it be done, if he obtained an automobile at once; or would a last moment lack of time prevent him from concluding the case successfully?

Surely, it was worth the effort, he decided. If he failed, Smith would, nevertheless, see that the trap was properly sprung in his absence; and if he accomplished his aim, the result would gain him something more than Superintendent Wainwright's mere approval.

In less than a moment after he had made his decision, Gilmore had headquarters, and had Tommy Rankin on the other end of the wire and was informing him of it; in answer to his first question, he learned that his colleague's machine was within reach, prepared for whatever he proposed.

"Meet me at the entrance of the Delaware River Bridge in twenty minutes," he ordered. "I'll explain when I see you, but we have a hundred-and-fifty-mile journey before us, between now and four o'clock, today."

A low whistle of surprise reached him. "That's an average of thirty miles an hour for five hours continuously," Rankin said. "Well, we'll see what we can do. At the bridge in twenty minutes. . . ."

As he rang off, Gilmore hastened from the Terrace Garden Apartments. In the driveway, a Yellow taxi was drawn up before the entrance, its driver conversing with the resplendent porter. They stopped speaking as he hailed it, and the man shook his head.

"I'm sorry, sir, but this cab is already engaged. I'm waiting for some people to come down from . . ."

The sight of the detective's credentials reduced him to obedient silence. He offered no objection to Gilmore's entering the car, and, at his order, took his place at the wheel.

"This is important police business," Gilmore said as he seated himself. "Drive me to the Delaware Bridge and never mind the traffic laws."

The shortest possible time for the trip proved to be five minutes more than the twenty he had allotted himself. The most direct route took the car along the Wissahickon drive, the narrow and winding character of which prevented such speed as Gilmore would have desired. Once on the wider park drive bordering the Schuylkill River, however, the chauffeur obeyed his instructions literally; with a reckless skill that seems inherent in taxi drivers, he left much of the townward bound traffic far behind and threaded an unhesitating course into the Parkway Boulevard. Disregarding traffic signals, he turned to the left at Race Street, on which is located Philadelphia's Chinatown; across eight or more intersecting streets, he reached to the opening of the bridge.

Rankin's car, with the engine running, waited on the avenue of approach. Money had long since been crammed into the driver's hand; not an instant was wasted in Gilmore's exchange of machines.

"It's quarter of eleven," was all he said to his colleague, as he took his place beside him. "That gives us exactly five hours, Tommy; that means you daren't fall under thirty. . . ."

By the time he had fully explained the sudden journey, the river had been crossed and the city of Camden was being left behind. On the other side of the bridge, they paused long enough to pick up an officer; his presence on the running board enabled them to thread the city traffic at illegal speed without interruption. Upper Broadway, however, with its early noon traffic, often held them up; so that ten minutes of precious time had been lost when the town's outskirts were reached. The officer dropped off at Gloucester. At Brooklawn, four miles out, the car swung into the Black Horse Pike, a main highway to Atlantic City, one branch of which leads to Cape May.

Had the occasion of the trip been less vital, Gilmore would have found much of pleasure in it. It was a warm day, with enough breeze to prevent the heat from becoming uncomfortable. The open country of southern Jersey, through which they were passing, was richly green and fertile; orchards and fields flashed by in quick succession. The open road stretched invitingly before them, a white encircling bed of concrete. But the detective, in his anxiety, had an eye only for his watch as mile after mile flew by; fervently he hoped that no mishap would delay their passage. And Rankin, engrossed at the wheel, had no attention to spare for the land's scenic beauties.

Though the latter fully accepted the invitation of the open road, Newfield, thirty miles out, was reached, according to Gilmore's schedule, a few moments late. Seven minutes of lost time had been recovered during the ride, but a series of towns and villages necessarily hindered their pace. Through Westville, Hurffville and the outskirts of Pitman, they traveled at a curtailed rate; Glassboro was passed at 11:25; then came Clayton, Franklinville and Iona. At Malaga they were stopped by the crossroad junction; but Gilmore recalled from Parker's tale of his race to Rockton, that the road to the right paralleled the railroad line into Newfield. Through the latter town they flew, regardless of the traffic.

Beyond Millville, an important center in southern Jersey, they arrived at Rockton. Through the larger town, a few more moments of invaluable time were again sacrificed; only Gilmore's knowledge of Rockton prevented a similar loss in their passage through it. Four miles out of town, still following the main highway, Jenny Belcher's and the dirt road that encircled Pelham woods, to the Marley farm, were passed. The pike crossed the railroad tracks shortly afterward, as Clem Marley had described, and paralleled it. The farmhouse, however, separated from the highway by a quarter of a mile of fields, was not visible. Marking, at fifty miles, two-thirds of the route in one direction, it was 12:28 when the machine flew by.

Between Rockton and Oldroyd, thirty miles farther on, there were further delays. The country through which they were now passing was unknown to them; except for Gilmore's journeys by train, and at night, they had never visited it. Lacking the opportunity to procure a map before starting upon the trip, it was necessary to depend upon the signposts on the road. These appeared only at crossroads, or important branch highways of which there were many; and every intersection required a halt. Several times, in addition, among many guiding signs, no information regarding Oldroyd was included; twice, inquiries of natives along the way became unavoidable. They approached the town at last, close upon twenty minutes after one.

It seemed to be little more than a secluded country hamlet, in which the railroad station was its most conspicuous building. The taint of salt in the cooler atmosphere told of the reflected significance it possessed, only by reason of its proximity to the ocean. A single main street alone gave it the cohesive qualities of a village; otherwise, it was composed of farm cottages, scattered in nearby meadows. The road led directly into its lone avenue, and passed beyond toward the shore resort.

"We're ten minutes behind schedule, Tommy," Gilmore said, as they followed it into town. "We'll have to make it up on the way back."

"We'll manage it," Rankin returned grimly. They were almost his first words during the course of the entire journey. "Now that we know the road, we won't have the same trouble on our return. . . ."

He drew the car up into the station driveway that wound itself about the rear of the depot. Before he had halted it, Gilmore was out and accosting a village ancient, who loafed upon the platform, smoking a pipe.

"I'm looking for a chap named Wally Berger," the detective said. "I understand that he's the driver of the depot jitney. . . ." Gilmore's anxiety made the placid tardiness with which the man replied, exasperating. Expectorating on the rotten wooden flooring, he went on calmly puffing at his pipe.

"Wally Berger?" he drawled at last. "Yes, he's the jitney driver, all right. He meets all trains, rain or shine. . . . I guess you'll find him 'round t' other side of the station, waitin' for that there train from Millville to . . ."

But Gilmore had already gone, behind the station platform.

Where the drive ended at the railroad tracks, a large, brightly polished Studebaker stood, receiving the attention of its owner. Evidently an object of pride to him, he was cleaning it with a cloth, until it glistened blindingly in the sunlight. The man himself was large-boned and tall; sharp and keen in a rustic manner, he was the possessor of lean features and twinkling eyes. Overalls protected his clothes. The nasal twang of his first words clearly proclaimed his rural origin and contacts.

The astounding adventure that befell Wally Berger probably had no equal during his uneventful existence. The sight of a stranger bearing down upon him from the other side of the station was surprising enough; that the newcomer was a detective, who insisted that he accompany him, was little short of bewildering. He literally found himself abducted, ere he could comprehend what was occurring; in an instant, he was swept into a car in which a driver waited, at the opening of the station road. Barely was he seated when the machine swept away at a tremendous speed.

"But," he protested vehemently, "I can't leave when the train's due. I must meet the passengers in ten minutes. . . ."

His vain objection came too late. Already the town of Oldroyd was being left behind; and with the approach of the open road, his words were momentarily drowned in the roar of the engine.

"You won't have any trouble on that account," Gilmore soothed him. "You'll be paid for your time and whatever losses you suffer."

Nevertheless, they were nearing Rockton before he succeeded in making Berger understand and accept the situation. Once Berger had grasped the necessity of these high-handed proceedings, he was only too willing to narrate his story, and answer the series of searching questions the detective put to him. While Gilmore satisfied himself that at no point had he erred in his deductions, mile after mile was reeled off in the furious race back to Philadelphia.

The northbound journey was, in a large measure, a repetition of that toward the shore. There were no delays, however, this time, as Rankin's familiarity with the road obviated the need of any halts. He permitted nothing to interfere with the uniform, constant pace, which he had adopted, of forty-five miles an hour. Rockton, Millville and Vineland swept by in quick succession. Utterly oblivious of traffic signals or dangerous curves on the pike, the car continued its swift course; that its occupants met with no mishap seemed miraculous. Newfield was reached at a quarter of three, and as the machine careened through the town, Gilmore said exultantly, "We'll make it yet, Tommy; thirty miles to travel and we're exactly right on schedule."

Nor was he in error. Between Newfield and Camden, Rankin gained ten minutes upon the schedule time that would necessarily be lost again in Camden traffic. It was twenty minutes after three when they turned from the Black Horse Pike at Brooklawn, three-thirty when the business center of Camden was reached, and not much later when they came to the suspension bridge spanning the Delaware. To Gilmore, the river never presented a more welcome sight.

As Tommy Rankin drew his machine up before the Post Office building at Ninth and Market streets, the clock on the City Hall Tower indicated that it was quarter of four.

The Post Office is a dirty graystone building that stretches its length an entire block along Ninth Street from Market to Chestnut. From the Market Street corner, a broad corridor within looking out upon Ninth Street, leads to Chestnut; at either end vestibules open into this passage. Directly inward from the entrances, through a series of doors, are large anterooms that open into various offices. The room on the Market Street corner has a wide staircase leading above, on the left; directly under it an elevator protrudes across the chamber. Under the stairs, telephone booths form three sides of a square, with the office door beyond them; in the open space before the elevator four pillars reach to the ceiling.

As Gilmore entered with the jitney driver, he observed a detective stationed outside; but no sign of recognition passed between them.

Smith, with Higgins beside him, greeted his superior and proceeded to describe the arrangements he had made.

"I've posted Jenks at the head of the stairs," he explained, "so that he will be coming down as the meeting is taking place. We can best watch what is going on, from behind the elevator or by the telephone booths; since Higgins will remain up forward near the front entrance, it's very unlikely that we'll be observed there. I suppose you saw Larry Beale posted outside, so he won't be able to escape through the door."

Observing that one standing behind the lift was not visible in the open space before it, Gilmore expressed his satisfaction.

"That will do excellently," he said, "particularly as we can appear merely by coming forward a few paces. You had best take a position in the corridor entrance, Smith, in case an effort is made in that direction. When Rankin comes, have him join us at the booths. . . ."

"Yes, sir," Smith agreed. "Here is the letter, prepared just as you've instructed."

The detective took from him a missive of ordinary correspondence size, addressed to the care of Elbert Higgins, on which were special delivery stamps. The smeared postmark, on first glance, might have been that of Boston; certainly the return address on it—821 Forum Lane—seemed to leave no room for doubt in that regard.

"This will be sufficient; Murray won't be able to do more than glance at it." He passed it to the butler. "You understand fully what you are to do, Higgins? You are merely to give him this; nothing further is required of you."

When all had taken their respective places, there was nothing to indicate that anything out of the ordinary was occurring. Berger, with the two detectives, appeared, to the casual observer, to be waiting for an expected phone call. In the corridor, one man waited, with the air of a loafer; outside, another, as though he had an appointment. The detective on the stairs was invisible from below. Only Higgins seemed, as the moments slowly passed, slightly nervous; but nothing about his conduct made him particularly conspicuous.

With an inexorable precision, the minute hand of Gilmore's watch moved toward the hour. Through the finely grilled bars of the elevator cage he peered closely every time the doors at the entrance began to revolve. A postman entered the anteroom toward the offices in the rear; a young lady descended the stairs, touching Jenks as she passed. A few moments later, a clerk brushed past them and hurried from the building; then several employees went into the parcel post room. But there was no sign of the man for whom they were waiting.

What if he had failed in this, which was to be his supreme effort! Gilmore was not aware that he had miscalculated at any point nor failed to provide for any contingency. He had applied the knowledge gained in Boston and made use of Higgins exactly as Mrs. Lorimor would have done. His quarry could not have learned of his inquiries in the Hub City. Though Allen Murray had not expected a letter, there could be nothing suspicious in the butler's receipt of one. And yet, every movement of the criminal had proclaimed his extreme cleverness; the safeguards he had raised clearly indicated that he was not to be trapped by ordinary means. Was it possible that, mistrusting his employee and the arrival of the letter, he had communicated with his housekeeper to learn if she had sent it?

The idea gave the detective a dreadful qualm; if that had occurred, the failure of his snare meant that, at the very end, he had lost the game. For, aware of everything that Gilmore knew, understanding that the detective had uncovered his identity and the motive for his crimes, he would most certainly flee. At this very moment, while Gilmore awaited him, he would be making his escape. And if later, by good fortune, he should be found, it would be impossible to bring his misdeeds home to him. Only a capture by surprise would successfully bring about that result.

No wonder Gilmore's appalling fears turned to a more dreadful conviction, as the minute hand touched the hour and crept beyond. Two, three, four minutes after four . . . and then the revolving doors turned again, and Gilmore felt a sudden tight clutch upon his arm.

"That's the man," Wally Berger whispered excitedly. "That's the fellow I drove last Monday night from Oldroyd to Newfield in time for him to catch the ten-thirty-five train back to Cape May."

The man who entered and accosted Higgins was clad in the dark blue coat and gray cap that Mrs. Pretching had described as the outfit of Ralph Burke's murderer. Nor had she been mistaken as to his mustache; he also wore a dark goatee. Pince-nez poised delicately upon the bridge of his nose. Yet, even though these items changed his appearance, he was undoubtedly the man, with clean-shaven, ascetic features, of the picture in Boston. Gilmore's impression of a fleeting, familiar resemblance to some one he slightly knew, was not strange; but it would have been surprising had he then recognized the features, aged by three years' imprisonment, and cleverly disguised by glasses and a natural growth of beard, of Dr. David Curtiss.

"I'm sorry to have been so late, Higgins," said the man Gilmore had known as Dr. Curtiss, "but I was detained by traffic. May I please have the letter?"

From behind the elevator, the detective stepped into full view; from the stairs, Jenks began a measured descent. The vestibule doors revolved as Beale entered, joined by Smith, from the corridor.

There was something admirable in Allen Murray's composure. Aware that he had been trapped, he made the effort that Gilmore had feared, to bluff his way through the situation. His feigned assumption of surprise appeared ingeniously genuine.

"It's quite astonishing I should meet you here, Sergeant Gilmore," he said evenly. "Something of a coincidence or . . ."

The words froze suddenly upon his lips, as his eyes leaving the man he was addressing traveled beyond to the jitney driver, who had just stepped into view from the telephone booths. Every vestige of color departed from his face; the contracting muscles of his mouth drew his lips together ominously. As though, for the first time, he realized how completely he was cornered, he stood rooted to the spot, his body taut with sudden confusion. The pince-nez fell with a tinkling sound to shatter upon the concrete floor.

"I arrest you, Allen Murray," said Gilmore, "for the willful murders of Philip Nixon and Ralph Burke and I warn you that anything you say will be used against you."

Still the other stood motionless, unstirring. Only his hands moved and swiftly, suddenly, they dropped to his pocket and were raised again toward his head. The cold evil gleam of steel unexpectedly flashed in his right hand.

"My God, stop him!"

Rankin's cry of warning came too late. Prepared as they were for any desperate effort to flee, this mode of escape took them unawares. Higgins, rooted to the spot in sheer horror, was in the way; even as Gilmore swung about him to grasp at his prisoner, the shot rang deafeningly in his ears, so close that its flame almost seared his face. In his very hands, the body of Curtiss—or Murray—collapsed; only his arms about him prevented him from falling.

For one brief instant, the terrifying violence of the act took its toll in a dreadful, pregnant silence. Then, as screams echoed through the building, there came the sound of running feet. As if by magic, spectators appeared in the comparatively deserted antechamber; from the street they poured, and from every corner of the structure, the offices disgorging their employees. They came crowding and cramming for places from which to witness the tragedy, until no space was left in the room except that occupied in the center by those concerned in it.

"Tommy, get a doctor and the ambulance at once," Gilmore ordered, as he gently lowered the body to the floor. "Jenks, call up Headquarters. Get some policemen together, Smith, and keep the crowds back to give him space. I'm afraid that he's finished, but we want to give him every chance."

Until the physician arrived, he did what he could; but it was little enough under the circumstances. Shaken by the catastrophe, he could only make Allen Murray as comfortable as possible. The man was unconscious and breathing so imperceptibly that, at any moment, it seemed life would be extinct. While Smith and two officers, whose attention had been drawn by the shot, evicted a portion of the throng and roped off the anteroom, he ministered to the stricken captive.

The examination by the doctor, whom Rankin procured, was brief. In a few moments, he rose from it, a serious look upon his face.

"I'm afraid that there isn't a chance he'll live more than two hours," he announced gravely. "The bullet traveled from the temple region, through the top of the head; in coming out again in the occipital region, it fractured the skull and caused an internal hemorrhage. Though he may regain consciousness for a few moments, and even be able to speak, there is certainly no hope for him."

The stratagem Gilmore had prepared to surprise his opponent into a betrayal had had distressing and calamitous consequences; but recalling Mrs. Lorimor and the child to whom Murray was so attached, he was not at all sure but that, after all, this was perhaps the happiest solution for all so tragically concerned.

25
THE HORRIBLE MISTAKE

"You understand," Gilmore was explaining to his wife, "that the address to which the telephone girl at the Terrace Garden Apartments traced Allen Murray's call was that of Dr. Curtiss. Then I knew that their identities were the same; but I was faced with the astonishing fact that the murderer was sitting beside me on the train that came upon Philip Nixon's body. That he had doubled in his tracks after leaving the seven-forty-five express was evident, though for what purpose I could not tell. If he had immediately started back to Newfield, he could catch the later train on which I was, in spite of the storm; he had seventy-five minutes between nine-twenty, when his train reached Oldroyd and ten-thirty-five, when mine left Newfield, to travel a distance slightly over forty miles. And then I remembered what the ticket agent at Newfield had said about Wally Berger, a jitney driver in Oldroyd, driving in with a passenger at ten-thirty. That told me how Murray had accomplished the journey and I knew Berger could identify him."

It was several days after the death of Allen Murray that the detective discussed the case with Mrs. Gilmore. Inevitably he did so, following the completion of every investigation, recounting, for her edification, his adventures. Mrs. Gilmore always wanted to hear of her husband's exploits; and now she sat with him in their parlor, the children having been sent to bed, placidly knitting while he spoke, but at intervals breaking the silence with some trenchant observation of her own.

Continuing his comments, the detective plunged into a narrative of his inquiries in Boston and how they had finally set him upon the correct trail. When he had described Allen Murray's motive for committing the crime, he went on:

"Viewed from any angle, it was a daring and dangerous undertaking. The police in Boston knew that he was an enemy of Russell Stirling; and they knew his reasons for that enmity. He had just been freed from the penitentiary; the police had his physical measurements, fingerprints and all the data that goes into a prison record. Should Stirling meet with violent death, immediately following his release, on him the first suspicion would fall. His movements would at once be inquired into; and the means of tracing him down were already at hand.

"It became vitally necessary, then, to bend every effort toward safeguarding himself while carrying out the crime; for the sake of his daughter, he could not afford to put his head into the noose. He had almost three years, while he served his prison term, to study how he would do it. Discarding some ideas, and adopting others, he carefully planned every barrier that would interpose a defense between him and the crime he would commit. In the end, protecting himself and deceiving the police became as important to him as killing Stirling, and strangely enough, that very thing finally gave him away. Like so many criminals, he had to embellish his trickery with further deceptions until he overshot the mark and brought about the result he wished to avoid.

"Consider, for a moment, his preparations. His clever disguise was brought about simply by adopting facial qualities different from the usual characteristics of his features. A normal beard, mustache and the pince-nez hid their austerity and added five years to his age. In addition, the strain of his prison term had aged him another five years. It was not surprising that I failed to link the picture Captain O'Connor showed me with anyone I knew; the face in the photograph was clean-shaven and young while Dr. Curtiss was at least middle-aged.

"No one except Mrs. Lorimor knew where Murray went after his release, and even she could not tell how to find him. In Philadelphia, he established an apartment, as David Curtiss, hiring a maid to keep house for him in the day. Until he had to draw funds from a bank, none of the acquaintances he must have had here knew of his presence; then, he chose some friend, so casual that he would never be located and questioned, to identify him at some bank. Allen Murray, gone from Boston, was swallowed up in Philadelphia. No thread connected him with his home except that single letter in which he instructed Mrs. Lorimor to write to him through Higgins.

"Stirling's butler served Murray in two ways. Murray could not afford to leave to chance the opportunity of carrying out his mission; he had to know with exactness all of Stirling's movements, what were his precise habits, when he could be found alone. Obviously, he could not be his own spy; and no one could supply him with this information better than Higgins. But in hiring the butler to keep in close touch with Stirling, he was also preparing another safeguard. Higgins was bound to be a safe go-between, you see; at Stirling's death, even if he suspected anything, he would never dare to tell what he knew, because of what he had done. And even if he did speak up, there was practically nothing he could tell of an employer who was to him merely an anonymous voice.

"As his greatest defense, Murray intended to make Stirling's murder appear a suicide. To every type of case, where death by violence is interpreted as suicide, he gave careful consideration. A suicide often merely turns on the gas because it is a painless means of ending life. Perhaps he hangs himself in his room, or leaps to death from some high building or bridge. It is not uncommon for him to shoot, either; and one found dead with the weapon in his hand is often taken to be a suicide. If Murray could arrange for the broker's death to occur in some such situation, with the requisite appearances present, he would have committed an undetectable crime.

"Unfortunately, though he might be able to prepare a convincing setting, one element he could not supply. He could not furnish his corpse with any reason for having killed itself. One does not commit suicide without cause— and Stirling had every reason to live. He had not been made morbid by the loss of some one dear to him; and in business, he had been successful and fortunate. In his case, therefore, this final shield was particularly necessary, or the police would find his death questionable and proceed to investigate. At the beginning, Murray hesitated to move without this essential part of his plan. That was why he delayed for more than three months, waiting and hoping that something would develop. In the end, I suppose, he would have gone ahead with his scheme without it, relying upon all his other precautions; but as it happened, the event for which he hoped actually occurred."

Gilmore paused at this point in his story to light his pipe and remarked directly to his wife:

"All these details I got from Murray himself, you understand. He didn't live any longer than the doctor said he would, poor fellow; but before he died he was able to explain the few points that I hadn't cleared up."

Mrs. Gilmore nodded, and, taking a few puffs, the detective continued the narrative.

"On the Friday before Philip Nixon died, Higgins informed him over the phone that Stirling was in difficulties on the market; and, by inquiry, he learned that, due to his short sale of Audubon Common, he was on the verge of ruin. His need had been supplied for him; from that moment, Murray doubled his vigilance, so that no opportunity would be lost to execute his revenge before the crisis had passed. Twice a day, now, he communicated with Higgins, instead of once, as he had previously done. No movement of Stirling's was too unimportant; to carry out his purpose, he was willing to follow him anywhere. And when he learned on Monday afternoon that Stirling was going to Cape May, he trailed him aboard the seven-forty-five express, in spite of the threatening storm.

"Murray took a seat in the last car, instead of sitting behind Stirling in the car ahead. While he could have kept a better surveillance from a position behind him, there was a chance that Stirling might turn around and recognize him. I, who had never met Allen Murray, might be deceived, but the broker, who had known him so well, might penetrate his disguise. There seemed, furthermore, no need of watching him until Cape May was reached; Stirling had purchased a ticket for the entire distance to the resort, and seemed safe until his destination was reached.

"Upon so inconsequential a decision rested his terrible mistake. For, failing to watch Stirling during the ride, he knew nothing of what subsequently took place. He did not see the broker leave the train during the five-minute halt at eight-twenty-five at Newfield. He never knew how close he was to losing him at the station. He observed nothing of the financier's arrival just before the train pulled out, nor of the two men reentering the car together. If he saw the financier at all, it was merely to note that some affable stranger from Newfield had taken the empty chair beside

Stirling. How was he to know that this meeting had been prearranged? But the most fatal result of Murray's act was his failure to see Nixon don his companion's brown overcoat and start toward the rear of the train.

"The first thing of which he was aware, as the financier passed through the car, was that the garment his enemy had been wearing had just brushed by him. By the time he had turned about and looked, Nixon had opened the door and stepped into the darkness. He caught only a glimpse of the broad back, in Stirling's overcoat, disappearing through the entrance. The broker had broad shoulders and a heavy body, and was wearing the clothes he so briefly viewed. With the belief that Russell Stirling stood alone on the rear platform came a realization of the opportunity that unexpectedly offered itself. If Stirling's body were on the track and struck by the train that came along in two hours, his death was almost certain to be considered an accident or a suicide. Death under the wheels of a locomotive is not an uncommon choice of a suicide. And accidents by the same medium are so commonplace that a suspicion of murder has never arisen under such circumstances.

"Murray committed the crime with no more unusual weapon than an umbrella he carried as a protection against the storm. It was ironical that the deed he intended as a revenge should have saved Stirling from ruin. The financier was bending over the rail; only his back was dimly visible in the enveloping darkness. The rattle of the wheels under foot completely drowned the sound of the door opening stealthily behind him. In a moment the act was finished, with a single well-placed blow with the knob of his umbrella, and a swift push that sent the body to the track below. Before he stepped back again into the car, he sent his weapon flying into the shrubbery lining the right of way."

Mrs. Gilmore looked up from her knitting. "He did not know, even after he had struck the blow, that his victim was not Russell Stirling?" she queried.

"He did not discover his mistake," the detective replied, "until two hours later, when, as Dr. David Curtiss, he bent over his victim to make an examination. There is nothing I admire more than the self-control he must have summoned to contain himself at that moment. The shock must have been stunning; particularly when he realized that his extremely dangerous return to the scene of the crime, whereby he attracted attention to himself, had been for a useless purpose. But he did not cry out or give himself away; he merely remained quietly on his knees until he had sufficiently collected his senses to continue his deception.

"Allen Murray should never have doubled in his tracks," Gilmore went on with his explanation. "And yet it is easy to understand the anxiety and suspense that drove him to make such a mistake. Like a man whose life has been threatened and who never feels safe, no matter how securely he is guarded, he, despite every effort to safeguard himself, became suddenly fearful that he had not provided for every contingency. Because he had committed the crime on the spur of the moment without sufficient consideration, he lost confidence in the precautions he had taken. For two hours, until the nine-fifty-five express destroyed the evidence, Russell Stirling's corpse would proclaim a murder had been committed. If the engineer of the train should discover the body! If it should be found by a trackwalker in the interim! Any number of events might destroy his every preparation; and he would be unable to prevent them. Indeed, if he went on to Cape May, he would not even know whether he was safe until the following day. Rather than endure such uncertainty, he far preferred to remain on the scene; if anything should go wrong, he would not be helpless then, to act in his own behalf. Nothing would satisfy him except to be aboard the later train when it wiped out all danger of peril and discovery."

"It seems to me," Mrs. Gilmore observed, "that whatever his motive was for returning to Newfield, it was a very clever and deceptive act. Why do you say it was an error?"

"Because, due to what followed, he made himself known to the police and myself. His final desperate effort to shield himself was as useless as it was hazardous; though he didn't know it, no link connected him with the financier. From Burke's account of what he had seen, we would only have had the criminal's description; had Murray not come forward, that would have been quite valueless. As it was, I was bound to recognize in Burke's story the man I knew as Dr. David Curtiss. Therefore, Burke had to be silenced; and it was the clue, left on the scene of the second crime, that finally gave Murray away.

"What occurred after he had, strangely enough, joined me at Newfield, justified his worst fears. The engineer actually discovered the body before the train passed over it, and halted the locomotive. Throughout the journey, Murray's perturbation was obvious to me, though, of course, I could not then understand the cause of it; he continually inquired how far we had gone. With the sudden halting of the train on the very spot where the crime had taken place, only defeat stared him in the face. He knew too well why the conductor entered the car and inquired if there was a doctor present. With a desperate and reckless disregard of consequences, he offered his services as a physician with the purpose of halting any possible investigation by pronouncing the death a suicide. And his deception would have succeeded had I not been present. And once Murray had involved himself so thoroughly in the case, he had to carry on with the pretense to the bitter end."

The detective fell silent as he knocked the ashes from his pipe. Mrs. Gilmore again rested her knitting on her lap.

"I find it difficult to believe that he could continue as a doctor for any length of time without giving himself away," she objected. "After all, he had no knowledge or experience of medicine."

"He didn't need either, my dear," Gilmore replied mildly. "You must remember that in the three months during which he delayed his plans, he had plenty of opportunity to study the best means of causing death. Such a study necessarily involved many of the scientific principles of medicine—certainly enough to make him familiar with many medical terms, connected with death. Furthermore, who should know better the cause of a person's decease than the man who was responsible for it? In both cases, he was called in to diagnose his own handiwork; he merely described what he had himself done, in sufficiently realistic terms. On the tracks, I could hardly expect a scholarly examination and was ready to accept whatever he could tell me; and at the second crime, he was far better prepared to meet the situation."

His wife looked unconvinced. "That may be very true with regard to you," she said, "but surely so experienced a surgeon as Dr. Sackett must have discovered that he was not genuine."

"Dr. Sackett never had the opportunity to find it out. As I recall it now, when Murray 'consulted' with Dr. Sackett on the cause of Nixon's death, he came after the coroner's physician had completed his medical report and not before; and he did not remain long enough to show his ignorance. At the inquest, his testimony was limited only to the finding of the financier's body; Dr. Ralston gave all the necessary evidence of the causes and manner of

Nixon's decease. As I have subsequently learned, the arrangement was by Murray's suggestion. Meanwhile, Murray instructed his maid that if any calls came for a Dr. David Curtiss, she was to say that she would pass the message on, but could make no appointments for him. He had not dared, you see, to give me an incorrect address; he could not chance the possibility that I might wish to see him sometime about the case."

Mrs. Gilmore's nod indicated her acceptance of his explanation. She listened quietly while Gilmore summed up his final opinion of the case.

"In many respects, it was the most amazing affair in the annals of crime, and without a parallel. Except for the fact that Nixon's murder occurred at the door of the Marley farmhouse, it contained not a single coincidence. Every development followed naturally and added another particular to the final result—the death of the wrong man. If Nixon had not had a narrow escape from the Ferris gang, there would then have been no occasion to leave his ruined overcoat at the farmhouse. It would not have been necessary to borrow Stirling's coat on the train. It was his condition after his flight that caused him to seek the air on the rear platform. Without the Marleys, on the other hand, he would never have caught the train. You see, had any single one of these items been omitted, the error never could have occurred. On the other end, too, with Murray following his enemy from Camden, every element conspired to the same tragic conclusion."

He shook his head slowly. "It was a distressing affair for everyone concerned. For Eleanor Nixon, in the first place, though, doubtlessly, she will find happiness with young Gardiner. For Martha Marley, too, though she still has her brothers to protect her and Eleanor's promise to care for her, if she will accept the aid. And for Murray's

little girl; luckily, she is too young to appreciate the tragedy of it."

"I am particularly sorry for her," Mrs. Gilmore remarked
gently. "Have you learned what is to become of her?"

The detective smiled appreciatively at his wife.

"Mrs. Lorimor will have more than sufficient to take
care of her. I was sure you'd be interested in knowing, Kate,
that Murray has made arrangements for both of them. He
had a very comfortable fortune, you know, and all of it is
left to Anna. Mrs. Lorimor will be appointed her guard-
ian. I sometimes think he must have tacitly understood
her secret love for him. . . ."

He broke off suddenly as he looked at his watch. With
a low whistle, he rose.

"It's half past eleven already," he said. "I had no idea
it was so late. I feel that I've earned a much-needed rest.
Shall we go to bed, or do you want to talk a little longer?"

COACHWHIP PUBLICATIONS

COACHWHIPBOOKS.COM

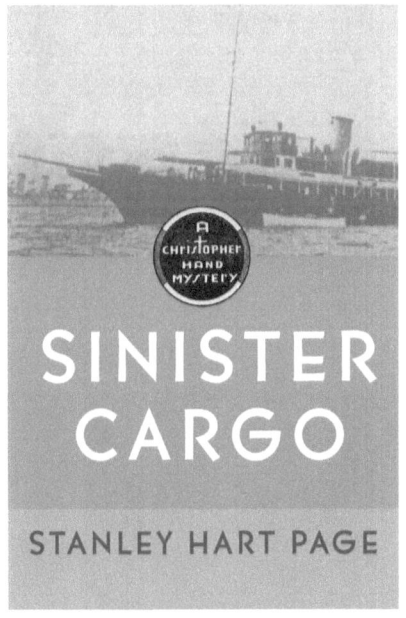

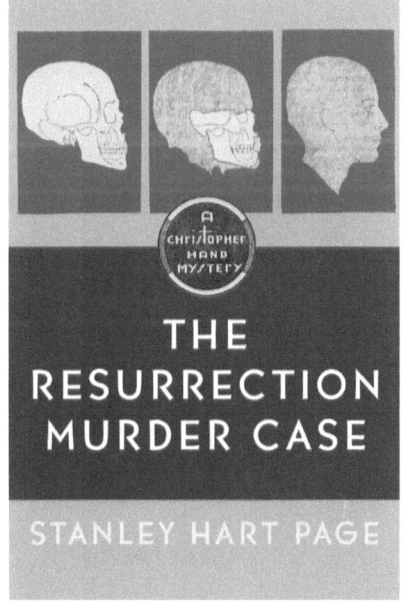

COACHWHIP PUBLICATIONS

COACHWHIPBOOKS.COM

CLUES OF THE CARIBBEES
being certain criminal investigations of Henry Poggioli, Ph.D.
T. S. Stribling

MURDER
IN A WALLED TOWN
Katherine Woods

VULTURES
IN THE SKY
A HUGH RENNERT MYSTERY
Todd Downing

LOUIS F. BOOTH
THE BANK VAULT MYSTERY
BROKERS' END

COACHWHIP PUBLICATIONS
COACHWHIPBOOKS.COM

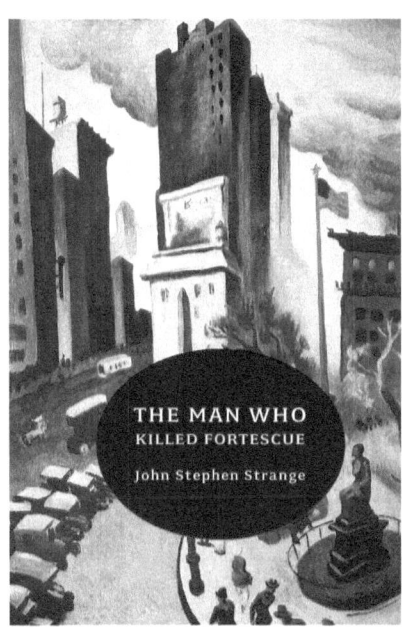

THE MAN WHO
KILLED FORTESCUE
John Stephen Strange

HENRY JAMES FORMAN
THE REMBRANDT
MURDER

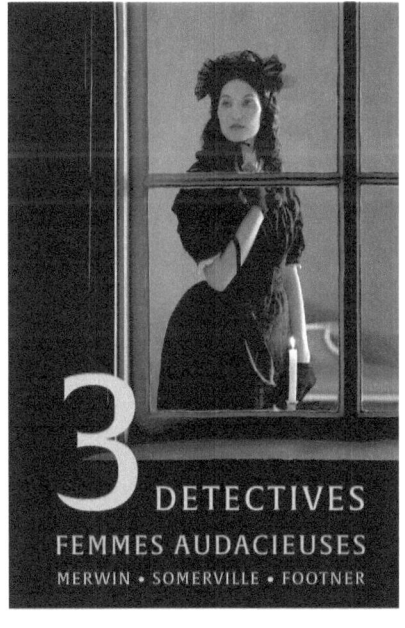

3 DETECTIVES
FEMMES AUDACIEUSES
MERWIN · SOMERVILLE · FOOTNER

MEDORA
FIELD
WHO KILLED
AUNT MAGGIE?

COACHWHIP PUBLICATIONS
COACHWHIPBOOKS.COM

THE HOUSE WITH
THE BLUE DOOR
HULBERT FOOTNER

The
Jekyll-Hyde
Murder Case
MADELON ST. DENIS

VIRGINIA RATH

DEATH AT
DAYTON'S FOLLY

THE 5.18
MYSTERY

J. Jefferson
Farjeon

COACHWHIP PUBLICATIONS

COACHWHIPBOOKS.COM

THE
BEACON HILL
MURDERS

∞

THE
BACK BAY
MURDERS

THE ROGER SCARLETT MYSTERIES
VOL. I

THE
SARA ELIZABETH
MASON
MYSTERIES

MURDER RENTS A ROOM

THE CRIMSON FEATHER

HELEN BURNHAM

THE MURDER OF
LALLA LEE

THE TELLTALE
TELEGRAM

THOMAS KINDON

MURDER
IN THE
MOOR

COACHWHIP PUBLICATIONS

COACHWHIPBOOKS.COM

THE MYSTERIOUS WAYS
OF WANG FOO

SIDNEY C. PARTRIDGE

MURDER
ON THE
BLUFF

ESTHER TYLER

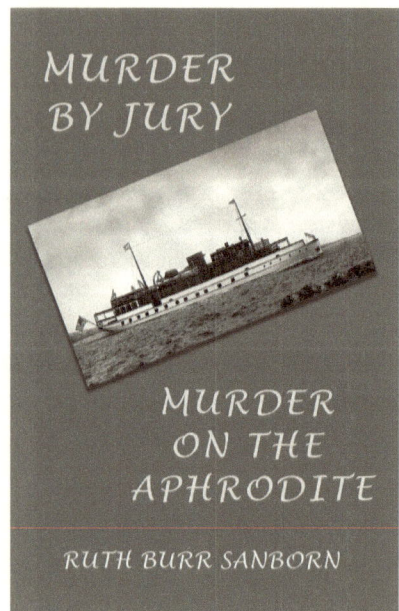

MURDER
BY JURY

MURDER
ON THE
APHRODITE

RUTH BURR SANBORN

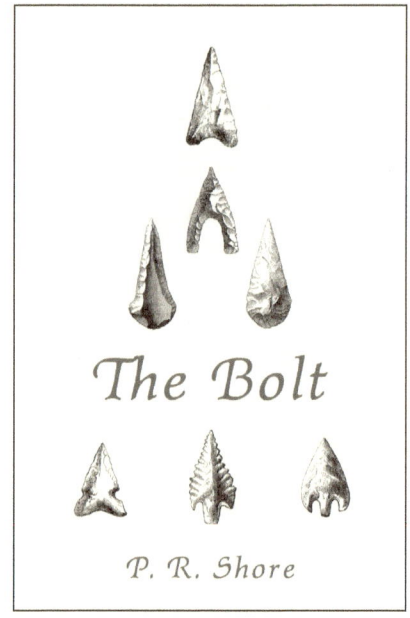

The Bolt

P. R. Shore

COACHWHIP PUBLICATIONS

COACHWHIPBOOKS.COM

COACHWHIP PUBLICATIONS

COACHWHIPBOOKS.COM